THE FOX HEIR

THRONES OF RUIN, BOOK TWO

BRIAR KNIGHTLY

BRIAR KNIGHTLY

THE
FOX
HEIR

Published by Fox & Thistle Press

Copyright © 2026 by Briar Knightly

Cover design by Damonza

eISBN: 979-8-9997857-2-5

ISBN (paperback): 979-8-9997857-3-2

 Formatted with Vellum

PART ONE

THE CASTLE

CHAPTER 1

THE TREES SHIVER. Their last leaves cascade around us as the icy wind howls through the Spires of Annwyn. It sounds like a pack of hungry wolves.

Above us, the sky darkens as black clouds roll over the mountain peaks. The oncoming storm feels like a living thing, tearing leaves from branches and hurling them through the darkening forest. Thunder shakes the ground beneath my feet.

We have to reach Gwyllion Castle before the winter storm swallows us whole. I haven't come this far just to die from foul northern weather.

Behind us, another massive pine crashes to the forest floor, cracking and splintering like breaking bones. The Dead Queen's skeletal hand flashes in my mind and my stomach roils. I shake the grotesque image away. As it is, I barely slept at camp last night with the nightmarish queen haunting my dreams. The dead don't need rest, so she traveled ahead of us. She's already at Gwyllion Castle by now. Waiting for me.

Tristan runs at my side, his eyebrows drawn together in concentration. His hands are outstretched, casting shadow power from his palms in swirling clouds of inky black. He's blasting fallen branches from the path ahead, but we're like moths caught in a turbulent sea. Thrashing will only keep us alive for so long before we drown. Once the storm gets here, no power—neither his shadows nor my light—will be enough to protect us.

He shoots me a glance, his gray eyes unreadable. I keep my mouth in a grim line. If I die out here, it will be just another tally to add to his long list of offenses. Tristan, the Wolf, is a liar and a cheat, and I haven't had sufficient time to lick my wounds. We both know that I'm only in Annwyn because of one thing:

The Wolf has outfoxed the Fox Heir.

Or the former Fox Heir, at any rate. Now, I suppose I'm just Sienna.

Fury prickles my skin, and I clench my jaw to keep from screaming in anger. Hail hammers through the tree canopy, knocking down whatever autumn leaves remain overhead. I hold my hands up to shield my eyes as hail bites my skin like tiny teeth. Mighty pines creak and rain their needles around us.

Above the sound of wind and crashing thunder, something else makes my skin prickle. First, it's just a distant howl so faint I almost mistake it for the screaming wind. But then Tristan stops, his feet sliding on the wet leaves scattered across the path. His arm sweeps in front of me like a barricade, forcing me behind him. The move is instinctive, protective. Infuriating.

"They're tracking us," he says, his voice low.

I listen. Another howl. Closer this time. And I'd bet my life these are no ordinary wolves.

"How—" I start, but Tristan's already scanning the trees.

I follow suit and grip the bronze hilt of my knife, drawing it from the sheath tucked into the ankle of my boot. The moths engraved along its silver blade gleam in the dim light. It looks delicate, but it's all the more deadly for it.

As heir to the Fox Throne, I've learned this above all else: men always see femininity as fragility. It's their favorite delusion, mistaking beauty for something that cannot bite.

Tristan's hand closes around my elbow, tugging me closer than I want to be. If these were ordinary wolves, Tristan could use his shadow power to stop their hearts in their chests, killing them instantly. But corpse beasts can only be stopped by severing the spine.

"Stay with me," he whispers. His breath is warm against my ear, and a reluctant shiver runs across my skin.

He nods toward the left, and I follow, darting off the main path and down a game trail. Out of the corner of my eye, I see movement, flashes of dark fur blurring between pine-green branches. Corpse wolves. My eyes strain to see them through the trees.

My ribs ache and the cold air makes me cough, but we can't stop. The silver moth necklace bounces against my chest as I sprint behind Tristan. I tuck it safely out of the way beneath the collar of my dress.

Up ahead, the first corpse wolf lurches onto the trail. It's massive, larger than any wolf should be. But that's not what makes me recoil. Its black fur is matted with dried blood. Several ribs poke out from its side, the muscles between them glistening with rot. Its maw is filled with broken, jagged teeth, ringed crimson with blood from a fresh kill. Luminescent eyes stare at us, devoid of life. Behind it, more shapes dart through the darkening forest.

"The trees," I say, my voice firm.

Tristan nods once before we bolt off the path. Howls echo around us, mixing with the crashing storm like an ominous symphony. My boots slide on dead leaves as another gust of freezing wind nearly knocks me sideways. Tristan steadies me with a hand at my back.

The temperature is dropping so fast my fingers are numb, but I don't loosen my grip on my knife as we sprint through the forest. Trees groan and bend under the onslaught. Branches snap above our heads and crash to the ground. I glance at the sky through gaps in the canopy. The storm front is closing in on us with a curtain of snow so thick it obliterates everything in its path.

I reach for my light power, but it slips through my grasp like fog. Ever since I exhausted my abilities escaping the battlegrounds of Llwyn, my power has been inaccessible. Burnout is a fickle thing. Even now, when I need my power most, it refuses to resurface.

We leap over fallen trees and push branches aside. Sticks slice at my skin, but I can't slow down. Speed is the only thing that will save us now. My red cloak whips around me with each gust of wind.

A corpse wolf lunges at me from the trees, teeth bared. I sidestep and slash out with my knife. The blade bites into fur and flesh, scraping against its shoulder bone. Black blood sprays, but the corpse wolf barely notices. I spin around, narrowly avoiding its jaws as it snaps at my throat. It bears down, bending its knees as it readies itself to pounce at me again.

We both startle at the sound of a thunderous crack. An enormous oak crashes to the ground, pinning the corpse wolf beneath it.

I stand there stunned, but not for long. Tristan catches up, and we continue running from the snarling wolves still on our trail. He yells above the thunder echoing across the sky.

"We're nearly there, Red!"

That's when I see her.

She stands motionless between two ancient oaks, her long, pale dress untouched by the violent wind. Her eyes are bottomless pools of black. Her long fingers curl around the trunk of the lichen-covered tree. When our eyes meet, her mouth stretches into a grimace that splits her face, revealing row upon row of needle-sharp teeth.

It doesn't seem possible, but my pulse races faster. There's something deeply wrong with this woman who remains untouched by wind in the middle of a northern snowstorm. She watches me with hungry eyes that make my skin crawl.

"Red!" Tristan's voice barely carries over the howling wind. "Look!"

I tear my gaze away from the woman and toward the break in

the trees ahead. Finally, Gwyllion Castle looms in the distance. Beyond it, a cluster of dim lights huddles against the falling snow. My stomach drops. It's a town, if you can call it that. Even from a distance, I see the sagging roofs, the listing buildings, and windows glowing with flickering yellow light.

It may look inviting compared to the raging storm, but I know better. The people of Annwyn would sooner kill me for being the daughter of the Fox King than offer me a warm bed or a cup of ale.

To my left, a flash of white draws my eyes. It's the woman again, but that's impossible. Nothing can move that fast. Her head tilts at an unnatural angle as she watches us. Snow stings my face, driven sideways by the storm. I blink it away, but when I look up again, the woman is gone.

"Did you see her?" I gasp. "The woman in the trees?"

Tristan shakes his head, but he isn't paying attention to me. Movement flickers in my peripheral vision, but when I turn, there's nothing but shadows and swirling snow. We burst from the forest, out into a wide valley. At the far end, the crumbling Gwyllion Castle sits upon seaside cliffs.

My foot catches on a rock, and I stumble to my knees. Gravel scrapes my palms. Before I can right myself, a nearby snarl makes my breath catch in my throat. Through the strands of my wind-blown hair, I glimpse black fur between the trees. The corpse wolf's eyes watch me, luminescent white in the growing darkness. My stomach lurches.

Tristan's hand seizes my arm, hauling me up as I hiss at the pain in my knee.

"We can't stop." His grip lingers a fraction too long before he shoves me forward.

We break into a sprint as the storm descends in full force. The pressure on my knee brings tears to my eyes, but I can't slow down. I hazard a glance behind us. More corpse wolves emerge from the forest—six, seven, eight of them. Their massive claws tear at the ground as they chase us.

The snow falls heavier, reducing visibility to mere feet. Ahead, Gwyllion disappears into a wall of white. The oppressiveness of it makes me feel claustrophobic, and I fight down the rising panic. Wind and snow sting my face as I squint through the whiteout.

I follow Tristan, trusting that he knows the way, even in the storm. Step after blind step, we push through, focusing on what's ahead instead of what's behind us. From out of the storm, a tall, stone wall appears, blocking our path into the castle grounds.

The corpse wolves howl.

"How are they still following us?" My voice is edged with fear.

"They're corpses. They don't care about the cold." Tristan grabs my hand and pulls me to the right. "The gate is this way!" He yells above the wind.

My eyelashes are coated in ice and my cloak is frozen. My hands and feet are numb, but we push through the building snowdrifts. Relief melts through my veins when a tall, wooden gate looms before us.

Remarkably, the gate is raised a few feet, as if someone was expecting us. Tristan shoves me to the ground first. My knee screams in protest, but I roll through the gap below the gate.

Tristan crawls under without a second to lose. A corpse wolf snaps at his heels. When I look through the gap beneath the gate, it leaps toward me. Its bloodied, rotted face scrapes against the wooden gate, and the bones in its jaw crack. Not that a little broken bone would stop the dead.

For once, the corpse wolf's unnatural size is its greatest disadvantage. I stare in horror as it attacks the gate, clawing, gnawing, and slavering against the wood. It forces its head through the gap along the frozen ground. Its dead, white eyes pin me as its skin scrapes away from bone in its attempt to fight through.

Tristan scrambles for a lever in the stone wall. The gate slams closed with an echoing thud, decapitating the creature on the spot.

I stare at the corpse wolf's bloodied, rotted head. Snow slowly buries it, covering its vacant white eyes, one snowflake at a time. The wolf is dead once more, its spine severed.

From my spot in the mud, I listen as more corpses arrive and attack the other side of the gate. I grab my silver moth necklace in one hand and hold it against my pounding heart. My limbs are trembling, but I refuse to let Tristan see how deeply shaken I am.

We've come closer to death than this, but something about being shut behind a heavy, locked gate keeps my relief at bay

Tristan drops to the ground beside me, panting.

My power stirs inside of me, so faintly I almost don't notice it. I try to access it, to pull it up from the depths, but it sputters out, silent. Good-for-nothing power.

I close my eyes and take a steadying breath. If I'm to face whatever waits for me inside the snow-battered walls of Gwyllion, I'll need every ounce of strength I have ... because this is the castle of the Dead Queen.

And a Fox Heir must keep her wits about her if she's to survive in a den of Wolves.

CHAPTER 2

BEYOND GWYLLION'S WALLS, the storm has lessened, though the brutal wind still stings my cheeks. My skin is numb, and I blink against the falling snow to see where we are.

Behind us, silhouetted against storm-black clouds, rises a castle that shouldn't exist. Its towers lean at angles that defy nature, and at least two of the wings have collapsed under the weight of time. Here and there, broken windows gape like mouths with jagged glass teeth. One turret lists so far to the side, its spire nearly kisses the tower beside it.

But its decrepitude isn't what's most alarming. Gwyllion Castle stands on a precipice. To the east, a cliff face reaches over a churning sea. I hear the waves crashing hundreds of feet below in an endless attack against the shore.

"It can't possibly stay standing in this storm." My words are torn away by the howling wind.

Beside me, Tristan's laugh is brittle as dead leaves. "It's stood for a thousand years, and it'll stand for a thousand more."

I want to ask how he knows this, but the question dies in my throat. My knee aches as I stand, taking in the full horror of this place.

A boom of thunder cracks through the air, and I flinch. It's a grim reminder that I'm not safe, not even close. But there's no turning back. I gave up everything for this: my title as the Fox Heir, my kingdom, my position as a healer in the battle-wrought borderlands ... Hunter.

Guilt scrapes at the walls of my chest, but I steel my spine. Somewhere inside this black and rotting castle lies the truth I set my world on fire to uncover. I just hope it's worth it.

Tristan and I press against the wind and swirling snow, toward the castle.

I'm truly in enemy territory now. Worse, the only assurance I have that I won't be killed on sight is the word of a single Wolf, Tristan. A Wolf who already betrayed me once. Those aren't great odds.

It feels like a lifetime ago since Tristan was sent to Caerwen Palace to sniff out rumors that the Heir to the North has returned. A lot has changed since then. Not the least of which is the fact that the Wolf is coming back empty-handed, without the Heir to the North in tow. Instead, he has me. A scrappy ex-Fox Heir that no one asked for.

Tristan misinterprets my unease. "It must look like a ruin compared to your palace in Caerwen and your copper-plated city." Tristan shouts against the wind. "Some say Gwyllion is cursed."

I squint over at him. His hair and clothes are covered in snow, like he's a fae creature made of ice.

"And why is that?" I shout back. "Is it the corpse wolves at the gate? The decaying castle? Or maybe it's the ghosts in the woods?"

He pauses mid-step and blinks at me a few times, dislodging snow from his eyelashes. "Ghosts?"

I shake my head and push through the snow. The last thing I need is Tristan thinking I'm seeing things that aren't there.

We're nearly at the castle doors when another crash echoes from the forest beyond the battlement wall. The sound is followed by a chorus of eerie howls. I turn back toward the castle and press on. Whatever horrors wait inside these walls, we're out of options.

As if on cue, the storm front swallows us in sheets of white again. In the last moment before the snow takes everything, I see movement in one of the highest towers, a pale figure behind shattered glass. The ghostly woman is watching us. She knows we're coming, and I can't help but wonder if she's been waiting.

Tristan pulls the heavy castle doors open, and I nearly tumble inside. He slams them closed behind us. The sound echoes low, like a sealed tomb, as silence envelops us. Tristan crumbles to the ground, breathing heavily with relief and exhaustion.

I stomp the snow off my feet, wiggle my toes, and rub my hands together. Gradually, sensation returns to my limbs as my skin burns like fire. I pray against frostbite, not that the old gods have ever done much for me.

After the howling winds outside, it feels as though my ears are stuffed with cotton. It's so quiet here. The entrance hall is empty. No rugs, no furniture, no lamps, no people. The only muted light comes from the tall windows on either side of the door. Outside, all I see is a sheet of white beyond the filthy glass.

Tristan stands up with a grunt, then limps toward me.

"Are you all right?" His voice is edged with what sounds like genuine concern. But with a traitorous Wolf, one can never be too sure. I wave away his fussing and stand tall, ignoring the ache in my knee.

My eyes search for any sign of life in the hall. When I find none, my chest tightens. In the Fox King's palace in Caerwen, you're hard-pressed to find solitude anywhere, let alone at the grand entrance. But here, the quiet is ominous. Even the air feels wrong, as if the castle is tainted with age and decay. Each breath tastes of metal and ancient stone.

"Are you sure we're welcome here?" I whisper to Tristan. I fight the urge to reach for the knife now tucked away in the sheath strapped to my ankle.

He grabs a torch from an iron sconce nailed into the stone wall and returns to me. "Hold this?"

I take it, confusion muffling my thoughts until I remember that here, in Annwyn, no one has the power of light, not even the noble-born. Here, everyone must rely on fire.

I watch as he strikes a match and lights the oil-soaked linen fibers wrapped at the end of the torch. The flame catches. Dread fills my chest as I watch it flicker and burn. It casts shadows across the great entrance hall. It's a reminder of just how vulnerable I am without access to my powers. And how out of place I am in the Dead Queen's kingdom, where shadow power rules.

I follow Tristan through the dark halls and empty chambers. Wind whistles down the chimney of a fireplace, scattering ashes across the floor. I shudder.

Out of the corner of my eye, something stirs in the shadows. I snap my head toward it, but there's nothing there except a ragged curtain that sways in an invisible draft. At the end of the long hall-way, an open doorway yawns like the maw of a beast. Someone is watching from the darkness. I can feel it. And yet, we don't encounter a single soul until we reach what must be the heart of the castle.

Outside a set of giant wooden doors, two men stand at attention. They look nothing like the guards in Caerwen. My father's King's Guard always took pride in their immaculate copper-plated armor. These men are dressed in worn leather and fur. Their only decoration is a pin on their chest—a silver wolf, the sign of the Annwyn court.

My gut tells me these aren't normal guards. They're Wolves, like Tristan. The Dead Queen's most skilled warriors.

For a moment, I wonder why they aren't fighting in the borderlands with the rest of the Annwyn fighters. Then I realize one of the men is missing an eye. The hole in his face is flesh-colored and hollow. When I look closer at the other guard, I realize his right hand is a jumbled mess of scar tissue and missing fingers. These Wolves did fight at the border. This is just what's left of them.

I watch the men warily, but they don't step aside. Either they don't know who I am, or they've been forewarned of the Fox entering the castle. One guard stares at the silver moth around my neck. He lifts an eyebrow at Tristan.

"We need to see the queen," Tristan says, his voice authoritative.

I swallow hard, waiting to see how the other Wolves will react.

After a beat, the men step aside and pull the heavy doors open. Tristan leads me into the room, his hand hovering against my lower back in a gesture that could be protective. Or possibly possessive. I decide not to dwell on that thought.

The throne room feels like a massive tomb. Our footsteps echo throughout the cavernous space. Shadows cling to the vaulted ceiling, and impossibly tall, arched windows line the eastern side. Along the left wall, ceiling-high tapestries sway in the frigid draft. They depict twelve variations of gnarled trees, from hardened cedars clinging to cliffsides to severed stumps in snowy meadows. Their branches shift and writhe in the flickering torchlight.

At the far end of the space, the Dead Queen sits upon a throne of blackened wood and molded iron. Her skeletal fingers twitch on the knotted armrests as we approach.

I straighten my spine.

She's dressed in voluminous silks of midnight that drape over the throne's weathered roots. Satin and brocade cover what I know to be a broken body of rot and decay. I've seen it only once, but the memory is forever seared into my mind.

Her white opalescent eyes bore into me from behind her sheer black veil. I swallow, unable to say the word that struggles at the tip of my tongue: Grandmother. The knowledge is still too new, and the pain of betrayal cuts deep in my chest.

Behind her stands a large woman, magnificent in her rugged

beauty. She's not dressed in corsets and silks like the ladies of the Caerwen court. Instead, she wears breeches and a weathered leather vest, all in earthy shades of brown. Her posture is rigid, and her dark blond hair is a wild tangle of curls escaping from a thick braid. But her most striking feature is the scar that cuts across her face, like she once kissed a blade and lived to tell the tale.

I don't miss how her eyes linger on the thin scar across my throat. I've met blades too.

No one needs to tell me this woman is a Wolf. Everything about her presence screams power and brutality. Her emerald eyes narrow as she regards me with open hostility.

Tristan kneels before my grandmother. "My queen." He nods toward the woman behind the throne, his body language tense. "Nalina."

I stand firm. I crossed Llwyn and the Spires for my grandmother, lost everyone and everything I held dear—only to discover she betrayed me. I loved my grandmother so deeply, it nearly killed me. That love that kept me alive all those years is now a hard, putrid stone in my chest.

Now, I hate her. It's a hatred that burns so hot, I'd kill her a second time if I had the chance. And this fury has no time for pleasantries.

"Why?" The word tears from my throat before I can think better of it. "Why did you leave me without an explanation? Why torture me like that?"

Behind her, Nalina stiffens, her hand ready at the silver sword on her hip.

The queen studies me through her sheer veil. Slowly, she stands, her bones cracking like popping coals. When she speaks, her voice is raspy and dry. "Sometimes, the path we walk requires great sacrifice."

I step forward, but Tristan places a hand on my arm.

"Sacrifice?" I balk. "You abandoned me to that monster! To a father who hated me, who made my life miserable." My voice breaks, but I refuse to cry. "You knew what he was, what he was capable of. And you still left me with him."

Nalina's gaze darts toward Tristan, narrowing further. The unspoken tension between them is almost palpable.

My fury burns through me, fueled by years of unanswered questions and bitter resentment. "I loved you. And you left me."

The Dead Queen's voice is maddeningly calm. "I did what I had to."

Bile burns my throat. Suddenly, the weight of the silver moth hanging around my neck feels unbearable. I grab it and tug, breaking the chain. I throw the necklace onto the ground. It clangs and skitters toward her feet. For a long moment, everyone in the room stares at it.

My heart is racing with anger. "Without you, he made my life a nightmare. He—" I choke on the words, the memories too painful to voice. He disowned me. He made an illegitimate son heir instead of me. He locked me in a dungeon to die. He sicced his foxhounds on me when Hunter saved me. He will stop at nothing until I'm dead.

Tristan's grip tightens on my arm. I can feel the weight of his gaze, silently urging me to hold my composure. But how can I, when the woman responsible for my suffering stands here? When she's wearing the face of the grandmother I once adored?

"Tell me what happened." My voice is sharp as a blade. I came here for answers. Once I get them, I'll leave this horrible place forever. I'll try to find a way to live, after existing in the shadow of death since I was twelve years old.

The Dead Queen doesn't speak.

"I deserve to know!"

"People don't always get what they 'deserve'. You should know that better than most."

She means my father. If he got what he deserved, then he'd have died a torturous death a long time ago. I can feel her dead eyes studying me from behind her black veil.

"I mourned you for years. I ruined my life just to find out

what happened to you." I take a step forward and speak through gritted teeth. "Tell me."

"No."

"No?" I scoff, incredulous.

"You aren't ready to hear that tale."

I turn to Tristan, expecting some backup, but he just stands still and stoic. Of course, he isn't going to help me. He was never my friend. Everything he did was driven by ulterior motives.

I stomp up toward the throne, but Nalina steps in front of me. In one smooth motion, she unsheathes her sword, pressing its silver tip to my chest. I glare past her, at the queen.

"Tell. Me." My voice has a pleading edge to it that makes me cringe. I'm not here to beg. I'm here to make demands. "I'll make you." I press closer, not caring that the edge of Nalina's blade bites the skin at my collarbone.

"You can't."

"I'll find a way."

Her tone is curious. "You plan to pry the story from my cold, dead lips, you mean?"

"That can be arranged."

"It's not so easy."

"I'm used to things being 'not so easy.' You'll find I'm rather industrious."

She shakes her head slowly. "I'm sorry to disappoint you, Granddaughter, but a Dead Queen can't be destroyed by mere strength of will."

"I've killed corpse beasts. I know *exactly* what to do."

"Decapitation, you mean?" She tilts her veiled head like a curious wolf. "It may work with a corpse beast, but it isn't so easy to destroy a queen."

I hadn't thought of that. That killing a corpse beast is simpler than killing a Dead Queen with immense shadow power.

"I'll learn how."

"I wish you luck." The Dead Queen says lightly. "Very few

people know that secret. And I'm not about to include you on that list."

"Then tell me what happened and be done with me. It's the only reason I'm here."

The queen sighs, a rattling, hollow sound. "I know you've suffered. Believe me, it pains me to see the scars you bear." Her gaze flicks to Tristan again, and something unreadable passes between them. His grip tightens on my arm.

I grit my teeth, fury rising in me. This woman doesn't care about my suffering. If she did, she wouldn't have left me to rot in Caerwen. Enough of this.

"My father. He did this to you, didn't he?"

The Dead Queen stills, then nods, just once.

My vision becomes a tunnel. I knew it. All along, my father was the one who killed her. The one who ruined my life. Who destroyed my heart and soul. It feels so obvious. I know now what I must do. Why I've survived this miserable life and sacrificed so much. This is my destiny.

"I'm going to kill him."

I will murder the Fox King. And when I'm done, I'll figure out how to kill the Dead Queen, too. Once and for all.

The Dead Queen's voice sounds hollow in my ears. "Perhaps. But you can't go back to Llwyn yet."

My head snaps up. "You can't stop me."

"I won't need to." The Dead Queen merely lifts one hand toward the tall, east-facing windows. The glass is darkened with a blanket of snow.

"Storms don't last forever."

She clucks as though I'm a silly child. It makes heat rush to my cheeks.

Nalina barely manages to hide a sneer. I glare at her and lean into her blade, daring her to doubt me. A trickle of blood slides over my collarbone. I can feel the trail of its warmth between my breasts.

"You don't know the north," the queen says. "But you will learn."

"And what's that supposed to mean?" I snarl.

Tristan's voice is low behind me. "It means, in Annwyn, winter is not so easily escaped."

I turn to look at him, but he simply watches me, waiting for me to understand. I don't.

"He means, you're stuck here." Nalina lowers her blade, her green eyes on me. "He means no one can survive out there until the snow melts."

"I've survived worse than a little snow."

Nalina outright laughs at that. "It is not just 'a little snow.'"

The Dead Queen speaks, and Nalina falls respectfully silent. "In Annwyn, winter means frozen lands throughout the Spires. Beasts grow mad with starvation. Snowdrifts grow so tall, they can cover a fortress." Once again, she gestures toward the high windows. From behind her veil, she turns her white eyes upon me.

"It means you are trapped here in Gwyllion until spring."

Chapter 3

THE CORRIDORS in Gwyllion Castle are a maze of shadows and stone. Cold drafts whisper between ancient tapestries that have long since faded into shades of muted gray. My boots echo each footstep as I storm away from the throne room. I don't know where I'm going, but I hardly care. It's one thing to trick me into traveling to Annwyn, it's another entirely to trap me here for the winter months.

Behind me, I hear measured, familiar steps. I don't bother looking back. After weeks spent traveling together, I'd recognize the cadence of Tristan's footsteps anywhere. He's wise to keep a safe distance behind me.

"Stop following me."

"We need to talk."

If I had any access to my power right now, I'd toss him head over heels down the corridor. Throw him out the tall, murky windows and into the swirling snowstorm. Make him sorry he'd ever stepped foot in Caerwen and tricked me into following him to this gods-forsaken wasteland. But this thought only infuriates me further, seeing as I haven't been able to use my power since it saved us from the wraith-infested borderlands. I used to be able to use it to heal the wounded and summon light in the darkness, but now ... nothing.

I whirl around. "Talk? Now you want to talk? After all your lies and deception?" My voice rises, catching in my chest. "You brought me here. To Annwyn. To *her*. You knew exactly who she was to me."

He doesn't even flinch. "Need I remind you that you wanted to find her?" He raises a dark eyebrow.

I shove a hand against his chest, but he doesn't budge.

He narrows his eyes. "You were practically begging me to bring you to her."

Blood boils in my veins. "No. You don't get to twist it around like that." I point one finger inches in front of his face. "I wanted you to *tell me* what happened to her."

"To bring you the answers."

My voice rises in fury, and I don't care who can hear me. "Which you could've told me without tricking me into crossing the entire country! Instead, you used me to get to the border."

Tristan stands his ground, but there's something telling in the way his fingers twitch, as if they want to reach for me. He just shakes his head. "No, not lies. I never lied to you, Red."

"You weren't honest with me either." The words come out like a blade, sharp and cutting.

"It was for your own good."

I take a step closer, close enough that the heat of him prickles against my skin. "Do you really expect me to thank you for ruining my life?"

"It was to save you from your father."

I laugh, but it sounds more like a sob. "Save me?! Look around, Tristan. I'm a Fox in a den of Wolves. This isn't a rescue. It's entrapment."

"I won't let them hurt you. I need you to trust me on that."

"Trust you?" My laugh cuts sharp as broken glass. "You're the last person I should trust."

I stare at him, wide-eyed. Does he take me for a fool? As if I could ever trust him again after what he's done. My head begins to throb. The anger is still burning inside me, but it's being slowly buried in an onslaught of painful betrayal. I don't want to admit how much I *did* trust him. And what it's cost me.

A vision of Hunter, begging me not to follow the Wolf, flickers through my mind. I shove it aside, unwilling to dwell on the colossal mistake I've made. I can't face that guilt. Not yet.

"For once, be honest with me," I say, exhausted. "Were you looking for me that day in my father's chamber? Did you think I was the mystical Heir to the North? That if you brought me here, I'd fix everything and save Annwyn?"

There is a moment of absolute silence. I can't read him, this Wolf with gray eyes. We've been traveling together for weeks and still, I don't understand him.

When Tristan speaks, his voice is steady. "No, Red. You're not the Heir to the North. That was never a lie."

"So, what? You brought me here as a political prisoner?"

"You're not listening." He growls. He levels his stormy eyes on mine. "Your father is a dangerous man. You know that as well as I do. I was trying to get you away from him. Away from the poisonous Fox Throne, because I knew you ..." He pauses, his eyes shifting away.

"Knew what?" I cross my arms. "What could you possibly know about me that I don't already know?" Frustration builds in my chest. I want to scream. Instead, tears prick at the corners of my eyes.

When Tristan looks at me, his eyes are defiant. "I know that you're better than he is." He lifts his chin, like he isn't sorry about any of it. "That you're a threat to his power, and he would do anything to get rid of you."

Something twists in my chest at those words, though I fight to cover it with a scoff. "Better than him? That's a low bar to clear." I take a half-step back, but he takes a step forward, refusing to let the distance grow.

My heart rate speeds up at the memory of the pitch-black dungeon my father threw me in. The place of forgetting. Of dying a cold, miserable death in a rat-infested pit no one would find me in. And no one would have, if it hadn't been for Hunter. A lump forms in my throat, and I turn toward a snow-covered window to hide how utterly destroyed I feel. How helpless and alone I am. It takes me several deep breaths to control the rising tide inside of me.

Tristan doesn't press me further. He just stands there silently, waiting. When he speaks again, his voice is soft. "I understand what you're feeling."

"How could you possibly know how I feel?" My voice cracks.

"I know what it's like to hurt someone you love."

It's the first time he's acknowledged what I did—leaving Hunter on a fiery battlefield surrounded by corpse beasts. The admission makes me pause.

He steps closer to me, his voice low. "The guilt. The fear that you're a monster for what you've done." Another step. He's barely a whisper away now. His words brush against the fallen curls at the nape of my neck. "And I know what it's like to lose someone you love. That bone-shattering heartache that never fully goes away."

My heart stumbles in my chest. There's something in those words, a depth of understanding that goes beyond mere sympathy. For a moment, the space between us fills with the impossible weight of half-spoken secrets.

I turn to face him again, my breath ragged. "You don't get to stand there and act like you understand anything I'm feeling."

Something in me wavers when I see the look on his face. It hints at grief, tended for years. I'd never noticed it before, but it's there in the grim line of his mouth and his quiet stoicism. Before, I'd mistaken him for cool and calculating. But now, I wonder if that's not the whole truth. If this Wolf has suffered and bears his scars openly.

The absolute certainty of my anger begins to crack, revealing something more complicated beneath.

Tristan nods once, then turns and walks past me. The brush of his hand against mine as he turns feels deliberate, like one last defiance. As if he knows he's leaving me with nothing but my misery and the howling wind beyond the castle walls.

———

The castle's corridors twist like the discarded skin of a serpent. Passages branch out in multiple directions and lead down darkened halls lined with tapestries. Their faded threads tell old stories that I can't fully understand. Knights in silver armor battle beasts and wolves. Fae creatures with black eyes watch from the shadows. Ladies dance naked in forests illuminated by moonlight. Each frozen image is but a glimpse of a story long forgotten. Annwyn heroes and monsters watch me as I wind through the unfamiliar corridors, like a fool stepping through a nest of vipers.

Before long, I'm lost. Completely, utterly lost. Pride keeps me from turning back and retracing my steps to the throne room to ask for help. My stomach growls. I haven't eaten since yesterday. Even then, it was just raw nuts and mushy apples. Very little still clung to the trees this late in the season.

Now, all I can think of is warm bread and hearty stews. It's the sort of meal you'd expect from a castle kitchen on a freezing winter day, but nothing in Annwyn has been what I'd call "expected." For all I know, these cold people with their grim frowns and sharp words eat nothing but snow and ice.

I'm hit with a sudden pang of homesickness, not for the palace in Caerwen, but for the kingdom in general. Llwyn, the southern lands where flowers bloom and heat caresses your skin on summer days. My eyes skitter over the endless snow-covered windows, most of them cracked. Wood planks block the light from coming in where the glass is broken entirely.

My footsteps echo down the empty hallways, each one swallowed by silence. Somewhere in the distance, something creaks. It could be a door or a floorboard. I can't tell. I don't see anyone, but the feeling clings to me like eyes watching from the shadows and from behind cracked doors.

I hear the kitchen before I see it. Pots clatter, knives cleave, and someone shouts orders in the distance. Then, the smell hits me: meat, herbs, and the warm sweetness of freshly baked bread. I follow my nose down a flight of stairs.

The kitchens, when I find them, are alive. Black cast-iron pots hang from thick hooks along the ceiling. A hearth large enough to roast an entire stag dominates one wall. Finally, here's the mess and noise of a great palace. Kitchen staff chop and shout, stir and wash. Voices rise over the din as chefs give orders and chastise slow kitchen maids. I stand in the doorway, watching the chaos. Heat from the ovens radiates clear across the room. It's the first time I've felt truly warm in weeks.

No one notices me until a young woman in a damp apron freezes mid-step. Her eyes grow round and her mouth drops open in a silent "O." The spoons in her hand clatter to the ground. The entire kitchen grows silent and still as every pair of eyes finds me.

I hold up my hands in what I hope is a universal sign of peace. "I apologize for interrupting. I ... um ... was looking for ..."

They all stare.

Apologizing again, I turn and run back out into the corridor. Around the corner, I slump against the stone wall and slide to the ground in defeat. Eventually, the noise of the kitchens returns, muted this time and laced with whispers. I wrap my arms around my knees and rest my head, staring at the worn flagstones.

Footsteps echo down the hall, but I don't look up until a pair of brown leather boots stop in front of me. The toes are scuffed and worn, but they're not Tristan's. I raise my head and squint up at the intruder.

Nalina stands like a warrior, her feet apart and shoulders back. She's watching me with narrowed emerald eyes. "You're lost."

I lift my chin, defiance rising despite my hunger and exhaustion. "I know exactly where I am."

Nalina's laugh is quick and unexpected, more of a bark. I get to my feet, wincing as my bones creak. We stare at each other for a long time.

Up close, I can see that Nalina is objectively beautiful, scar notwithstanding. She's a large woman whose broad stature belies immense strength. She's clearly not the type to care about primping or dressing to impress. Her clothes are worn and practical, allowing for easy movement. Her leather vest and breeches are scuffed. Her only adornment is a silver wolf brooch pinned to her chest, a reminder that Nalina isn't any ordinary guard. She's a Wolf, like Tristan, and just as deadly.

"Come," she says. "The guest rooms are this way."

Too worn down to protest, I rise from the cold stone floor and follow her. The hallway she leads me through is colder than the rest of the castle, if that's even possible. Drafts slip through cracks in the mortar, stirring the thin tapestries that hang limp along the walls. A sense of unease tightens in my chest, and I start to wonder if I'm walking straight into a trap. But then Nalina pushes open a heavy wooden door and my breath catches.

The room opens to a wall of tall, arched windows, their glass blurred with frost. Even through the drifting snow, I can see the Spires in the distance and the mountain path home to Llwyn.

"It's beautiful," I whisper, before I can stop myself.

Nalina watches me with an unreadable expression.

The room itself is utilitarian. There's a single chair, an empty hearth that whistles with wind, and a massive bed covered with thick furs. But with that view, who needs gilded sconces or elaborate portraits?

I clear my throat, remembering myself. "Thank you."

Nalina's lips pinch, as if she's trying to decide whether she should speak her mind or not. She nods. "I'll ask someone to bring up firewood and a meal."

My stomach growls in response.

Her eyes flicker over my soiled red cloak and mud-caked boots. She turns to leave before pausing. "And warm water to bathe."

I'm far too grateful to care whether that's a veiled insult or not.

CHAPTER 4

MOONLIGHT POOLS ACROSS THE FLOOR, turning everything to silver and shadow. I can't sleep. The fire in the hearth has long since gone to embers, and the silence is too thick.

"*Trapped.*" The word echoes in my mind like a prison sentence.

As much as I hate it, the Dead Queen was right. There's no traveling through the Spires back to Llwyn, now. Not that I'd be welcomed back.

I slip from beneath the fur-lined covers, my bare feet cold against the stone floor. Outside, the storm still rages. I trace my fingers along the frozen windowsill as I ponder my situation.

If I return to Llwyn in the spring, I'll be on the run. My father wants me dead so my illegitimate brother can grow up to inherit the Fox Throne instead of me. Do I let him? I never wanted to rule to begin with. Do I just disappear into some forgotten corner of the world, always looking over my shoulder? Always afraid he'll find me?

The Fox in me recoils at the thought of running. Submission has never been my nature. I must find allies, fight, and challenge a throne I've never loved, in a kingdom that never felt like home. Even as I think it, I know it's not the kingdom I hate. It was my father poisoning everything in it. What if Llwyn could be different? What if I could build something better? I've never loved my kingdom. But perhaps I can love what it could become ...

After I kill my father.

The storm outside seems to whisper seductively ... *Kill the Fox King. Take the throne ... Be the true Fox Heir.*

Winter stretches before me. Months of waiting. Months of not knowing what's going on in Caerwen. Months of wondering what happened to Hunter after I crossed the Annwyn border without him.

A sting of grief and regret seizes my chest. I swallow it down like bitter medicine. After all, I deserve this pain. But these months will feel unbearable if all I do is wallow in it.

Instead, I need to use this time more productively. I need to prepare for whatever will come with the spring thaw. My fingers curl into fists against the cold glass. The storm continues, indifferent to my resolve. I may be trapped, but I am not defeated.

My red cloak hangs by the door. I pluck it from its hook but pause before putting it on. Something about it is different. I hold the fabric up to the moonlight to examine it. It's ... clean. The rips from the forest have been finely mended with red thread. Tiny stitches run here and there, like veins. Even the mud stains have been washed off. But how? No one came into my room. Had I fallen asleep after all? Even if I had, it's not possible that someone could've retrieved the cloak, washed it, dried it, and mended it so quickly.

It seems I still have much to learn about Gwyllion Castle.

I pull the cloak around my shoulders. There's no point in pacing in this room all night.

The hallway outside is lit only by moonlight. The pale glow filters through frost-laced windows, and the light casts strange patterns across the flagstones. The wind howls outside like a vulture circling low over the castle.

As I roam, every corridor looks the same. Shadows stretch across the walls as the moon shifts behind clouds. The tapestries lining the halls seem to breathe with each draft, their heavy fabric stirring. It feels as though they might reach for me if I walk too close.

Then I hear a new sound, small and quick, like footsteps. The skin on the back of my neck prickles and I hold my breath as I listen.

Silence.

I turn, but there's no one there. Only the empty hallway behind me, stretching long and cold. Could it have been mice? My gut twists. No. My dormant power stirs uneasily beneath my ribs in a subtle warning.

My steps are more cautious as I walk now. I scan the dark corners where moonlight doesn't reach and strain my ears against the shrieking wind.

Around the next corner, at the far end of the corridor, a door slowly closes.

I rush forward, heart hammering in my chest. My hand reaches for the door, pushing it open.

Inside the room, white cloths drape over furniture like shrouds. Dust coats everything, thick and undisturbed. Even the floor is covered in a layer of dust, not a single footprint in sight.

And yet, I know I'm not alone.

Still, I tell myself it was the wind. Just another draft slipping through the stonework, making the old bones of this castle creak and groan.

As I stand in the doorway, clouds swallow the moon and the room grows dark. I wait, staring. The darkness grows so thick, it feels like a living thing pressing against my skin. My heart pounds wildly, echoing in my ears.

But still, I am alone.

I fumble backward, one hand pressed to the cold wall as I feel my way blindly back toward my room. Once my bedroom door is latched, I spin around to search the room. Another winter storm rages outside the large windows, the bedcovers are rumpled, and the room is still.

But one thing is not as I left it.

My eyes snag on a flash of white on the bedside table. It's a note. The paper is wrinkled and the handwriting is scratchy, but the message is clear.

"Leave."

Oh, how I wish I could. I snatch up the paper, crinkle it into a ball, and throw it into the hearth to burn when I light tomorrow's fire. Even as fear curls tight in my chest, I'm certain of one thing: Gwyllion holds secrets. And if I'm to be trapped here all winter, I may as well uncover them.

————

Morning comes, but without much light. The darkness gradually shifts to gray, and the shadows soften.

Despite my sore limbs, I get out of bed quickly. My eyes snag on the hearth, searching for the flash of white paper in the ashes, but the note is gone.

When I shiver, it has little to do with the chill. The stone floor is like ice beneath my feet as I tiptoe to the massive windows in my room. The storm has ceased, leaving behind a pristine landscape of immaculate white. It's beautiful, even if it is deadly.

My thoughts darken as Hunter floats to the forefront of my mind. If he's alive, he's out there somewhere in the cold winter, beyond the Spires. I hope with all my heart that he survived the fire and corpse beasts of Ellyll, but I know it's unlikely. Even if he did survive, we're now worlds apart. Separated not just by mountains, but by secrets and betrayals too big to overcome.

Guilt sends waves of nausea cascading through me. It was a mistake leaving him behind. Even if he refused to travel into Annwyn with me, I shouldn't have trusted the Wolf. The price for answers about Grandmother was too high. Now that I know what happened to her, I see how foolish I was. I should've let the dead stay buried. But it's too late now, so I swallow down the guilt.

I can't survive a winter in Annwyn, simpering and whining about my mistakes. I need to own them and move on. It's time to take control of my situation. I may have been tricked into coming here, but I refuse to be a captive.

Besides, foxes are famous for outwitting traps.

My door creaks as I make my way out into the empty halls. I note subtle differences in the tapestries and doorways as I create a mental map of my surroundings. This castle is huge. It must have been a place of immense power in centuries past, back when the human kings of the North ruled. Long before the Dead Queens took their place. Now all that remains are the Wolves and the servants of the Dead Queen.

This is disorienting, considering the tales I grew up with. I'd always believed Annwyn was filled with armies of death-wielding warriors with shadow power, killing every living thing in their way. In Llwyn, even children know the Dead Queen raises corpses from their graves to continue fighting for her. But I haven't seen a single undead human in Gwyllion, apart from the queen. And then there were the borderlands. Each time we were attacked, it was by corpse beasts. Not men. And certainly not human corpses.

Realization blooms within me. The Wolves here are all wounded, and there are very few servants for a castle this size. Now that I'm here in Annwyn, I see the truth. There aren't many Annwyn fighters left in this desolate land. If Wolves refuse to revive dead humans, as Tristan swears is true, then they have no choice but to rely on beasts. And they won't be able to keep my father's soldiers out of Annwyn for much longer.

Hinges groan in protest as I push against a door that leads outside. It presses into a snowdrift, but I manage to open it just enough to slip out. The snowfall is up to my knees, but I high-step my way out to the perimeter of the castle anyway.

The world is so quiet, it feels as though my head is underwater. The air hovers around freezing, but it's not so cold that I must return indoors.

I push through the snow, carving a path along the castle's edge. Beyond the battlement wall, the Spires rise to the south. As I continue, my feet grow numb in my soaked boots.

I'm just about to turn back when I stumble upon a long glass building, half-buried in snow. A narrow path has been cleared, leading from a castle door to its entrance. I push my way through the snow, nearly spilling onto the cleared path. My legs burn with exertion, and my heart is pounding. After catching my breath, I reach for the glass door and step inside.

It's a greenhouse. But unlike the ones back home filled with exotic flowers, this one holds planter boxes lined with vegetables. Carrot greens, fennel stalks, and curly parsley rise from the soil in neat rows. Lettuce and herbs cluster together in varying shades of green, white, and purple. Overhead, bundles of chamomile, lavender, and other drying plants hang from the rafters, likely for teas and tinctures. No doubt they were gathered to last through the long winter.

I stare at all the colors in awe. So far, Gwyllion has felt like nothing more than the empty husk of a castle, cold and dead. But here, in the middle of a harsh winter, plants bloom.

"They're medicinal," a voice says.

I jump and turn. An old woman watches me through narrowed eyes, her skin wrinkled and browned from the sun. She's standing at the far end of the greenhouse, her posture wary.

"Though I doubt a lady such as yourself would recognize such plants," she says, her voice thick with contempt.

"I know a thing or two about healing," I say. Her words sting because she's right. I don't know what these plants are used for. My bloodline is gifted with the greatest power of healing in Llwyn. What use were plants when I could cure a fever with a touch, or knit flesh and sinew back together in moments?

The old woman eyes me warily. "I'm sure you do." She sniffs. "But not what those plants are good for."

After a moment, I concede. "You're right."

She nods, her face still wary. Her hair escapes from beneath a worn scarf. It's white and wild like the landscape. She wears layers upon layers of worn wool, everything the color of dried leaves and earth. The curve of her back and the lines on her face hint at a life of harsh winters and laboring summers, but her eyes are clear as a mountain stream.

"You're the Fox Heir," she says. It's not a question.

I say nothing.

Her hands are gnarled, with fingers twisted like roots. She digs them into the planter box in front of her, then pulls up several small beets. She knocks them against her thigh to shake the soil loose, then tosses them into a waiting basket.

"I'm Sienna."

She pauses, eyeing me again for a long time before she says, "Tabitha." She plucks a curved knife off a nearby potting bench. She ignores me as she grabs handfuls of kale and cuts them at the stems.

"Can I help?"

She pauses, watching me. "You? Want to 'help'?"

I nod.

She scoffs, shaking her head. "Well, that's a new one."

Her sharp dismissal stings. "We've only just met."

"Aye," she says, cutting the greens more vigorously. "But I know you, Fox Heir. I've known you all your life."

My stomach drops. "How could that be true?"

"I know your people." She tosses her greens on top of the beets in the basket, then kicks it further down the line of vegetables. She scoots to follow it as she continues working. "The Fox King, and the Fox King before him. The greedy, selfish Llwyn royals, intent on taking the lands of my people. No matter the cost." Her hands are shaking, her knife cutting less carefully with each new handful.

"I'm not like my father." I lift my chin, even though I'm not so sure she's wrong about me.

She scoffs again, ignoring me.

I watch as she moves on to cutting stalks of asparagus. Each slice is crisp and precise despite the gnarled hand holding the blade.

My voice is quiet and earnest when I ask, "What has it cost you?"

She looks up at me. "Everything." Her voice trembles with emotion. "Your bloody throne has cost me everything."

She slices another bunch of greens, but her knife slips, slicing into the palm of her hand. The knife clatters to the ground. Her eyes are wide with shock as she takes in the trickle of blood, dripping down her fingers and onto her feet.

I rush forward on instinct. "I can help." Before I even touch her skin, she pulls back, her eyes alarmed.

"Don't you touch me!"

"It's alright," I say, reaching for her hand again. "I can heal you." It's only now that I remember I can't. My power is still infuriatingly unreachable inside of me.

"I'd rather die of infection!" She scrambles back, smearing blood on the potting bench behind her. She scurries around the planter bed, watching me with anxious eyes. "Don't you dare touch me with your filthy hands!"

I freeze in place, confused. "I only meant to help."

Her face is dark with rage that I don't understand. She spits, her saliva hitting me in the cheek. I'm too shocked to do or say anything before she slips out the door and back into the snow.

CHAPTER 5

I'M STILL in the greenhouse when I hear footsteps crunching through the snow outside.

Nalina walks through the glass door. Her curly blond hair is tied back in a braid, but she's dressed in the same scuffed brown leathers as she wore yesterday. Her mouth is set in a thin line of irritation when she spots me. "There you are."

"Here I am." I continue sweeping the spilled soil from the greenhouse floor with a broom and dustpan I found tucked into a corner.

The look on her face suggests I'm due for a scolding, but she hesitates, taking in the room. Where there had been broken pottery and piles of dead leaves, the greenhouse is now clean. I'd spent most of the morning clearing debris and stacking it in a far corner. The potting benches are tidy, their tools organized neatly in empty clay pots. Even the paths between planter beds are swept clean of soil and scattered leaves.

Nalina blinks once, twice. "What are you doing?"

I shrug as I dump the last pail of spilled soil from the ground into a large bucket. I'm not sure if it can be re-used, but I didn't know where else to put it. "Cleaning."

"Cleaning ... dirt?" Nalina looks at me as if I'm the strangest person in this strange land.

I cross my arms in front of my chest, refusing to be belittled. "What else am I supposed to do in this dilapidated castle all winter long?"

She pauses, considering, then shrugs. "Thankfully, that's not my problem." She gestures for me to follow her. "The queen is waiting."

My stomach drops. Of course, I knew I couldn't avoid my grandmother all winter, but I'd hoped to draw it out a little longer. With a resigned sigh, I return the broom to its cobwebbed corner and trail after Nalina as she leads me out of the greenhouse and back toward the castle.

I expect her to turn toward the throne room, but the hallway she takes is unfamiliar. We wind through the castle until we reach a narrow spiral staircase, its steps worn smooth with age. It's one of the castle's many towers. I follow her up the steps, boots squeaking slightly on damp stone. At the top, we stop before a wooden door. The first thing I notice is the moth carved into its center. The same moth that's on my grandmother's necklace.

Nalina opens the door and steps aside.

I blink at her. "Aren't you coming?"

She grins wickedly. "I'm not the one who was summoned."

I glower at Nalina as I step into the tower room. The space is round with tall, arched windows that face every direction. From this height, I can see the roiling sea to the east. It churns beneath a jagged line of cliffs that stretches for miles. A narrow strip of beach lies below, scattered with boulders and pummeled by waves. In the north, thin tendrils of smoke rise from crooked chimneys in the village, with the wild sprawl of Annwyn beyond. I imagine that's where most of the Gwyllion people live. The castle halls are far too empty to house many.

At the far window stands the Dead Queen. She's tall and unnervingly slender, draped in a black gown that pools around her like spilled ink. She turns as I enter, lifting her eyes toward me through a sheer black veil. Dressed entirely in shadow, she might be mistaken for a wraith were it not for the glint of silver at her breast. The moth necklace catches the light.

The sight of it twists something inside me, and I fight the bile rising in my throat. I wore that necklace for months, dreaming of her. Longing for answers. Wishing I knew what happened.

Now I wish I didn't.

The Dead Queen nods to me. "Granddaughter."

I pinch my lips together, refusing to call her "Grandmother." She isn't. Not anymore. She's the Dead Queen now.

"You sent for me."

She nods. "I trust you had a restful evening."

"Not really."

"Pity."

A distant roll of thunder breaks the silence. My eyes flick to the tall windows. Another storm is already gathering over the peaks of the Spires to the south. A strong draft cuts through the room, making me shiver. It whistles from a narrow wall along one side of the tower. I turn and find it lined with narrow cracks.

No. Not cracks. They're too orderly for that. They're thin gaps in the stone, barely half an inch wide and no more than three inches tall. It's just enough to let the wind in. Odd. No stonemason would have made such an error, especially in a place with winters like this.

"I apologize for the chill," the Dead Queen says. "I no longer feel the cold."

I sniff and pull my cloak tighter around my shoulders. We face each other in silence until the wooden door opens behind me, making me jump in surprise.

Tristan brushes past me to kneel before the Dead Queen. "My queen." She nods to him, and he rises before turning to me. "Red."

I mask the heat rising to my cheeks with a scowl, irritated with myself for the flicker of relief I feel at seeing him. I shouldn't be pleased. He's my captor. The trickster. The Wolf I rescued from the edge of death in my father's kennels, no matter how regretfully.

Today, he looks different. His strong jawline is clean-shaven, and his dark hair is no longer dusty from weeks on the road. He's wearing black leathers and a fresh shirt now. They're tailored to fit the Dead Queen's court, showing off his broad frame and legs that are used to climbing mountains. A silver wolf pin now gleams from his chest. My eyes dip lower, to the leather belt around his waist and the silver sword sheathed there.

He seems taller, more composed, but his eyes are the same stormy gray. When they find mine, my chest tightens and my breath catches. I hate that he has that effect on me.

The Dead Queen turns to me. "It has come to my attention that you recently came into an unusual amount of power. But it seems you've burned it out just as quickly."

I shoot Tristan a glare before responding, since he's the only one who could've told her. "I have."

"Would you explain it to me?"

"There isn't much to tell."

From behind her sheer veil, I can see the queen's white eyes studying me. "When you were a little girl, I wondered if you were more powerful than him." Her voice lowers meaningfully. "Than any of them."

I blink several times. "Them?"

"All the Foxes before you."

I scoff. "How could you possibly have suspected that?"

She shakes her head only once. "You haven't answered my question."

I look at Tristan again, but his expression is stoic. Distrust looms at the back of my mind. I may not trust the Dead Queen, but I'm not exactly in a position to bargain.

"I don't know how I accessed it," I admit. "It happened twice. We were facing death both times."

Tristan catches my eye. He nods slightly, urging me to continue.

"It happened first when wraiths chased us in a battle-sacked village." I swallow hard. That night, my power exploded out of me in a blaze of light, and I was burned out for days after.

As far as I know, this newly awakened power was only triggered by need. I had to save the Wolf, because he was the only one who could help me discover what happened to my grandmother. Even if he brought me here under false pretenses, I can't ignore that he nearly died trying to rescue me from the wraiths.

And if I'm being honest with myself, I needed to save him because I couldn't stand to watch him die. And that is why his betrayal cuts me so deeply.

"Go on," the queen says.

"The second time was on an old battlefield. Among the dead who didn't know ..." My voice fades.

They didn't know they were dead. I swallow hard. The dead had been cursed to remain trapped there eternally. Lost. Abandoned. And rightfully angry.

And *she* did it to them.

I clear my throat. "We narrowly escaped. My power has refused to cooperate ever since."

The Dead Queen nods, perhaps sensing the anger rising in me over what she'd done to those people. "It is regrettable, war."

"Regrettable?" I stare at her in disbelief. "Those souls will be punished forever. Both Llwyn and Annwyn fighters."

Tristan's eyes dart between me and the Dead Queen, his expression neutral. He was there on the battlefield too. He should be as outraged as I am, but he says nothing.

I narrow my eyes at the Dead Queen. "There is nothing *regrettable* about what you did. It was abhorrent."

"Yes," she says. "It was." The Dead Queen watches me for a long time as I try to regain my composure. "Sometimes creatures can be saved. Other times ..." She leaves the rest of her explanation hanging, like a criminal at the gallows.

Her dismissal of the living leaves me feeling ill. But, I need to remember I'm not speaking with my grandmother, I'm speaking with the Dead Queen. Perhaps it shouldn't be so unexpected.

Another gust of wind whistles through the narrow slits in the wall. I glance toward the sound and catch a flicker of movement. Something small is forcing its way through one of the gaps in the stone. It's not until the creature takes flight that I realize what it is. A moth, pale as bone, drifts on the draft. Its ragged wings look too damaged to fly, yet somehow it does. It glides over the Dead Queen and settles on her shoulder, delicate as snowfall. For several heartbeats, it rests there, its tattered wings fluttering open and closed. Then, silently, it lifts into the air and flies toward the rafters above us.

I watch it rise before I notice something that makes me gasp. Far above our heads, the rafters are moving. At first glance, it looks like a living, breathing ceiling. I squint at it, trying to understand what I'm seeing. It's not the rafters themselves that give the illusion, but countless pairs of wings.

Moths cover every surface above us. Brown, gray, striped and solid. Cabbage whites, speckled leopards, fuzzy silks, orange atlases, and even great lunas. They crowd the beams, fluttering for better purchase. Their wings—some whole, some ragged as crumpled leaves—stir softly in the draft. For a moment, it feels like they're watching us. Thousands of unblinking eyes, casting judgment from the darkness above.

I stare up at them, amazed. "Impossible ... it's winter. They should all be—"

"Dead?" the queen asks.

Of course. Here I am, in a crumbling tower owned by a dead regent who rules legions of corpse beasts, and I'm surprised that she has a menagerie of undead insects?

"I give them refuge," the Dead Queen says nonchalantly.

"But why moths?" My voice comes out strained.

I think of the silver moth blade tucked into the ankle of my boot. Moths were Grandmother's favorite creatures. For some reason, seeing the Dead Queen with them makes my stomach turn, like she's defiled Grandmother's memory somehow, just like she's defiled her corpse.

The Dead Queen studies me. "You know why."

I shake my head, refusing to believe it. "My grandmother had a connection with moths when she was alive."

"*I* had a connection with them, you mean."

"No." My voice is hard and brittle as obsidian. "*You* are not my grandmother. You're masquerading in what's left of her body."

The Dead Queen shrugs. "Maybe so. Still, I had a connection with them in life. Thus, I have a connection with them in death."

Nausea rises in my gut. Moths were sacred to me because Grandmother loved them so much. Now ... my eyes drift back up toward the fluttering rafters.

The queen's voice is clipped now. "Regardless of how you feel about me, I didn't request an audience with you to discuss the moths."

I drag my eyes away from the moving ceiling. From the other side of the room, Tristan studies me as if waiting to see how I'll react.

"Your power," the queen says. "You must learn to reclaim it."

Instantly, I'm wary. "Why is that any of your business?"

"Because someday, you may need to wield it in defense of your kingdom, not just to save your own skin."

I bristle at the implication that I'm selfish, even as a voice in the back of my mind tells me it's true. I square off with the Dead Queen of Annwyn, my gaze challenging. She's not *my* queen after all, only my host until spring. Until I can leave this cursed place and kill the Fox King. Then, I will come back and end her.

"And why would you care about the people in Llwyn?" I challenge.

She tilts her head to the side, like a curious predator. "Because I am going to help you take the throne from the Fox King."

———

It's an odd thing, realizing people believe in you when you hardly believe in yourself. It's especially strange coming from your mortal enemy.

There are many reasons I've never desired the Fox Throne, regardless of my royal bloodline. Sure, I have exceptional power to heal and cast light. Or at least, I used to. That's the only thing I can thank my father for. But it's more than that. When you grow up hearing what a disappointment you are, again and again, you start to believe it's true. I never loved Llwyn because it never loved me back.

But I've come to understand something. My father may wear the crown, but he is not Llwyn. Not even close. Llwyn is the grieving families who mourn loved ones lost in an unending war. It's the rebels who gather in secret, daring to speak against the throne. It's the people who despise the Fox King as much as I do.

And I left them behind.

Just like I did to Hunter on that bloody battlefield two weeks ago. I left my home for an undead woman in a tower filled with moths.

"Red."

I look up from the warm bowl of soup in my hands. I'd finally found the great hall with its long wooden tables and delicious smells emanating from the adjoined kitchen.

Across from me, Tristan slides onto a bench. He leans forward, resting his elbows on the table as he watches me. The dim lantern light casts shadows across his face, making him look older, but no less striking. I wish it did.

A wave of anger rises in me at the sight of him, but I squash it down. My spoon scrapes the bowl as I turn my focus back to the long-awaited meal in front of me. Last night's cold cellar rations did nothing to fill the emptiness left in my belly after weeks on the road.

"What do you want, Wolf?"

His lips press into a thin line at the title. He must've grown used to me calling him by his real name while we traveled. But that was before.

"I wanted to make sure you're alright."

I stare at him over the spoon hovering in front of my mouth.

"It's a lot. I know." His eyes flicker behind me. No doubt he's looking for eavesdroppers, but there's no one here but the nervous serving maid hovering near the kitchen. She fiddles with the hem of her apron, looking like she'd rather be anywhere but here, near the despised Fox Heir. I can't blame her. I'm not the best company.

I shove the spoon into my mouth and resume eating.

Tristan watches me, calculating. I ignore his stone-gray eyes. The serving maid tiptoes by, bringing another plate of food. She sets it in front of Tristan, and her gaze flickers up to his face. Only now do I realize that one of her eyes is clouded white, blind.

"Thank you, Elisandra." He nods to her.

I look up, shocked. This Wolf, one of the Dead Queen's most trusted advisors, knows the name of a serving maid.

Elisandra's face flushes, and she curtsies before scurrying away.

Tristan tears his bread and dips a piece into his bowl of soup. He chews, then moves to shove the other piece into his mouth before his eyes meet mine. I'm gaping at him like a stunned fish on a dock.

"Is there a problem?" he asks.

"You know her name?" My ears are humming.

He looks back at the serving maid, who's returned to her station near the kitchen door. "Yes? Did you think I made it up just now?" He squints at me.

I shake my head, swallowing the lump rising in my throat. "No, it's just ..."

Just what? That the knights and nobles in Caerwen never spoke to the servants unless giving an order? That the idea of calling a kitchen maid by her first name had never even crossed my mind until now?

"Just?" His gray eyes are on me, making heat rush up my neck.

I swallow. "Just different. Everything here in Annwyn. It's different." I sigh and push my empty bowl aside. "I don't really know how to behave here. What to do. Or say." I shrug.

He surprises me by chuckling.

"Excuse me?"

Tristan grins, and my heart stumbles at the sight of the dimple in his left cheek. Had that always been there, hidden beneath the stubble he wore during our long days on the road? I try to remember the first time I saw him, before he was shot with a crossbow and dragged into my father's dungeons. It was at my engagement ball just a few months ago, when he was dressed in immaculate black. But he hadn't smiled. He had no reason to.

He tears off another chunk of bread. "I heard you had a less than warm welcome in the greenhouse."

The heat I felt a moment ago switches to irritation. "And who told you that?"

He shrugs. "It's a big castle, but not *that* big. Word travels fast."

The memory of the old woman in the greenhouse still stings. "She said I had cursed hands."

Tristan shrugs. "It's a common sentiment in these parts. That the Llwyn light power is cursed."

"But why? Light power can help her."

"Not in the way she needs it."

I huff and throw my hands up helplessly. "I don't understand this place with your creepy, empty halls and cold, bitter people."

Amusement flickers in his eyes as he smothers another grin. "We may be cold and bitter, but you know why."

A hollow moment hangs between us. "My father."

He nods. "The woman you met is Tabitha. Her son and his wife died in the war. As did her husband. And every other relative in her family except for her young grandson. She's terrified the war will take him too."

My face pales. "That's awful."

"It's an all-too-common experience here, I'm afraid." Tristan watches my face intently. "I hope you can excuse my people's poor manners. They aren't accustomed to looking a Fox in the face. All they know is the death that follows in your wake."

My hands are shaking on the tabletop. I tuck them under my thighs, hoping the pressure will steady them. Of course, I had nothing to do with the deaths in Tabitha's family. But I can't blame her for hating my entire country because of it. Myself included.

"You've seen us now," Tristan says. "The real Annwyn. Our castles aren't filled with walking dead. Our treasury is empty. Our queen is not bloodthirsty."

I roll my eyes. "Well, I don't know about that."

He chuckles, then sighs. "You should talk to her. She's your grandmother, after all."

I breathe deeply, then shake my head. "No, she isn't. Not anymore. She stopped being my grandmother the moment she was reanimated."

He doesn't argue. I wonder just how much he knows about the woman my grandmother used to be. The woman who was adored by every servant and palace worker I ever met. Who taught me to sneak out at night so we could dance in the moonlight. Who taught me how to climb trees and run through the meadow without a care in the world. The woman who saved me from my father's cruelty again and again.

My hand reaches up toward my collarbone, to the place where her silver moth necklace used to rest. My fingers only find bare skin. I forgot how I'd thrown the necklace at her feet.

"Come with me." Tristan shovels the last of his bread into his mouth as he stands.

I raise an eyebrow.

"It's time you had an official tour." He holds out his hand toward me. "We can't have you falling into pits of corpse mice or running into our amateur undead theater troupe."

I blink up at him from my seat on the bench.

"Are you ... is that ...?"

"A joke, Red."

Despite myself, I sigh in relief. "If that's what stands for comedy in Annwyn, I'd hate to see what you consider tragedy." I stand but refuse to take his outstretched hand. I may have to play nice here in this den of Wolves, but I certainly don't have to touch one. My refusal just makes his irritating grin widen.

He laughs. "You're right about that."

Tristan leads me into the cavernous halls. Light beams through a break in the clouds and past the oversized windows, warming the stone beneath our feet. It's a rare treat to feel this warm.

Now that we're closer, I can see the hilt of Tristan's sword where it sticks out of its scabbard at his waist. It's a practical design made of silver, with few embellishments aside from the head of a wolf stamped above the cross-guard.

Our steps echo as we walk. Tristan points out various rooms and passageways. The path that leads to the throne room. The door that will take me out to the stables. The wing where the servants used to live.

"Used to?" I ask.

"They all chose to travel back and forth from the village now."

A pit forms in my stomach. "Since when?"

He shrugs. "It's a new development."

"It's me." It's not a question. I know in my bones that I'm the reason they left.

Tristan pauses, turning toward me. "They'll learn," he says with a conviction I can't quite muster. "You're not the enemy. If I could recognize that, they will too." He waggles his head back and forth. "Eventually." He resumes walking.

The note left in my room last night comes to mind, but I decide not to tell him. The last thing I need is for the Wolf to pity me. Still, there's mystery here in Gwyllion. Maybe more than one.

Tristan might be the only person who could help me figure out what's going on.

"Last night," I say, my voice hesitating. "The castle was so quiet. I wondered if they left for an entirely different reason." My mind wanders back to the footsteps I heard, and the doorway that I was sure someone hid behind. And the emptiness I found instead.

"And what reason would that be?" He gives me a quizzical look.

"I thought perhaps they were afraid it's haunted."

To my surprise, the Wolf doesn't laugh. His eyebrows lower thoughtfully. It takes him a full minute to speak. "They do say this castle is haunted. But not by ghosts."

"What then?"

He watches me from the corner of his eye, reading every line in my face. "By the fae who used to rule these lands."

A shiver runs through me that has nothing to do with the cold. Something in his words resonates deep in my chest, where my power lives.

"And do you believe that?" My voice is barely above a whisper.

He draws his lips into a thoughtful line, then shrugs. "Maybe." He gives me a wry grin. "I prefer to keep an open mind."

"So, the fae just ... linger here?" I think of the eyes I felt on my skin last night. Could it have been fae, hidden deep in the shadows?

"Not exactly." He leads me through the empty entrance hall that I found so intimidating when we first arrived. Now, it just strikes me as sad. "There aren't many fae left, not like there used to be in the age before the Dead Queens and the war. Those that remain cause minor mischief. Take what they want. Torment those they despise." He looks at me sideways. "There are a lot of illegitimate children who've been explained away by the mischief of the fae."

I scoff. "Naturally."

"But ..." He sighs. "The fact remains that there are many unexplainable events that happen here in Gwyllion. Not that I believe the fae can be blamed for all of them."

"Why do you think they're still here?"

He nods, pondering for a moment. "I suppose they're just ... waiting."

Tristan stops outside a simple wooden door. I lean out a nearby window and see a familiar sight. A training yard covered in snow. Frozen, straw-filled dummies and bags of sand hang from ropes, like nooses.

"Waiting? For what?" I raise an eyebrow.

"For the Heir to the North to save us all, of course."

CHAPTER 6

An hour later, the training yard is choked with shadows. They swirl around my legs and creep up my spine, curling into my hair. The shadows blind me, thickening with each failed attempt to summon my power. I plant my feet and reach inward again, clawing for the spark buried deep in my core. Nothing. Only the familiar emptiness.

Frustrated, I spin in place, heart pounding, eyes scanning the shadows for the Dead Queen. But she's vanished into the void, leaving me alone, grasping for light that refuses to come.

"You must learn to banish the darkness." Her voice is close, but I can't see her through the oppressive black.

"I'm trying," I grumble through my resentment.

Day one of training, and I already feel like a helpless child. I close my eyes and try to focus on the place where my power used to live, curled like a sleeping creature behind my sternum. But all I find is stillness. I grit my teeth, dig deeper, and drag it forward with everything I have.

The most I can manage is a faint stirring in my chest. A feeble spark, like a match about to sputter out. Then it dies, vanishing as if it never existed at all. A colorful curse slips from between my lips.

Somewhere behind me, the Dead Queen tuts. "And here I thought you were the Fox Heir. The woman with the power to heal legions and ignite battlefields."

"You heard exaggerations." I rip off my gloves and throw them onto the frozen ground. The cold bites instantly at my skin, but I ignore it. Pressing my fingertips to my temples, I take a deep breath and refocus. Slowly, my power begins to stir. It pools in my chest so sluggishly, it's torturous.

A dark wind snuffs it out like a pathetic candle.

"How is this teaching me anything?!" I yell, whirling around, trying to find the queen in the pitch blackness. "You won't even give me a moment to get my bearings!"

"And neither will your Fox King father," her voice whispers, smooth like black velvet. "He will murder you on the spot."

"I already know that!"

I can't see anything in the snow-covered training yard, but I pick a direction and start walking. If I can escape the queen's shadow, maybe I'll find some clarity at the edge of the yard.

"Perhaps. But I did not know how weak you've become in my absence," the queen says.

Her words grate like broken glass against my nerves. Absence? She abandoned me for a realm that was never hers, for a throne that stands in direct opposition to the one I was supposed to inherit. The kingdom I was going to rule before my illegitimate newborn brother was handed my birthright. Now, I stand to inherit nothing. Unless I take it for myself.

My feet are freezing, but I keep walking, careful not to slip on the icy ground. "You say that like I had anyone to help me after you ..."

Left me, I almost say, but I don't. I will never again grieve for this woman. I believed her dead and gone, and I suppose that's still true. Whatever stands in this yard now, speaking to me as if she still knows who I am, it isn't my grandmother. It's her corpse.

My shins slam into a crate filled with blunt, wooden practice swords.

I smother another curse and hop on one foot as I rub my aching leg. My boot stomps the snow-packed ground like I'm a temperamental child. "What good is learning to fight against your powers when I should be worried about my father's?" I shout.

"If you can't control your own light, then how do you expect to battle his?"

Instead of responding, I gesture silent curses into the darkness. My frozen breath disappears into the black mist around me.

"Control. That's how." She says evenly, as if she can see my rude motions through the darkness. "You must learn to control yourself and your power. To use it to its best advantage, in order to defeat the Fox King and his knights."

"And his entire army," I mumble. I start feeling my way around the crate of practice swords, toward what I hope is an exit from the yard. All I run into is a damnable sand-filled bag swinging from a rope. I hit it with both of my fists. It barely swings from the assault. I lean my head against it, smelling the cool canvas and the damp sand inside. "This is a mistake."

"No," the Dead Queen says simply. "It is destiny."

I scoff. "Destiny? Destiny is nothing more than a story told around the campfire to keep spirits high on the eve of battle."

"And what would you call this?"

"An experiment in torture?" I offer.

The Dead Queen says nothing, but I sense a sigh behind her silence.

In a split second, the darkness disappears, leaving me more disoriented than I was in pitch blackness. Sunlight reflects off the snow, blinding me. My legs wobble, and my head spins with vertigo from the sudden change.

Across the training yard, the Dead Queen watches. Unfazed and unruffled by the exercise, while I'm left squinting and exhausted.

"You need to work on your endurance," she says.

"Noted." I lean forward, bracing my hands on my knees as I let my heartrate return to normal.

"Stamina can only be earned through practice and constant vigilance."

"Got it."

"You will begin physical training." She turns to walk away, then calls over her shoulder. "With Tristan."

A protest rises in me, but before I can voice it, someone else cuts in.

"No."

The queen pauses mid-step.

"No?"

Tristan steps out from the castle walls where he's been watching my embarrassing display. His face is grave, and his arms are folded at his chest. "No."

The queen turns to him, her head tilted at a curious angle. "You would dare disobey a direct order from your queen?"

"I would if I suspected it was a mistake."

"Mistake." Her voice is even, thin.

He nods. "You can trust me to always tell you the truth, my queen. Even if it hurts to hear."

She pauses, considering. The stillness of her body reminds me she's dead. Her chest doesn't rise with breath, her feet don't shift for balance, and her fingers stay unnervingly still. I wouldn't be surprised if she didn't blink beneath her veil.

"Regardless of your concerns, I insist." She waves a hand, slow and dismissive, as if wafting his words away like smoke.

The corners of Tristan's mouth turn down in distaste.

"This is too important a mission to fail," she says. "We have only *one* weapon against the Fox King." Her head nods in my direction. "And she is weak."

Heat rises up my neck. "I'm a weapon now, am I?"

"And what else should you be?" The Dead Queen asks this as if she's merely curious. This irritates me further.

"I don't know." I shrug. "A living, breathing human being?"

She scoffs at the reminder that I'm not one of her undead legions. "You are more than that, Granddaughter. Or, you could be more if you only embraced your birthright. A weapon has power."

My skin prickles at the affectionate name. It sounds unnatural on her undead lips. "A weapon also has a wielder."

The Dead Queen shrugs. "Perhaps. At least until the weapon becomes its own master. But that," she turns her head back in Tristan's direction, "will take time and practice."

She glides through the castle doors, leaving me with a furious Wolf.

Tristan paces, kicking up slush from the muddy ground near the castle wall. He clearly wishes he could say more to the queen than he did. Something in the way he resisted her request irks me.

"Am I truly so despicable?" I ask.

He doesn't even pause his pacing. "No."

"I'm starting to wonder if that's the only word you can use today." I glance toward the Spires, their peaks swallowed by a storm thick with snow. I wonder how long before it reaches us.

He exhales sharply and throws up his hands. "No, you're not despicable." A beat. "Quite the opposite, actually."

The words make me flush, but there's a war inside of me. Hate battles against an attraction that I refuse to accept. Something in his gray eyes makes me feel naked, vulnerable. But I will *not* let this Wolf take my guard down. Never again.

I clear my throat. "How are you going to train me exactly?"

He looks around the frozen yard with its practice swords and balance posts. I'll feel ridiculous thwacking a straw dummy, but if he thinks it will help me defeat my father, then I'll do it. I'll do anything to kill him.

"I don't know yet."

"Then how do we start?"

"Not how, when."

"Okay, when?"

"Tomorrow morning. At dawn. I'll figure something out by then."

"Dawn?" My heart sinks.

A hint of a smile brushes his lips. "Yes, Red. Dawn. Meet me at the front gates."

Then, he turns and follows his queen out of the training yard, leaving me feeling very much like an annoyance and a burden.

So much for being a weapon.

———

After supper, I return to my room. Grateful for a moment of peace, I shut the door behind me and close my eyes. Dead Queens, corpse moths that gather in towers, crumbling castles held together by ancient spells ... When will I finally stop being surprised by this place?

A small scratching sound makes me open my eyes.

I follow the sound to the fireplace, where faint golden embers still glow from the day's fire. They're moving.

I drop to my knees and peer closer. A tiny creature, black as coal, rolls in the soot like a bird in a bath. It's round, like a mouse, but has no tail. It scoops up embers with its tiny hands and tosses them over its back, scrubbing soot into its fur. It wiggles its rump, then dives headfirst into the red-hot flames still burning in the remains of the firewood.

I startle, sure I've just watched it burn itself alive. But a moment later, it pops back out of the flames, looking thoroughly pleased with itself. I stare at it, wide-eyed.

It's fae, I realize with a rush of awe.

When its black eyes lock on mine, it freezes. We stare at each other, neither of us quite knowing what to do next.

I break first. "I won't hurt you."

At the sound of my voice, the tiny fae creature darts for a crack in the fireplace wall and disappears. I stare at the spot for a long time. How many fae creatures are in this castle? Or in all of Annwyn? My head whirls with the realization that I know so little about this place. It's at once exhilarating and overwhelming at the same time.

When I'm sure the creature isn't coming back, I cross the room to the towering windows. The view steals my breath as the sun sets over the mountains in the west. Storm clouds ignite in violent shades of pink, orange, and red. The snow-covered peaks reflect the blaze in a dazzling display of light. Reflection, it seems, can be nearly as powerful as the source itself.

I squint but can't look away. The jagged mountains shift with sun and shadow, changing from molten gold to deep violet. In the distance, a pack of corpse wolves howls into the encroaching dusk.

After twilight fades into night, I turn my gaze toward the south. It feels like I can see Llwyn there, just beyond the Spires and storm-heavy sky. My thoughts drift to the palace in Caerwen, where my father is no doubt still seething over my escape.

And even though Elena betrayed me by calling her son my father's heir, I still hope she survived my father's curse of inconvenient women dying too soon. No matter how wrong things went between us, I never wanted to see her trapped in my father's web.

No one deserves that fate.

A knock on the door brings me back from my thoughts. I turn from the darkened windows, and I'm surprised to realize there are tears on my cheeks. I wipe them away hastily, then open the door.

Nalina stands there, like a mountain topped with a thick blond braid. She thrusts something toward me.

"Here. For you."

There's a clump of black leather in her outstretched hands. I take it warily. It unfolds in my grip, showing itself to be a pair of leather breeches like the ones she wears.

I lift an eyebrow. "Oh, um ..."

"He insisted."

"Pardon?" I look up at her, wondering if I somehow misunderstood something.

"Tristan."

"Ah." I force a smile. "Thank you, but I'm not sure they're—"

"He wouldn't take 'no' for an answer." She sighs her disappointment. "Believe me, I tried."

"Hm." I purse my lips, unsure what to say.

"They were an old pair of mine. I had them taken in. You're not as tall or strong as I am."

I ignore the insult. My legs itch just at the sight of the tight, black leather. How does Nalina wear these every day? "Why do I need them?"

She shrugs. "I didn't ask. But he said they're for tomorrow. For training."

"Of course. Training." I mumble. I am not looking forward to whatever the Wolf has in store for me. It's bound to be unpleasant.

Nalina turns to leave, then looks back at me, her hand resting on the enormous sword at her hip. "I hope they know what they're doing." I must look confused because her mouth turns down even further. "With you, I mean."

I nod. "You and me both."

She studies me for a second longer before stomping back down the hall.

I close the door and hold up the breeches. Black leather, slightly scuffed. These were clearly not her favorite pair. They don't hold nearly as many scratches and repairs as the ones I've seen her wearing.

I toss them onto the bed and fumble beneath my skirts to remove my stockings. It's probably best to try the leathers on now, before I'm expected to wear them for whatever torture Tristan has in store for me next.

Another knock sounds at the door, softer this time. I pull the stocking off my foot as I call out.

"Just a moment!" With one foot bare and freezing against the stone floor, I open the door.

There's no one there.

I look down the hall in both directions, but whoever knocked hadn't wanted to wait. After closing the door again, I reach down to wrestle with my other stocking. I barely have time to slide it over my knee before another knock sounds. This time, I open it within seconds.

Still, no one.

I pause, waiting. All is silent. But as I turn to close the door, a flash of white on the ground catches my eye. At my feet, there's a torn slip of paper. The handwriting is messy, but familiar. I saw it once before.

"Get out."

My power rumbles a low warning in my sternum. Some-where, there are eyes watching me. I can feel an invisible gaze inching over my skin. I slam the door closed again.

No knocks follow.

CHAPTER 7

I'VE NEVER FELT MORE EXPOSED.

The black leather breeches cling like a second skin, tracing every movement and every curve of my body. It's not that I'm a prude, but I'm not used to parading my thighs through a castle full of watchful eyes. Or my ass.

Still, there's nothing to do but square my shoulders and wrap myself in false confidence like armor. Nalina doesn't seem to give a damn what anyone thinks of her. She may be grumpy, fearsome, and unapologetically herself, but there's something to admire in that kind of defiance. I bunch up my red cloak and carry it under my arm, refusing to let anyone see me shrink.

The sun hasn't risen yet, and already there are a handful of townspeople in the castle at dawn. Sleepy-eyed men carry stacks of logs toward the kitchen. Yawning serving girls rush after them to cook breakfast for anyone who wants it. I'm far too nervous to eat, so I skip the kitchens and head straight for the front gates.

When I get there, Tristan is waiting, leaning against the stone like he's been there for hours. He looks perfectly at home here in this dark, crumbling castle with his black clothes and silver Wolf pin. He tilts his head when he notices me. His dark hair falls over one eye. "Took your time."

"The sun has barely risen."

"But it *has* risen. Hence, it's after dawn."

I cross my arms over my chest. "You didn't exactly give me a precise time."

He stands straight, brushing the stone dust off the back of his shoulders. "Noted for tomorrow." He pauses, seeming to finally notice what I'm wearing. His eyes travel down my legs and back up again.

I stand firm. "I heard you insisted."

He merely nods, then walks out the door. Reluctantly, I follow as I throw my red cloak over my shoulders to brace against the cold.

For all his whining about it being past dawn, the sky is only barely lightening. Thankfully, it isn't snowing and there's only a slight breeze. The world is silent as we trudge across the snow-covered ground, toward the stables. But instead of continuing toward the horses, who snort loudly in their stalls, he opens what appears to be a storage shed. I wait outside as he knocks things around wordlessly. After several moments, he emerges carrying an armful of weapons. He tosses me a tarnished silver sword. I barely manage to grab it without slicing my hand.

He watches me with a pained expression.

"What?" I demand, straightening. "I wasn't exactly trained with a sword."

"No," he says. "I seem to recall you are more adept with knives." His eyes drift down my legs again, to the ankle of my boot where I hide my moth-engraved knife. My skin flushes as his eyes trail the length of me, but I lift my chin, refusing to shy away from his lingering gaze. Heat builds low in my belly.

Tristan raises an eyebrow at me, questioning. "I assume you have your vicious blade hidden down there?"

I cross my arms again. "You'll just have to find out."

A sly grin crosses his face. "Don't tempt me."

I refuse to blush at the implication. "What exactly are we doing today, anyway?"

"Hunting," he says as he grabs a sling of arrows, followed by one of the bows.

"Hunting?" I balk. "I thought you were supposed to train me in endurance."

"Exactly." He nods toward a hook on the inside of the open door. It's cluttered with a variety of sheaths, holsters, and buckles. I grab a thick leather belt and tie it around my waist before sliding the tarnished sword into its scabbard. It hangs against my leg, clunky and annoying. How does anyone get used to wearing one of these?

Tristan pulls the sling of arrows over his shoulder with practiced ease. "The best way to build stamina is by doing something practical. There's nothing more irritating to me than jumping around and lifting bags of flour to build muscle when you could do something useful."

"Like hunting."

"Precisely."

I sigh and take the bow from his outstretched hand. I pull it over one shoulder like I've seen hunters do in Caerwen.

He watches me with those storm-gray eyes. "Our hike across Llwyn and through the Spires was a good start. At least you've built up some muscle in your legs ..." His eyes drift down again. "And lungs." His eyes move higher, lingering on the swell of my breasts beneath my wool shirt.

I stiffen, instinctively wanting to wrap my red cloak around myself like a shield. But I stop. That urge belongs to a girl I no longer am, a girl trained to be modest, obedient, pleasing. I refuse to be that person. I'm done with being someone I'm not.

Instead, I keep my arms at my sides. Let him look. The secret truth is, I like it when he looks at me that way.

When Tristan's eyes meet mine, I stare him down, daring. The heat low in my belly smolders a little hotter, despite my hatred for the Wolf.

He turns and heads toward the looming battlement wall

surrounding the castle grounds. When we reach it, he pulls a lever and a heavy door reinforced with iron swings open.

Alarm shoots through me as I remember what happened last time we were outside the castle walls.

"We're going out there?" I ask, trying to mask my fear. "What about the corpse wolves?"

"They mostly stick to the south." He points west, toward the tree-lined forest. "We're going that way." He walks through the heavy doorway and, reluctantly, I follow.

Out beyond the castle's walls, the world is white. We trudge through the knee-high snow, across a wide valley. In the distance, the dark western forest waits. I scramble after him, the sword thudding against my legs with every step. After the third time I stop to readjust it, Tristan stomps back toward me.

"We're never going to get to the hunting grounds if you can't even cross a meadow without pausing."

"You're the one who insisted I wear this infernal thing."

He reaches for my waist. Fingers brush the curve of my hips beneath my red cloak as he adjusts the scabbard on my belt. The shift angles the sword away from my legs. His eyes drift back up to mine.

"There," he murmurs, his voice low. "That should feel better."

His hands linger there, beneath my cloak. Heat seeps through the fabric of my clothing, blooming across my skin. I'm hyper-aware of his touch. It burns and aches with something forbidden. I shouldn't feel this way about the Wolf. I hate him.

Still, I hold his gaze longer than is strictly appropriate.

He pulls his hands away and steps back, but I don't miss the way his fingers stay splayed, like they've been burned. Without a word, Tristan turns toward the trees. His boots carve a path through the snow.

As the world lightens around us, my eyes dart to the cloudless sky above.

"If you're thinking of running, I would reconsider."

I jump, irritated that the Wolf seems to be able to read minds now. "And why's that?"

"This area is enchanted to keep most of the storms at bay. But it doesn't go beyond a few miles' radius from the castle." He points to the east, where dark clouds seem to roil above the turning sea.

"And I'm supposed to believe you?" I ask even as my eyes dart to more ominous clouds hovering above the Spires in the south.

He studies me. "I think you already do."

I roll my eyes. "If there's an enchantment protecting this place, then why is this crumbling castle continuously battered by storms?"

"I never said it was strong enough to keep out *all* the winter storms." Tristan pauses at the tree line, peering through the branches for a path to follow. "Even the strongest, oldest power can't protect us from the worst the world has to offer." He gives me a long look. "I assure you, to leave is certain death." He pushes past a bushy fir and holds the branch aside for me to follow.

Inside the forest, it's like another world entirely. Pine needles glisten in the rays of sunlight that fight their way past the canopy overhead. Snow makes the branches droop, as if every tree were bowing before a dance. The silence here is less ominous and more ... peaceful.

"Who even has power strong enough to enshroud an entire castle in a protective circle?" I ask.

"The fae."

This stops me in my tracks. "The fae?"

He nods. "It's why we're all trapped here, in this 'crumbling castle'. It's the only place left that's safe for us. Everything else was taken or destroyed by your ancestors."

He doesn't say it to be a jibe, but I feel a stab of shame anyway, even if there's not much I can do about the past. "I thought there weren't many fae left."

"There aren't." He takes off one of his leather gloves and

presses it to the bark of an old tree. "And those that remain no longer have that level of magic."

"Then how ..."

"It's been enchanted for centuries, Red."

My eyes grow wide with wonder. "But power doesn't work like that. Power doesn't linger."

"We're not talking about human power, Red. Fae magic. It's different from ours."

"But that sort of power ... the amount of strength it would take for it to last centuries ..."

"Was immense. Yes."

My mind whirls. No wonder light and shadow power still live on in our blood. It lingers, like booming thunder echoing off mountains.

"That's impossible," I whisper in awe.

"For us, yes." Tristan shrugs. "But the fae were far more powerful than we could possibly understand." He nods toward the heart of the forest. "Come on, we've got tracking to do." He moves beneath the trees, his footsteps muffled by the snow.

We walk west. Our tracks leave a trail for us to follow when we return, but something tells me Tristan doesn't need them. By the way he peers at the trees and crouches to the ground in concentration, he seems to know this forest as well as the castle.

"We can't go much further in this direction, or we risk leaving the protective barrier," Tristan says, his voice quiet.

Up ahead, the forest turns gloomy with shadows. A thought crosses my mind. I haven't seen a living creature since we entered the forest.

Tristan puts a finger to his lips in the universal sign for quiet. He pivots, taking us north. My legs ache from walking through the heavy snow, but I don't complain and I don't slow down. Next to me, a large pile of snow falls from a branch overhead, nearly catching me underneath. I peer up into the trees, squinting. The boughs ahead of us are moving, bouncing and shaking piles of snow from the pines.

At first, I think I see a family of squirrels overhead. But when I look closer, I see something else. The small brown creatures are similar in size to a squirrel, but they have no bushy tails. Their limbs are human-like, but bent at strange angles. Their bodies are round and covered in thick, patchy fur, like a winter cloak gone to moths. The creatures have wide faces with squashed noses and mouths that turn down slightly in a permanent frown. But what truly gives them away are their long fingers and beady black eyes.

"Fae," I whisper in awe.

I watch as they hop from one overhead branch to the next, knocking snow down along their path. They pay us no attention as they continue on their journey west, toward the storm-dark trees beyond the protected area. Before the last one vanishes from sight, it turns around to stare at me. Its face is almost curious. We lock eyes for a moment before a long tongue reaches out to lick its eyeballs like a frog. It's vision cleared, it leaps out of sight.

For a long while, I stare into the darkened forest where the fae disappeared. Tristan touches my elbow, and when I glance at him, he's crouched low, nodding toward the opposite direction. That's when I hear the grinding sound that echoes against the trees. I crouch beside him, on alert.

Through the underbrush, I catch sight of a giant moose. It rubs against a thick cedar tree, its muscles rippling beneath its hide. The animal must be eight feet tall, with antlers of ice-covered bone that top even that. It scrapes them high up on the tree and bark rains down like shattered glass.

Nothing in the south grows this big. My heart hammers in my chest.

Beside me, Tristan slides the bow from his shoulder and draws an arrow from his sling. To my surprise, he hands it to me.

I hesitate. He arches a brow and jerks his chin at me. I take the arrow and pull my own bow off my shoulder. Tristan grabs another one from the sling and draws it back with practiced ease, muscles flexing. He nods for me to do the same. I study his hands, trying my best to ignore the shape of his strong fingers and the way he pulls the string of the bow back effortlessly.

My arms tremble as I knock my own arrow and draw the bowstring back. I hold my breath and steady my aim at our target. The tension in the string takes far more strength than I anticipated. My arm strains and my fingers grow white with effort as I try to hold position.

"On my count," he whispers. "Three ... two ..."

I can't hold the string back any longer. The rope snaps back, stinging my wrist as the arrow slips through my fingers, arching wildly into the trees. I stumble, losing my balance and crashing into Tristan. His arrow, released in the chaos, strikes the moose high on its flank. Tristan and I look up from our heap on the ground.

The moose bellows, a sound that seems to shake the ground beneath us. It rears back, its hooves digging into the snow. Then, instead of fleeing, it stops and turns in our direction. Steam bursts from its nostrils with each breath. Its brown eyes narrow in on us as it stomps the ground in fury.

Tristan shoves me off him and grabs my arm, hauling me to my feet. We break into a sprint.

Hooves pound behind us as we dart between trees. The moose barrels after us, splintering branches with its massive antlers. I veer left, trying to escape its path, but a sickening crack stops me cold. I glance back, panic seizing my chest, as the moose tosses Tristan aside like he weighs nothing. He hits the ground hard, rolls through the snow, then scrambles to his knees.

In one swift motion, Tristan draws another arrow and shoots. It bounces off the moose's thick hide. The moose skids, hooves carving deep ruts into the frozen dirt. Then it turns, antlers lowered, preparing to charge straight at Tristan.

"Go, Red!" Tristan yells without taking his eyes off the animal.

But my feet are glued to the frozen ground. I can't leave him in danger, that irritating, infuriating Wolf. Suddenly, I realize there might be another way.

I can't outrun the moose or help Tristan from the ground. So, I look up. The snow-capped trees sway above us, and an idea strikes me. I toss aside my red cloak and scramble up the nearest spruce. Turns out, these leather breeches were a good idea after all.

Below, Tristan weaves between trees, the moose lumbering after him. He knocks another arrow, but the shot glances off an antler and vanishes into the trees.

Finally, I reach a long snow-covered branch and shake it.

Nothing happens.

I need better footing, and there's only one way to get it. Higher. I grit my teeth and climb, muscles burning as I haul myself up past the next branch.

Then, I jump.

My boots slam onto a snow-covered limb, jarring it so hard it crashes into the neighboring tree. Then another. Branches sway in a chain reaction as snow drops in a thunderous hush. Snow falls like a curtain of white over the moose and Tristan below. It blinds them both, just long enough.

I unsheathe my sword and leap out of the tree—right onto the moose's shoulders.

It's disoriented in the whiteout, but it knows enough to try to knock me off. I hold tight, my thighs squeezing the animal's neck as I loop one arm around an antler. It's all I can do to hold on as it bucks.

Tristan rolls out of the way of the creature's hooves. I swipe my sword toward the beast's neck, but all I manage to do is slice its skin. At this angle, with only one available hand, it's not enough.

With a curse, I throw the infernal weapon to the ground, then reach into my boot to retrieve my trusty knife. The silver blade flashes in the sun before I stab the creature in the neck, dragging my blade across its artery.

Blood gushes over the snow, turning the whiteout red. The spray of warm blood coats my arm and face as the creature finally slows. There's just enough time for me to roll out of the way as its 2,000-pound body crashes to the ground with a thump. The moose looks toward me with surprise, then the light fades from its eyes.

My hand instinctively reaches up to my own neck, touching the thin scar there. I just killed a creature the same way my father tried to kill me.

For a moment, all is silent.

"Why didn't you tell me you can't shoot a bow?" Tristan stomps toward me. His hair is a mess, and his face is red with fury. "Didn't they teach you anything at that fancy palace?" His face is wild with anger.

I glower at him from my spot in the frozen mud. "Why would they when my father has guards watching me at all times?"

Tristan pinches the bridge of his nose before letting out a gruff sigh. "It's like you're a baby," he mutters under his breath.

My face and arms are covered in blood, and I just took down a veritable giant. I may not know how to be a northerner, but I'm not a child. I seethe. "In case you failed to notice, I killed it."

"And could have died in the process. That was stupid. And reckless."

"And I saved your life. Again!"

We stare at each other for a long time before I start to piece things together. He could have stopped the charging animal in a heartbeat if he truly thought he was about to die. He's a Wolf with immense shadow power. Heat flashes in my cheeks at the realization. Now that the chaos is over, I see this exercise for what it was.

Training. Pure and simple.

He never bothered to use an ounce of shadow power, because we were never in real danger. What is one measly moose against a Wolf?

Tristan sighs. "Well, at least now I know where to start with you."

"Meaning?" I cross my arms in front of me petulantly.

"The archery range." His eyes dart around, looking for the discarded sword. He spots it a few feet away, then picks it up. "And we'll need to work on sword basics."

"Seems to me, I should stick with what I'm good at." I twirl my moth blade in one blood-soaked hand.

After a moment, he holds out his hand to help me off the ground. I don't take it. Instead, I get up on my own, even though my knees and hips crack in protest.

"Are you hurt?" he asks.

Every muscle in my body aches. No doubt my skin will be speckled with bruises when we get back to the castle. Even my tailbone hurts.

"I'm fine."

He holds up his palms in frustration. "I have no idea what to do with you."

I glare at him as I retrieve my red cloak from the snow and stomp back toward the castle.

CHAPTER 8

THE CASTLE DOES little to warm the sting from my frozen fingers and toes. I stomp through the main doors, dripping and half-numb. My boots leave slush in their wake. Halfway back from the forest, the ice storm broke past the fae barrier. It pummeled me with sleet that soaked through my cloak and froze in patches. Now the wet fabric clings to my skin. My hair drips steadily down my back, tangling in icy knots. A villager taking shelter glances up as I pass, then quickly looks away. He doesn't even comment on the blood and mud streaked across my clothes.

After a day like this, all I want is to go back to my room. I need to stare out at the mountains and dream of spring, when I can go back to Llwyn. Back to Caerwen Palace to kill my father. Happy thoughts. Warm thoughts.

As I walk, frigid drafts slip through invisible cracks in the walls, carrying the scent of damp stone. I hate this damn castle and the chilly Annwyn people in it. My heart longs for warm summers and the clear skies of Llwyn.

I pivot, making a rash decision. If I'm going to be stuck in this miserable castle for the next three months, I might as well make myself at home.

As I pass the kitchen, the staff are tidying up the remains of a modest midday meal. The clink of tin plates echoes through the corridor as I hesitate near the open doors. Inside, a scullery maid is scrubbing a pot at the washbasin. Steam rises in lazy tendrils as she leans over it, sleeves damp to the elbows.

The staff ignore me, though I feel their wariness. I can't blame them. I'm a mess. The ice in my hair has melted and so have the crusted mud and blood on my cloak. Warmth radiates from the hearth and I look at it longingly, but turn away. If I'm right, the cellar should be nearby.

Beyond the kitchen, near the outermost wall of the castle, I spot a low wooden door with rusted iron latches. My knees groan as I crouch, muscles tight from the cold. I grasp the iron ring and heave the door open, the hinges groaning. Cool, stale air rises from below. Beyond the door there's a dark stone staircase that descends into pitch blackness.

I wrench a flaming torch from a sconce along a nearby wall, then descend into the cellar. My footsteps echo with each step down.

At the bottom, there's a veritable treasure trove of food. One would never guess that Annwyn has a problem with hunger by the look of this stocked cellar. Salted meat hangs from hooks along the ceiling. Baskets filled with carrots, potatoes, and other root vegetables overflow along the left wall. Bushels of dried herbs hang from pegs and, below that, shelves are filled with blocks of salt, crates of apples, and rows of pickled and preserved produce. There are even boulder-sized wheels of hard cheeses coated in protective wax, some with tiny bites out of them from mice.

It strikes me that this cellar might be more valuable to the people of Gwyllion than any royal coffer or bank back in Caerwen. No wonder the villagers all seem to take meals in the castle, even if they don't live within its walls. To them, this cellar *is* a treasure trove.

My eyes peer through the room as the flickering flames create shadows that sway with each movement. Finally, I find what I'm looking for. A wooden door waits at the back of the room. When I open it, it reveals aisles of ancient wooden shelving.

The wine cellar.

A small smile spreads across my lips. It feels foreign on my frozen face. I can't remember the last time I genuinely smiled. Maybe not since Llwyn. Maybe not even then.

I reach out and grab the nearest ceramic jug with my free hand. Shining black eyes peer back at me from the empty space.

"Ack!" I stumble backward, dropping the precious jug of wine. It cracks when it hits the dirt floor, leaking wine in a dark burgundy pool.

The tiny gray creature stares at me with unnaturally dark eyes that shine like polished coal. Its short, pointed ears twitch, catching every sound. A squashed, wrinkled face gives it the look of a bat, though it has no wings, just spindly limbs. When it grins at me, rows of impossibly white teeth gleam beneath its upturned nose, each one small and needle-thin.

Anger flares up in my chest. All I wanted was to drink wine alone in my room without another damnable thing happening to me today.

"Shoo!" I wave at it. "Why can't you lot just leave me alone?"

My nerves are long-since fried today. I do *not* have the patience to deal with more of Gwyllion's infernal strangeness.

"Go away!" I yell at the fae, waving the torch in front of it. It doesn't budge. I grab another jug as it stares at me. "What are you, the cellar guard or something?"

A second pair of watery black eyes appears in the hole. Then a third. The fae creatures just sit there staring and grinning. I take a deep breath to give them a piece of my mind.

Behind me, someone clears their throat.

I spin to find Nalina watching me from the doorway. Her strong frame casts a long shadow behind her. As if this day could get any worse.

"What are you doing here?" I snap.

She lifts an eyebrow. "I might ask you the same, but I think I can see why." Her eyes travel to the jug of wine in my arms. I hug it protectively. "You know theft isn't taken lightly here in Gwyl-lion. We all share supplies; it's how we ensure everyone survives. Maybe it's different where you come from?"

I scowl. "If you only knew the day I just had, you'd understand."

"Oh, I can hazard a guess." She looks at my face pointedly.

Right. I'm covered in the blood of a moose. I wipe my cheek self-consciously.

"Training with Tristan?" she asks, clearly already knowing the answer.

I draw my mouth into a thin line. "Some might call it that."

She cocks her head to the side. "And others?"

"Cruel and unusual punishment?"

She nods, but I see the faintest flicker of a smile at the corner of her mouth. "Well, training looks ... different on you."

I glare at her. I'm filthy and uncomfortable. All I want to do is go back to my room and try to forget how Tristan looks at me like he wants to devour me and punish me all at the same time.

I just nod.

She crosses her arms across her chest. "To answer your question, I heard sounds of alarm. So, I figured I'd come down here to check on the damsel in distress."

"I wasn't in distress."

"No? It sure sounded like it from up there." She nods back toward the cellar stairs.

A growl escapes my throat. "It's just the damnable fae! They're everywhere. I'm not used to them sneaking up on me all the time like this."

Nalina studies me. "No?"

I can feel a blush rising, along with the need to defend myself. "There aren't any in Llwyn. There haven't been for generations."

"That's because your people killed them all."

She's not wrong. Now that I'm here, I'm beginning to question all the stories I've been told. Stories of terrible fae.

Murderous fae. Fae that stole children from their beds and kept maidens in underground chambers in the hills. How many of those stories were true? Sure, I find these wine cellar bat things annoying, but they hardly seem worth killing in droves. Even if some fae were cruel, how many were just like the cinder fae in the fireplace? All he seems to want is to roll around in the warm ashes at the end of a good fire. He can't be much more devious than a mouse who nibbles the choicest rounds of cheese.

Nalina just stands in the doorway, staring at me like she's studying something unusual. Like she thinks I might be losing my grip on reality.

"I'm fine!" I huff. "I just ... wasn't expecting this."

"Hm."

"Look, if you don't mind, I'd like to go back to my room now. I need to clean up." I point to my bloodied face.

She doesn't move. "It's not normal to see them, you know."

"Pardon?" I hug the wine jug closer to my chest.

"The fae. Most people can't see them."

I blink at her, not sure if I heard her right. "Oh," is all I can think to say. Yet another thing that makes me odd around here.

Something in my voice must make her take pity on me. "It's the royal blood. The traces of fae magic in your veins. It's why you can see them."

"Like you?"

She scoffs.

I blink at her. "I thought, since you're a Wolf ..."

"Annwyn isn't like Llwyn." Her face grows dark. "A woman can gain power and position through more than mere blood. I worked hard to get here, and I didn't need nobility or shadow power to do it."

I nod. "It must be nice."

She raises an eyebrow at me.

I clarify. "To be respected because of something you did, I mean. Rather than the family you were born into."

After a moment, she sniffs and gives me a curt nod. "Anyway,

I may not be able to see the fae, but now that I know where they hide, you won't catch me down here ever again." She shivers like the invisible fae give her the creeps.

A small laugh escapes me. "Not even for the wine?"

She gives me a reluctant sideways grin. "I don't much like the idea of something watching me while I sin. Happy drinking, Fox." She turns to leave.

I nod, a bit bewildered that she isn't criticizing me. "Right." I follow her out with the jug in hand, past the rows of wine and shelves of potatoes and cheese.

At the top of the cellar steps, she turns to look at me. "I'll ask someone to bring a bath up for you."

I glance down at my blood-soaked clothes, then nod. "Thank you."

She pauses, peering down at me. "I have to say, you surprised me. You almost look like you're from Annwyn, covered in sweat and blood like this."

It's a compliment, I know, but I'm not sure if I like it.

CHAPTER 9

WELL AFTER MY bath has grown cold, I remain submerged in the tub the staff brought up for me. It feels almost obscenely luxurious, soaking in a bathtub in a crumbling castle while people freeze and starve outside. But, given the brownish-pink color of the water I'm sitting in, I know I needed it. Badly.

Now that my body has rested, everything hurts. And I'm sleepy. But I blame the half-empty jug of wine on the floor next to me for some of that. Tonight, I might just be tired enough to skip supper. Luckily, the castle staff also brought up a selection of breads and cheeses when they delivered the tub and buckets of hot water.

I'm sure I have Nalina to thank for that too. It may be a strange joke, given the wine she saw me steal, but I'm not complaining. I'll take wine and cheese over an empty belly any day.

There's a knock at the door.

I groan. Not again.

"Go away," I say halfheartedly before slipping beneath the surface of the water. Even with water in my ears, I can hear the knocks grow more urgent. I sit up, splashing water over the edges of the tub.

"What do you want?" I yell.

Nothing. Then, more knocking. Louder this time.

Swearing under my breath, I stand. Every muscle in my body protests the movement. The air in the room is frigid, despite the new fire in the fireplace. I shiver and wrap a thick dressing gown around me.

The knocking continues ceaselessly.

"I'm coming!" I yell as I press the water out of my long auburn hair with a linen cloth.

Tiptoeing across the freezing stone floor, I make my way to the door. Water drips from my hair, and I try not to slip. That's the last thing I need today, an injury from being drunk and sloppy. Nalina would love that.

I open the door. Predictably, the hallway is empty.

I slam the door closed again and stifle an irritated scream. Limping, I walk back across the stone floor, but I don't get far before there's another knock. I growl and run back to the door, throwing it open.

"You know," I call into the empty hallway. "I've had enough drama for one day. Just do me a favor and come out already, or just leave me the hell alone."

A scurrying sound catches my attention. I peer down the gloomy hallway lit by flickering lantern light. There's no one there, just shadows and drafts from the howling storm outside. I sigh and start to close the door again, but pause. At my feet, there's a small jar.

I bend to pick it up, my sore muscles aching. The lid takes some effort to unscrew. Inside is a dense, waxy balm. I sniff it cautiously. It smells of beeswax, sharp peppermint, and something floral underneath. Lavender, maybe.

As if on cue, a muscle spasms along the side of my neck. I dip my fingers into the cool balm and rub it into the knot. A sigh escapes me as warmth spreads through the sore muscle. This was a gift. It's a far cry from the ominous messages left for me. Gods, Gwyllion gets more confusing by the day.

"Thank you," I say into the empty hall. I'm not fooled by the silence. Someone—or something—is watching me.

At the end of the lantern-lit hall, a door hinge squeaks. I lean out of my doorway to squint past the shadows. A shadowed figure peers out from behind a partially opened door at the end of the hall. It's only a few feet tall, like a child, and yet I know instantly that it's not. Its hand on the door frame is thin and pale, almost blue. Its eyes glisten black in the lamplight.

I lift the jar and nod toward the creature. No, not creature, I correct myself. Fae.

It shuffles back out of sight, but not before I catch the unmistakable shape of a smile.

It seems I have unexpected allies here in Gwyllion Castle.

PART TWO

THE WRAITH

CHAPTER 10

WHEN MY EYES snap open in the middle of the night, I know I'm not alone.

Moonlight drifts in through the tall windows, casting beams of silver onto the stone floor. It must be after midnight. The silence is all-consuming, suggesting everyone has long-since gone home for the night.

I sit up, my blankets pooling around my waist. Goosebumps prickle all along my skin, and my breath makes misty clouds in front of my face. This cold is unnatural, even for Gwyllion.

At the far side of the room, a shadow stirs.

Instinctively, I reach for the moth blade on my bedside table. My eyes are wide as I try to peer past the streaming moonlight and into the shadows beyond.

"Who's there?"

Slowly, a pale figure emerges from the darkness. Dread pools in my stomach. I've seen this woman before. It's the ghost from outside the castle gates. Her long dark hair floats on an invisible current, and her torn white gown billows around her.

The wraith hovers at the foot of my bed. Her dark eyes bore into mine, silent and unblinking. She doesn't show her ghastly teeth this time, just watches.

"What do you want?" My voice trembles. My hand is slick with sweat where it grips the bronze hilt of my knife. I'm not sure the blade would matter, not against something like her.

I've faced spirits twice before and nearly died both times, but my gut tells me this woman is different. She doesn't appear to be mindlessly bloodthirsty or trapped in an endless death loop. There's no gnashing teeth, no wailing or shrieking, just calculating stillness. Like she's sizing me up, same as I'm doing to her.

We stare at each other for a long, breathless moment. Then, without warning, she turns and slips through the door like smoke.

My heart pounds, loud and urgent. Something pulls me to follow her. It would be wiser to stay here, within the supposed safety of my room, but there's something odd going on here in Gwyllion Castle. I can feel it. I see it in the tightness around the villagers' eyes, and hear it in the brittle silence that fills the halls. Whatever the secret is, I intend to find it.

I wrap a blanket around my shoulders, slip my feet into boots, and follow her into the hallway.

The wraith lingers at the end of the corridor, hovering like an invitation. Then she turns left, vanishing from sight. I rush to follow. She doesn't glance back as she glides into a different wing of the castle. She knows I'm behind her and keeps just far enough ahead to stay visible, but never quite reachable.

Eventually, I find myself in a long hallway on the opposite side of the castle. One wall is lined with the remains of portraits. Ripped canvases show grim, faded faces of important people long-since dead. Whoever they were, they're now forgotten here in this dusty corridor that has a distinct smell of dead rodents in the walls. I wonder if this used to be additional living quarters, back when Gwyllion was a bustling fortress. Before most of Annwyn was laid to waste in the Llwyn wars.

I'm beginning to wonder if the wraith has a purpose beyond leading me in circles. But just when I'm certain she's playing some silent game of cat and mouse, she slips through a doorway and disappears. I draw the blanket tighter around my shoulders, then reach out to open the door.

The hinges creak, as if they haven't been used in a long time. Inside, the wraith has disappeared.

The room seems to be a rather ordinary bedroom. Or was, before it fell to ruin. Now, everything is coated in dust. A small hole in the window seems to be a passage for birds seeking shelter from the weather. Beneath it, scraps of nesting material lie scattered in a loose heap.

Tiny creatures have chewed away portions of the bedding, and the curtains around the wooden bedposts are dulled from age. At the center of the ceiling, an ornate chandelier droops. Cobwebs sway lazily from its crystals, illuminated by the moonlight streaming through the filthy windows.

This was clearly once the room of a lady. I open the wardrobe to see moth-eaten silks and furs hanging limply. Some have fallen to the floor and become homes for mice. The clothes used to be quite fine. The cuts and colors suggest a young woman wore them once. Maybe not more than a decade ago, based on the fashion.

I move toward the window, unsure why the wraith would lead me here of all places. Outside, the view overlooks the southern forest and the path to the front gates. Was this the wraith's room when she was alive?

"What are you doing in here?"

I spin toward the voice. Tristan stands in the doorway, his expression outraged. His dark hair is disheveled, and his chest heaves beneath a loose white shirt that clings to his skin. The hem hangs untucked over black trousers.

He storms toward me. "You are *never* to come in here. Do you understand?" His voice is tight, seething.

I meet his glare without flinching. "Don't tell me what I can or can't do."

"You think this is a game, Red?" His tone cuts, sharp with anger. "You're being reckless. This isn't Caerwen!"

"You think I don't know that?" My chest is heaving beneath

my nightclothes. How dare he lecture me? As if I don't know I'm an entire kingdom away from Llwyn and the Fox Court. As if I'm not reminded every second of every day that I'm stuck here, in this awful, freezing place.

His hand closes around my wrist, and he drags me out of the room, slamming the door behind us. The sound echoes through the corridor.

I twist free of his grip and whirl to face him. "You don't have to manhandle me!"

"I wouldn't have to if you'd just stay out of places you don't belong."

"I don't belong anywhere!" The words slip out before I can stop them, but it's too late to quiet the storm raging inside me now. "Isn't that the point? I'm not a Wolf. I'm not even really a Fox anymore. I'm nothing." I glare at him, daring him to tell me I'm wrong.

He glares back, gray eyes dark and threatening. His chest heaves with each furious breath, but he doesn't protest. He doesn't defend himself or his people for making me feel entirely unwelcome in Annwyn. The look in his eyes tells me he knows I'm right.

He turns and braces his forearms against the thick wooden door, his fists clenched so tight his knuckles are white. He lowers his head against them and shuts his eyes. His shoulders are tense, and they rise and fall with each seething breath. Every line of his body radiates contained fury, like a storm caught inside a cage. He doesn't answer me. He just stands there with his back to me, rigid.

When he finally speaks, his voice is low and even. "How did you find this room?"

Something warns me not to show all my cards. The wraith is trying to tell me something, and I suspect Tristan doesn't want me to know what it is.

"I was exploring."

Finally, he whirls around to look at me. He knows I'm lying. His eyes are dark with fury and mistrust. But there's something more there. Something familiar and deeply unexpected: grief. Heart-wrenching, soul-tearing grief. I should know. I've experienced it myself.

For a moment, we're too close. The corridor feels small with his body so close to mine. And yet, I don't step back.

His gaze drops to my mouth, lingering there for only a heartbeat. His eyes snap back up to mine. "Go back to your room. The castle isn't safe to 'explore' after dark."

I purse my lips but decide not to argue with him. I turn to leave.

He calls after me. "And don't come back here again."

I give him a heated glare over my shoulder.

"Please," he says in a less demanding tone. Something in that word pulls me in a way I wish it didn't.

I make no promises, but I find my way back across the darkened castle to my room. And, just as I suspected, there's a new note waiting for me when I return. It sits on my bedcovers, bathed in moonlight.

"Go now!"

My eyes dart around the darkened room, but I know I won't find anyone hiding in the shadows.

Who is leaving these messages? The wraith seems an unlikely suspect. A being who floats through walls seems hardly capable of holding a quill. Nalina? She's ominous and hates me enough to stoop to intimidation. But she knows it's certain death for me to leave Gwyllion Castle in the middle of winter. Are fae literate?

There's more here than meets the eye. On top of that, I can't help but wonder why the wraith brought me to that dilapidated room. It could've been a set-up. Maybe she knew it would upset Tristan to find me there. But why?

A chill runs down my spine as I remember the fire that crossed Tristan's eyes. Perhaps the wraith was trying to issue a warning. Maybe the Wolf is not what he seems.

CHAPTER 11

THE THRONE ROOM looks different today. Daylight streams through the tall, narrow windows along the eastern wall. Dust drifts between the beams like tiny sprites.

When I glance up at the arched ceiling, I notice the carvings along the molding are more intricate than I first thought. Owls hunt mice as elk graze among maple trees. Hares crouch in thickets as fish swim through winding streams. An opossum hangs from a branch with its rat-like tail, and wolves prowl around carved boulders.

There are other creatures too, ones I don't recognize. Fae, most likely. I can't help but wonder if they still exist, all these centuries after the castle was built.

Along the western wall, the tapestries look different too. They still show the same gnarled, black trees, but the scenes around them have changed. Their roots and twisted branches are blanketed in snow. Red berries tempt birds in one tapestry, while a cruel wind blows branches nearly horizontal in another. On a third, a yellow-eyed fox stares out at me from the entrance of a burrow beneath a stump.

This is clearly the work of old fae magic.

Tristan walks a few steps behind me, like a perfect guard dog.

Despite his icy temperament last night, his foul mood seems to have passed. He didn't mention it this morning when he came to fetch me, but his sleepless night is etched all over his face. His skin is drawn and pale, and there are dark circles around his gray eyes.

Upon the dais, at the far end of the room, the Dead Queen waits. She's sitting on the gnarled black wood and iron throne. It unfolds from the ground, as if it grew there from beneath the castle. The last time I saw it, I thought it was the work of a master craftsman. But now I'm beginning to recognize fae magic. It's everywhere in Gwyllion, if I only take the time to look.

"Granddaughter," the Dead Queen says. "I've called you here to request a report."

"On?" I fold my hands in front of me like a polite court lady.

"Your training."

I keep my voice light, almost cheerful. "I was nearly killed, if that satisfies your requirements."

She nods slowly, her face hidden beneath her long black veil. "It does. There's no surer way to gauge someone's competence than to put them to the test."

"And is that what it was?" I narrow my eyes at Tristan. "A test?"

He tilts his head from side to side. "Of sorts."

The Dead Queen turns to her Wolf. "And what have you learned about our weapon?"

The word makes my skin prickle with irritation. "I am *not* your weapon."

The queen and Tristan both ignore me, which only makes my irritation burn hotter.

Tristan clears his throat. "Her upper body is too weak to wield a sword. Or hold a bowstring for any length of time."

I bristle. It may be true, but he doesn't need to be quite so blunt about it. "I don't need one of your bloody swords. I work better with a knife."

The Dead Queen turns to me, just for a second. "If you want to kill the Fox King, then you'll need more than a knife."

I bite my tongue to keep from arguing further. She's right, and I hate it.

The queen turns back to Tristan. "What else?"

"We've learned that she's stubborn. And she pokes her nose where it doesn't belong." He gives me a pointed look.

"How disappointing," the Dead Queen says. If corpses could breathe, I suspect she'd sigh at that. Her hand strokes the silver moth necklace where it hangs above her dead chest. This simple gesture makes me bristle.

To my surprise, Tristan shakes his head.

"Not quite." He turns to me, his gray eyes meeting mine. "She is also curious, intelligent, and incredibly determined when she puts her mind to something. Admirably so. And she wields a knife as good as—if not better than—anyone in Annwyn. Even if she does fight like a scrappy fox." Whether that's an insult or a compliment, I'm not entirely sure. There's a hint of a smirk at the corner of his lips. "She doesn't shy away from danger. And she won't give up. Possibly ever."

The queen nods slowly. "I see."

My heart pounds in my chest, and I have no idea what to say to this. I expected to be torn to shreds. Back home, I was called a failure so often that I expected the same here. But even after my tongue-lashing last night, Tristan has been more than fair to me.

When I look at him again, I see something I haven't recognized before. Tristan is infuriating, yes. Grumpy, cold, and full of secrets. But he is also noble and honest. And in this world, those traits are not easy to come by.

Up on the dais, the Dead Queen stands. "Come. I have something to show you."

When I glance at Tristan's face, I see that he's just as clueless as I am.

We follow the Dead Queen out of the throne room, past villagers who bow as she passes, and out into the snow-covered yard. Despite the clear skies, the air is bitter cold, but the queen doesn't even flinch at the biting wind.

I pull my red cloak tighter around me and follow her. Her long black gown drags over the snow like liquid night, and her thin veil ripples in the wind.

Surprisingly, she leads us to the stables. Inside, we're sheltered from the icy breeze, but the horses still puff clouds of mist from their nostrils. At the sight of the undead queen, they grow nervous, dancing and whinnying as they back further into their stalls. They want to get as much distance from the Dead Queen as they can.

I don't blame them. She's unnatural. She shouldn't exist, and someday she won't. Not if I can help it.

The queen leads us to the furthest stall, then unlatches the gate. She steps back. "For you," she says, her veiled face turned toward me.

I hesitate.

"Go on," she says somewhat impatiently.

I step forward, my boots crunching on the straw-covered ground. In the back of the stall, standing as still as stone, is a horse I could never forget.

"Nell?" I whisper, confused.

It can't be. My beloved horse was torn to pieces by corpse wolves months ago. There's no way ... I lean in to take a closer look, and there's no mistake.

It is Nell. But it isn't.

Her brown fur is patchy and her nose glistens with blackened blood. Her dark mane is matted and littered with forest detritus. Decayed leaves, clumps of mud, and small twigs are knotted in her hair. My eyes drift over her body, and I take in the gaping hole in her side. Where once there were strong muscles and ribs, there's now a rotten hole where the corpse wolf devoured parts of her. I fight the urge to vomit.

Nell looks up, noticing me for the first time. Her eyes are the worst thing of all. They're the horrible opalescent white of the undead.

"I wanted to give you a gift," the queen says behind me, her voice flat and devoid of emotion. "To help ease your home-sickness."

When I say nothing, she adds, "Her body froze before too much decay set it. I had my sentries fetch her before the worst of the storms arrived."

My ears begin to hum. "This ... is severely misguided," I whisper.

The queen looks back and forth between me and the horse that was Nell. "Was she not your favorite horse?"

I close my eyes, banishing the sight from my mind. Nell is yet another beloved friend who's been defiled by this horrible place.

"Please." I wince at the pleading in my voice. "Put her back in the ground. She deserves peace."

The Dead Queen tilts her head to the side, as if I'm a curiosity. "You don't like her."

Nausea claws at my stomach. "No!" I shout, anger clouding the edge of my vision. "I don't like that you brought her corpse back to life. She isn't Nell. She's one of your undead pets!"

The Dead Queen watches me for several seconds, as if trying to process my words.

It takes all of my strength to regain my composure, to keep from flying off the edge. "Look," I say, my voice shaking. "I recognize that this was intended to be a gesture of love, but it's horribly, terribly twisted."

She nods once, then steps back so I can leave the stall. She latches the door behind me.

On the other side of the stable, Tristan watches us with an unreadable expression, his arms folded across his chest. His Wolf pin shines in the dull light.

"You're wrong," the Dead Queen says behind me.

I swallow the urge to scream. But before I can get a word out, she cuts in.

"It is not a gesture of love."

My fury dies in my mouth, tasting like bitter ash. I must have misheard her. Why else do this if not for love?

"I do not feel love," she says, watching my face through her veil. "Not anymore." She rests one black-gloved hand on the stall door. "And I do not ask you to love me, either."

The words shouldn't sting, but they do. When my grandmother was alive, she was filled with love for me. Overflowing with it. Her entire life revolved around me and making sure I knew how much I was adored. That loss scarred me deeply. And while I don't consider the reanimated version of her to be the same woman, perhaps a small part of me still clung to the shadow of a dream. A hope that her love somehow remained for me, even after death.

My eyes flicker to the silver moth necklace that rests against the black silk of her bodice. I swallow hard, banishing the memories of the woman who once wore it. She is dead. And this abomination is wearing her skin, like a grotesque theater costume.

"We'll put your horse back to rest," she says.

"Thank you." When the words come out, they sound slightly strangled in my throat.

"But I wonder." She pauses, thinking. "Do you truly think the Annwyn people are so different with our monsters than you are with yours?"

I blink several times. "You mean the foxhounds?"

She nods slowly. "They are living, but monstrous all the same."

I can't argue with that logic.

The Dead Queen watches me for a reaction. "And would you pardon the living for murder, yet punish the dead for killing in self-defense?"

I never thought of it that way. If I had to choose between death at the hands of my father's soldiers or at the jaws of a corpse wolf, what difference would it make? In the end, it's the same thing. Death.

My temples throb. Nothing I grew up believing about this place is true. Right and wrong blur until I can't tell them apart anymore.

"I don't know," I whisper.

She drums her fingers on the stable latch. It's an oddly human motion for a corpse. "I only meant to bring you comfort. I see now that it was misguided."

I merely nod.

"Your mother loved all of the earth's creatures too."

The mention of my mother is so unexpected, so sharp, pain shoots up my spine. Panic seizes me. Suddenly, I realize there's a question I need to ask. To clear the possibility from any future doubt.

"My mother. Is she like you?"

If this queen could reanimate the frozen corpse of my beloved horse, then who else has she tried to bring back?

The queen tilts her head. "Dead?"

"Yes, but not just dead."

She hums low in understanding. "No, Granddaughter. Your mother is truly gone." She turns away from me, staring back into the horse stall. "We do not reanimate people. To do so is high treason."

Her face lifts toward Tristan in the back corner. He nods in affirmation.

"Except for new Dead Queens to replace the old," I say.

She stands unnaturally still for some time before her veiled face dips into a slow nod. "Yes. As difficult as it is to lose someone you care for, that is the end." Silence stretches between us, unbearable and filled with grief. "Your mother was a far better queen than I am. But she is truly gone. And we both have your father to blame for that."

I scoff. "I'm no fan of the Fox King's, but even I can't blame him for a woman dying in childbirth."

The Dead Queen turns toward me sharply. "Your mother did not die in childbirth."

All around us, horses snort and stomp their feet anxiously.

My heart begins to race as I slowly process her words. "But I thought ..."

"You thought what?"

My words come out slowly with confusion. "I thought *I* was the one who killed her."

She shakes her head impatiently. "And your father told you that, did he?"

I nod, a long-tended knot of guilt tightening in my gut.

She leans forward. "It is a lie." The Dead Queen does not breathe, but I still smell the scent of rot and decay on her words.

I blink several times as the world swims around me. "That's not possible. What's the benefit in making me believe such a thing? I *must* have killed her."

"No, Granddaughter." The Dead Queen shakes her head slowly. "Your mother's death was not your fault."

I should have suspected this. Women in my father's circle never last long. But to make me think my mother's death was my fault is cruel beyond comprehension. All those years as a mother-less child, believing I killed her. Believing I didn't deserve a mother because of what I did to her. A dense ball of emotion catches in my throat, burning there like a hot coal.

I hate him. And if it's the last thing I do, I *will* kill him.

The queen begins to walk away from Nell, toward the stable door. Pain clutches at my heart as I watch her leave. It unleashes a fresh wave of grief. I had no mother, and then I lost my grand-mother. How much loss is one person expected to bear?

"I mourned you," I whisper. "For so long, I was in agony over your death."

In this fragile moment of honesty, I wish I could see her face behind the veil. But that isn't the truth. I've already seen the corpse she's become, all rot and bone and putrid decay. She's nothing like the woman I loved. What I truly long to see is my grandmother's face as it once was. I miss her more than anything in the world.

"You were right to mourn me, to believe me dead," the queen says, her voice thinning to a rasp. "Because I am. The feelings of the living are lost to me now ... except fury." She takes a shuddering breath. "That is the one emotion that refused to die with my body."

As we pass the stalls, the horses' restlessness grows into terror. They stomp the ground and kick their walls, trying to escape their enclosures. They huff wildly, their breath hovering, frozen in the air. They sense a change in the atmosphere. I feel it too. It's dark. Dangerous.

"Death strips you to your basest self," the queen says as she glides past them. "I cannot hide that I seethe. That I rage. That I crave the blood of my enemy for what he did to Llwyn." Her spine crackles as she straightens to her unnatural height. "For what he did to my daughter."

Her words take on a deep, hollow quality, like a curse.

"When I was alive, I wore masks. A different face for every occasion. The doting grandmother to you, the obedient mother-in-law to your father, the defiant leader to the Sympathizers. But now there is only this." She gestures to her veiled face. "Grotesque. Vengeful. And so, so angry."

I stand frozen in the face of her thunderous wrath. She may have lost all other human emotions, but her rage has multiplied a hundredfold. It's the closest thing I've ever seen to the spite that's buried in my soul, to the fury that's ruined me.

"And I remember." Her words echo unnaturally against the surrounding stables.

A shiver needles down my spine. "Remember what?" I ask, despite my better instincts.

Behind me, Tristan shifts. He's tense. Watchful ... protective.

The Dead Queen halts and turns toward me with unnatural speed. "You." Her voice is almost a hiss. "How you used to cry after your father's cruelty. How you hid with that boy of yours in the library, reading histories and fairy tales for hours. Wondering why you were never good enough."

My heart seizes with guilt at the mention of Hunter. Tears sting at the corners of my eyes, and I hate myself for them. "I *wasn't* good enough, it turns out."

The Dead Queen leans in, far too close. Her words curl around me like smoke. "Of course you were. It was never that you weren't good enough. It was that you were *too* good. Too clever, too brave, too strong, and too powerful for him."

I say nothing.

"And it made him afraid."

"I was a child," I whisper, disbelieving. "What could he possibly have feared from me?"

"That you would overshadow him." Her words are sharp as shattered glass. "That you would burn brighter than he could, or any other Fox King or Queen before him. And he couldn't stand that possibility. Small men can't bear to be eclipsed by a woman."

Her face hovers so close to mine, I have to steel my spine against the urge to back away. Behind her veil, I can see the hint of her opalescent eyes fixed on mine. They're wide and insistent. They're eyes that hold more power in a single gaze than most mortals could command in a lifetime.

"Tell me," I say. "Tell me what happened. Why you left me. How you became the Dead Queen."

"No." Her voice is barely more than a whisper, yet the word is final.

"Please."

She stills, assessing me. "You don't understand what you ask."

"Of course, I understand!" My voice cracks as I throw my arms up in frustration. "For years, I've been searching for answers. For years I've been tortured by not knowing!" My breath hitches. "I want to move on, but I can't. I need to know."

The Dead Queen steps toward me, her fury radiating from her rail-thin body. Her veil trembles as she shouts. "What do you know of torment, Fox Heir? What do you know of *need*?"

I dig my heels into the soft dirt of the horse stable, refusing to budge. "If you had been there, you would know I understand more than you think. Tell me."

She shakes her veiled head. "Some knowledge is better left buried. Some truth can destroy you."

"I'm already destroyed!" I shout. Tears of rage sting my eyes. "Or haven't you been listening? My entire life is in ruins! All because I was searching for answers. All because I was searching for you!"

Her voice cracks through the air like a whip. "DO NOT ASK ME AGAIN!"

Out of the corner of my eye, I notice Tristan's hand shift to the hilt of his silver sword. His posture is rigid, muscles tense. He watches us, ready to interfere if this goes too far. But I can't tell whether he intends to protect his queen, or me.

The horses scream in their stalls, kicking the walls and pounding the straw-covered ground with their hooves. Dust and frost churn in the air. Chaos erupts all around us, but I hardly notice it. My eyes lock on the veil, on the lifeless gaze I know lies beyond it.

I should be terrified in the face of her anger. My limbs tremble, my mind buzzes, and my breath is strangled. But I am not afraid. I'm angry. Furious. Enraged.

I know in my bones that I will kill this undead woman someday.

And in this moment, I know that I am a lot like my grandmother. Even in death.

CHAPTER 12

MY FOOTSTEPS ECHO through the stone halls of Gwyllion Castle. My thoughts have always come easier with motion. When I was younger, Hunter teased me for constantly pacing. I wandered the kitchen while I ate and roamed the palace grounds, lost in thought. I'd walk and plan, daydreaming of the Fox Kings and Queens who came before me, wondering how I might one day live up to their name.

Through it all, Hunter would be there. Perched on a stool or a bench, nose in a book, offering comfort with nothing more than his steady presence. He understood that I thought best on my feet. But now he's gone, and I walk alone. I find it far less comforting.

Gwyllion weighs on me with its unfamiliar customs, bewildering rules, and overwhelming expectations. I walk, passing cracked windows shrouded by snowdrifts and abandoned corridors draped in dusty cobwebs that sway in the cold air.

Mid-step, I falter. My body goes still before my mind can name why.

Music.

Faint and distant, it drifts in and out of earshot, like a phantom song that's too thin to hold. Someone is singing. The melody is both haunting and wistful, like a lullaby soothing a heartache. I listen, holding my breath.

There it is again, low chimes and a silky voice. The words dissolve before I can catch them.

I turn to see if anyone else hears it, but I'm alone. The halls in this wing of the castle are empty. The windowsills are clouded with grime, and the paintings along the walls are faded with age. My restless wandering has carried me into unfamiliar territory.

My heart beats faster, though not from fear. Curiosity pulls me forward. Without thinking, I follow the path toward the sound. The music grows clearer with each step.

As I draw closer, the voice begins to take shape.

"... When fate calls, the soul must answer.
A heavy burden for dreaming dancers.
None shall know what the Fates foretold
But fae and the kings and queens of old ..."

A heavy wooden door stands at the end of the hallway. I press my ear to the ancient wood and close my eyes. The voice and the haunting music are coming from the other side. My hand reaches for the doorknob, but I hesitate. I shouldn't intrude, yet something in me insists I follow.

I push the door open.

Light spills out, silver and strange, as if the door has opened onto another world. It blinds me, and I lift a hand to shield my eyes. But the moment I step across the threshold, the song dies and the glow fades. The silence is so abrupt it nearly unsteadies me.

I blink hard, and the space comes into focus.

The room, it turns out, is more of a courtyard, hidden in the depths of the castle. High above, a glass ceiling rises in peaks and valleys, its panes buried under snow like distant mountains. No sunlight could reach this place. And yet, moments ago, it had glowed.

I peer through the gray and my breath catches in my chest.

Lichen-covered boulders are scattered across the ground, etched with carvings eroded by time. Gravel paths wind between them, circling up a central mound. At the top, a gnarled, black tree twists upward, as if reaching for the sky. Silver windchimes sway from the branches, echoing a low, hollow hum that reverberates in my bones.

The singer, whoever she was, is gone.

Disappointment wells up in my chest. It feels as though I just missed something important, and the opportunity may never come again.

Behind me, I hear slow, heavy footsteps. I whirl around as Tristan steps through the wooden doorway. He doesn't look surprised to see me here.

At the sight of him, my guard snaps back into place, though slower than it should. This courtyard and the music have weakened my resolve. There's a sense of peace here, as if nothing bad can happen.

"I wondered how long it would take you to find this place," Tristan says. His face is drawn, like he hasn't slept in many nights. My heart stirs, wondering what's kept him out of bed ... or maybe restless within it.

"Are you following me?"

He merely shrugs, confirming my suspicions.

I sigh. "I suppose the queen doesn't trust me."

"You are her mortal enemy, Red. A Dead Queen can't trust a Fox." He says this lightly, as if it's of no consequence.

"Hm." I purse my lips. "And here I thought I was her treasured granddaughter and biggest weapon."

He steps closer, the faintest smile tugging at his lips. "Two things can be true at once."

The space between us hums with that truth. I know too well that I am many things, and not all of them good. Heir to the Fox Throne, yet granddaughter to the Dead Queen. Selfish enough to abandon a friend at the edge of the world, yet guilty enough to punish myself for it. Furious at the Wolf who tricked me, yet inexplicably drawn to him despite it.

"I'm not so sure about that."

His tired smile tugs something low in my core. This Wolf affects me in ways I'd rather not think about.

I turn away from him, fixing my attention on the nearest carved boulder. It's hard to make out the details, but there was a symbol here once. The other stones around the courtyard have them too, each one unique.

"What are they?"

"The crests of ancient families." Tristan leans close to look at the pattern. He runs one finger over the cuts and grooves on the stone. "These monuments represent powerful fae who did great deeds. Returned the sun from endless night, calmed storms that threatened to flatten entire coastlines, ravaged monstrous foes ... you get the idea."

I nod. "We tell similar stories about the Fox Kings and Queens in Llwyn."

One side of his mouth turns down at the mention of my ancestors, but he doesn't berate me. Those so-called "great deeds" usually resulted in the deaths of hundreds of Annwyn people over the past centuries.

I step away from him, toward the tree in the middle of the courtyard. Oddly, the wind chimes aren't the only decoration hanging from the tree's branches. Dozens of mirrors of all shapes and sizes dangle from its limbs. Some are faceted and some are framed with silvered edges, dulled and tarnished with age. Others are little more than broken shards hanging from rusted chains. Below the tree, glass speckles the ground surrounding the tree's roots.

"It represents the Tree God," Tristan says. "Protector of the northern forests. You've seen him before."

"In the temple at the abandoned village, in Llwyn."

He nods. My cheeks flush with the memory of the faded tapestry. Two deities tangled in lustful abandon, the goddess in a sheer white gown, exposing her breasts to the moonlight. I look away too quickly, hoping he doesn't notice.

"But where's the Moon Goddess?"

He tilts his chin upward. "The glass ceiling. It was meant to let her light through." He studies the filthy windows overhead. "Back when the fae priestesses still cared for this place, they would've kept the glass clear, so the lovers could be reunited each night." His eyes flick briefly to mine.

I look away, toward the ceiling, though the press of his gaze lingers on my skin. The story of the God and Goddess hangs between us—two beings kept apart, reaching for each other within fragments of light and shadow.

Something in my heart aches. It's a beautiful story. Lovers separated by circumstance but brought together in darkness. Together, their love created the Northern Kingdom before it was Annwyn. Before the Dead Queens and the endless war with Llwyn. Their forbidden love created the fae. And the wolves who out-survived most of them.

My eyes drift from the glass ceiling to the tree. It feels oddly familiar.

"It looks like one of the trees from the tapestries in the throne room."

"That's because it is."

I turn to look at him.

He meets my gaze. "It's the first tapestry to the right of the throne."

"And the others?"

"Those trees are spread across Annwyn. Each is sacred."

"Sacred to whom?"

"Fair point." He nods. "Sacred to *some*. The fae kings and queens worshiped here long before the humans took power."

He trails his fingers along the carvings on another boulder. This one has the vague shape of a bear with antlers. It stands on its hind legs, ready to attack.

"Some people still pray here," Tristan says. "Mostly hoping their savior will return, bringing an era of prosperity again."

"The Heir to the North."

He nods once, letting his hand fall. The motion is sharp, almost dismissive, though his eyes hold mine a beat too long. I wonder what fae family the carving represents. What deed earned them the right to be remembered in a temple built for a god?

"It sounds like a beautiful fairy tale."

Tristan shrugs. "Some people think it is. Others ..." His words fade, but I know what he means. One person's fairy tale is another person's faith. It's all a matter of perspective.

Above our heads, a rumble makes me flinch. Snow falls from the ceiling's highest point, cascading from the peaks to the valleys. The small avalanche clears a window to the sky above. Sunlight beams through, igniting the tree in a glorious halo. I lift a hand, shielding my eyes from the brightness.

I hold my breath as I take in the sight. "The mirrors," I whisper. Each shard of glass reflects the light a hundredfold.

It takes me a moment to realize the ground is glittering too. Quartz stones push up from the soil and moss, some no larger than peas, others the size of human skulls. I crouch to pick one up, brushing dirt and lichen from the stone to examine it. I can only imagine what the courtyard was like before the castle around it fell to ruin. How sacred it must have felt when priestesses scrubbed the stones and lit candles in the moonlight.

"I can see why people worshiped here."

When I glance up, Tristan's eyes are on the tree. The mirrors above shift, scattering light in fractured patterns. One catches his reflection, and in it, his gaze meets mine. We stare at each other through the glass, as if through another realm. My heart beats faster, and a tight cord coils inside me. I can't keep my imagination from wandering to the time when this temple was reserved to worship lovers. When it was sacred to a goddess made of moonlight and a god as immovable as a tree.

"These mountains are ancient," Tristan says, breaking the spell.

I blink and look away from his reflection, heat rising to my cheeks.

He nods toward the stone in my hand. "Quartz. It survives pressure most things can't."

"It makes them sparkle." I turn it in my palm. The thought sticks in the recesses of my mind like honey. Maybe *I* changed under the Fox King's pressure. Perhaps I emerged luminous, even. "Too bad for my father."

Tristan tilts his head. "Why's that?"

"He always believed pressure makes people crumble."

"The Fox King is a fool." His voice is low but certain.

I let out a hollow laugh. "Maybe. But so far, his methods seem to be working."

"To keep building his empire."

I drop the quartz to the ground. It bounces off the mossy patch and lands with a soft clatter on a gravel path.

"That's the thing about empires," I say. "The bigger they are, the more trouble they cause. Just ask the old fae kings and queens."

Tristan's mouth twists in something that's not quite a smile. "Tell that to your father."

I hesitate, and he catches it. His eyes flick to mine, sharp and curious.

"I have," I say earnestly. "Even before you came to Caerwen. I tried."

The humor leaves his face. His jaw sets, and the light in his eyes darkens. "I know, Red." His voice dips lower. "I know."

Something within me stirs at that. Maybe it's this courtyard with its haunting chimes and fractured mirrors, but my guard slips. He tricked me into coming to Annwyn. I haven't forgotten that. Yet when he looks at me with those tortured eyes, I begin to understand him. His home is crumbling. His people are dying.

And his queen believes I'm a weapon that can save them all. Maybe he does too.

As terrifying as it is, I'm beginning to wonder if they're right.

Something sparks between us, sharp as flint to steel, and my skin prickles as if charged with lightning. My eyes linger on the Wolf. His dark hair falls across his eyes, and his hands are curled into fists at his sides, as though he's holding back something dangerous.

And gods help me, I want to touch him. His gaze pins me with the strength of an oncoming tempest. I want to step into the storm I know will break me.

But I can't. I can no longer deny that I want this Wolf, but there are too many secrets between us. Too much is at stake.

I am the Fox Heir. He is the Dead Queen's Wolf.

Together, we would only end in ruin.

CHAPTER 13

I SIT UPRIGHT in bed long after the fire has burned to embers.

I'm waiting.

Outside the tall windows, wind rattles the glass in its panes like a beast begging to be released from its cage. Clouds drift across the crescent moon, drowning the chamber in shifting shadows. The darkness is all-consuming, making my ears strain for every creak and groan of the ancient castle. The cold presses in around me, oppressive and suffocating. No one is awake this late, in this cold. No one except me.

It's well past midnight when I see her. The wraith appears at the foot of my bed as though she's been there for hours, watching.

"No," I say quietly.

Her hollow black eyes don't move. Her pale dress floats up and around her like a current around a drowned body.

"I'm not going to follow you." My arms fold over my chest. I will not play her games. They only lead to trouble.

The shadows around her eyes darken, and her fingers lengthen. She swipes at me with cracked fingernails. But I don't flinch. I refuse to be intimidated by a dead girl made of mist.

"Go away."

She lashes out again. This time, her nails slice a thin scratch across my cheek. I reach up and feel a warm trickle of blood. The sting only sharpens my defiance. I refuse to be bullied by the living; I certainly won't be pushed around by the dead.

"You think you can intimidate me just to lure me into another trap?"

The wraith withdraws a step, dark hair stirring like smoke. Her gaze flicks sideways to the dressing table, to the silver moth knife glinting in the moonlight.

"What good is a knife against—"

Before the words leave my mouth, the wraith grabs the knife. The blade glimmers in her pale hand for the span of a breath, then she slips out the door.

For a moment, I can only stare, stunned. I didn't think ghosts could even hold objects, let alone steal one.

Panic jolts me upright. "Hey! Bring that back!"

I throw the covers aside and dart into the hall. At the far end of the corridor, the wraith waits, her form half-dissolved into shadow. She gives me a sly grin before slipping around the corner. It's a game of chase, and I have no choice but to play. My grandmother's knife is at stake.

The castle is so silent, it feels abandoned. My eyes are wide as I peer through the dim hallways. As I follow the wraith past the quiet kitchen, I pause. Given the bone-deep shadows of this place, I'd rather keep firelight with me. Here and there, long-cold torches wait in iron sconces along the wall, and I grab one. I dart into the kitchen, hoping the wraith will wait for me. In the giant hearth, the barest flicker of embers still glows. For a moment, I'm not sure they're enough, but when the torch ignites, I breathe a sigh of relief.

Just as I expected, the wraith is waiting for me when I step back out of the kitchen. She casts me an impatient look before continuing around another corner. At the end of my torch, the flame sputters as if in protest, but there's nothing to do but follow.

The wraith lures me through cobwebbed passages and past

windows laced with ice. She leads me down an old staircase, into the castle's depths. Even with the torchlight, my eyes strain against the dark. At my approaching footsteps, rats scurry away through holes in the crumbling walls. Somewhere unseen, water drips, slow and steady. The air down here smells of wet dirt and mildew, like a soggy grave.

The spiral staircase ends in another corridor. When I step down, I kick something in the darkness. It skitters just out of the reach of my light. When I bend to get a closer look, my breath catches in my chest.

It's a human bone.

I hold up my torch to see the corridor more clearly. The walls are lined with skeletons still bound in chains, prisoners of some forgotten sin.

A shiver creeps through me. The nearest skeleton is draped in the tattered remains of a gown. It's faded, filthy, and covered in holes, but I can tell it was once quite fine. The fabric's delicate floral pattern is still visible through the filth. A courtier undone by royal intrigue, maybe? Or an ambitious lover passed over for a younger woman?

As I walk, the air seems to press tighter around me, and dread blooms in my chest. Everything in me is telling me to turn back. To return to my icy room and leave the wraith to her twisted games. But every time she appears ahead of me, Grandmother's knife glints in her ghostly hand. I can't leave it. It's all I have left of the grandmother I loved.

Further down the corridor, another body lies collapsed in a heap of bones. Its arms are pinned high above the pile, its wrists shackled to the wall. Faded linen molders away with the remains. When I look closer, I realize it's the remnant of an apron. A scullery maid? A woman from the kitchens? It's hard to tell, but it leaves me feeling deeply unsettled.

A sudden realization hits me like a slap.

They're women. All of them.

At the end of the corridor, the wraith watches me. She's

standing in front of a door. At first glance, it looks much like any prison door with aged wood and a barred grate in the center. Except for one thing: it's wrapped in thick iron chains. They're woven together and locked with heavy bolts.

Someone truly doesn't wish for this door to be opened ... or to let whatever's inside out again. On shaky knees, I approach the door and peer in through the grate in its center.

At first, all I see is blackness. Then, a voice thick with disuse calls from the darkened corner.

"Well, aren't you a pretty bug?"

I jump back from the door, my heart in my throat.

The strange voice in the darkness laughs low.

I push my torch through the iron bars and into the cell. Inside, a creature scurries toward the farthest corner and huddles away from the light.

"Get it away!" It hisses.

I pull the torch back, but only slightly. The creature is thin and knobby, almost human if not for the unnatural angle of its limbs. He's wearing nothing but a torn loincloth around his waist, and stringy hair hangs limp from his pale skull. His skin is ashen gray, and when he glowers at me through the flickering light, I see that his eyes are black.

Fae.

He's standing on a massive nest made of what appears to be straw ... and human bone. The sight makes bile rise in my throat. I take an involuntary step back, pulling my torch out from the grate.

From behind the darkened door, I hear the creature limp forward. Each step pops and grinds as it walks, like its joints no longer fit in their sockets. My skin prickles at the sound as it echoes down the corridor behind us. From the darkened cell, long fingers, tipped with cracked, black claws, curl around the iron bars. He leans forward, squinting against the light.

"Does the little bug like my house?" His wide eyes gleam with interest as his mouth stretches into a grotesque grin. A hundred tiny points glimmer along his blackened gums like razor-sharp baby teeth.

I shake my head. "I was just leaving."

"So soon, little bug? But we haven't had dinner yet." He tilts his head in mock disappointment.

I pause, willing my heart to stop racing. I glance around, remembering the wraith that led me here, but she's gone, disappeared back into the shadows.

I turn back to the fae in the cell. "Who are you?"

He laughs, his face twisting in a horrible grin. "Who am I? I've nearly forgotten, so long have I been down in this dungeon."

"That isn't an answer."

"Isn't it?" He blinks at me with his wet black eyes. "Ah, but it's no bother. I love my cozy little bed in this dark corner of the world. It keeps away the pests ... and the light." He squints at my torch warily. A strand of stringy black hair falls over his face.

"Why are you kept down here?"

"Kept? I just told you; I likes it down here." He pauses. "As long as the pests bring me my dinner."

"Pests."

It nods, looking me up and down.

"People."

He twists his face in distaste. "Humans! Blech. They are only good for one thing."

"And what's that?"

He smiles, and rows of sharp baby teeth glint in the light. "Dinner, of course." The creature licks its lips with a pointed, black tongue.

Unwittingly, my gaze drifts to the skeletons lining the hall. The torchlight flickers across what remains of their bodies. "You ate them?"

He grins wider, excited that I finally understand him. "Delicious. But I do have standards, of course. Mens taste icky." The creature gags, illustrating his dislike.

"You eat women."

He nods enthusiastically.

Fear makes my breath grow shallow. There is nothing between me and this woman-eating fae except a wooden door covered in iron chains.

"Why?" I ask.

He glowers at me as if my question were ludicrous. "Why do humans eat squirrels and rabbits or ... apples?" He punctuates the last word with another gag. "But I don't eats them all. No, only the supple ones. The ones with clean hair."

I can't control the grimace on my face. "Your standard is clean hair?"

His eyes grow wide, and he nods enthusiastically again. He grips the bars of the grate tightly, as if he can barely control his excitement at the thought.

My eyes dart back to the looming nest in the back of the cell. "What else is in there with you?"

The fae cocks his head. "Wouldn't you like to know, little bug? Open the door and I'll let you in." The creature gives me a horrible childlike grin.

I shake my head.

He pouts. "Oh, but I don't offer that to any little bug who comes to my house." Saliva drips from his tiny teeth as he growls. "It has been such a long time since I had my last meal." He pauses, squinting against the torchlight. His eyes trail over my auburn hair where it's braided over my shoulder. "Your fur is dirty. It's not gold, like they usually send me. But, I likes it. What is it?"

He squints, leaning closer to the bars. His eyes widen. "No, it cannot be! Copper-hair like a fox? Ooooo, I must add you to my collection."

I take another step back, my heart racing as the fae's laughter bounces off the stone walls. The sound makes me cringe. He's unnatural, like something that doesn't belong in this world. I try to swallow, but my throat feels tight, dry. The air is thick with rot and mildew, and my pulse is hammering in my ears.

It's time to leave.

The fae pauses, eyes lingering on me. "You think that you're safe there, on the other side of this door." His finger drifts lazily down one of the bars before his gaze lifts to mine. "Safety is only an illusion, fox-haired bug."

In an instant, the door and its iron chains dissolve into nothing. Fae tricks. I should have expected it. I should have been more careful. Now there's nothing between me and the hungry fae who feasts on women.

He giggles, high and strange, covering his mouth like a coy child before clapping his hands together. "Oh, you're frightened." His grin spreads, teeth glinting. "I can smell it. You want to run, but I want something first."

I glance over my shoulder toward the spiral staircase at the end of the long corridor, measuring the distance. My legs tense, ready to bolt, but I know better than to turn my back on a predator.

The fae's grin stretches wider, his jaw cracking at the joints with a pop. "We'll see how long you last, little bug."

He lunges. I barely register the movement before claws slice the air. I step back, but not fast enough. He shears through several strands of my hair. I stumble back, caught off-guard by his speed, and catch myself against the stone wall.

He lands on all fours behind me, blocking the corridor. Slowly, he lifts his hand and drags my cut hair beneath his nose. He lets out a shuddering breath that makes my stomach twist.

"Filthy, dirty girl." He rubs my hair all over his sallow face. All across his body, his sickly pale skin twitches with pleasure. The front of his loincloth tents.

His eyes snap back to me. "I must have you."

He leaps at me again, and I'm driven backward, deeper into his disgusting lair. My foot slips on a brittle bone, and I fall back onto the creature's nest, narrowly avoiding dropping my torch. The stench is revolting, a blend of rot and centuries of decay. Then my free hand closes around something soft. I glance down and raise a fistful of the fae's nest toward the torchlight. It's not made of straw.

It's blond hair.

Golden strands spill all around me, tangled with white bone fragments. Thousands of heads of human hair, some twisted and braided, form a plush bed. I resist the urge to scream as I throw the hair aside and scramble to my feet. I bite back the rising panic and turn my attention to the fae. He's watching me with interest as he rubs my auburn hair over his skin. Saliva dribbles down his chin.

"Don't worry, little bug. I always make them scream before I cuts their hair."

My power lies dormant and useless in my core, but I will *not* go down without a fight. I will not be the next woman to die at the hands of this revolting fae with a fetish for hair and female flesh.

His laughter cuts through the air, cruel and sickening. "Oh, you'll be a delicious little bug."

"I'm no bug," I say, steeling my spine. "I'm a Fox."

I run at him, swiping my torch.

The fae cringes back, covering his black eyes with a hand. "It burns!"

"Good." I thrust the fire toward him again. This time, I don't hold back. I set his loincloth aflame.

The scent of burning flesh fills the room within seconds. The fae screams and writhes, the fire consuming his loincloth and catching on his skin. I duck aside as he rolls to the ground, writhing into his awful nest. The dry golden hair ignites. Acrid burning hair turns into smoke.

"No!" he shrieks, still burning. "You ruined it. You ruined everything!"

The fae and I both begin to cough.

I don't waste any time. I run past the wall of dead women, toward the spiral stairs, not daring to look back. Behind me, skittering claws follow.

"You horrible little bug! I will rip you to shreds!" The fae's voice is ragged from smoke and anger. "I will suckle your fleshy female bits and make them bleed!"

I skid to a stop and whirl toward him, my torch held in my outstretched hands. He freezes a mere ten feet behind me. His skin is raw and blackened, but he's no longer aflame. He's trembling, whether from fury, or pain, or fear, I can't tell. Behind him, his nest of golden hair still burns. The flames throw wild shadows across the corpses strung up in the corridor.

"You will *not* touch me." My breath comes fast, my chest heaving, but I force my voice steady. My heart pounds like a drum, each beat echoing in my ears.

The torch fire crackles in my hands. The fae's black eyes watch it warily.

"You will never take another woman again," I warn, my voice low and hard. "Or I will come back to finish what I started here."

Slowly, his face shifts, melting into that strange, childlike lightness. He giggles, head tilting at an unnatural angle.

"Does the mortal bug think she can outwit a fae who's lived for centuries?" He shakes his head slowly, tutting like a scolding parent. "I do not take."

I frown. "What?"

His clawed hand gestures down the hall toward the line of dead women. "I do not take. They *give*."

I stare past the flames into the fae's dark eyes.

"They. Give." He grins. "I. Eat."

My breath comes too fast, and my brain can't keep up. It must be another trick. "No."

He only nods, stepping back toward his smoke-filled nest. "They know better than to keep me waiting. All I must do is bide my time. Sooner or later, the mens always bring me my next dinner." His shoulders twitch with a shiver of delight. "And it will be a good one, after all the trouble you caused."

My voice sounds hollow in my ears. "And if they don't?"

His face hardens. "Then they break a promise." A growl

rumbles in his throat as he steps back into the smoke. "And fae do not tolerate broken promises."

I turn and run down the corridor and up the spiral stairs. The smoke claws at my lungs, but I force myself to keep going. The fae doesn't follow me.

Through the dusty corridors, I retrace my steps, my mind reeling. I nearly died, so I should be furious at the wraith for bringing me down there. But even so, something gnaws on me. The wraith *meant* to show me the fae. The thought leaves me feeling sick. Someone in this castle feeds blond women to that creature. And they've done it for years.

Does the Dead Queen know? Does Tristan? If so, why haven't they mentioned this to me? If there's a reasonable explanation, it seems like something they'd warn me about. Unless they don't want me to know. And if that's true, what else aren't they telling me?

When I reach my room, I'm not surprised to find another message. But this time it isn't left on a wrinkled piece of paper. The stone floor is covered in ash from the hearth. Letters spell out the message.

"Run!"

All around the room, tiny black footprints leave a trail from the intruder.

Fae.

I stare down at the letters for a long time. The messages weren't meant to intimidate me. They were intended to warn me.

Across the room, my eyes catch a glint of silver. My grandmother's silver moth knife waits at the center of my pillow. I pick it up, gripping it hard. Damn wraith.

From now on, I'll keep the knife on me at all times.

CHAPTER 14

At dawn, I tie my auburn hair into a tight braid before I pull on my leathers. Yes, it's practical, but the real reason is I can't stand the feeling of hair touching my face after last night. It takes all my willpower to push away the mental image of the fae rubbing strands of my hair all over his wrinkled, pale skin.

My head aches, and my limbs are stiff from the cold as I walk through the castle's echoing corridors. Outside the tall windows, the sky is only barely beginning to pale with dawn.

When I arrive, Tristan is waiting in the stone archway, his silver sword sheathed at his hip. One foot is braced behind him against the wall, and he arches an eyebrow like he's been expecting me.

"Let's go," I say. "We're wasting daylight."

The Wolf smirks. The sun has barely risen, but it seems he approves of my impatience. If he notices the scent of smoke on my skin or the scratch on my cheek from the wraith, he doesn't mention it. We both have secrets, and he knows it.

Tristan tosses me the heavy practice sword that's resting near his feet. I fumble but manage to grasp the hilt without dropping the dull blade on the flagstones. Wordlessly, he leads me out onto the frozen castle grounds.

When we reach the frost-covered training yard, the snow sparkles like shattered glass in the pale morning light. Long shadows trail behind the straw-filled dummies where they lean, their heads dusted in last night's snow. Someone must've been out here before dawn, because the ground at the center of the yard is already cleared in a wide circle. My grip tightens around the hilt of my sword.

Tristan pauses in front of me and unsheathes his silver sword. Tendrils of smoke-like shadow dance along the blade.

My eyes widen at the sight.

He holds it up to give me a better look. All along the blade, shadows swirl and dance against the silver. "A weapon can be enhanced with power, making it even more lethal." He spins it in his hand, and the shadows twist and bend with his movement. "But you'll need to master the weapon first."

My heart sinks. "And my power."

"Yes, well. First thing's first." Tristan clears his throat. "You need to learn how to handle your weapon properly." He demonstrates, holding out his sword so I can mimic his grip on mine.

"Then, two positions." He shuffles his feet, bracing his sword in front of him. "A basic block." He pivots, turning his sword to the side in a graceful arc. "And a basic attack." He nods toward me.

I do my best to move between blocking and attacking, but the movements feel awkward and the sword feels heavy and clumsy in my hands. Each movement makes my wrists and shoulders ache. How can anyone stand to fight with a sword? Knives are far more graceful.

Tristan nods as I repeat the steps again and again. "It takes years to master the footwork involved in sword fighting."

"Well, we don't have years," I grumble, my arms burning with exhaustion.

"Exactly." Then, without warning, he lunges toward me. His sword is a blur of silver and shadow as it arches through the air. I stumble backward. My sword clashes against the frozen ground, and the sound echoes off the stone walls. I wince.

Tristan closes his eyes for the briefest moment, his weapon frozen in mid-air. "Again," he growls.

I pick up my sword, my face burning with embarrassment, and step into the defensive posture. My breath mists in front of me with every exhale.

The Wolf lunges a second time, his silver and shadow sword swinging right. Our blades clash, but my grip is too weak. The blow of his sword on mine knocks the hilt right out of my hands, and the sting of the impact lingers on my palms. I shake it off and bite back a particularly graphic swear. If I'd had a sword in the fae's dungeon last night, would it have made any difference?

Tristan's eyebrows are lowered in concentration. He nods for me to pick up my fallen sword.

Does he know about the fae under the castle? As the Dead Queen's Wolf, he must. He probably knows all the dangers lurking in Gwyllion. The thought sends an arrow of distrust into my gut. Why didn't he tell me?

"Again," he orders, his tone rough. "Feet apart. Balance. You're holding it like it's going to bite you."

I adjust my stance and ready myself for another attack.

His body blurs in motion. With a flick of his wrist, and a twist of his foot, suddenly his silver blade is slicing toward my side. I barely bring mine up in time. The force of impact rattles through me, and the clang of metal makes me grit my teeth. Tristan nods sharply, then steps away.

"Practice your attacks."

He nods toward a straw-filled practice dummy. I roll my eyes before getting in position and swinging at the inanimate object, over and over again. Within minutes, my arms tremble and sweat prickles my brow, but I won't complain. Tristan walks away, examining the practice equipment scattered about the yard.

My arms are screaming for me to take a break, but I refuse. I hack and jab at the dummy, straw falling to the slush beneath it.

Every muscle in my body aches. My eyes dart to the Wolf. I know he's waiting to see how long it will take me to give up. I grind my teeth.

It's time to make things more interesting.

I keep my face placid as I stab the dummy in the chest. "What do you know about the fae who still remain in Gwyllion?"

Tristan freezes, his back to me. For a moment, all I hear is the icy wind howling over the castle's leaning turrets.

"Why do you ask?" His breath curls in the morning air.

I feign nonchalance as I swing my dull practice blade again. "Call it curiosity."

He gives me an assessing look over his shoulder. He knows I'm lying. The Wolf tosses his gleaming silver sword into the air. It twirls before landing back in his hand. He turns back to me and stands in a fighting posture.

I give up on the dummy and mirror his stance, keeping my eyes on his face. Watching for any hint of a lie.

He frowns. "All I know is some remain. Hidden, mostly." He raises his free hand and makes a gesture for me to ready myself. Before I even register his movement, he lunges toward me. I step aside, barely managing to leap out of his sword's path.

I know he's going easy on me. My face burns with frustration. My feet step back into the fighting stance and I give him a nod to continue.

"Are they dangerous?" The icy slush seeps through my boots, but I steady myself. I'll have to start practicing on my own, build up muscle and balance. How does he make it look so easy?

The Wolf lunges, light on his feet. This time I manage to block him, though my arms tremble and my feet slip on the icy mud. We stand with our swords crossed between us, and shadows twisting around our blades. The Wolf's eyes are piercing, as if he's trying to read my secrets.

He shrugs. "Everything can be dangerous in Annwyn."

He knows about the fae in the dungeon. I can see it in the

tightness of his jaw and the way his breath is quickening. I'd bet he knows something about the wraith too.

Quicker than seems natural, he whirls away, his silver sword arching right back toward me in the span of a breath. The impact rattles up my arms, but I don't stumble this time. The thrill of success makes me grin. Progress.

Tristan exhales sharply through his nose. Not quite approval, but not disdain either. "Better."

The moment stretches. The silence between us hums as his gaze pins me in place. This is how I want him to see me. Strong. Confident. Not weak or incapable just because I can't wield a sword. He should know me better than that by now. After all, he'd be dead without me.

His storm-gray eyes search mine. "You've relied too much on other people to protect you. You need to learn to protect yourself."

Fury wipes the smile from my face. "I don't rely on other people to protect me."

"No?"

"No." I step back, swallowing a wave of defensiveness.

He folds his arms across his chest. "Then what were all those King's Guards doing lingering in your shadows at Caerwen?"

"It's not like I had a choice," I bite back. "I didn't want them to follow me."

"Are you sure about that?" He raises an eyebrow. "It seemed like you quite enjoyed it. Dancing with your handsome groom, dressed in fine silks, always surrounded by adoring knights in copper armor."

I grit my teeth. "It wasn't like that!"

The Wolf uncrosses his arms and takes a step toward me. "Then what was it like?"

I hold my ground and lift my chin, so I can meet his eyes. "It was a prison."

He scoffs lightly. "No, I think you're misremembering, Red. *I* was the one in a prison, remember?"

"Not all prisons are in a dungeon." I clench my fist around the hilt of my sword.

Tristan merely smirks. "I've seen my fair share of prison cells, but I've never seen one covered in crimson silk."

I drop my practice sword to the ground and shove him in the chest, throwing my entire weight into it.

He barely shifts, only sighs and slides his silver Wolf blade back into its scabbard. The swirling shadows extinguish like a candleflame in the wind. His refusal to meet my anger only infuriates me further. Heat floods my face as I clench my fist and draw back, aiming for his perfect, smug mouth.

But before I can strike, the Wolf moves.

His hand shoots out, catching my fist mid-swing. In one fluid motion, he twists my arm behind my back. In the span of a breath, his other arm snakes around my chest, dragging me flush against him.

I thrash against his hold, but his muscles are iron. He doesn't even strain. He simply waits, immovable, until my struggles break into panting curses. His breath warms the shell of my ear, and an involuntary shiver slips down my spine. I gasp, hating myself for it.

I refuse to turn my head, refuse to meet his eyes. I can't decide if it's because I'm angry, or if I'm afraid he'll see what's really pulsing through my veins. Because the fire that's heating my body now isn't just anger anymore. It's an entirely different kind of passion. One that I refuse to admit.

He leans his head down to whisper in my ear. "What do you want, Fox?"

The question takes me off guard. No one ever asks what I want. Hell, *I* barely know what I want.

"I want my power back." I say, my pulse fluttering at the sensation of his breath on the skin of my neck. "And I want to use it to kill the Fox King."

I want you, I don't say. But something molten heats between my legs, anyway.

He nods, as if I said the right thing. Finally, he releases me. I whirl around to face him, my feet automatically planting a fighting stance, as if on instinct.

A flicker of something unreadable crosses his face. It could be satisfaction, or perhaps hunger. His voice drops an octave. "And what do you fear?"

I stare at him, unblinking. He stares right back, his gray eyes drinking me in. His gaze drops slowly down to the thin scar along my neck—to the spot where my father held a knife to my throat and promised to kill me. My skin grows warm beneath his gaze, and my pulse quickens. Something dark and dangerous burns low in my belly.

I swallow. "I fear failure."

His eyes flicker back up to mine, and he tilts his head ever so slightly. "That you will fail the queen? Your people?"

"No." I shake my head, irritated that he doesn't know me better than that. "I fear that I will fail myself."

He nods slowly. I'm distinctly aware of his body so close to mine. How easy it would be to close that gap again. My heart thumps erratically in my chest. There's something deep inside of me that feels like I'm coming alive, bit by bit, in the face of this Wolf.

Suddenly, darkness surges forward. A twisting mass of ink and shadow curls around my ankles, then rises to swallow all sunlight. Walls of darkness shift, pressing in. I try to draw my power, but only a flicker burns in my core. I fight back a wave of hopelessness. I am *not* weak. Even without my power, I'm something to be feared.

"You don't need the light," Tristan says through the blackness. "Fight like the scrappy fox I know you are."

A thrill rushes through me as I kneel to feel for my fallen practice sword again. I tighten my grip on its hilt and grin.

I strike in Tristan's direction, but the Wolf is faster. Even in the darkness, his blade deflects mine with ease. My frustration mounts as I press forward into the shadows, striking blindly again and again.

I feint right, then pivot, but I'm always too slow. Tristan appears from the shadows, his face suddenly a breath away from mine. Before I can react, he hooks a foot behind my ankle and wrenches me off balance. My back slams into the icy ground, the air rushing from my lungs.

Then he's there, kneeling above me, his sword at my throat. Thick shadows swirl around the blade, waiting for his command.

I freeze. My pulse thrums against the blade's cool edge. The shadows swirl lazily between us like tendrils of smoke. I can't take my eyes off the rise and fall of the Wolf's chest, or the pulse thrumming in his neck. It sends a shiver through me.

He watches me for a beat too long. Then, slowly, he lowers the blade, dragging the tip down until it rests lightly against my collarbone.

"Dead."

I don't know what possesses me, but I lift my chin in challenge, just enough to test the edge of the blade. The steel grazes my skin. His breath catches.

He stands, sheathing his sword. Regret floods through me, leaving a hollow ache at the loss of his body over mine. He offers me a hand. This time I take it. His palm is rough and warm against mine as he pulls me to my feet.

I don't let go right away. Neither does he.

The tension thickens between us. Even the shadows seem to still, like they're waiting to see which of us will break first. Tristan's breath is heavy, and his eyes search mine in a way that can only be described as hungry. And, old gods forgive me, but I want him to devour me.

Tristan drops my hand and steps away. His movement is so sudden, it's disorienting.

The shadows around us recoil, bending in on themselves in swirling clouds before disappearing entirely. The sunlight is momentarily blinding. We stand frozen in the middle of the training yard, but something is shifting between us. I know deep in my bones that he feels it too.

A door creaks open, and we both turn. Silently, a dark figure walks back into the depths of the castle. The voluminous black gown is unmistakable.

How long had the queen been watching us? Heat flushes my cheeks.

Another flicker of movement catches my eye. Nalina lingers in the shadows, her mouth set in a hard line. She turns without a word and follows her queen into the crumbling castle.

CHAPTER 15

ELISANDRA, the kitchen maid, sets a cup of ale in front of me at midday, when Tristan finally lets me take a break from training.

The great hall is dim, despite the beeswax candles melting on the long wooden tables. A draft moves through the air, making the flames gutter and bend. A handful of villagers sit scattered throughout the room as they eat. They give me a wide berth. Whenever I'm around, they whisper among themselves and shoot me nervous glances. I've been here for nearly three weeks now, but most people still eye me with distrust.

No matter. The watery ale may as well be the finest vintage of wine after the morning I just had.

I sigh and give Elisandra a smile of thanks. "Bless you." My arms are so tired, I can barely lift the mug to my lips.

Elisandra curtseys, her cheeks growing pink. "You're most welcome."

At a nearby table, a grizzled man in a sheepskin vest snorts, glaring at me. To my surprise, Elisandra glares right back, looking all the more menacing for her one clouded eye. The man grumbles, picks up his mug, then limps to a different table. He sets his mug down with a clatter next to a group of old women. They push their heads together and whisper, no doubt about me.

"Ignore them," Elisandra says. "Like most things in the north, they're slow to thaw."

Her unexpected kindness takes me by surprise. I glance at her sidelong, lowering my voice so no one can hear. "You don't need to defend me if it'll cause you trouble."

She shakes her head and tucks a wayward strand of hair behind her ear. "It's nothing I can't handle, Fox Heir."

Hearing my old title makes my skin prickle. "Is that what everyone's calling me?"

She tilts her head questioningly. "Isn't that who you are?"

I take another gulp and swallow slowly. "I suppose so. Kind of." I shake my head. "Not anymore."

She must sense my discomfort because her face melts into empathy. "I imagine it's a great burden, having a name like that."

I nod, unsure what to say.

Across the room, someone clearly mumbles something that sounds remarkably like "Llwyn whore."

Elisandra casts another glare across the room, then turns back to me with a sigh. "You must think Annwyn is a terrible place."

I shrug. "Well, there is a lot of doom and gloom."

"And ice. And snow."

"And corpse wolves."

A grin flickers at the corner of her mouth. "Yes, those too." She exhales again, softer this time, and studies me with a look caught somewhere between pity and mischief. After a moment, she stands straighter and taps her hand on the table. "Come. I want to show you something."

I take a long swig of ale, emptying my cup before I stand. My legs ache, but I stifle a groan and follow her. We ignore the stares and whispers as we walk out of the great hall. The second we're out the door, I hear the hum of conversation resume. Elisandra takes me through familiar castle halls without a word. Other villagers nod to her as we pass, but none spare me a glance.

We stop in front of a heavy wooden door near the throne room. She pauses with her hand on the handle.

"Don't mind the mess."

She pushes the door open. Inside, a cavernous room is stuffed wall to wall with such a random assortment of odds and ends that it's staggering. My eyes widen as I take in the sight. There are barrels filled with empty spools for thread. A mountain of fireplace pokers and ash shovels clutter an entire corner. Old furniture is piled on top of more old furniture. On top of that, there are moth-eaten bolts of holey fabric, which spill down to the floor below like faded waterfalls.

"What is this place?" I ask.

We pass a gilded mirror leaning against a stack of crates, and its cracked glass reflects fragments of my face. My eyes are haunted and strange in the splintered glass. I hardly look like myself anymore.

"It used to be a ballroom," Elisandra says as she closes the lid of a trunk filled with old clothes and spiderwebs. "Now, it's storage."

I look down toward my feet. Sure enough, beneath the dirt, there's a mosaic floor in shades of black and white. For a room this size to have such intricate flooring, it must have been a spectacular ballroom. It's difficult to believe such a room was ever used in Gwyllion, given the state of the castle now.

Elisandra pushes an old boot out of our path with her foot. "We can't afford to get rid of anything, so it ends up here." She looks up at the hundreds of years' worth of broken chairs, bolts of stained cloth, tables, even cradles. "We come here to find replacements for anything too broken to use. Or if we need wood to burn." She points toward a pile of furniture that's been chopped down into kindling. "But this isn't what I want you to see."

We wind our way through the clutter, squeezing past wardrobes missing doors. Elisandra pauses to run a finger over an ornately carved cabinet. Wood-carved trees seem to shift in a breeze, raining flower petals over two lovers lounging together beneath their limbs. It's an idyllic scene that feels remarkably out of place in Gwyllion with its cold stone walls and winter storms.

It makes me wonder what Annwyn is like when it's not coated in snow and pounded with ice storms.

Next to me, there's a crate filled with disintegrating straw. I brush the straw away, and something sparkles.

"It's ... crystal." My breath catches with surprise. I rub away the grime with my thumb to reveal green glass decanters so delicate they must be the work of a master craftsman. They're empty, of course, except for dust.

"We used to be a fine castle, you know." There's a note of defensiveness in Elisandra's voice. "Though that was long before I was born."

I look around with new eyes. This room isn't filled with mere junk; it's the archive of a great era. Sure, it's nothing like the organized archives back home in the palace at Caerwen, but it's a historic collection, nonetheless. I lift a heavy blanket from a mound and uncover a chandelier with teardrop glass in shades of rose and lavender.

I have to blink away the disbelief. "It's hard to imagine something like this hanging at Gwyllion."

Elisandra's expression softens. "Every time I come here, I wish I could have seen it." Her voice sounds almost wistful. "Royals, both human and fae, spent their summers here by the sea. There were feasts every night. Hunts and garden parties by day. The balls were the stuff of dreams. It was second only to Ellyll, the main residence of the Fae Kings and Queens."

"Before the humans usurped them."

"Yes." Her voice sounds far away, lost in the fantasy of the past.

"This was a summer palace?" I ask.

"The sea gives a lovely breeze in the warm months." Outside, the wind howls, rattling the windows in their panes. Elisandra shrugs. "It was mostly shut up in the winters, given the ..." She gestures toward the snow-frosted glass.

I drop the blanket, letting the chandelier sink back into its dark slumber. Nearby, I spot piles of velvet curtains faded to ghostly shades of plum, rose, and forest green.

Elisandra tilts her head. "Just a little farther."

Beyond a mountain of broken relics lies a collection of paintings and books piled to a precarious height. I pick up a book whose cover is so faded the title is long gone. The spine cracks when I open it. The title page is lettered in loops and curls: *Fae Ladies and Their Lovers.*

I lift an eyebrow. "This one looks like it's been read sometime this century."

Elisandra gives me a sly smile. "I have no idea what you're implying." She nods toward it. "But you're welcome to borrow it anytime."

I grin. "Maybe another day." I set the book aside for another. *"The Horticultural Wonders of the North."*

Her face brightens. "The summer gardens here were legendary. Visitors came from as far away as the western deserts to see it."

"I didn't even know there were deserts in the west."

Elisandra gives me a long-suffering look. "That's because you grew up in Llwyn. Your people can't see past their own noses, let alone to the lands beyond the Spires."

"I suppose that's fair."

Elisandra sighs deeply. "Annwyn, on the other hand, cherishes its vast and dramatic landscapes."

"I'd love to see it someday." I'm surprised when the words leave my mouth, because they're true. I would like to see more of Annwyn. It can't all be crumbling castles and impenetrable mountains.

"Me too," Elisandra says.

I blink at her. "What do you mean?"

She trails a finger through the dust on top of a curio cabinet. "I've never been anywhere but Gwyllion. On account of the ..." she gestures toward her blinded eye.

"I'm sorry to hear that."

She shrugs. "We all have our fates."

"Maybe yours will change someday."

"Maybe." Her voice is sad, and her gaze is far away.

I lean down to pick up another book from the ground. "*The Faerie King and His Brides*. More than one bride?"

Elisandra shrugs, the light returning to her face. "The fae had a very different culture. More ... open to experiencing all the delights life has to offer."

I raise an eyebrow. "Well, perhaps longer lifespans meant they needed a bit of excitement."

We share a grin.

"As lovely as the old books are," she says, "these are what I really wanted to show you."

She leads me to the stacks of portraits. Some remain in gilded frames; others are canvases nailed to rough boards. I lean close as she flips through them.

Families in grand attire gaze back, their beauty still ethereal even after all these centuries. Flecks of gold foil cling to the edges, and the paint remains impossibly vivid, as if fae magic still lingers in the pigment.

"But the fae haven't lived in Annwyn since before the human kings," I say, bewildered.

Elisandra nods. "These portraits are thousands of years old."

"It's not possible."

Her voice softens. "You've been in Gwyllion long enough to see what remains of fae magic. Protection from winter storms. Ancient castles that refuse to collapse. Anything is possible."

As I gaze down at the faces of long-dead families, something about the portraits unsettles me. Their eyes gleam in unnatural shades of violet, blue, and green; their skin glows faintly, like moonlight trapped in paint. I trace the jawline of a woman with silvery hair. Her posture is regal, her gaze proud and unflinching. Though she's been dead for thousands of years, she feels alive, made immortal by paint and fae magic.

I exhale. "They're remarkable."

"And those are just the portraits. Come see the landscapes."

I follow her to the shadow of a wardrobe carved with lilies and tulips. She flips the canvases one by one, balancing the weight against her hip. The paintings steal my breath.

The wild, raging sea, caught forever mid-storm. A canyon drenched in sunlight so golden it glows. A meadow thick with wildflowers so real I almost feel the brush of petals against my skin. And then, a castle perched upon a cliff, sunlight spilling over its towers against a flawless blue sky.

I blink. "Is that ...?"

"Gwyllion." She nods.

"It's hardly recognizable." Entire wings that have long-since crumbled stand whole again, bright with gleaming windows. Turrets stretch toward the clouds, tiled with patterned shingles. Gardens spill in lush waves of green, with statues of maidens and fae creatures draped in climbing roses.

"This is how I know the stories are true," Elisandra whispers. "And this is why we fight so hard to save this place from the Fox King."

"But you can't bring back the past."

"No," she sighs. "We can't." Her eyes lift to mine. "But *they* can."

"Who?"

"The fae."

"I don't understand."

Her eyes bore into mine, begging me to see. "It's why so many of us still pray to the old gods. The Moon Goddess gave us the Dead Queen to restore the balance between humans and fae. If the fae return, they could change everything. They could restore Gwyllion, and more."

Her gaze drifts across the room. "And this is only the beginning. Gwyllion was a summer palace, but Annwyn holds far more: sirens and sprites, gnomes and great forests, caverns older than even the fae. Waterfalls so high their rivers vanish into clouds. Deserts so vast, no living thing has crossed them. The peace, the joy, the magic."

"The magic?"

Elisandra closes her eyes, lost in a daydream. "Annwyn was glorious. In ways we can't even imagine anymore." Her voice trembles. "Someday, we hope to see it returned." She turns to face me straight-on. "*That* is why we stay. Why we refuse to stop fighting for our home."

She straightens, sniffing once. "The Heir to the North will help us. When the Dead Queen finds the Heir, they'll sit on the human throne again and bring everything back to life." She gestures toward the broken mirrors and tarnished silver, the moth-eaten fabric and the splintered bedframes. "Someday, the Heir will stop the Fox King, make peace with the fae, and restore Annwyn to its former glory. Then we'll have no need of Dead Queens anymore."

I whistle softly. "Sounds like a big job."

She nods, her expression dimming. "It is. But the Heir to the North can do it." She pauses. "We have to believe. Without hope, we have nothing left."

CHAPTER 16

WE RETURN to the great hall reluctantly. Elisandra has to go back to her duties in the kitchens, and I'm still hungry after my morning with Tristan.

Thankfully, no one pays me much attention when I sit back down at one of the long tables. Elisandra leaves me with a plate of stew and warm bread. But before she turns away, she gives me a small smile.

As impossible as it may seem, I think I've made a friend here in Annwyn.

I eat in silence, lost in thought for several long minutes before footsteps approach. I turn to see three of the queen's Wolves walking toward me through the hall. They're a grizzled lot. All three are broad-shouldered and covered with furs, each wearing a silver wolf sigil pinned to their chest. Snow still clings to the hems of their cloaks, melting into dark patches along the stone floor. But their scars are the most menacing thing about them. These are men who've been to the borderlands and lived to tell the tale. I eye one man's hand, where three of his fingers end in stumps.

The Wolves stop in front of me. "The queen wishes to see you," the tallest one says from behind a thick black beard.

"Can it wait?" I ask as I take a bite of an herb-roasted potato.

The guard looks at me, incredulous. "No one makes the Dead Queen wait."

I shrug. "She's dead. She has all the time in the world."

The room falls silent.

The guard's face flushes. "Now."

I take another bite before I stand. Casting one mournful glance back at my hot meal, I follow them out of the great hall. Behind me, benches scrape the ground and whispers ignite like oil to flame as the Wolves lead me out the doors.

They lead me through the castle, then up to the throne room. They open the doors and I step through, but they don't follow me.

I turn back and raise an eyebrow at them. "Not coming?"

Their faces remain expressionless as they close the door behind me with an echoing bang.

The throne room is more ominous today. The windows are dimmed by the dark storm clouds moving in. In the distance, I can barely see the Spires through the storm raging there. As I step further into the cavernous space, hail begins to pelt the glass like pebbles. Vicious winds make the castle creak. I've come to think of this sound as the music of the north.

This time, I pay closer attention to the tapestries hanging along the left wall. The trees are much the same as they were last time I was in here, though more are blanketed in snow. One seems to be coated in a glistening cocoon of ice. Just where Tristan said it would be, the twisted black tree from the temple courtyard stands in the tapestry to the left of the throne. Its many mirrors are dim from lack of sunlight. Now that I've seen it in real life, the image feels stiff, as if even fae magic can't preserve the sacredness of such a place.

Upon the twisted black throne, the Dead Queen waits. She watches me through her black veil as I walk toward her. The silver moth necklace rests upon her hollow chest and her gloved fingers tap a restless rhythm along the throne's iron armrest. To her right, Nalina stands tall, watching me with distrust. The scar across her face makes her look even more menacing. Her hand flexes on the hilt of the sword at her hip.

I don't miss the massive silver greatsword strapped to her back. It's a strong woman who can wield not one, but two heavy swords. No wonder her biceps look so powerful beneath her brown tunic. If I had to wield that monstrosity, I'd topple over.

"You seem quite intrigued by our tapestries, Granddaughter." The Dead Queen's voice echoes throughout the hall. It rolls through the chamber like thunder.

I sniff as I stop at the foot of the dais. "Merely interested in the artwork."

"Mmmm."

I clasp my hands in front of me. "You summoned me."

"I did."

The plink of the hail sharpens against the windows as the storm intensifies. The great tapestries ripple in the draft, their embroidered trees shifting as if they're alive.

The queen stops tapping her long fingers on her armrest. Her head tilts, veil stirring with the movement. "I wanted to give you a warning."

I raise an eyebrow.

"To be careful." Her voice is no nonsense. "To remember what's at stake if you get ... distracted."

Beside her, Nalina shifts on her feet, the leather of her boots creaking. Her gaze never wavers from me, but her face remains impassive. They must teach that trick to all the queen's Wolves.

"Noted," I say lightly.

"This isn't a game." The Dead Queen's voice is low, threatening.

"Of course not. If it were, all players would start with an equal advantage."

The queen leans forward on her throne, and the dim light glints off her silver moth necklace. "And what disadvantages do you have?"

I list them off, counting on my fingers as I go. "Adequate

training, similar skill sets, prerequisite knowledge ... That's a big one."

"You think we're hiding something from you."

I stare pointedly at her in answer.

The queen reclines slowly back onto her throne. "Well, let us amend that. What is it you need to know?"

I let out a low whistle. "Oh, so many things."

"Start with one."

"Alright." I nod. I can't ask about the wraith or the dungeon fae without showing my hand. I'll need to start at a different angle, then make my way around. "How about the Sympathizers?"

"What of them?"

"Who are they? What do they do exactly? Who is their leader now that you're, you know ..."

"Dead?" the queen says humorlessly.

"Exactly."

Next to the queen, Nalina narrows her eyes at me in silent threat. Her fingers curl tighter around her sword's hilt. I can practically feel her disdain for me, the Fox in Wolf territory.

The Dead Queen doesn't seem as ruffled. "Sympathizers are Llwyn people who seek to overthrow the Fox King. You know this."

"That isn't enough to understand them."

She pauses, studying me. Though her eyes are hidden behind the black veil, I can feel the weight of her gaze on my skin. "Alright. They meet in secret. Distinguished only by the sign of the silver moth. Which I believe you've already guessed."

Her eyes flicker to the hilt of my silver moth knife where it sticks out of my boot. Its bronze handle is strapped against my ankle. Without the skirts to hide it, it's on full display like all the other weapons in this court.

She continues, "Sympathizers exist in every city, every town. Even the palace at Caerwen."

Nalina stiffens, no doubt fearing the queen is telling me too much. The queen ignores her hesitation.

"Besides you, who else was a spy in the Fox King's court?"

"Your mother."

I blanch outright at that. My mother, the woman who has an ornate, marble mausoleum in the royal cemetery. Who was the Fox Queen, if only for a short while ... she was a Sympathizer.

"You seem pale."

I blink several times. "Yes, well. This is quite a revelation."

"You wanted to know."

"I did." Then I add, "Thank you for being forthright."

I didn't truly expect the queen to tell me the simple truth. My beloved grandmother, before she was reanimated as the Dead Queen, was the leader of the Sympathizers. And my mother, the Fox Queen, was her spy.

"How?" I ask.

"How what?" the queen asks, her tone annoyed. "Be more specific."

I sputter. "How did you do it? How did your daughter become the queen of Llwyn?"

"That is a story for another day, I'm afraid."

But I'm not done yet. There are too many unanswered questions whirring in my brain. "How did father not see what you truly were?"

"Your father ... he had his suspicions. Then, he found out the truth."

"That's why he killed you, isn't it? You were trying to destroy the Fox Throne. *My* throne."

She nods slowly. The motion is so slight, I almost don't notice it.

While I understand hating my father, I'm struggling to see why my own grandmother would work to destroy a legacy I was supposed to inherit. A throne that I was someday supposed to sit upon. Maybe things would've been better once my father was out of the picture. Maybe I could have actually been a good Fox Queen, like my mother. But there my grandmother was, loving me one moment, then destroying my future the next.

Outside, the wind picks up. The clouds are so dark with swirling snow, the windows show nothing but a blanket of gray. The tapestries shudder against the stone wall, threads like shifting leaves in a storm.

I take a deep breath, realizing I've been holding it for too long. Dizziness plucks at the edges of my vision, but I force myself to focus.

The outline of the Dead Queen's opalescent eyes are barely visible beneath her veil, but I can feel them studying me.

"Do you feel betrayed, Granddaughter?"

"Yes," I whisper, because it's true. Ever since I discovered who she is—*what* she is—I haven't been able to love her. And I spent my entire life loving her memory. Fiercely. Obsessively. I no longer know who I am now that I know the truth.

"You shouldn't." The Dead Queen's voice echoes throughout the hall, sharp and unemotional. It grates like a knife against bone.

"And why not, exactly?"

"Because I did it all for you."

My ears ring. "Me? How could I possibly have anything to do with this?" I wave toward her grotesque body hidden beneath midnight silks. We both know that behind her veil, her gown, and her long gloves is a body of rot and decay. A skeleton without a soul.

My voice rises in pitch. Without even meaning to, I'm yelling. All the anger and hurt inside of me is spilling out.

"You're trying to overthrow the kingdom that I was slated to rule one day! How was this for *me*?"

She watches me for a long moment. "Because you deserve a better world than one ruled by greed and monstrous men."

I breathe deep, trying to steady my heartbeat.

The queen stands from her throne, bones popping with the movement. Her black gown sweeps the ground like smoke. "I hope you understand that I have shared this information as an olive branch. You do not trust me. But I assure you, I have your best interests at heart."

For some reason, the mention of her heart makes my stomach turn. She doesn't have a heart. Only a twisted, rotten organ inside her chest.

She lifts a hand to dismiss me.

I step forward. "I have one more question."

She lowers her hand and settles into a patient stillness. "Go on."

"What happened to the fae?"

She cocks her head. The movement is sharp, birdlike and unsettling. "You know what happened to them. Your ancestors chased them out of Llwyn. In the north, they died out. Dwindled to negligible numbers."

I shake my head. "Dwindled maybe, but not gone."

She nods in agreement. "No. Not entirely gone."

"What fae are left? Why don't they help fight my father's armies?"

The queen pauses for a long while. "You did not grow up with the fae, Granddaughter, so I will forgive your ignorance in this. As all northern children know, the fae are allies against the south, in a sense. But they are not to be trusted."

"Why?"

"Because some fae are fickle and take joy in creating mischief ... and worse."

"Then why tolerate them here in Gwyllion?"

The queen stills. "Be careful, Sienna," she warns, her voice low. "If you keep thinking like that, you'll turn into your Fox King father."

My cheeks burn, and I snap my lips closed.

The queen walks past me, her steps unnaturally graceful as she crosses the throne room. Nalina trails behind her, her boots striking hard against the stone. She glances at me once, sharp and appraising, before she vanishes through the doors.

Outside, the storm howls on.

CHAPTER 17

THE RUINS of an old temple stand haloed in the moonlight. Frozen vines curl around the ancient stone pillars, peppering them with decayed purple flowers that must bloom here in the summer. The vines wind through the crumbling masonry like veins through a corpse.

Along the one remaining wall, shattered stained glass still clings stubbornly to a windowpane. What's left of it glitters in shades of green, brown, and yellow. A tree bathed in sunlight, perhaps. I'd guess it represents some portion of the Tree God myth. Now the image is fractured, broken into shards that catch the moonlight.

Tristan walks beside me, silent as a shadow. For the past two weeks, he's kept his distance. Even during our dawn trainings, he barely speaks unless it's to correct my form. I wonder if the queen warned him too. Still, his gaze prickles my skin when he thinks I'm not looking.

He refuses to touch me now. There's no brush of knuckles when we spar, no firm grip at my waist to adjust my posture, no steadying hand when I slip in the icy training yard. The physical denial hums between us, taut and hot. I hate it, and I crave it all the same.

"Why have you brought me here?" I ask, my breath turning into white mist in the cold.

"It's time to put what you've learned to the test." Tristan kicks aside rubble, clearing a smooth area in the center of the temple. "If you're going to kill the Fox King, you'll need to practice the killing part."

I cross my arms in front of my chest. "A giant moose wasn't enough?"

He gives me a dark smirk. "As much as I enjoyed watching you murder a moose, that was nothing compared to the Fox King."

I tsk. "Pity. I'd assumed he'd bleed the same."

"For one thing, your father has an army."

I kick a pebble, and it skitters across the ground. The sound echoes through the stone temple. "And you think I'm useless against him if I can't access my powers." It's not a question.

"Yet." His voice is confident, firm. "You can't access your powers *yet*."

"How are you so sure I will again?"

Tristan stops clearing away rubble and turns to face me. "Because I've seen you fight, Red. You don't quit. In the end, that's who wins."

The words hang heavy, stirring something fierce in me. I take a deep breath. "I've tried, Tristan. I don't know how to bring my powers back."

Tristan shrugs as he continues clearing away frost-speckled rubble. "The queen believes you just need focus and control."

"Easy for her to say."

Above us, moonlight spills into the temple. The ceiling fell apart at least a century ago, leaving the star-strewn sky visible from our place at the white marble altar. I clear off the snow to find it's cracked, and the corners have crumbled away. But I can still make out faint details. The smooth surface was decorated with stars and moon phases before the gold foil washed away with centuries of rain.

This temple must have been beautiful once. I can feel the

sacred weight of this space. Feel what it used to represent before people left and nature reclaimed it.

Tristan looks through the shattered stained-glass tree at the crescent moon that shines in the distance. "Your powers of healing and light are strong. Stronger, perhaps, than anyone else in your bloodline. It will come back. I'm sure of it."

I wish I were as certain of myself.

My fingers trail over the gold moon inlays on the marble altar. "And how do you expect me to practice murder here tonight?"

His eyes dart around the darkened temple. "With a creature that's been spotted here lately. It's been terrorizing the villagers. Stealing their livestock."

A shiver runs up my spine. The shadows between the broken pillars feel darker now, more ominous. "What is it?"

He shakes his head slowly. "Nothing natural. A creature bred between fae and animal, most likely."

My skin prickles. "That's possible?"

His mouth pinches in a thin line. "It shouldn't be." The way he says it makes me think he's already preparing for the worst.

"But?"

"But the fae sometimes act in unfathomable ways." He grimaces. "Whether this creature was made intentionally or by accident, it's hard to know."

I nod, trying to dispel the image of the dungeon fae from my mind ... and his morbid fetish for blond women. The memory lingers, like the taste of bile at the back of my throat.

"Then again ..." Tristan pauses.

I raise my eyebrow at him, urging him to finish his thought. "Then again, what?"

He gives me an odd look. "Then again, I suppose that's how *we* were made, humans with light and shadow powers. When high fae mingled with human nobility."

"It creates monsters."

He gives me a small laugh. "Maybe so, Red. Maybe so."

A branch snaps in the distance, sharp as a bone breaking. My breath hitches. Tristan's posture instantly shifts to alert, like a cat ready to spring. He holds one finger up to his lips and gives me a pointed look.

I nod, swallow hard, and flex my fingers over the daggers strapped to my thighs. Several this time. I won't be caught unprepared again, not after the dungeon fae. I'd found a measly armory during one of my sleepless nighttime walks. There wasn't much there, a handful of rusty swords, axes with broken handles, bits and pieces of tarnished silver armor. But I took the best of the daggers, polished them, and sharpened their blades.

When I first arrived at dawn training with silver blades strapped to both thighs, Tristan didn't even blink. I'm becoming more of a Wolf each day, it seems.

I unbuckle my cloak and let it slip to the ground. If I'm expected to fight, I need to move. The scarlet fabric pools like spilled blood at my feet. Tristan's gaze flickers toward it, then back to me, quick and sharp. He gives me an approving nod. I adjust my stance to match his, two predators ready to hunt.

Snow crunches beneath Tristan's boots as he steps over the shattered remains of a stone archway. As I listen for the sound of an approaching animal, the air grows colder. Unnaturally so. It prickles across my skin, settling into the hollows of my bones. I shiver, one hand resting lightly on the hilt of a dagger.

"You feel that?" I whisper, breath curling in the cool air.

Tristan nods as he unsheathes his silver sword. Shadows coil along the blade. "It's close." He shifts nearer. The awareness between us burns hotter than the cold air.

A sound splits the stillness, a low, bone-deep growl that thrums in my chest. Outside the temple, a creature steps out from behind an overgrown elderberry bush. At first, I think it's an enormous emaciated polar bear. But it's no such thing. It moves in impossible ways. Its joints bend too far, like limbs pulled by marionette strings. Its fur shimmers like frost, and jagged spines of ice ripple down its back.

The creature halts, noticing us through the ruined window.

Every nerve in my body is on alert as it pushes its heavy front paws into the icy ground and stands on its hind legs. It lets out a howl that sounds so unnatural, I cringe and cover my ears with my hands. The sound rattles through my ribs, and stars pop in front of my eyes. The temple walls groan and dust falls on us like rain.

The creature moves fast, catching us both off-guard as it charges into the temple through a crumbled wall. Stone explodes around it in a spray of ice and grit. It lunges, claws scraping stone as Tristan's sword flashes, shadows writhing. He slices a jagged arc toward the beast's face. Shadows bite deep into its flesh, but the creature barely flinches. Breath mists from its jaws, spreading crystalline frost across the floor.

My heart is racing, but I steady myself. I try to summon my power, but nothing comes. It stays silent in my chest.

"Focus!" Tristan yells, twisting to evade another swipe. The beast's claws slam into the marble altar, cutting deep grooves into the stone. "Control your power!"

"I'm trying!" I grit my teeth. My voice cracks with rising panic.

Infuriated, I try to call it forth again but fail. This is useless and I'm wasting time.

Enough. I'll have to handle this creature a different way. I dart toward the bear's flank, quick and quiet while it's focusing on Tristan. My feet slide along the icy ground as I slash the creature's hind leg with one of my daggers. With my other hand, I land a second cut in its side. The blade sinks deep into its fur, but instead of blood, shards of ice spray outward, racing up my arm like splintered glass. Panic blooms in my chest.

"Red!" Tristan slams his blade into the beast's ribs. Shadows pour into the wound, spreading like poison. The frost bear growls, and the sound shakes what's left of the temple. The walls tremble, rubble spilling from cracks above. For a heartbeat, I think the whole ruin might collapse on us.

I grit my teeth and shake the ice from my arm. Frost burns my fingers, but I don't stop moving. I jump out of the path of another powerful swipe of claws.

Tristan swings his shadow-laced sword again, but the beast kicks out, sending Tristan skidding across the icy floor. He hits hard, sliding to a stop at the foot of the altar. I lunge toward him on instinct, my hand outstretched to help, but he's already pushing himself up. There's blood on his lips and a storm in his gray eyes. His dark hair hangs wild across his brow, and his jaw is set. The sight sparks something sharp in me, something hotter than fear.

I fling a dagger at the creature's head. It slices the beast's ear before clanking to the ground on the other side of the temple. The creature twists to look at me, taking its attention off Tristan for a moment.

I withdraw another dagger from the straps along my thighs. Across the room, Tristan wipes blood from the corner of his mouth. There's pain behind his eyes, but he doesn't let it slow him down. He advances again, sword flickering with shadow. This time, when he strikes, his dark power tightens around the beast. The creature stops advancing toward me, pinned by the weight of shadows. But even as it staggers, its jaws yawn wide. Rows of jagged teeth glisten with frost.

The creature's unnatural howl makes colors burn across my vision, violent and dazzling. My knees buckle as the world swims. Tristan shouts something, but his words are lost in the roaring echoes that bounce endlessly off the stone of the ruined temple.

I rise, trembling. The creature lunges at me again. I throw another dagger as I dive out of its path. The blade lodges in the creature's eye. Shards of ice spatter from the wound instead of blood, shattering when they hit the ground.

Tristan doesn't hesitate. With a final strike, he drives his sword deep into the creature's heart. Darkness rushes from the blade, flooding the beast with writhing tendrils of shadow that flicker behind its eyes and out its nostrils.

The beast howls once more, and the sound bounces off the

stone columns, destroying what remains of the window. For one breathless moment, it's still. Its remaining eye fixes on me. Then it collapses, its body exploding into fragments of ice that skitter across the temple's marble floor. Outside, the winter wind carries its last echoing howls away.

I turn to Tristan, relief swelling in my chest, until I see him stagger. His sword clatters to the ground, and he presses a hand to his ribs.

"Tristan!" I rush to his side, heart hammering. "You're hurt."

He grimaces. "I've had worse."

"Sit down."

He doesn't move. "It's fine."

"It's not." My voice is sharper than I mean it to be.

Our eyes meet and, for once, he doesn't argue further. That alone tells me how much pain he's in. He leans against a nearby pillar and slides to the ground with a quiet exhale, his jaw tight.

My eyes flicker up to his. "I'm going to have to get a better look."

He nods curtly.

Gently, I pull the fabric of his wool shirt up over his stomach. He hisses in pain but doesn't stop me. My eyes grow wide at the sight. His ribs are a mottled mess in the moonlight. No doubt he has at least one cracked rib, likely more. I suck in a breath. At any other time, I'd use my powers to heal him. I've relied on my gifts my entire life, but now I have to admit that there's nothing I can do.

Guilt and shame tumble inside me. What good is a Fox Heir with no power? Who am I if I can't even heal bruised ribs? My chest tightens until I can hardly breathe.

"I'm sorry," I whisper.

Tristan's stomach muscles flinch, and he lets out a tight groan. "It's not your fault."

I move my hands over the mottled swelling. My fingertips hesitate, hovering just above his skin. Something stirs inside of me, faint as breath on glass, but it's gone before I can grasp it. With a pang of regret, I pull away.

"It's alright, Red." He sounds almost disappointed. As if he thought the sight of his injury would trigger something in me. That it would make my powers surge back to help him. But my core is just as hollow as it's been since I arrived in Gwyllion.

"No, it isn't."

He shrugs, then winces. "I'll heal like I always do. With time."

"That isn't the point."

His cut lips press into a thin line, but something soft flickers in his gaze. He pulls his shirt back down over his ribs and slowly rises to his feet. My eyes drift up to his face to find that he's staring down at me. He holds out a hand. I hesitate before grabbing his calloused palm. He lifts me to my feet and, for a breathless moment, we stand there, inches apart.

I swallow, hard. My heart is hammering in my chest, and my skin is prickling beneath his gaze. Under my tunic, my body flares with heat. I blink away the mental image of me, leaning into him. Of my hands taking him by the collar of his shirt and pressing my lips to his. Of the feel of his hard body pressed against mine in this ice-filled temple, where there's no one around to witness the awful, delicious things my body craves to do to him.

I suck in a breath and start to turn from him, but Tristan catches my wrist. His eyes find mine again. My wrist burns where he's touching me, but not from pain. His fingers tighten just enough to remind me how easily he could pull me closer. And how much I want him to.

The ruined temple is silent around us. It feels as if the icy north is waiting to see what choice we'll make, here, alone in the darkness of a ruined sanctuary.

I want him. And the look in his eyes suggests he'd like nothing more than to press me against the temple's altar and take me right here. My body responds to the thought. Heat pools low in my belly, and my nipples harden. Every inch of me begs to give in, to surrender to instinct and desire.

Yes, I want him. But I can't let that happen.

"Your power will return." His voice is steady, assured.

"Why do you have so much faith in me?"

His eyebrows draw together over his gray eyes. "Because I see you, Red. Not your power, not your family's throne. You." His voice is tinged with something dangerously close to longing.

My heart stills. "Do you still see a spoiled heir?"

He shakes his head slowly. "No. I see a woman who's going to bring kingdoms to their knees and leave blood in her wake."

"Sounds ominous."

"Only to those who get in your way."

A thrill rushes through me at his words, but I tamp it down. "Right now, it looks like I'm in my own way."

He gives me a dark smile. "Just a temporary diversion on your path of ruin."

The temple fades around us as heat unfurls low in my belly. His breathing is uneven now, mirroring mine. He shifts just enough that the distance between us narrows. Just enough that I can feel his warmth radiating through the chilled air. His gaze drops to my lips, then back up to my eyes.

Suddenly, the queen's warning echoes in the back of my mind. This is a dangerous game we're playing, and I can't afford to get distracted. I jerk my wrist away. For one long moment, we stare at each other, daring one other to make a different choice. But we don't.

I turn, pick up my cloak from the icy ground, and walk out of the temple as I try to gather the pieces of myself that have just come undone. Even so, I feel his presence behind me. He doesn't speak, doesn't reach for me. He doesn't need to. The weight of what just passed between us follows me like a shadow, impossible to ignore.

I still don't trust him. Not completely. But in this moment, I realize something far more dangerous.

I want to.

CHAPTER 18

A COUPLE OF WEEKS LATER, Gwyllion appears to transform overnight. The castle is more alive than I've ever seen it. Old men and women rush through the halls carrying beeswax tapers and armloads of firewood. Boughs of evergreens are hung in the main corridors, and holly is strung above archways. Wreaths of thorns and red berries sit at the center of every table in the great hall, candles lit in each one.

For the first time since I arrived, the castle feels warm. Like a tiny spark of life has ignited, however simple. Gwyllion has finally woken up. It's brighter, louder. Alive.

In Caerwen Palace, these decorations would have been scoffed at for their simplicity. Nobles would say they're just items found in the forest, strung up like trash in the royal halls. But here in Gwyllion, it feels beautiful in its simplicity. The halls smell of pine instead of cold stone, and the scent of stewed apples and cinnamon drifts out from the kitchens.

I follow my nose and linger near the kitchen door, languishing in the scent of cider drifting from a large pot on the hearth.

Elisandra notices me and nods toward a pile of tableware in the universal look of, "Make yourself busy."

I pick up a linen rag and begin drying the freshly washed items. Then I sort them into piles of knives, forks, and spoons. Elisandra stands by one of the grand kitchen hearths as she gathers rolls of bread into a wide wooden bowl. The firelight casts a warm glow across her face. Her sleeves are rolled up to her elbows, revealing pale forearms dusted with flour.

"This bread is special for the Midwinter Full Moon," Elisandra says matter-of-factly when she catches me eyeing the cinnamon-sprinkled rolls.

I blink at her, fork in hand.

"Don't tell me it's not celebrated in the south," she says, pausing long enough to give me a look of pure incredulity. A stray curl escapes from her braid, falling over her blinded eye.

I shake my head. "No. It isn't."

Then again, in Llwyn, we don't suffer the extreme winters that they do here in Annwyn. Maybe prolonged suffering makes people eager to celebrate something in the middle of the harshest season.

She scowls, an unexpected expression on her usually composed face. A genuine laugh bubbles out of me before I can stop it. I like this feisty side of Elisandra.

"It isn't funny," she huffs, holding the bowl against her hip and fixing me with a mock-glare. "It's a tradition older than this castle. I can't believe you've never even heard of it."

"Please enlighten me," I say, stepping aside as she brushes past me. Her brown homespun skirt whispers against the door frame as she rushes out into the great hall. She turns and nods for me to follow. I gather the dried tableware and head after her.

"Technically, it isn't *exactly* mid-winter," she says. "But it's the first full moon after we've passed the harshest part of the season. We still have weeks to go of cold, but the worst is over and we can look forward to spring."

She weaves through the hall as she sets bread rolls on tin platters spread along the tables. Each seat is marked by a pewter goblet and a linen napkin. It's a far cry from the usual bare-bones place settings. The Midwinter Full Moon must be an important occasion to warrant such a display.

I trail behind Elisandra and lay a knife and fork beside each plate.

"It's the night we honor the Moon Goddess and her blessing of light in the darkness," she explains, her voice softer now, though no less animated. "We feast, we drink, we make merry. It's an evening to let down our hair and toss aside our inhibitions."

My eyebrows lift at that. "Lowered inhibitions, you say?"

Elisandra glances over her shoulder and gives me a wicked grin. "I didn't mean it in that way. Though some ..." Her smile turns sly, and the mischief in her eyes makes me laugh.

"Sounds like trouble." I set another knife into place.

"The best sorts, usually." Elisandra places the last roll on a platter with a flourish and straightens, brushing flour from her hands. "After nightfall, we gather down by the shore where we can see far out into the night sky. There will be music, and dancing, and all manner of merrymaking."

"All manner?" I echo, feigning innocence.

She gives me a sideways grin and snorts. It's a sound I haven't heard from her before. I'm struck by how much she's opened up to me. Just weeks ago, she was distant and fearful. Now, she's teasing me like an old friend.

"Maybe in the old days," she shrugs. "There aren't many eligible young men in Gwyllion anymore, seeing as they're all in the borderlands."

I look around the hall at the people who still live in Gwyllion. Men and women too old to fight, children too young, and the wounded. For the first time, I realize why Elisandra is here in Gwyllion instead of at the borderlands. Her clouded eye very likely saved her life.

"You'll see," she says, turning back toward the kitchen, her braid swinging against her back. "You'll learn to love our northern customs."

I lay the final fork and knife next to a bread plate and fall into step beside her.

———

The moon hangs high above the crumbling castle. It bathes the frozen world in a silver light. Along the snow-packed paths that wind over the cliffs and down to the pebbled shore, hundreds of candles flicker in iron lanterns. The air is sharp with cold, but the storm clouds have passed for now. The midnight-blue sky is clear, exposing millions of stars. Over the great black sea, the northern lights sway hypnotically.

I grew up in the land of light. Every noble in Llwyn can create it. And yet I've never seen such an awe-inspiring display. I can almost see why the ancient people in Annwyn worshiped the Moon Goddess. There's something in the moon that feels sacred.

Elisandra walks beside me, her breath puffing white in the air. Her cheeks are flushed with excitement. "It's even grander than last year," she says, her voice soft with awe. "The whole village must be here."

As we reach the edge of the cliff, I pull my red cloak tighter against the wind blowing off the sea. Below us, a celebration unfolds in a riot of sound and light. Bonfires burn brightly against the snow-crusted beach. Their flames crackle and spit sparks into the cold night. Fiddles and drums carry over the wind, and laughter mingles with the crash of waves against the ice-lined shore. It's like I'm seeing a whole new side of Gwyllion, one reserved just for the people of Annwyn.

I glance sideways at Elisandra. Her eyes glow with reflected firelight as she drinks in the sight. Her guarded edges are gone. Tonight, she looks young and carefree.

"Come on," she says, grabbing my hand and tugging me toward the shore.

I lift the hem of my wool dress and follow her, stepping over icy mounds of hard-packed snow. The cold bites through my boots as we step onto the beach, but no one else seems to care. People dance in wild circles around the fires, boots kicking up snow and pebbles as they spin to the music. Others gather in small groups, passing bottles of spiced liquor and trading stories. Children chase each other and throw snowballs, their laughter high and bright.

Near one of the largest fires, I spot the greenhouse caretaker, Tabitha. We've given each other a wide berth since our initial meeting. Tabitha doesn't seem the type to warm up to anyone, certainly not a Fox. But here, she seems different. Her lined face is soft with affection as she watches a young boy. Her grandson, I presume. He tosses icy pebbles into the sea, running away each time a wave crashes to shore.

Tabitha must sense my gaze. Her eyes flicker to meet mine, and a cloud passes over her face. She whistles sharply, and her grandson runs back over to her. She gathers him like a mother hen, ushering him back into the protective crowd, away from me.

"Elisandra!" a warm voice calls.

We turn to find a young man leaning on a cane a few steps away. His cheeks are rosy, probably from a combination of cold and the liquor everyone keeps passing around.

Next to me, Elisandra's grip tightens on my arm. At first, I think she's wary, but I quickly see that I'm mistaken. She has the unmistakable pallor of a girl who just learned a handsome young man knows her name.

The man's windswept hair flutters across his forehead, and he stutters like he's gathering courage. "I—uh, I wondered if you'd like to dance?"

Elisandra stills. She looks from me to the young man and back again. She wants to, it's clear across her face. She just needs a gentle push.

"Well, don't keep him waiting," I say, extracting her grip from my elbow. "I don't need you to protect me all evening."

Her face melts with relief. "You're sure?"

I smile. "Go. Have fun."

When the man holds out a hand for her to take, I'm mildly afraid she's going to faint, but she doesn't. She takes his hand as a wide grin spreads across her face. He leads her toward the nearest bonfire, where several couples twirl and laugh with the music. He has a pronounced limp, and Elisandra does most of the dancing, but neither of them seems to mind.

My heart fills at the sight. I'm happy for her.

I watch them for a while before I leave to walk through the crowd. Most people avoid my eyes. They turn away or walk to another fire when I pass. It's clear I'm not welcome. I'm still an outsider. I settle near the farthest bonfire to watch the festivities. It's a calm sort of loneliness, at least.

Someone approaches from the darkened beach. "May I speak with you?"

I spin to find Nalina standing right behind me, tall as a mountain. Her tight braid has come undone with the wind, and golden strands fly around her scarred face. She doesn't bother to brush them away.

I nod curtly.

"I assume you're not the dancing type," she says.

"Nor you?"

"Most certainly not." She side-eyes me. "Nice dress," she says in a tone that tells me she does *not* think my dress is, in fact, nice.

I scowl. "It's a party. I didn't want to wear my sweaty leather pants."

She looks down at her own clothes and shrugs. "Works fine for me."

We watch as nearby dancers stomp and twirl and grab hands. Almost all of them are children, but there are a few older men and women. No doubt they're remembering the many partners they've lost to the unending war. The husbands, wives, parents, and friends who went to the borderlands and never returned.

A memory strikes me like a stab to the heart. The last time I danced was with Hunter, at our engagement ball. It feels like a lifetime ago. I bite the inside of my cheek and swallow away the wave of guilt that washes over me. There will be no more dancing for me. Not ever.

I need to let him go. Even as the thought crosses my mind, pain shoots through my heart. It's time to move on. Time to let the past die. It can never come back.

I toss a sideways glance at Nalina. "So, what's this visit really about?"

"I just wanted to remind you."

"Of?"

"Your promise."

I scoff. "I don't recall promising anything."

She purses her lips. "Perhaps you should have." She leans toward me and whispers. "Do not get distracted. You have a job to do."

I pull back just enough to look her in the eyes. "You think I've forgotten?"

"You don't seem to be taking your situation as seriously as you should."

"And what situation are you referring to?" I ask. "The one where I'm trapped in Annwyn until spring? Or the one where my father tried to kill me, making my false infant brother heir to Llwyn instead? Or maybe you're speaking of the situation where my dear grandmother turned out to be the Dead Queen, my sworn enemy?" A dark laugh escapes me. "There are just *so many* situations. I can't follow which one you mean."

Her brown eyes narrow. "Careful, Fox Heir, or you might become the victim of prophecy."

I drop all false lightness. "What prophecy?"

The glow from the bonfire casts flickering shadows over her face. "Oh, he didn't tell you?"

I refuse to take the bait.

She continues. "You're so busy out here trying to become a northerner, I'd assumed he'd tell you all about our lore."

I'm truly starting to dislike Nalina. "Either you're going to tell me or not. I'd rather skip the games."

Waves crash on the rocky shoreline behind us as she considers whether to tell me. I think she's trying to torture me with suspense until she finally gives in.

"Every northern child grows up whispering the prophecy. About the Wolf who will save the kingdom by bringing back the Heir to the North. The Wolf who's destined to kill the Great Fox."

A chill runs down my spine. When we were in Llwyn, Tristan told my father he was there to find the Heir to the North.

I shake my head. "I don't believe in prophecies."

She sucks her teeth. "You're in the north now, Fox Heir. Maybe it's time you start."

A figure steps around the bonfire, and my heart stumbles in my chest.

"Red." Tristan steps toward us, his eyes narrowed. "Nalina." His voice is quiet and edged, like a subtle warning.

The confidence in Nalina's eyes flickers. "We were just discussing fairy tales and folklore."

"I'm sure."

When she looks back toward me, her eyes are dark. "A fox can't be tamed. It will always be wild at heart. Vicious, sneaky." Her eyes flicker to Tristan. "Remember that, Wolf." She walks away, the dancers parting in her wake.

Suddenly, I don't want to be here anymore. What once felt like a welcome break from the monotony of life at Gwyllion, now feels like a mistake. My unease must show on my face.

Tristan leans in toward my ear. "I want to show you something." His voice is a low whisper. His warm breath on my neck sends a shiver down my spine, but I can't ignore the spark of distrust that flares inside of me.

I pull back to study his face. "What is it?"

He nods his head toward the darkened shoreline, beyond the glow of the bonfires. "You'll have to come with me to find out."

I size him up, then decide I would rather be anywhere but here, at the edge of a party that no one wants me at. I nod.

Without another word, his hand finds mine. The memory of his skin makes my heart flutter in my chest. But if it affects him, he doesn't show it. Tristan pulls me gently away from the crowd. His grip is steady, but there's a possessive edge to it, as though letting go isn't an option. We leave the fire's warmth, the music fading behind us as the cold night closes in. Overhead, the northern lights twist and pulse in their endless dance.

We walk along the shore until the loudest sounds are the crashing waves and our boots stepping along the sand. It's a relief to be away from the fray, but a small shadow nips at the back of my mind. I'm alone with the Wolf. And now I know for certain that he hasn't been entirely truthful with me. I'll need to tread carefully.

"I suppose I should thank you," I say, breaking the silence.

He gives me a curious look. "For?"

"Rescuing me."

He huffs a quiet laugh, but there's no warmth in it. "You're not the sort who needs rescue. I suspect you can handle your own." His words curl in my chest, unsettling and reassuring all at once.

"Then where are you taking me?"

His face changes to an expression I can't quite read. "To a place I've been meaning to show you."

I tilt my head, challenging him. "I see you at dawn every morning, yet you couldn't find the time to take me here in daylight?"

He shrugs, then winces at the pain in his ribs. "This seemed like a good opportunity."

"You don't like parties either, I gather."

The faintest hint of a smile flickers at the edge of his lips, but it's gone in an instant.

An icy wind sweeps in from the sea, and without thinking, I step a little closer to his side. He doesn't pull away. Music and laughter drift on the wind, but it's distant now, like a dream we've left behind. The cold gnaws at my fingertips, but I barely notice, not when Tristan's hand is still wrapped around mine.

Old gods help me, because beneath the light of the moon and the shimmer of the northern sky, the world feels a little less cold. Even if deception and secrets still nip at the back of my mind, refusing to be forgotten.

CHAPTER 19

WE WALK IN SILENCE. The rhythm of our footsteps blends with the rush of the waves over the ice-crusted sand. Peppered across the shore, weather-beaten rocks glisten with frost. Without a word, Tristan leads me toward a narrow opening hidden between two boulders that must've been tossed against the cliff in a long-ago storm. I hesitate on the moonlit shore for a long moment. Tristan watches me, waiting to see if I'll decide to follow.

I do.

The cave is dark. Tristan disappears for a moment before a flame ignites, briefly blinding me. He holds out a lantern that was stashed behind a large rock.

"I keep candles and a striker here."

So, this is a place he comes to often. I store this information for future use. As he leads me deeper into the cave, my eyes flicker back toward the exit. I can just make out the moonlit waves that crash against the shore. He pauses and holds out his hand again. I take it, following the Wolf into the darkness.

The air is damp with the scent of the sea. The roar of the water fades to a murmur behind us as it's swallowed by thick cliff walls. My boots scrape against the uneven ground, and I stumble on a loose rock.

"Careful." Tristan's hand tightens around mine.

My heart thuds against my ribs. The walls of the cave glisten where beads of moisture cling to the jagged edges. Streaks of salt and minerals gleam like veins beneath the cliff overhead.

We move carefully, our footsteps echoing against the stone. Pools of seawater lie eerily still in the hollows of the floor. They reflect the golden glow of our candle flame with such precision, it feels like looking into a dark mirror. The deeper we walk into the cave, the quieter it becomes. Gradually, only the distant drip of water remains, falling like a heartbeat in the dark.

A sudden realization hits me. "It's warm."

At first, I thought the temperature change was because we left the biting wind behind, but even so, it's definitely warmer in here than seems normal. It's the middle of winter. The pools should be frozen solid, but they're not.

"It's the springs," Tristan says. "Heat rises from deep inside the ground. It keeps everything in here the same temperature all year."

"It's amazing ..."

Tristan smiles to himself as he helps me step over a wide tidepool.

"Do you bring many people here?" I ask, my voice barely above a whisper.

He casts me a sideways glance. "No. Just you."

Finally, the passage widens, opening into a hidden chamber. It feels vast, the ceiling arching high above us. At the center of the chamber, a still pool of water gleams like polished glass. The sight of it is enough to steal my breath.

"I'm going to blow out the candle," Tristan says softly.

"Wait, what?" The thought of being in pitch darkness sends a shot of terror up my spine. I grew up in a palace where almost everyone could summon their own light. I've rarely been in true darkness. Even then, I'd always had the safety of knowing I could summon light in an instant. That isn't the case anymore.

"You can trust me," he says.

I'm not sure "trust" is the right word for what I feel for the Wolf, but I'm in too deep to turn around now. My heart stumbles against my ribs, and I nod.

He looks me straight in the eye to make sure he has my consent. Then, in a single puff, he blows out the candle. For a moment, nothing but blackness surrounds us. I blink, trying to adjust my eyes, but my vision swims with ghostly spots of light. I think it's a trick of my eyes until I realize the lights aren't fading.

They're growing stronger.

All around us, hundreds of tiny lights speckle the cave walls, glowing in shades of blue, purple, pink, and yellow. They stretch across the ceiling, glittering softly against the dark stone. Even the the pool glows with luminous sea stars that cling to the rocks beneath the water's surface.

I draw a breath. "It's beautiful," I whisper.

Tristan releases my hand and climbs onto a large rock. His face grows tight for a moment, and I know his ribs ache, but he won't say as much. He pats the space next to him. I sit, grateful that my red cloak protects me from the chill of the damp stone. His gaze drifts across the glowing cave, his face lit by the light of a hundred sea stars. When he finally speaks, his voice is quiet.

"I used to come here when I was a kid. When I needed some-where to hide away from the world."

Something about the way he says it makes my chest ache. I glance at him through the dim light, searching the hard lines of his face. This is a side of him I've never seen before. He's being vulnerable, letting down his guard.

"You hid here?"

He nods once, his jaw tight. "It was the only place where I felt safe. Like the outside world couldn't touch me."

The sound of dripping water echoes around us. He's right. Here, in the heart of the cave, the rest of the world feels impossibly far away. There's no danger, no responsibilities, only the two of us.

I shift closer, keenly aware of his thigh pressed against mine. "Why did you bring me here, Tristan?"

For a long moment, he doesn't answer. His eyes catch the light, and I see that he's struggling to come up with an honest answer.

"I don't know," he admits. "Maybe I wanted to share something with you. Something that no one else knows."

The words hang between us, sweet and intimate.

"I know what it's like to lose someone," he says suddenly, his voice thick with emotion. "My sister, Isadora. She was twenty when she died."

I inhale sharply. "What happened?"

He hesitates before speaking, his shoulders tightening. "It was sudden."

My heart cracks then. I had no idea that he knew what loss felt like. That he's suffered grief so deep that it fractures your entire life in two: before and after.

His gaze drops to the glowing pool. "When she died, everything fell apart. My father, Corrin, and my mother, Ilsa ... they didn't last long. Grief hollowed them out. I watched them fade away. And when they were gone, I was alone. I was only twelve years old."

The same age I was when I lost Grandmother. My heart aches for the boy Tristan was. The boy who had to suffer the loss of his entire family at such a young age. I know that particular flavor of despair.

"That must have been unbearable," I say.

His jaw clenches. "It was. I hated everyone and everything." He turns to give me a sidelong glance. "I suspect you might know about that."

I swallow hard. "I do."

This conversation feels fragile, like it could collapse at any moment. Tristan has never opened himself up so completely before. It feels like a rare gift.

"You surprise me," I say.

He tilts his head. "What do you mean?"

"Half the time I think you hate me."

His eyebrows furrow. He lifts a hand to my chin, tilting it up until my gaze meets his. My skin tingles at his touch.

"I could never hate you, Red."

My cheeks burn, but I keep my eyes fiercely on his. "You're a difficult person to read."

A faint smile tugs at the corner of his mouth. "Maybe I don't want to be read like a dusty old book."

This makes me laugh. "Some of us happen to love books."

"And what of wolves?" His voice is hesitant when he says it, like he hadn't meant for it to come out. But it has. And some words can't be pushed back into the depths of our secret souls.

He moves his hand to where mine rests against the cold stone. His fingers curl through mine, steady and certain. The world outside might be cold and isolating, but here, beneath the light of a thousand glowing sea stars, I feel wanted.

"Why do you refuse to call me by my name?" I whisper.

"Because it reminds me of him. The Fox King."

"I'm not my father."

"No. But you *are* the Fox Heir."

I give my head a small shake. "Not anymore."

"Maybe not to him. But to us, you'll always be. He can't take that away."

Something painful claws at my heart. I'm afraid to say the words, but in this moment of vulnerability, I do anyway.

"What if I don't want it?" I take a deep, steadying breath. "What if I'm afraid it would make me cruel, like him? Like all of the Foxes before me."

His eyes grow fierce as they search mine. "Foxes are known for being cunning and cruel."

I scoff. "You're starting to sound like Nalina."

"No," he says firmly, his hand gripping mine tighter. "You're not those things. That much was clear to me, even back in your father's kennels. You're more than your family, Red."

"But 'red' is just a color."

He looks taken aback. "That's not true. Red is the color of fire. Of power and ... passion."

"Also love." The word slips out before I can consider the repercussions. Or, maybe I no longer care.

His gaze locks on mine with an intensity that makes my breath catch. "Yes," he says quietly. "That too."

Something between us has shifted, something undeniable. And this time, I don't think either of us can ignore it.

He leans closer. "You're more than your family, Sienna."

The way he says my name—my real name—lingers between us. This isn't just a conversation anymore. This is something else. His presence fills my senses until he's all I can focus on. The smell of him, cedar and salt, clouds my mind. It feels like being lost in a dark forest, yet deep in a stormy sea.

"Sienna." There's an unfamiliar tremor in his voice. "Do you ever wonder what we could be if we weren't ..." He pauses, his warm breath brushing against the shell of my ear. "If things were different?" His lips are inches from mine.

"Yes." The word slips from me before I can stop it, a midnight confession brought to light. "But we can't change who we are."

His lips draw into a tight line. I see something flicker in his eyes, something almost like regret, but it's gone before I can be sure. Then his hand rises, slowly brushing a strand of hair from my face. His fingers linger against my jawline and a shiver runs through me.

The distance between us vanishes.

His mouth crashes onto mine, hot and insistent. My body moves before my mind catches up. I lean into him, my hands clutching at the fabric of his shirt, pulling him closer. His lips are soft, but the kiss is rough, and I match his frantic desire with my own. Every vessel, every nerve, every inch of my skin hums with need. It feels like the world has cracked open around us, like by denying ourselves these past few weeks, we've only fueled the fire burning inside.

He winces, and I draw back, gasping. "Your ribs."

He grabs my face in his hands. "Fuck my broken ribs." He pulls me back into him, and that's all the permission I need.

I lose myself in him. I savor the taste of sea salt on his skin, the scent of the bonfires lingering on his clothes, his soft moan against my mouth. There's a heat between us that no amount of cold can extinguish. Every part of me is alive, straining toward him, desperate for more.

His hand finds my waist, and he draws me onto his lap with a force that leaves me breathless. He grunts at the pain in his side, but that doesn't stop him. His mouth ravages me, kissing down my neck as he unclasps my red cloak to expose the neckline of my gown. My breath comes in wild gasps as he trails his fingers across the exposed skin of my breasts where they're pressed high beneath a simple corset. A shiver courses through me, making gooseflesh prickle every inch of my skin. I gasp and my eyelids flutter.

I pull away, just long enough to see his gray eyes filled with hunger. For me. The Wolf wants me as much as I've wanted him.

In the next breath, our lips come together again. My fingers dig into his chest, above where I know his star-shaped scar marks his perfect body. I can feel the frantic pulse of his heartbeat against my skin. There's a desperation in the way we move against each other, as if we both know that this moment is fleeting.

But for now, I don't care.

As if my body has a life of its own, my hips grind into his, feeling how stiff he is with need. Our lips crash together as his hand finds the hem of my gown, then slips beneath it. I feel his fingers graze up the length of my thigh, where it's wrapped around his waist. His touch burns like fire across my skin, filling me with an uncontrollable need. I want, need his hands on me, everywhere.

Without thinking, I bite the taut skin of his neck, and he lets out a low, rumbling moan.

He pulls away only for a moment. "Gods, I want you, Red." His voice is deep with longing.

"Why not take me then?" I ask, a seductive lilt in my voice.

Tristan lets out a shuddering breath and his hands tighten on my thighs. He swallows hard, but I know what he's thinking. It's written clearly across his face: the tight jaw, the veins straining in his neck, the hard look in his eyes.

A Wolf and a Fox can never be together. He would lose the trust of everyone in Gwyllion, not to mention the other Wolves. Nalina would loathe him. And the queen ... I hate to think about what she would do if she found out he betrayed the Annwyn people.

"We can't," I say, answering my own question.

The words taste bitter on my tongue, my body begging for the relief it craves. But it's true. We can't take this any further. Not when the world would tear us apart because of it. This illicit moment would be damning enough, if it were ever discovered. I can't have him. Not really. Not in this world.

His eyes are dark, tortured, but he gives me a firm nod. "We can't."

His eyes drop to my mouth and linger there before traveling back up, as if dragged away from unspeakable temptation.

This can never happen again. I know this. But right now, I can't bring myself to care about the consequences. I'm like a drowning woman in need of breath. I reach above the waves and pull his body back to mine.

Chapter 20

As I lie wide awake in my room, the wraith appears.

She hasn't visited me since the incident with the fae creature in the dungeon. I'd assumed that was all she needed to show me, like unfinished business finally put to rest. It seems not.

She floats at the end of my bed, long after the bonfires were doused and the villagers retreated back to their homes.

All I want to do is sleep. And maybe, if I'm lucky, dream about a certain cave bathed in the light of a hundred sea stars. Of the strong hands of a Wolf at my waist. And, if I'm still dreaming, even lower.

The wraith's eyes darken, as if she knows I'm considering throwing the blanket back over my head so I can resume dreaming. Begrudgingly, I sit up against the pillows. It's not like I can sleep after what happened tonight, anyway.

"What do you want this time?" I sound like a petulant child, but I don't have it in me to be polite to the ghost who nearly got me killed.

The woman's long, dark hair floats around her head in an invisible breeze. She opens her mouth as if to speak, but no words come out.

I sit up a little taller. Can she speak? But even though her mouth moves, no sound comes out. It's as if she's talking underwater or behind thick glass.

"I can't hear you."

Her eyes narrow. Her mouth moves again, like she's saying the same sentence over and over, but I still can't hear her. I shake my head, concern welling up inside me as she grows more frustrated by the second.

"I'm sorry."

She points toward the window. I turn to look, but there's nothing out of the ordinary. The moon is still bright, though I can't see it from this side of the castle. The Spires are bathed in silver, as if they're glowing. A storm hovers on the horizon, blanketing the mountains in a new, thick layer of snow.

I turn my eyes back to her and shake my head slowly.

The wraith closes her eyes, as if she's trying to rein in her irritation. There's something different about her tonight. She seems less menacing and more ... I'm not sure. Afraid? Can ghosts even feel fear? There's something in her black eyes that screams of desperation.

I throw the blankets off my legs and get out of bed.

"Show me."

Something like relief flashes across her pale face. I grab my red cloak and follow her out the door. The wraith leads me through the darkened corridors and out into the castle yard. The castle grounds are eerily silent at this time of night. I look up to see that all the windows are dark.

The wraith floats ahead of me, leading me toward the east side of the castle, where the cliffs meet the sea. A thick fog has blown in from the water, coating everything in swirling mist. The farther I follow her, the thicker it gets until I can barely see three feet in front of me.

But I *can* see her. Even through the fog, the wraith remains impossibly visible, as if natural elements don't affect her.

"Where are you taking me?" I call out, even though I know it's useless. She can't speak, and our game of charades wasn't helpful.

I can't see where we're going, even though the mist is bright with reflected moonlight from the clear sky overhead. It's beginning to feel like there's a blanket over us, muffling all sight and sound. Despite the cold, sweat coats the back of my neck. I'm getting nervous. Memories of the borderland fog and the hungry cursed wraiths flicker across my mind.

Something deep and primal sends a warning jolt through my spine. I stop walking.

As if sensing my hesitation, the wraith turns around to face me. She begins gesturing ahead, pointing in the direction she was leading me. Her mouth opens wide, as if screaming for me to follow. Her fingers curl into claws and her long white dress billows around her like she's caught in a storm.

But it's her eyes that frighten me the most. They're wild and black with a frantic energy that I don't know how to interpret.

I shake my head. "No!" I yell back at her. "I can't follow you any further. I can't see anything!"

All around us, the fog swirls. Panic claws at my chest. Where are we?

The wraith just keeps screaming, silent and terrifying, as she points ahead toward a point I can't see.

Something grabs my wrist.

I whirl around, my heart in my throat. Tristan is there, his eyes wide with fear.

"Red! What are you doing?!"

I grab onto his shoulders. "Do you see her?!"

Concern etches across his face. "What? Who?"

"The wraith!" I'm yelling now. My heart hammers in my chest. I turn to point back toward the woman in white, but she isn't there. And neither, I realize with a start, is the fog.

A sudden strong wind blows a mix of snow and rain that pelts my face. I look down and see that I'm soaking wet. My red cloak hangs from my neck, heavy as a noose. My feet are bare and white with snow. Only now do I feel the sharp bite of cold against my skin.

A mere three feet ahead of me lies the edge of a cliff.

The sea crashes below, while a tumbling maelstrom thunders overhead. Icy whitecaps crash so far up the shore that white water sprays up into the sky. Lightning flashes overhead. There is no moon in sight. No fog. No ghost.

Just the edge of a cliff and a raging storm.

Tristan pulls me back from the cliff's edge. "Red!" he yells above the thunder and the crashing sea. "Step back! The cliff isn't stable!"

But I'm frozen in place, bewildered and afraid. "I don't understand!" I yell out into the rain, hoping the wraith can hear me.

Tristan yanks me back. "What were you thinking coming out here in a storm? You could have died!" I don't miss the sharp edge of fear in his voice.

"Tell me you saw her!" I yell, feverishly.

"Who?" He's still trying to pull me back, away from the cliff's edge.

"The woman!" I yell, my voice edged with fear. Am I losing my mind? "The one that led me out here!"

His face is pale, his gray eyes wide. Icy rainwater streams over his face as he shakes his head slowly. "I didn't see a woman."

Thunder clashes overhead and we both flinch.

"No, not a normal woman." I growl in frustration. "A ... a ghost. Or specter? Something ... not human. At least not anymore."

He stares at me for a long time, his expression unreadable as icy water streams down his face. "I didn't see anyone. Only you, walking through the storm."

My body begins to tremble, whether from the cold or the

shock, I don't know. I rub my palms over my eyes. Am I going mad in this awful place?

"How did you even find me out here?" I ask. It sounds accusatory.

"I saw you from my window."

I don't need to ask what he was doing staring out his window in the middle of the night. No doubt he couldn't sleep either.

"I saw you walking through the storm. I recognized your red cloak." His eyes drift over my cloak as it whips around me in the violent wind and pelting frozen rain. "I followed you."

"I swear. She was here." My voice is pitched high, almost hysterical.

He pulls me toward him, and I allow myself to fold into his chest. Why would she do this? Why torture me? Why try to kill me again?

Far below us, waves hammer against the stones scattered along the shore.

Beneath my cloak, my white nightdress is soaking wet. I look down to see it's translucent, clinging to my body like a sheer second skin. I should be ashamed to have my nakedness on full display out here. But all I feel is afraid. How could I have been so easily fooled? I'm vulnerable in a way I've never felt before. What must he think of me, standing on these cliffs of death in nothing more than a nightdress, in the middle of a winter storm?

"Come on," he says, tucking me under his arm. "You'll catch your death out here."

But even as I turn to go with Tristan, the memory of the wraith's panicked gestures makes me pause. I stop.

"What is it?" Tristan asks.

"I—I don't know." I turn back toward the sea and shield my eyes from the pelting rain and snow. The sky is dark with storm clouds, the sea a roiling force below. Lightning flashes, and something makes my breath catch.

Am I seeing things again?

I stand stock still as Tristan tries to pull me back toward the castle.

"No!" I point out past the cliffs and the pounding shore.

Lightning flashes again, and Tristan sees it too. "That can't be ..." his voice is lost to the wind.

Thunder booms, and we watch as a ship is swallowed by the raging sea.

CHAPTER 21

BY DAYBREAK, the bodies start washing up on shore.

The storm ceased soon after it capsized the ship, as if satisfied with its catch. Its belly full of dying men, it dissipated as if it had never been there at all.

Dawn arrives without the usual fanfare of blazing colors, but rather with the gradual lightening of a gray world. Tristan sounded the alarm, gathering men from the town while I changed out of my wet clothes and warmed myself by the fire. Even now, as feeling returns to my limbs, I can't stop shaking.

I've seen death before. Many times, in fact, but I've never seen the sea take an entire ship in one swallow. One moment it was there, tossing violently among the waves. The next, it was gone.

Someone knocks on my open door. I turn to see Tristan, his face pale and gaunt from lack of sleep.

"You asked me to tell you when we're going to shore."

I nod, standing on tired legs. "I'll follow you."

Tristan leads the way down the steep path, down to the sea. In the hazy light of a cloudy dawn, I can see the shore is littered with what's left of the ship. Splintered wood from the hull, casks, and crates speckle the coast.

And, of course, there are the bodies.

Tristan turns to me. "You don't have to—"

"I'm coming."

He nods, assuming my answer before giving me a way out. I'm a healer. I've seen bodies mangled and torn before. Drowning is a new one though, battlefields being mostly inland.

The first body we see is a man dressed in a waterlogged cloak. There's sand in his hair, his clothes, and his ears. His skin is pale and puffy, with the disturbing pallor of the drowned. His eyes stare up at the sky. I hope he doesn't have to replay his last sight over and over again in the afterlife. I place my hand over his eyes to close them forever.

A short distance away, Tristan kicks away tiny shoreline crabs who've already begun feasting on another dead man. The corpse's mouth gapes open in a small pool of water.

"They're from Llwyn," Tristan says, breaking me out of my stupor.

My head shoots up. "How can you be sure?"

He points to the sword still strapped to the waist of a nearby body. "The hilt is bronze."

I rise to my feet to get a closer look. True enough, the man's weapon is a muted shade of copper and decorated with the face of a growling fox.

"Why would they be out at sea in Annwyn waters? In the middle of winter?" I turn to Tristan.

He shakes his head. "I have no idea. It's a wonder they even made it this far north, this time of year."

My head swirls with possibilities, each more terrifying than the last. Did my father send them on a suicide mission to capture more territory from the sea? Are more Fox Soldiers approaching from other directions, winter storms be damned?

The impossibilities are endless. And yet, here lie the bodies of his men, washed up on the Annwyn shore in the middle of winter. Sheets of ice slide gracefully over the smooth pebbles, between the bodies jostled by the waves.

Tristan turns to three old women who are assembling a pyre to burn the dead.

"That can wait," he says, his voice laced with urgency. "Open the crates and casks. Look for anything that might give us a clue as to why Llwyn soldiers were so far north."

The women drop swollen bodies and the shredded remnants of the ship's sail. One of the villagers produces an axe. Another has a pry bar. They get to work opening anything that's still sealed. Ale spills, the scent mixing with salty seawater as it foams in the waves. One of the casks holds animal feed, making me cringe. More than people died on that ship. Horses, likely. Depending on how long they were planning to stay in Annwyn, possibly farm animals as well.

Another crate cracks open with a soggy thump of an axe. From inside, copper-plated armor spills onto the rough sand. My family's emblem stares back at me like a ghost from the past. The fox makes me shiver as if it were my father's eyes watching me, plotting his next attempt at my life.

I can't help but wonder what's happened in Llwyn since I fled with Hunter and Tristan last autumn. Is my father's new bride, Elena, still alive? And what of her son, my alleged brother? Has he survived his first few months in the care of a monstrous king?

I've been detached from my homeland over the past couple of months. With the Spires and the storms between us, Annwyn is uniquely cut off from the rest of the world.

More detritus washes up on the shore as the waves courier secrets from the wreckage. Waterlogged travel biscuits. A soggy boot. The torn remains of a sail. There must be something here that could tell us what's happened in Llwyn.

A short distance away, one of the villagers turns over another body with his crutch. He pauses, staring down.

"This one's alive!"

It takes me a moment to register his words.

The man starts to wave his free arm while leaning on his crutch. "This man's still breathing!"

All around me, people run toward the body on the ground, but I'm frozen in place. Not because of fear. Not because I'm worried what that man might say about my homeland or my father. I'm paralyzed because I recognize that head of sopping blond hair. That bulky, tall frame, and the cut of the man's jaw. I ought to, since I've trailed my fingers over it enough.

It's Hunter.

My vision blurs. He didn't die on that flaming battlefield in Ellyll. He wasn't mauled by corpse wolves or murdered by my father's soldiers. Finally, my feet catch up with my brain. I sprint across the beach, then kneel beside him in the wet sand. His face is unnaturally pale; his breath shallow. When I touch his cheek, his skin is as cold as death.

"No." I shake my head. "No, Hunter, this isn't how you die."

Not after what I've done to you, I think. This man is the purest soul I've ever known, and I treated him abysmally. Guilt makes my breath catch in my chest. This can't be it. This can't be how his life ends. Not after everything we've been through.

My brain whirs through the hundreds of medical procedures I've seen the non-noble healers use in the borderlands, from sewing sutures to herbal remedies for infection. But we never had patients who were half-drowned on the battlefields. I don't know what to do.

My face scrunches up with a confusing mix of frustration and panic. I push Hunter full in the chest. He doesn't respond.

"Wake up!" I yell. I push him again. "Hunter, wake up!"

There's a small crowd forming around me, keeping a short distance. They watch me with pity in their eyes, but I refuse to be pitiful.

I bend forward and speak into Hunter's ear. "You have a long life of wooing pretty maids in seaside towns ahead of you, remember?" I wipe the wet hair away from his eyes. "You're going to marry one of them, and have a dozen babies, and grow old, and tell your grandchildren stories about being a great knight in the King's Guard."

He doesn't even flinch. His skin is beginning to take on an unmistakable blue tint. I growl in frustration and fight back the tears that are building behind my eyes. But I can't cry now. If I start, I know I'll never be able to stop.

If I am anything, I'm stubborn. And I refuse to watch my only friend die here, on a frozen shore, in a foreign land far from Llwyn. I close my eyes and place my hands over his chest. His breathing is dangerously shallow, and his wet skin sends a shiver through my arms. From deep within my core, I try to reach for my power.

"Please," I whisper to it. "Please."

At first, all I sense is emptiness, that all too familiar hollowness in my chest. Then, I recognize a small spark in the darkness. I focus on that small flame of hope, coaxing it, drawing it out of the depths of my core. It eases into my chest, filling me slowly, then faster. I gasp, unable to control it as it returns with an unexpected force.

Light power surges through my veins in a rush of heat. Golden power bursts through me, traveling up my chest and down the length of my arms. It doesn't so much pool in my hands as it rushes like a waterfall, engulfing Hunter.

Only now do I realize how close to death he truly is. I can feel his heart beating, so painfully slowly, it's as if it's already giving up. His life force is still there, barely hanging on by a thread. One foot already into the abyss of death.

"Come back," I beg.

Power laced with panic floods my mind. I think of nothing else, just Hunter. How much I've missed him. How he saved me from my father when we were children. How he rescued me when I was locked in the dungeon. How he crossed the entire Llwyn Kingdom for me.

How I need to save him. Desperately.

Even if I forget all else, I could never forget this: I love Hunter. I always have. And here, on the frozen coast of a forbidden land, I know that some part of me always will.

Under my palm, Hunter's heartbeat begins to grow steadier, stronger. He takes in a shuddering breath.

"Please don't leave me." Even as I say it, I understand the irony of the words. I'm the woman who left *him*. Not once, but twice.

Suddenly, his hand shoots up to grab my arm. His eyes flutter open.

I breathe a sigh of relief.

He stares at me, his warm brown eyes not fully focused. "Sienna ..."

"Yes, it's me."

His eyes flutter closed again, and his grip on my arm loosens, but he's no longer on death's door. I can feel his heartbeat growing stronger, his breaths growing deeper. He's unconscious, and I know it's for the best. His body desperately needs rest.

My power slowly eases back into me, sliding up my arms and returning to my core. Just as freely as it erupted, it slumbers again. But this time, I can feel it waiting there. The hollow emptiness in my chest is gone. My power has returned.

I finally sit back on my heels in the wet, grainy sand. When I look up, everyone is staring at me, their eyes wide with a mix of fear and awe.

"We need to get him to a fire," I say, back in healer mode. I need them to stop staring at me. Heat flushes my cheeks. "Someone, make a sling to carry him back to the castle. The rest of you, check the other bodies. Make sure there are no other survivors."

Wordlessly, they nod, taking direction as if they needed it. Several of them watch me warily as they retreat. I bring my attention back to Hunter as I breathe a sigh of relief. That's when I notice something odd. He's wearing layers of wool, likely to keep the freezing ocean air at bay. But there's an odd lump under his jacket, near his heart. I reach forward and unfasten the buttons. When I lift the fabric from his chest, I see a pocket sewn into the inside lining. I fish out the hard rectangle inside.

It's a small thin book. But not just any book. It's the one the librarian, Merle, gave to me the night before my father locked me in the rat-infested dungeon. The silver moth on the green cover shines in my hands.

The Silver Moth Society. How did Hunter find it?

I blink in wonder several times before the skin on the back of my neck begins to prickle. My eyes search the shoreline. They fall on the Wolf, standing a short distance away. Behind messy strands of dark hair, his gray eyes are filled with pride ... and the unmistakable glint of jealousy.

Somewhere in the distance, a seagull laughs.

PART THREE

THE HEIR

CHAPTER 22

HUNTER SLEEPS FOR THREE DAYS.

I rarely leave his side, riddled with guilt as I am. I sleep in the bed next to him, watching his breath, making sure it doesn't hitch or stop altogether. Fever keeps returning, like Death's insistent knocking. Every few hours I set my hands on Hunter's chest, his cheek, his forehead. I touch him wherever the heat rises, threatening to pull him back under the waves that tried to claim him. I won't let him die on my watch.

As he sleeps, I read and re-read the thin green book Hunter brought all the way from Caerwen for me: *The Silver Moth Society*. I'd set it as near to the fire as I dared, pages splayed to dry them as best I could. The book doesn't close flat anymore, damaged from both salt and water, but most of it is still legible.

This book is proof that the underground Sympathizers in Caerwen exist. That Grandmother was their leader. That there are more of them somewhere, hidden behind the Fox Palace walls and within the city.

I flip open the green cover to read the first page for the hundredth time.

The Silver Moth Society
A treatise on the demands of the Llwyn people in favor of the
permanent destruction of the Fox King and all future despotic
rulers.

My fingers linger over the names written inside the front cover. Most are still legible, though blurred. A few washed away completely, but not the first name, the one that started this entire journey: Áine. My grandmother.

The door to Hunter's room opens with a bang as it hits the wall.

"Enough." The Wolf storms into the room and opens the thick, faded curtains. Sunlight streams in and I wince. "You can't abandon all the progress we've made because the golden boy has shown up again."

My skin prickles with irritation. "I'm not abandoning anything. He needs me."

"To sleep? I don't think so." His jaw muscles visibly clench as he crosses his arms in front of his chest.

"If the fever returns—"

"Then you can heal him again, after you're finished with training for the day."

As much as I hate it, I know he's right. Hunter is out of danger, at least for now. He just needs rest. He'll wake when he's ready.

Tristan tosses a pile of clothes at me. I hold them up to find my leather pants and a clean tunic. My body aches in protest. I've barely stretched in days, let alone practiced with weapons.

"I'll meet you in the usual place," Tristan says, his voice even, before he walks out of the room.

I hesitate for a long moment, my fingers curling around the edges of the little green book. Finally, I change into my leathers, but I pause at the door. My eyes linger on the salt-stained book I left on Hunter's bedside. In a rush, I snatch it up again and tuck it into a pocket sewn into the lining of my cloak. This book has travelled a long way to return to me, and I don't want to risk losing it again. Something tells me this book is more important than I ever realized.

When I find Tristan at the castle's entrance, he doesn't lead me out toward the training yard. Instead, I follow him around the perimeter of the castle. The snow glistens with a thin layer of ice on top, and our feet crunch through with each step. The gray sky suggests there's more freezing rain and snow to come. It hovers along the edge of the Spires, as if waiting for the right moment to crash in on Gwyllion.

Tristan leads me to a wing of the castle that's so crumbled it's practically in ruins. There's no roof to speak of anymore, and trees grow out of buckled cracks in the slate floor. I stare up at the remains of fortress-like towers and leaning buttresses. Vines scale up their walls, barely holding together what was meant to fall ages ago.

A cold, bitter wind blows. How many more winters does the castle have before its fae magic fails entirely, leaving the rest to crumble to dust?

Tristan leads me around piles of rubble until we come across a thick, wooden door. Its hinges are no longer attached to the door frame. It leans against the entryway at a steep angle, a snowdrift covering half of it. Tristan makes quick work of removing the frozen layer of snow, then pulls the door away from its resting spot. Inside, there's a dark hallway leading into the forgotten depths of the castle.

I raise an eyebrow at him in question. "Are you sure this is safe?"

"Not at all." He walks into the corridor, disappearing into the dim interior.

"Lovely."

I eye the doorway, then follow the Wolf into the dark. I reach inside of me to ignite my orb of light, but Tristan interrupts my concentration.

"There's no need."

I'm not sure about that, but I quiet my power in my core, anyway. Darkness, it is.

My eyes widen as I try to make out details in the crumbling corridor. I follow Tristan into a large, open space, like a cavern beneath the ground. Our footsteps echo against the stone.

"What was this place?" I ask. The air is so still, it feels frozen in time.

Next to me, I feel Tristan shrug. "Likely some old ballroom or great hall. It's hard to know now. Much of this castle was built upon the remains of the castles before it. As far as we know, this might be the fourth or fifth version."

I blink at the darkness. The shadows are so consuming, all I can make out are different shades of black. I know the ceiling is tall because the shadows darken up above. How wide the room is, I couldn't guess. The only light comes from the distant doorway that leads outside.

Damp air clings to my skin, thick with the scent of earth.

"Why bring me to a dark pit when you can create shadows yourself?" I ask.

Tristan circles me, his boots scraping softly against the uneven floor. I watch him move gracefully as a panther. "Because today, you'll be using your light as a weapon."

"What?" I shake my head. "My light isn't a weapon, you know that."

"I know that's a lie. I've seen you use it."

I throw my hands up into the air. "Those weren't normal circumstances. It just ... happened!"

"Therefore, you can do it."

"Not intentionally!"

"We shall see about that."

I wonder how much the Wolf can see in this darkness. I throw out a rude gesture, just to test him.

"You're wasting time, Red. Ready yourself."

Jaw tightening, I unclasp my cloak and let it fall to the

ground. It thuds with the weight of the book. I step into a defensive stance. My pulse thrums in my ears.

"Call forth your light. What little you can of it, in any case."

I bristle at his words but say nothing. I lift my hands, summoning a glowing orb into my palm. The familiar sight sends a thrill of pride through me.

Tristan snuffs it out.

I gasp, stepping back.

"Again," he commands.

I summon my light once more, focusing with all my strength. It's brighter this time, pushing against the darkness. For a moment, it holds, before Tristan's shadow slips through, devouring it. My frustration spikes.

Before I even ignite another orb, there's a sudden shift in the air and a wall of darkness collides into me. Tristan's shadow takes me by surprise, and I lose my balance. I hit the ground hard, my breath rushing from my lungs.

I sit up, rubbing my hip where it hit the ground. That will leave a nasty bruise.

Tristan stands over me, unimpressed. "You would be dead right now if this were a real battle."

Anger sparks hot in my chest. "You cheated."

Did I seriously kiss this man a few days ago? The Wolf stands over me, his posture distant and unforgiving. It's like I'm a stranger to him.

"The world doesn't play fair, Red. Get up." His words are clipped, sharp.

I push to my feet, fists clenched. "This isn't training. This is humiliation."

He steps closer, shadows coiling at his feet like snakes. "You think I'm being cruel? I'm trying to keep you alive. Because one day, someone will come for you, and they won't wait for you to be ready."

I swallow hard, but the anger doesn't fade. "And you think breaking me is the best way to teach me?"

"I'm not trying to break you. I'm trying to make you stronger."

"Because everyone here thinks I'm so weak, is that it?"

"That's not what I said."

"Are you sure you're not trying to punish me for something?"

His jaw tightens. I've hit a pressure point. He doesn't respond.

I cross my arms in front of me. "This is about Hunter, isn't it?"

Silence stretches between us, thick and suffocating. My chest heaves, frustration twisting inside me.

"This is about learning to use your power."

I scoff. "Well, I can't control it like that. Do you really think humiliating me is going to change that?"

"You can do it!"

I step up to him, my skin radiating with fury. "I can't!"

"Stop saying that!" He runs a hand through his messy black hair in frustration. Then, after a moment, he turns back to me, intense and close. "I saw you use your power to bring a man back from the edge of death."

"That was different." I sound petulant, but I don't care.

"How? How was that different, Red?"

"I ..." I stumble over my words. The truth is, I don't know. When I saved Hunter, my instincts took over. It's as if everything in me needed Hunter to stay alive. "I don't know."

Tristan watches me for a long moment. "Well, that's what we need to figure out."

If only it was that easy. I don't know how I was able to call my power back from burnout, but I'm not sorry about it. With its warmth safely in my core, I'm finally starting to feel more like myself again.

"Let me ask you something." Tristan studies me, crossing his arms in front of his chest. "What you did to Hunter on the beach, how is that any different from reanimation?"

"What?" This change in direction has me slightly stunned. "That was healing, not reanimating a corpse."

"From where I stood, it looked a lot like bringing someone back from the dead."

"It wasn't." I hiss. "It isn't the same."

He raises an eyebrow, watching me.

"He wasn't dead!"

"So, the difference between your light power and my shadows is just perspective? A slight change in the subject's circumstance?"

I glare at him through the dark. "I'm not going to dignify that with an answer. You're just trying to bait me."

I'm done with this conversation. I turn to walk toward the exit, back toward the light. Back toward Hunter.

The Wolf's voice follows me. "And why would I do that?"

I whirl back toward him. "Because you're jealous!" The second the words leave my mouth, I regret them deeply.

His face grows still, and I swear I see the smallest flicker of hurt cross his gray eyes.

"I'm sorry. I shouldn't—"

"Do you love him?" he interrupts.

"What?" My face freezes.

"You heard me, Red. Do you still love him?"

"I ..." My brain is whirring, trying to come up with a simple answer to that question. "It's complicated."

Tristan shakes his head. "No, Red. It really isn't."

"And what would you know about love?"

Tristan swallows hard. "I may not be Hunter with his flowery words and his grand gestures, but do *not* mistake me for being any less of a man." He takes three steady steps toward me and pauses, just out of reach. "And I *do* know the sting of love. For me, it isn't that complicated."

He stares at me for a long moment as my pulse quickens and my heart races in my chest. His voice drops to nearly a whisper in the darkness. "And I think you already know that."

Tristan passes me and doesn't look back.

CHAPTER 23

WHEN I RETURN to the room, Hunter is sitting up in his bed, awake.

The second I step through the door, I hear his voice. "Well, I have to admit. I'm a little confused."

In an instant, all my tension dissolves into a puddle of relief. I rush to his side and throw my arms around his shoulders, like old times. I am so blissfully happy to see the glow in his cheeks, I could cry. In fact, I do cry. It's messy and gross, and I don't care.

"I'm fine." He tries to pry my arms from around his neck, but he's weak and I'm holding on so tightly, I may not ever let go.

He coughs. "You're suffocating me."

I pull away slightly and give him a giant kiss on the cheek. He stiffens, but, given his brush with death, I'll forgive him that.

I wipe my tears roughly from my cheeks and sit back on his bed. Dim light from the overcast sky makes the room feel cold, even with the fire in the hearth burning strong. I shiver beneath my red cloak, then pull Hunter's blankets higher up his chest. He pushes them back down. I know I'm fussing, but I can't help it.

His eyes widen as he takes in my leather pants for the first time. His eyes drift up to mine, one eyebrow raised.

"They're practical." I sound defensive.

"I bet." He squints at me, studying me for a long moment. "A lot has changed over these last two months."

"It has."

He leans back into his pillows and closes his eyes. Exhaustion etches his face. "I don't know where the hell I am, but they sure have nice pillows."

I laugh. "You and I both know these pillows are shit."

"I was trying to be polite." A weary smile cracks his face. To me, it shines like the light of a summer day in Llwyn. He opens one eye to look at me. "I sure would like to know what happened."

"We'll get to that, but first, are you sure you're alright?"

He nods. "I am."

I punch him in the shoulder as hard as I can.

He shoots straight up, his eyes accusatory. "Ow! What the hell, Sienna?"

I point at his face, my finger a mere three inches from his nose. "What were you thinking, sailing a ship north in the dead of winter?!"

He snaps his jaw shut and rubs his arm where I hit him. I hope it leaves a bruise.

"At least you have the decency to look chagrined." I glower at him. "Seriously, Hunter, of all the harebrained, foolhardy, misguided things you've ever done, this—"

"It was for you," he says evenly.

I stop, mid-sentence. "What?"

"I stole a ship and sailed north for you."

I can't hide the bewilderment I feel. I blink at him several times. "Wha ... I ... how ..."

He sighs and leans back into the pillows again. "They all died, didn't they? The men? My crew?"

I nod slowly.

"We knew it would be dangerous. I just thought we'd at least make it to shore before we all died."

"Hunter, it wasn't just dangerous. It was suicidal." I stare at him hard. The past couple of months have changed him too, I realize. He's thinner, and his eyes have dark circles beneath them. I'd wager he's had more than a few sleepless nights since I left him on the battlefield at Ellyll.

"We didn't have much of a choice," he says, the corners of his mouth turning downward.

I bite my lip, thinking of how to proceed. There are a million unspoken words between us. How I broke my promise to marry him. How I convinced him to help me save the Wolf from my father's prison. How he gave me his body and soul before I abandoned him on a burning battlefield, to follow the Wolf into Annwyn.

I heave a weary sigh. "Hunter, but why come here? We both know I made my own choice to leave Llwyn."

To leave you, I don't say. Still, behind his deep brown eyes, I can see the words there. The pain of betrayal shows when he looks at me.

"I swore an oath to protect the royal family, and I intend to keep it."

"You're not a member of the King's Guard anymore," I remind him.

An involuntary look of disgust crosses his face. He tries to hide it, but not well enough. He turns his face to look out the window. "You wouldn't understand. Some of us value our words. Our promises."

Shame, thick and heavy, burns its way through my chest. I've broken many promises in my life, especially to him, but I never did it without a reason. Someday, I hope he'll be able to see that.

The fire crackles in the hearth, doing little to cut the sudden chill between us.

Hunter's eyes stare out at the snow-covered landscape of Annwyn, but I don't think he really sees it. It's just an excuse to keep from looking at me. Out his window, the frozen north awaits in an immense forest. He doesn't even know about the fae yet. How they're real. How they can be both whimsical and utterly terrifying. How they're out there, in the wilds of Annwyn, just out of sight.

When he speaks again, his words are raw, honest. "An oath doesn't mean you give up when the path gets too difficult, or complicated. I may not be a King's Guard anymore, but no one can break the oath I made to the rightful ruler of Llwyn." His brown eyes shift to meet mine. "You."

"Don't you mean my father?"

He shakes his head. "Your father lost his right to the crown when he disowned the rightful heir and used the Llwyn people to feed his lust for power."

He sits up and reaches for my hand. I suck in a breath. I thought I'd forgotten, the feel of his skin on mine, but I didn't. The memory of it comes crashing back into me, like the sea in a storm. My hand knows his. My skin remembers the warmth of him, the hard calluses from years of training with swords, the surprising sureness of his grip ... but something isn't the same. There was a time when Hunter's touch sent shivers down my spine. When his voice sent my heart skittering.

Now, he's familiar, and yet not. There's a distance between us.

"Hunter, I can't just be the heir again. My father disowned me. He tried to kill me."

He shakes his head again. "It's not a matter of if you can or cannot. You *are* the rightful heir. You may not have chosen this life, but it chose you. And I chose you too. Even if I won't be your husband, I will always be a knight in your service. Until death takes me."

Hunter's eyes burn with determination and sincerity, like a warm flame. I know this look. I know this man. He believes in honor and virtue above all else. When faced with a difficult choice, he will always do the right thing, even if it comes at his own expense. It's why I fell in love with him all those years ago. It's why I had to let him go.

"Whatever happened to living a quiet life?"

He shakes his head slowly. "That was a fiancé's promise to his betrothed. We're not those people anymore. They died back in the borderlands, in the fires of Ellyll."

In many ways, he's right. I certainly don't feel like the same woman who crossed Llwyn on a mission to find her grandmother. Now, I want only one thing in life: to kill the Fox King.

I'm almost afraid to ask, but I do anyway. "What happened after Ellyll?"

He nods and chews his lip for a few seconds before deciding where to start. "I couldn't go back to Caerwen. I'm a fugitive." His eyes flicker up to meet mine. There's no blame in them, but I feel the bite of guilt all the same.

"Mostly, I traveled from village to village, asking for odd jobs. There were plenty of farmers in need of a strong back to finish the last of the harvest or ready their fields for winter. I meant what I said when I told you I wanted to be a fisherman. To live a simple life."

I nod. "I know you did." It's why we never would have worked.

He sighs, growing weary again. "But then the snow came, and there was no need for hired hands. After Ellyll, things were different. You were gone. I suppose I just ... drifted."

It's difficult for me to imagine Hunter wandering from town to town with no mission, no purpose. It couldn't have been easy for him.

"But then, I started to notice something ... concerning."

"More concerning than normal, you mean?" I raise an eyebrow.

He nods. "The soldiers are heading toward the borderlands. There were so many of them. And King's Guards too." He gives me a meaningful look. "I knew he was up to something. And it wasn't good."

My face pales.

"So, I went back to Caerwen. To the Fox Palace."

"Hunter, you could've been killed!"

He nods, looking sheepish. "I was careful. But I couldn't just sit back and pretend nothing was happening. I needed to find out what your father was up to."

Of course, he did. A pang of fondness strikes my heart. Hunter, forever the noble knight, with or without his copper armor.

"And did you?" I ask, almost afraid to hear the answer.

His mouth forms a grim line. "I heard stories. None of them good."

Fear strikes my heart, and my body stiffens. "Tell me. I can handle it."

Hunter studies me for a reaction. "Your *brother*," he says the word like he knows it's a lie. "Is fine, it seems. Or, as fine as any child can be when he's raised by nursemaids and an evil father."

"Fennec is still a baby. My father can't do much damage yet."

He shrugs. "Maybe not. But, Elena ..." his voice breaks.

My heart sinks. I know where this is going. No woman lasts long with my father. Hunter's cousin wouldn't be the exception.

He nods, sensing I know. "She disappeared."

"Dead?" The word sounds hollow in my mouth.

"I think that's safe to presume, knowing the king's track record."

I suspected as much, but hearing it aloud makes it feel real. Elena, despite being my father's mistress, had once been my friend. She didn't deserve the life she got. Nor the end. I remember the cold, dark dungeon that my father locked me in when he left me to die. I refuse to think of Elena there, dead with hundreds of rats in that damp darkness.

I reach out toward Hunter hesitantly. When he doesn't flinch away, I set my fingers gently over his where they rest on the blanket.

"Hunter, I am so, so sorry."

He takes a deep breath and nods. "I wish I'd asked her more questions. I wish I'd been there for her. Instead, I was too concerned with becoming a King's Guard. I suppose on some level I was embarrassed. My cousin was the King's mistress." He

BRIAR KNIGHTLY

closes his eyes and shakes his head angrily. "Now I know there was more to it than that. But I was too blind to see it."

"The moth ring?"

He nods. "The ring."

I hesitate, not sure this is the right time to bring it up, but there's no such thing as perfect timing. "Hunter, when we found you on the beach. In your pocket, you had a book." I level my eyes with his. "*My* book, as it happens." I take the little green book out of the pocket of my red cloak. The silver moth on the cover flashes in the dim light.

He takes a deep, relieved breath, then coughs. "I was afraid I'd lost it."

"How did you find it?"

He gives me a sheepish grin. "Do you really think I'd forget the place you used to hide sweets in when we were kids?"

My mouth drops open. "You snuck into the palace? Into my room?" I stare at him wide-eyed. "Hunter, you could have been caught!"

He shrugs. "I figured if you had any useful information, you'd hide it beneath the floorboards."

It's so ridiculous, I laugh. "And here I thought it was the perfect hiding spot."

He waggles his head back and forth. "It is, but you keep forgetting how well I know you."

A relieved smile tugs at my lips. I am so glad to see him again. "Still, you shouldn't have gone back there. It wasn't worth it."

"I had to. I couldn't ignore what was happening. Not after everything we went through." He takes a deep breath, like he's bracing himself to tell me the worst. "There's something you need to know. The increased soldiers at the borderlands, it's a renewed effort to 'protect Llwyn from the invading corpse armies.'"

I scowl. "Even though *we* are, in fact, the true invaders. It was never Annwyn."

He pinches the space between his eyes. "Yeah, about that."

I raise my eyebrows, suspicious.

196

Hunter takes a deep breath and gives it to me straight. "Your father is using your disappearance as an excuse to send renewed forces into Annwyn. To take revenge for your kidnapping."

I blanch. "My ... what?"

"You know your father. He will spin anything to his advantage."

"And what of Fennec, the new heir?"

Hunter shrugs. "He's just a footnote in the king's new tale. The Dead Queen and her Wolf stole you, the heir to the Fox Throne. He's out for blood." He scrunches his face. "More than usual, at any rate."

I pause, thinking. "None of this makes any sense. He hates me. He tried to kill me. He made Fennec his heir."

Hunter shakes his head. "Maybe in writing, but few people know that. All the Llwyn people know is the Wolf stole you away on the eve of our wedding. And your father will murder every last person in Annwyn to get you back."

My brain is humming with adrenaline. "But he doesn't want me back. Not really."

"No. But he *does* want to kill the Dead Queen. I don't think any of us truly knows why."

I might, but I'm not sure it's the right time to tell Hunter this. Nothing could be more humiliating to my father than a woman outfoxing the Fox King. This fight has little to do with me. My father will stop at nothing to get revenge.

My stomach roils just thinking of all the Llwyn soldiers dying on the borderlands. I've seen enough of them to last a lifetime, and yet my father sends more. It's too much to think about right now.

I turn the conversation back to Hunter. "None of that explains why you presumably stole a ship and sailed north in the middle of winter."

"The Spires are impassable this time of year. The sea was my only shot."

"And the men? The ship?"

"Let's just say I knew a few people who owed me favors from my time on the King's Guard."

"Sailors?"

"Pirates."

"Ah."

He looks toward the window, at a rising storm that has finally made its way past the enchanted border.

"But, why did you think I needed saving to begin with?" I ask. "I went into Annwyn willingly. You were there, you know that."

He drags his gaze away from the window reluctantly, landing on mine. His warm brown eyes are sad. "I didn't come here to save you from the Wolf, Sienna. I came here to warn you."

"Warn me?"

"Your father's men are camped at the foot of the Spires. Ready to march here the second the roads are passable. He knows where you are, Sienna."

I shake my head. "It doesn't matter. They won't get past the border. The Annwyn people have been protecting the border for centuries—"

"And losing territory by the year."

"They won't get past the Spires."

Hunter levels his brown eyes on me. "This time, they will. He brought the Fox Army, Sienna. All of it."

The news settles on my shoulders, cold and heavy. As isolated as I've been out here in Gwyllion, I actually managed to feel safe this far out of my father's reach. I should have known better. Nowhere is safe from the Fox King.

Behind us, the door opens. Instinctively, I stuff the little green book into the pocket of my red cloak, to keep it out of sight. I don't know why, but something tells me this isn't the sort of book that should be left out for anyone to see.

We both turn to see Nalina step in, her face grave. Her brown leathers are dusty and her blond braid is frizzy. I wonder if she's been in the training yard, hitting things.

"Good. You're awake," she says. She doesn't sound glad.

I stiffen.

Hunter sits up. "Yes. Thank you for your hospitality."

Nalina gives him a suspicious look. "I had nothing to do with it. If things went my way, I wouldn't tolerate southerners here in Annwyn." Her eyes shoot toward me.

Hunter nods. "I understand."

"Do you?" she asks sharply.

I feel the words slice through the air as surely as a dagger. "None of this is his fault, Nalina."

"No, you're right." She turns to me slowly. "It's yours."

I stare at her for a long moment. "Did you need something? Or are you just here out of morbid curiosity?"

"The queen wants to see him."

I shake my head. "No. It's too soon. He only just woke up."

Nalina holds the door open wider. "Oh, I'm sorry. Were you expecting tea first?"

I roll my eyes and turn to Hunter. "There's a lot I need to tell you. Meeting the queen won't be what you expect."

Hunter moves the blankets off his legs and shifts to step out of the bed. "It's fine. I saw her before, in Ellyll." His knees tremble when he stands.

I rush to help him, but he waves me off. "No, I don't mean that she's frightening. There's more to it than that."

Hunter locates a pair of boots by the hearth and steps over the cold floor to retrieve them. "Sienna, I can handle it." He bends to tie his laces. "I'm not an invalid. I'm just tired. Do me the decency of allowing me to make up my own mind about the Dead Queen."

"Hunter, I need you to sit down, to listen to me—"

He holds up a hand, irritation clear on his face. "Please stop." He gives me a level look. "I don't need you to protect me."

My lips snap shut. All I can do is follow a step behind him as he trails Nalina through the cold, dark halls of Gwyllion Castle. Toward the throne room.

Toward Grandmother.

CHAPTER 24

THE WINTER STORM is in full force when we enter the throne room. Wind howls through cracks high above us, and tiny flecks of snow drift down from the rafters. The tapestries depicting sacred trees flap and sway, as if dancing to the music of the storm.

Not for the first time, I'm reminded of how inhospitable this castle is. No one should live here, but there aren't many places for the people of Annwyn to go. I'll have to explain this to Hunter.

Next to me, Hunter's eyes dart from window to window as hail pelts the glass. Nalina doesn't even flinch when thunder booms, followed by a floor-shaking crack. Outside, something heavy tumbles to the ground. I wonder if it's a crumbling stone wall or one of the many leaning towers. Hopefully, no one was in it when it fell.

Upon the dais, the Dead Queen waits.

Her long veil drapes over her face and black gloves cover her arms, but I can't shake the memory of what's underneath. Scars and festering wounds. Skeletal hands and dead flesh. She sits on the blackened wood and iron throne, her posture straight and unbreathing. The throne suits her. A cold, dead throne for a cold, dead queen.

"A Hunter has arrived in the den of Wolves." The queen's

voice booms in this cavernous space, and I notice Hunter flinch out of the corner of my eye. The Dead Queen leans forward as we approach. "Did you think you could sneak into my kingdom? You are no fox. Deception does not become you."

I expect Hunter to hesitate like most people would when confronted by the infamous Dead Queen, but he doesn't. When we reach the dais, Hunter kneels, ever the courtly knight, despite his lack of armor.

"Your Highness, thank you for taking me in and saving my life."

The Dead Queen laughs humorlessly. "You have your Fox Heir to thank for that."

Nalina passes us and walks up the dais steps. She stands in her usual spot behind the throne, settling into the posture of a guardian with her shoulders back and head held high. Her mouth is pinched in its usual way. Now she has two southerners to tolerate. I can only imagine how much fun this is for her.

"You may stand." The Dead Queen waves a gloved hand impatiently.

Hunter rises to his feet, trembling slightly. I study his face. It's grown pale, but I don't think it's from fear. He's still weak, but if I know Hunter, he'll never admit that he's weary. The only hint of emotion I catch is when his eyebrows draw together in momentary confusion. I follow his gaze and see his eyes are resting on the silver moth necklace around the queen's neck. The necklace he once gave me to remember Grandmother by.

My stomach twists. There wasn't enough time to prepare him for what's coming. But, then again, I suppose there's not enough time in the world for that.

The queen continues, "I have a gift for you."

My internal alarm bells ring.

Hunter tilts his head to the side. "A gift?"

The Dead Queen holds out a hand toward Nalina, whose eyes grow dark with concern.

"My queen, perhaps it would be wise—"

The Dead Queen turns her face toward Nalina. "Do not question me again." Her voice is low, that unnatural, haunting element returned.

My skin prickles, and my eyes dart to Hunter to watch his reaction. The corners of his mouth are pulled down in a worried expression, his eyes locked on the Dead Queen.

Nalina hesitates, but she doesn't protest further. She reaches behind the black wood and iron throne and retrieves something that steals my breath away.

Nalina places a long silver sword in the Dead Queen's open hands. Its pommel is molded into the face of a copper fox with ruby red eyes. The fox wraps around the cross-guard, ending in a silver-tipped tail. This is no ordinary sword. It's also strikingly familiar.

Hunter's eyes grow wide. "My father's sword. But how did you ... it was on the ship ..." His voice is filled with reverence.

"It washed up on the shore with your men."

The dead men, she means. I try not to think about the swollen bodies of the drowned scattered about the pebbled shore like driftwood. Another gust of wind howls through the rafters overhead as tiny snowflakes rain down on us in slow motion.

The Dead Queen holds the ornate sword out toward Hunter.

He walks forward as if in a dream. He's only feet away from the Dead Queen when a horrible thought crosses my mind. What if she means to kill him with it? When she doesn't, I let out a breath.

Hunter reaches forward to take his father's sword from the queen's black-gloved hands. "I don't know how to thank you."

"There's more."

Hunter's face pales further. "More?"

The Dead Queen raises a hand. Behind us, the doors to the throne room open. Two Wolves dressed in black furs enter the room, carrying a crate between them. Their steps echo on the stone floor as they approach. They set the crate before the throne.

"Open it," the queen commands.

One of the guards uses a pry bar to remove the crate's nails. The wooden lid pops open. Inside, lies a copper man. Or, rather, just the shape of one. Hunter's copper-plated armor rests on a bed of soggy straw. All that's missing are the copper-plated gauntlets that his father melted in the fires at Ellyll.

Hunter stumbles up to it, then trails one hand over the helm with its decorative plating. He holds his father's old sword up in front of the armor, as if he can't believe this is all real. He turns back to the Dead Queen with wide eyes.

"Why would you give these back to me?"

Her words are careful, measured. "Let's call it a show of good faith."

Fear begins to needle its way into my gut. I have no idea which way this encounter will go, but I'm certain there's more to this show than 'good faith.' Like a skilled card player, she still hasn't revealed her hand. Her secret identity. She's playing a game, and I don't like being an unwilling pawn. I need to speak up.

My voice has an undeniable edge to it. "I have a feeling there's a price to this generosity."

Hunter and Nalina turn toward me, blinking as if they forgot I was here.

"Everything comes with a price, Fox Heir." The Dead Queen's voice is low with warning.

"Then it's hardly a gift."

From behind her black veil, she clucks. "Such a rude guest."

"You and I both know I'm no mere 'guest'."

"No." The haunting edge has returned to her voice. I can sense those undead eyes on me from behind her veil.

"Then tell him plainly," I say. "What do you require in exchange for this generous gift?"

Hunter's eyes dart between the Dead Queen and me. I stand firm, daring the queen to be forthright.

She lets out a weary sigh, as though I'm a tedious child. "Fine." She turns her head to Hunter, her veil swaying in a draft.

"In exchange for safe harbor and the return of your armor, I have one request."

"And that is?" Hunter's voice sounds hesitant, as if he's not sure he wants to know.

"Fight for me," she says simply, as if it is nothing. "Help me destroy the Fox King's empire."

The silence of the room is torture. Cold drafts make the tapestries sway and the guards behind us shift uneasily. From her spot next to the Dead Queen, Nalina watches us with fury in her eyes.

"How am I supposed to defeat an entire empire?" Hunter asks.

"Not alone, I assure you." The Dead Queen nods toward me. "The Fox Heir will help."

Hunter turns to me, his eyes wide. "You're helping the Dead Queen now?"

"It's complicated."

He gives me an incredulous look before turning back to the queen. "And how am I supposed to fight a force like the Fox King?"

The queen shrugs her bony shoulders. "By swinging around that pretty little sword of yours. And ..." She pauses, weighing her words. "Doing what you do best. Protecting the Fox Heir."

Hunter scoffs. "Why can't you have your corpses do that for you?"

The queen's voice is sharp as a blade. "Because they're not enough!"

The room stills in the wake of her words. Hail pounds on the windows and thunder rumbles in the distance.

Then, just as quickly as she erupted, the Dead Queen gathers her composure again. "You may not know this, but my people are barely surviving." She trails her bony fingers along the armrest of her twisted throne. "The Fox King takes more territory each year. We are losing this centuries-long war. And losing it badly." She sits back as if to rest her weary bones. "We need a new plan. The dead cannot fight all the battles for the living."

"And what is this 'new plan'?" Hunter asks.

"A new weapon."

I stiffen. I'd wondered when it would come into this.

Hunter looks down at the sword in his hand. "This? It's a sword, nothing more. It's not enough to turn the tide of war."

The Dead Queen tuts. "Never underestimate the might of a single sword, Hunter. For a single blade can change the world." She shakes her head. "But that is not the weapon I was referring to."

"Then what?"

The Dead Queen laughs lowly.

Hunter frowns. "How is any of this amusing to you?"

"Because I know something you don't."

"What?"

"Our tides have just turned."

He throws out his arms. "How?"

"We have the Heir to the North."

Silence.

My heart is racing in my chest. I'm not the Heir to the North. Tristan told me as much. I stand to inherit the Fox Throne in the south. I'm not even sure I believe in this mythical human heir that comes from a lineage older than the reigns of the Dead Queens. That story is steeped in legend, not fact.

Hunter shakes his head in disbelief. "The Heir to the North is nothing but a fairy tale mixed with nostalgia for the past." Hunter narrows his eyes at the Dead Queen. "A past when humans sat upon that throne, not Dead Queens."

The queen doesn't look bothered by this confrontation, but Nalina does. She looks angry enough to take the greatsword off her back and kill something. Or someone.

"That is for me to worry about," the queen says. "Right now, you must decide. Will you protect the heir to the Fox Throne?"

Hunter watches the queen for a long moment before he gives

her a curt nod. "Of course, but not for you. I swore an oath to protect her."

"Your motives do not matter to me, as long as you do it." From beneath her veil, the Dead Queen gives him a long, assessing look. "You know, you haven't changed much since you were a child, running around the palace with her." She nods in my direction.

Dread fills my veins. For a moment, I actually allowed myself to believe she wouldn't tell him.

Hunter takes a step backward. "How would you know that?"

"Hunter—" I start to intervene, but the Dead Queen talks right over me.

"I wonder if you remember me."

Hunter's face melts into confusion. "How could I forget? You saved us in Ellyll."

"No, from before. From the palace in Caerwen."

I reach toward Hunter, suddenly desperate to steal his attention back from the queen and the horror I know is coming. "Please, let me tell him."

Hunter shakes my hand from his arm. "No. What are you trying to hide?" His words are sharp and accusatory when he looks at me.

I bite my lip, willing tears not to fall. I will not cry in front of this horrible queen. I will not let her get under my skin.

He turns back to the queen. "I never met you before Ellyll. I'd remember."

The queen laughs darkly. "We'll see about that."

The Dead Queen rises from her throne, her bones popping with each movement. She walks down the dais, graceful as a shadow, and stops before us. I know it's coming, and my heart breaks for Hunter in this moment of revelation.

The Dead Queen raises her veil, revealing the rotted, destroyed face of a woman we both loved.

Hunter's face crumbles into horror as recognition takes hold. "No." He shakes his head, backing into the crate of copper armor.

"No, it can't be." His eyes dart between her massacred face and the silver moth necklace hanging at her breast.

The Dead Queen stares, her pearlescent eyes revealing no emotion.

Hunter turns to me, disbelieving. "You knew?!"

I shake my head, reaching out for him again. He scrambles away from me like I'm made of hot iron, fresh from the forge.

"I had no idea, Hunter, I swear it. Not until I got here."

"All those years trying to discover who killed your grandmother, and she wasn't even dead?"

I look pointedly at the splitting, pale flesh on the queen's face. "She is dead, Hunter. Like the corpse wolves."

"But she *isn't* dead, is she?"

I huff in frustration. "It'll take time. You'll come to understand."

"No." Hunter shakes his head firmly. "No. This is one thing I will never fully understand." He turns to the queen, fury distorting his face. "How is this possible? Why are you here?"

"That isn't a story I wish to tell."

He huffs. "Well, I didn't wish to see someone I loved turned into a monster."

Bang! The sound cuts through the rising tension like the swing of an executioner's axe.

We all turn to see the throne room doors swing open. Tristan walks across the flagstones, his steps swift and determined. Despite our fight earlier, relief floods me at the sight of him. Maybe he can fix this before everything goes to hell.

"I asked you to wait for me," Tristan says.

I'm not sure who he's speaking to until Nalina steps forward. "I did as I was bidden."

"And a simple warning was too much to muster?"

Nalina gives him a long look. It's clear she had no intention of bringing him into this meeting. When he reaches us, Tristan kneels before the Dead Queen.

"My Queen, I apologize for the interruption."

The Dead Queen waves his apology away. "It's no matter." When she speaks, her black, desiccated tongue is visible through the remaining flesh of her fetid jaw.

Tristan rises and turns to me. "Are you alright?"

I nod.

"You!"

We all turn to Hunter.

He's staring at Tristan like he's going to erupt. "How dare you show your face in front of me again?"

Tristan holds out his hands defensively. "Red followed me into Annwyn willingly. You can ask her yourself."

Hunter points a finger at Tristan's face. "You're a liar. You tricked her, just like you tricked me into believing you were a decent human being!"

Tristan raises an eyebrow. "'Decent' is a relative word, I've found."

In a whirl, Hunter raises his father's fox sword. "Decency isn't open for interpretation."

Tristan doesn't look concerned about the sword in the slightest. "What are you going to do, Hunter? Kill me?"

"I'd sure like to." Hunter swings.

Tristan jumps out of the way, looking appalled.

"Hunter!" I shout. "I can explain everything, just give me time!"

Hunter swings again. Tristan spins away and draws his own sword from the scabbard tied to his belt. Shadows twist along the silver blade eagerly. "I really don't want to do this, Hunter."

"Well, I do."

The two men swing at each other. Silver clashes. The sound echoes throughout the throne room as the men completely lose their senses in the fight. So much for Hunter feeling weary after his brush with death.

"Stop!" I shout.

Tristan thrusts his blade toward Hunter, silver and shadows cutting through the air. Hunter spins around, out of reach as he angles his sword to jab it toward the Wolf. Tristan avoids it, then jumps over the crate of armor to get closer to his target.

"That's enough!" I shout.

Clang! Clang!

Hunter nearly draws blood as he swipes his fox sword toward Tristan's thigh.

Tristan's jaw tenses, his face transforming with fury. "Oh, I don't think so, Golden Boy." He attacks with a force and speed that frightens me.

"Tristan! Hunter!"

They ignore me.

"For the love of the old gods, stop!"

Someone grabs me from behind, and I stumble back into them. Nalina's strong arm wraps around my chest, tight as a vice. I recognize the cool touch of an unexpected blade against my neck.

"I will slice her pretty little throat." Nalina doesn't yell. She doesn't have to.

The two men freeze, both swords raised. Two pairs of eyes dart toward me, and I'm shocked to recognize the expressions on both men. Concern. Panic. Worry. I'd expect as much from Hunter, sure. He's always been protective of me. But Tristan?

Nalina presses the steel tighter into my neck. "Really?" she asks, but her words are directed toward Tristan. "This is how you behave in front of your queen?"

Near the dais, the queen stands still, watching. She doesn't appear concerned, but then again, I'm not practiced in deciphering the expressions of corpses.

"I beg your forgiveness," Hunter says first. He walks to the crate of armor and sets his sword inside. "I should have known better than to raise a blade in front of a queen."

"Yes," she says evenly. "You should have."

After a beat, Tristan sheaths his sword and his shadows extinguish in mid-air. He clenches his fists as he says, "Apologies, my queen."

I stare at the two men. Since when does Tristan lose his composure? And since when has Hunter turned vengeful?

Nalina removes her blade from my neck and releases me roughly. When I give her a reproachful look, she gives me a resentful one in return.

She narrows her eyes at Tristan. "I expected to see the fear in *his* eyes," she nods toward Hunter. She walks toward Tristan, then stops mere inches from his face. Her whisper is so filled with spite, it may as well be a shout. "But not in yours."

She turns and leaves the throne room, slamming the doors behind her.

CHAPTER 25

AFTER WE'VE GONE our separate ways to calm down, I go in search of Hunter. We need to talk. But he isn't in his room, nor is he in the great hall.

Eventually, I find Hunter outside in the training yard, hitting things. The storm has quieted, leaving only the soft shiver of falling flakes over the crates, targets, and straw dummies. It's surreal to see him here, in the space Tristan and I have used for practice over the last couple of months.

Someone has strung three frozen sandbags from a wooden beam in the middle of the yard. They sway heavily on their ropes like hanged men. Hunter attacks them with a practice sword, as if they're Fox Soldiers like the ones we met on the battlefield in Ellyll. A knot forms in my stomach.

I don't announce myself. I stand beneath the long shadow of a ruined arch and watch him work. Snow gathers in his tousled blond hair and melts at his temples, then trickles down the hard plane of his cheek. His breath steams in ragged bursts as he twists and strikes with the energy of a man who's been betrayed. It breaks my heart to see him this way.

After his brush with death, he's not ready for this much physical activity. His skin still has the pallor of the drowned and he coughs between swings. He strikes, pivots, strikes again. The sand-bags jolt on their ropes, creaking, and spitting a dusting of snow with each impact.

Hunter's grip fails and his sword clatters to the ground, but that doesn't slow him down. He attacks the sandbags with his fists instead. The first blow lands with a dull thump. He grunts and hits it again, and again. As I watch, his knuckles grow red and raw with the impacts.

I know I should intervene before he hurts himself, but truth be told, I'm afraid. Afraid of hurting him even more by saying the wrong thing. Afraid of chasing him away. But everything is already such a disaster that I doubt it's possible to make things worse.

One of the ropes frays with each hit, threads popping. Hunter kicks it once, hard, and the rope tears free. The bag crashes to the ground and splits, spilling frozen grit across the snow. Hunter stands over it, chest heaving.

"You should rest," I say quietly.

Hunter startles and turns. When he sees me, his face grows tense. "Go inside, Sienna. You'll freeze standing around out here."

I shrug and step out of the shadows to approach him. "I've been cold for months. But a few days ago, you nearly drowned." The second sandbag turns in a lazy arc, brushing my shoulder as I pass.

"What do you want me to do?" he snaps, the words misting white in the air. "Lie down? Take a nap? Brave men boarded that ship with me. Believed in me. And I—" He breaks off, eyes dark with grief. "I brought them here to die."

"This won't bring them back," I answer softly. "Hurting yourself won't help."

He looks past me toward the direction of the roiling gray sea. "I was a fool to follow you."

"I never asked you to."

"And you never need to. That's the whole point, Sienna."

We stand in the hush of falling snow, the flakes large and fluffy as feathers. I ache for him, for all the ways I've hurt him. But we will never get out of this pit of darkness if we can't speak plainly to one another.

"Talk to me. Please."

Hunter kicks his fallen sword. It skitters a few feet before landing in a snowbank.

"About what?" His laugh is low and humorless. "How your grandmother is our sworn enemy? How the Wolf and I nearly cut each other to shreds? How I'm here on a fool's errand and every decision I make seems to end in death?"

"Yes. All of it."

He drags a weary hand through his damp hair. His shoulders are shaking with exhaustion. When he finally speaks, the anger has cooled to a hard, steady heat.

"I don't know who I'm more furious with. Your new queen. The Wolf. Your father. Myself." He lifts his eyes to mine. "Or you."

The pit in my stomach deepens. "I know. And I deserve it."

"I should hate you."

I nod. "You should. But I need you to hear why I'm doing this. Why I've sided with Annwyn."

He looks away and shakes his head in disappointment and disgust.

"Nothing about Annwyn is what we thought." I step closer, my voice urgent. "This place is not a realm to be conquered. There are fae in the cellars and old magic lingering in every ruin."

He raises his eyes to study me. To him, the fae are still folklore and fairy tales. But I need him to see how wrong we've been. About everything.

"Yes, the people here are ..." I search for a polite word. "Thorny."

Hunter raises a skeptical eyebrow at me.

"But they love this place so fiercely, they'd rather die protecting it than flee to the south. Gwyllion used to be so much more than this crumbling castle. I've seen the paintings. I've read old books about what Annwyn was like two thousand years ago, when the fae and humans lived in peace. It was *real*, Hunter."

I search his eyes, trying to make him believe. His eyebrows are drawn together, like he's not sure what to make of me. But I know this man. I can see the cracks of doubt in his warm brown gaze and in the curve of his mouth.

I reach out and touch his arm. "That's why the people here still fight, even though they're worn down to rags. They dream of making Annwyn safe again. Of stopping the endless war." I look past him to the Spires. "And my father will destroy what's left of them."

Hunter chews the inside of his lip for a long moment while he considers my words. "Your father is up to something. He wants to take Annwyn, and it's more than just a family legacy." He heaves a weary sigh. "It doesn't help that he hated your grandmother, and now she sits on a throne."

"No, it doesn't." I swallow hard. My father is like a fox in a henhouse. Nothing is safe until he's taken his fill. "But, Hunter, Grandmother *is* dead. I promise you that. The queen may wear her face, but she's not the same woman."

He draws a breath and coughs, then leans his arms on one of the sandbags. Snow has gathered along his shoulders and in his hair. "I don't trust her."

"And you shouldn't." My voice is firm. "She's no saint. The Dead Queen has ulterior motives, I'm sure of it." I swallow. "But so do I."

"Such as?" He turns his head to watch my face.

"We may need her now. But, someday, I will destroy the Dead Queen."

He studies my face for a long moment before nodding. He knows me as well as I know him. I don't mince words, and I am not one to threaten lightly. When I promise to do something, I do it.

"So," he straightens. "You are a basilisk waiting for an opportunity to strike?"

"I can't let her keep Grandmother's face for all eternity."

"No," he agrees. "She deserved better."

"She did." I clear the knot in my throat. "We're allies now because we have to be. Annwyn's living need the dead to protect them. At least until we can survive without her. When it's over, when the border is safe and my father is dead, I will end her." I straighten, meeting his eyes. "Then we'll give Annwyn back to the living."

His gaze flickers. "Does the Wolf know you plan to kill his queen?"

"Tristan knows what I am." My heart stills. "He knows I'm loyal to no one but myself."

Something sad crosses Hunter's face. "You sell yourself short."

I scoff. "Says the man who I left on a battlefield to die."

He shakes his head slowly. "I think you pretend to be selfish to hide the hurt in your heart."

My eyes flicker away from him, too embarrassed to admit that he hit close to the bone.

He isn't deterred. "You say you can't trust anyone in this world the way you can trust yourself. But here's the thing, Sienna." He leans toward me, meeting my eyes. "You *can* trust me."

"I want to." The words come out in a whisper. I straighten my spine and face him. "And I need you to trust me now, despite everything that's passed between us. We *must* save Annwyn from my father, Hunter. There's more at stake than any of us truly understand. I can feel it in my bones." I press my hand to my chest, where my heart beats with certainty. "I know my father is up to something. I'm sure the Dead Queen is too. And we can't let either of them win."

"Why?" His question is so sharp, it takes me aback. "Why bother saving this place?" He gestures toward the crumbling castle. "What's here that's truly worth saving? Truly worth risking everything for?"

It's a valid question.

The world around us is dusted in shades of white, and the

silence is all-consuming. Large, fluffy snowflakes stick to Hunter's hair, his shoulders, his eyelashes. It's ... beautiful. The thought surprises me. For the last couple of months, I've hated this place with its frozen landscape and icy people, but somehow, I find my heart has changed.

Hunter watches me as I raise my face to the gray sky. Snowflakes kiss my cheeks as they float all around me, like the gentle caress of a moth's wing. It's peaceful.

"All I've seen of Annwyn is snow," I admit. "But as cold and inhospitable as it is, it's also beautiful."

Hunter scoffs. "It's not beautiful." He turns back to hit another sandbag. "This place is miserable." He punches. "Cold." He hits it again. "Dead." He kicks the sandbag and it swings wildly between us.

"That's what I used to think too," I say, almost to myself.

Hunter turns to squint at me. His breath puffs out in bursts of fog. "Used to?"

I pause. Somehow, I'm no longer at odds with this place. I no longer hate it. Something in my chest tugs, insisting I be honest with myself. Amid this frozen, stormy landscape, I've found that I *care* about Annwyn. I admire its fierce loyalty, its wild lore, and the magic that winds through every folktale, every cellar, and every ruined castle corridor. I care about this land. And I care about its stubborn, headstrong people too. How they managed to worm their way into my Fox heart, I will never understand. But here we are.

I let out a shaky breath, and nod.

"And now, you wish to fight for them." He studies me.

I swallow hard. "I do."

"I just ..." He pinches the bridge of his nose, then sighs up at the gray sky. "I can't believe it's her. After all these years of searching. Your grandmother is ..." He stops, as if he can't bear to say the words.

"The Dead Queen, yes."

He shakes his head at the snow-covered castle.

"It was difficult for me to come to terms with that, too."

His shoulders sag as he studies me again. "How did you?"

"I didn't. Not really." I shake my head, trying to keep the bubbling anger from rising up in me again. "I just can't dwell on it. She isn't the same person. She isn't alive."

Hunter stares at me for a long time. Snow falls silently around us, muffling all sound but for the two of us.

"It must have been terrible for you," he says finally. "Finding her after all this time. Like that."

I swallow and blink away the tears. Beneath my red cloak, I wrap my arms around myself. "It was," I whisper.

Hunter heaves a sigh and tilts his head up toward the sky. Snowflakes fall across his flushed face, reminding me of how I used to touch his skin, kiss his lips. My fingers twitch, wanting to reach for him again, but that time has long since passed. It will never be again. Like how I've had to accept that Grandmother is gone, and the Dead Queen sits in her place, I will have to find a way to accept this loss as well.

Hunter is not gone. Not completely. But in many ways, he will never be the same. Not toward me, in any case. And I have no one to blame but myself.

Snow catches on his eyelashes as he turns back to me. "I'm still angry. But ..." He exhales heavily. "I didn't come here to drag you home. I came here to keep you breathing."

"Then keep me breathing *here*." I try to keep the pleading tone out of my voice. "Fight for Annwyn with me. Help me stop my father."

He looks down at his raw knuckles. "If I say 'yes,' I'm not saying it to her. I will not kneel to the thing that wears your grandmother's face."

"I understand completely."

Hunter's eyes are warm despite everything. He steps closer, close enough that I can see the green flecks in his brown irises, the tiny white crescent of an old scar beneath his left eye. Snow gathers on the shoulder of my red cloak; he reaches up without thinking and brushes it away. The small, familiar touch unspools something terrible and tender inside me.

Hunter takes a deep breath, then turns from me to face the ruined castle. The snow continues to fall around us, coating everything in a blanket of white. After a few muttered swears, he turns back to me.

He sniffs. "Alright."

I raise an eyebrow. "Alright?"

He rubs the snow out of his tousled blond hair, as if in frustration. He stares at me, considering his words. "My entire life, I've trusted you above all others. You're reckless. Stubborn. And, at times, infuriating. But I've never known you to be wrong. Especially when it mattered."

My throat tightens, and I'm too afraid to say anything. Afraid I may break whatever spell this gentle snowfall has cast over us.

"I don't like it." He hits the sandbag again, for good measure. "Actually, I hate it." He turns back to me. "But I trust you."

I let out a shaky breath. "Even after ..." I can't finish the sentence. After we crossed Llwyn together, and I abandoned him on the fire-engulfed battlefield at Ellyll. After we made love in an enchanted forest, and I broke his heart.

He sniffs, and nods. "What's happening here, between Annwyn and Llwyn, it's bigger than us. I have to keep everything in perspective."

"Of course." He hasn't forgiven me. But he's a bigger man than most to put that aside for the greater good.

"I don't know how we can stop your father." He squints up at the crumbling stone and shuttered windows of Gwyllion. "This castle is in shambles, and the people here are no match for the Fox Army."

"But we have to try."

"Unfortunately, I think you're right." He nods slowly. "I'm going to do this, Sienna, but I want you to understand one thing."

Snow falls harder all around us, and the wind picks up again. I look up to search his face and find his eyes boring into mine.

"I'm going to do my best to help save Annwyn. For the oath I made to serve the Fox Heir for the rest of my life." His mouth twists. "For you. Even if 'for you' hurts."

I squeeze my eyes shut for a heartbeat. The ache of relief is almost enough to make me cry. I let out a shaky exhale. "Then I have a condition."

He arches a brow, amused despite himself. "Of course you do. Aren't *you* the one recruiting *me*?"

"Yes." A slight smile catches me by surprise. "You need to go take a nap."

Hunter's laugh is laced with exhaustion, but I've never heard a warmer sound.

I tilt my head toward the doors. "I don't want to steal you back from Death a second time."

He studies me for a long moment, then nods once. "Only if you promise me something in return."

"What?"

"Don't let this place turn you into a monster."

"What makes you so sure I'm not one already?"

In reply, he reaches out and brushes a snowflake off my cheek. My heart stills. The touch lasts just for the slightest moment, but it's enough. It has to be.

I think of the Dead Queen's black veil, of the silver moth that rests against dead flesh. I think of all the horrible decisions I've made in my life and all the heartache I've left in my wake. I'm not convinced I'm *not* a monster already. But if a brave, truehearted Hunter believes in me, maybe I can believe I'm not completely lost yet.

"I promise."

We stand there too long for friends and not long enough for lovers, while the snow blankets the world and the wind whistles through the Spires.

I've ruined everything with Hunter. And I truly don't deserve him. Yet here he is, standing before me in the gently swirling snow, the wilds of Annwyn behind him. Wherever this journey takes us, whatever the spring thaw brings, I know one thing will always be true.

Hunter is the greatest man I have ever known. And I am the luckiest woman in the world to know him.

CHAPTER 26

THAT NIGHT, I toss and turn, my mind racing. Everything is in ruins. Hunter and Tristan are at each other's throats. My father wants to kill me. And the Fox Army is waiting for the first sign of spring to cross the Spires and take Gwyllion, the last remaining fortress in Annwyn. If the Dead Queen loses this castle, they lose the entire war. Not to mention their home.

And somehow, I'm supposed to fix everything?

I rub my palms over my eyes. There's no use in staying in bed with my mind a jumbled mess. I swing my legs to the ground and throw my red cloak over my shoulders.

I'm already at the door to the courtyard temple of the Tree God before I realize where my feet have carried me. Light streams through the crack in the door, illuminating the dark, dusty hallway. I push the door open and step inside.

The first thing I notice is the sacred tree bathed in muted moonlight. Reflections bounce off the mirrors that hang from its branches. They twist and sway, flashing like fireflies. I glance up at the snow trapped against the skylight. It's a filter, keeping the Moon Goddess from fully reuniting with her beloved Tree God.

The second thing I notice is that I'm not alone.

Nalina kneels on the moss in front of one of the large carved stones. The etching on the boulder depicts a crescent moon with swirls emanating from it.

She must have heard my approach because she speaks first. "I've always wondered what this symbol meant."

I step out of the shadows near the doorway. As I near, I sense her weariness. I've never seen Nalina like this, on her knees, her shoulders slumped. It's unnerving to see someone so strong appear so broken.

For one horrible moment, I realize I might have interrupted her praying. "I didn't mean to disturb you."

She shakes her head slowly. "Everyone is welcome in the temple." She draws her eyes away from the etching and squints toward me. "Even Foxes." There's a slight humorless smile in the corner of her mouth. She stands with a sigh and levels her gaze at me. "Just don't get used to it."

I nod, feeling like my presence here is sacrilege somehow.

Nalina turns toward the tree, and we both stand in silence. The filtered moonlight dances between the slowly spinning mirrors. There's an ache in my chest, like a longing for something I never knew to begin with. I wish I could see this place in its former glory. I wish I understood why it still feels so holy, even centuries after it was abandoned. Did the old gods feel pain when they lost the faith of their people?

"What are you doing here?" Nalina finally asks.

I shrug beneath my red cloak. "I'm not sure. I couldn't sleep. My feet brought me here." I pause, taking in the moonlit court-yard. "Maybe I was led here by old fae magic."

I say it as a joke, to lighten the mood, but Nalina eyes me skeptically. "You know, the fae used to believe magic was sacred. That it made its hosts divine."

I laugh lightly. "Funny to think of Tristan as holy."

I expect this to bring a smile to her face. Tristan is, after all, her friend. But it doesn't. A crease forms between her eyes and she frowns.

"He's not what you think he is."

I turn toward her. "How so?"

Nalina narrows her eyes at the tree as she thinks. "He used to be joyful. Sunshine incarnate."

A laugh erupts from me. I can't help it.

Nalina glowers.

"Sorry." It takes a moment for me to regain control of my face. "That's just hard to believe."

"There are many things about us and our history that you don't know."

I nod slowly. "I'm sure that's true. But I've spent so much time with Tristan these past few months. It's hard to imagine him as 'joyful'."

She thinks for several moments before responding. "No one in Annwyn has escaped suffering at the hands of your family, Fox Heir. I thought you'd have figured that out by now."

"Could you tell me?" I ask, deciding to be bold. "How have you suffered? I would like to understand."

She chews her lip and crosses her arms over her chest. "My twin sister was taken from me."

I blink over at her. "I didn't know you had a family."

"I don't anymore. That's the point."

"I'm sorry."

"She sacrificed herself for the safety of the kingdom." Nalina's voice is thick with pain. "She was the best person I ever knew. The strongest. The bravest. I should have known that she'd do anything to protect me."

I nod. "I suppose that's the thing about love. It makes us braver than we could ever imagine."

Nalina turns to face me. "Tristan lost someone too."

"I know. He told me. First his sister, then his parents."

Nalina shakes her head, like I somehow got it all wrong. "You think you can waltz into Annwyn and understand everything about us."

Her sudden sharpness stings. And here I thought we were

making progress. "I know I don't understand everything. I'm trying."

"Hm." She studies me, uncertain.

"Nalina, can I ask you something?"

She sighs. "That depends on what it is."

"Why do you hate me so much?"

She raises an eyebrow in an isn't-it-obvious expression.

I shake my head. "I know you hate my father. My ancestors. My entire kingdom. And I understand why. You lost the person you loved most in the world."

Nalina's expression doesn't change.

I continue, "But you also hate *me*, specifically. I can see it in your eyes."

Nalina's face remains stony for several beats. She turns to face the sacred tree again, as if she can't stand the sight of me. "It's the way he looks at you."

"Who?"

"Don't play coy with me."

I'm almost afraid to say his name. "Tristan?"

Her mouth draws into a thin line. "He's betrayed his own people. With a Fox, no less."

"He hasn't betrayed you. He hasn't betrayed anyone. He's loyal to Annwyn."

"And what would you know of loyalty?" Her words are cutting, bone deep. "You're the one making promises to usurp the Fox Throne. The one who betrayed your Golden Boy. More than once, I hear."

I steel my heart. "It's more complicated than that."

"So you said in the throne room." She scoffs. "But how? Either you're loyal to your country—to your people—or you're not. Which is it?"

I throw my hands up in frustration. "Would you rather I sit back and watch while my father destroys what little is left of Annwyn?" I ask, my anger bubbling to the surface. "I'm trying to save your kingdom."

"Save us?" Her eyes bulge. "You're the reason we're all in this damn mess. You and your power-hungry ancestors."

"I am not my family!"

"And what would you know of family? Of the sacrifices someone makes for the people they love?" In her anger, her face grows red. Her long scar pales against the flush.

"I've made sacrifices too, Nalina."

"Have you?" Nalina turns her body toward me, her voice low. "Have you walked your sister into the jaws of death? Did you watch her bleed so your people could be safe for just a little while longer? Until someone else had to make the same sacrifice all over again?"

I blink at her. "What are you talking about?"

"I know that you know about him."

"Who?"

"The fae!"

My heart pounds in my chest as fear claws at my throat. Deep in my sternum, my power flares in warning, as if it's afraid too.

Nalina's hand clenches the hilt of her sword. "I followed you. Watched you go down into the dungeon, but you made it back out alive."

"You know about him." My voice sounds hollow to my ears.

She laughs humorlessly. "We all know about him." She spits in disgust. "So many women have died because of him. *That* is what true loyalty and sacrifice look like."

My ears hum as I try to put all the pieces together. "But why not kill him?"

She kicks at the gravel beneath our feet, scattering tiny chips of quartz. "Haven't you wondered how the castle hasn't toppled over yet? Or how the worst storms hover along the horizon?"

"Yes, but Tristan said it was ancient fae magic."

"It *is* ancient fae magic." Her voice is level. "Fae are territorial. After your father pushed us back to the brink of extinction, we had no choice but to trespass on this territory. This is his nest."

I blink several times, trying to understand what she's telling me.

Her expression grows tight. "He moved in after the castle was abandoned by humans. He wasn't exactly keen to give it back."

The fae in the dungeon, the disgusting creature who tortures blond women, is responsible for the ancient magic holding Gwyllion together.

"How can that be?" I ask. "The castle was abandoned centuries ago. If that's true, the fae must be—"

"He's older than any of us could fathom."

I shake my head. "That's not possible."

She purses her lips. "Not for humans."

In front of us, the mirrors sway in the draft, shining light into far corners of the courtyard.

My mind is whirling. "How long do fae live?"

"That depends," she shrugs. "How powerful are they? A simple cellar fae might live a century. Two at most. But something like him? Or the fae kings and queens of old? Thousands of years."

"And somehow, we've managed to kill them all off."

She actually laughs. Her shoulders shake and her eyes grow bright. "You think they're all dead?"

I sputter. "Well, obviously there are *some* still hanging around. The dungeon fae for one."

She gives me a pitiful look. "They're only sleeping, Fox."

My power begins to hum in my sternum, like it's listening.

Nalina studies me, her head tilted like I'm a curious creature. "Why do you think so many people still visit their old temples?" She gestures to the sacred tree and the carved stones that represent ancient fae families. "Or feed the fae that remain?"

"I don't know."

She leans toward me, her voice a rough whisper. "Because we're afraid."

I blink at her.

"The fae of Gwyllion are only a drop in the bucket. And if

one ancient fae can keep the storms from tearing down this castle, what do you think the royals can do?"

"But they're dead. They must be."

She raises an eyebrow. "Why do you think your father wants to take our lands so, very much?" She lets out another hollow laugh. "You've been here long enough to see we aren't rich in resources." She holds out her arms, gesturing to the decrepit castle that surrounds us. "We don't have anything he wants. But that's because he doesn't want *us*." She gives me a meaningful look.

"He wants them?" I ask, my voice sounding thin. "The fae?"

She nods.

All this time, I just thought my father wanted to live up to the expectations of his ancestors. And then, once I found out about Grandmother, I thought he wanted revenge. Revenge against the Dead Queen. Revenge against me.

But it's more than that. Of course, it is. How did I not see it all along? Yes, my father is vengeful. He is power-hungry and feels like he has something to prove. He wants to be the mightiest Fox King that ever lived. The Fox who finally ends the Dead Queen of Annwyn. But my father always has an ulterior motive. He has plans within plans. And humiliating the women who defied him is only the beginning.

"But why?" My voice sounds afraid. And I suppose I am. My father always had that effect on me.

"You tell me. What does any greedy despot want?" She stares at me for a long time, waiting for an answer, but I'm too afraid to give it.

"More power," she answers. "And if he releases the ancient fae from their slumber ..." Nalina shakes her head slowly. "Let's just say, those fae kings and queens will be grateful to him." She gives me a long, meaning-filled stare. "And very, very angry at the rest of us."

CHAPTER 27

The high fae have unusual appetites, each relishing in the indulgence they favor. They will do almost anything to satiate their particular hungers, whether it be for revelry, flesh, or blood.

I'M LOUNGING on a chair in front of the windows in my room after yet another grueling training session with Tristan. It's like he's trying to torture me or something.

The fire in the hearth crackles softly, casting faint, dancing shadows across the stone walls of my chamber. Outside, the wind howls, scraping against the castle like a beast at the gates.

While it is well known that the fae loathe lies, they are also masterful tricksters. Be wary of making any deal with the fae, for you are most certainly going to get more than you bargained for. This author advises against making any such ...

Bang! Bang! Bang!

I nearly drop the book in my hands. It sounds like someone is trying to knock my door down. A growl works its way out of my chest.

"No, thank you!" I yell toward the door before bringing the book back up in front of my nose.

"I need you to come with me!" Nalina's unmistakable voice answers.

"Don't care!"

The banging continues.

"Go away!" I yell.

"No."

I put the open book over my face and scream into the pages.

My door bursts open and the Wolf from hell walks in, her boots stomping against the floor with the gravitas of a woman on a mission. She strides toward me without a word, her expression grim as she reaches down and rips the book out of my hands.

"Let's go."

"Maybe you could try asking nicely." I say through a grimace.

She grabs my arm in an iron grip. "Or I could just drag you."

"I can walk myself." I yank away from her with a sharp twist. "You know, manners would do you a world of good."

She steps back, her lips pressed together in a thin line. "We don't worry so much about niceties in Annwyn, Fox. On account of the short lifespans."

I roll my eyes but don't argue. She doesn't expect me to, and frankly, I'm too tired to waste breath on it.

"Come with me." She doesn't wait for my reply as she turns on her heel and walks out of the room. I pull my boots on hastily, then grab my red cloak before I step into the hall.

Nalina leads me through the castle. We head toward the castle's grand entrance, where the cold air presses in from outside. As we step through the massive doors, I feel the sharp bite of winter. The snow falls fast, like a thousand needles. The world beyond the castle walls seems to vanish in a blizzard.

"Where are we going?" I shout over the howling wind.

"The village!" she calls back, her voice barely audible over the shriek of the storm.

I've never been to the village. I always thought it was best to keep my distance since most of the locals hate me.

I jog to keep up with Nalina's long strides as she leads me beyond the castle's stone wall. She doesn't seem bothered by the storm, while I'm struggling to shield my eyes. The wind keeps trying to blow the hood of my cloak back, but I hold it tight to protect my face from the stinging snow.

By the time we reach the village, I can't feel my fingers or my toes. The small thatched houses are barely visible through the swirling white. Their windows glow faintly from lit fires within. I wonder how anyone would rather survive these storms in thatched-roof houses instead of the fortress just beyond the wall. Then I remember who lives in the castle: the dungeon fae and the Dead Queen. And me, the Fox Heir.

That's why they keep away. And I can't say that I blame them.

Nalina walks up to one of the houses and pushes the door open. She turns back to me, her face hard as stone.

"Stop dawdling."

I'm hardly dawdling. My legs burn with the effort to keep up with her and my face stings from the biting wind. I say nothing, just step inside and shake off the snow that's built up on my shoulders. Nalina shuts the door firmly behind her and I take a look around. The home is small, no more than three rooms. A crackling fire blazes in the central space.

Before I can register who else is here, a young woman runs up to me and throws her arms around my shoulders.

"Thank the old gods, Sienna. I'm so glad you're here." I'd never realized just how thin Elisandra was. Now that her arms are wrapped around me, I see she's as delicate as a bird.

"Elisandra, what's going on?"

She pulls away, shooting Nalina a wary glance. "I asked her to bring you. We need your help." She steps aside to reveal the rest of the room.

A middle-aged man leans heavily on a cane in front of the hearth. At his feet, on a bed of quilts, there's a boy. His face is deathly pale, and he appears to be asleep. With a start, I recognize him. He's Tabitha's grandson.

The old woman walks in from the next room, carrying a wet cloth. When she notices me, she freezes mid-step.

"Get out," she growls. Her withered face contorts with rage. She points to the door. "I said, 'Get out!'"

I glance at Nalina, unsure what to do. But the infuriating mountain of a woman just stands there, calm as can be. No doubt she's been waiting for an opportunity to toss me out into a blizzard.

Elisandra shakes her head. "No." She grabs my elbow possessively.

Tabitha's eyes narrow. "I will *not* have that Fox in my home, Elisandra. You should know better than that."

"I do." Elisandra nods. "But we have to at least try."

My eyes dart to the boy lying on the quilts. Even from a distance, I can sense his fever. I can feel Death calling him. With sudden clarity, I realize what this is about.

"Let me help him." I shrug off my red cloak, which has grown damp and heavy from melted snow. Elisandra takes it before hanging it on a hook near the door. "Nalina was right to bring me." I shoot her a glance, but her face reveals nothing. These damn Wolves and their stoic expressions.

I take a step toward the boy.

"Do not touch my grandson!"

I stop.

The man near the fire eyes me with a look of resignation. "Tabitha, it may be the only way."

She glares at him. "Jona will heal."

"He will not." I say it with a certainty that I know deep in my bones. My power already hums inside my sternum. It knows too. I turn to the man. "What happened to him?"

He gives Tabitha a warning look as she takes a breath to protest. "He fell from the roof while he was fixing a hole in the thatching. He hasn't woken."

"When did this happen?"

"Yesterday."

My eyes grow wide with disbelief. "Yesterday?" I look to Nalina. "Why didn't you summon me sooner?"

She speaks through gritted teeth. "In case you haven't noticed, Fox. You're our last resort."

I try not to take offense.

Tabitha shoots the man a traitorous glare and kneels down next to her grandson. She puts one gnarled hand on the boy's forehead. His skin is damp with sweat and his cheeks are dangerously pale.

Next to me, Elisandra wrings her hands. Her desperation is obvious. In this land of cold people, she's the only person who has shown me kindness. I will do anything she asks, I realize. Even if I need to throw Tabitha out into the blizzard myself.

I hold up my hands toward the old woman, pleading. "Tabitha. I know you don't like me, but I promise I can help."

"I don't want your filthy Fox paws on my kin."

The man speaks up, his voice stronger this time. "And would you rather he die?"

Tabitha's body stills, her hand on the boy's cheek.

The man limps toward her, his cane tapping the ground heavily with each step. "Because that's what's coming for him. Death. Unless you let the Fox Heir try. You have to make a choice here, Tabitha. Death, or your own damn pride." He rubs a weary hand over his eyes. "We've already lost so much."

He doesn't need to remind us what this town has lost. There are no healthy young men or women in Gwyllion anymore. Only the very young, the injured, and the very old. It's a terrible price to pay in the hopes that the survivors can someday live a life without war. Without the Fox King taking more, and more, and more.

For several moments, no one speaks. We watch the old woman think as the room falls still. Tabitha's breath catches, and I see pain flash across her face like a dagger. I know that feeling; I've felt it too many times. The agony of loss, the fear of helplessness.

"Fine," she whispers. "Save him. If you can." She gets to her feet again, her knees cracking. "But I can't watch."

Elisandra gasps in relief. "Thank the old gods ..." she whispers under her breath.

The man nods. "I'll stay with him."

Tabitha walks into the next room. She slams the door closed.

I rush to the boy's side and kneel on the ground. One touch of his forehead and I know his fever is dangerously high. I touch his skull tenderly, looking for injury.

"Did he hit his head?" I ask the man.

He lets out a shaky breath. "We're afraid it's his spine."

And they waited a full day to ask for help? I swear under my breath. The injury is far worse than I feared. I hold my hands over his chest, summoning my power. It slinks out through my veins, and I can feel the wound there. His spine is severed in two places. It's a miracle he lived this long.

I look toward Elisandra where she waits a few paces away. "I don't know if I can save him."

Her chin quivers as she says, "Please try."

Next to her, Nalina narrows her eyes at me, as if daring me to refuse. Not that I would. If she knew anything about me, she'd know that I'd never leave a person to suffer. I'm not as proud as some.

The man kneels beside me with a wince and sets his cane aside. "We've heard of your family's great healing feats; surely you can help one small boy?"

My heart clenches in my chest. "My power has been a little unreliable lately."

The man puts a shaking hand on my forearm. "Please." His eyes dart to the closed door where Tabitha just retreated. "She has no one else."

I know that feeling all too well. I take a shuddering breath and nod.

"Thank you." He says, with tears in his eyes.

I turn my attention to the boy on the ground. His breathing is too shallow; his heartbeat is weak. I can feel the heat of the injury on his back. It blooms from the breaking points along his spine in both directions. Nerves are already dead, limbs already disconnected and limp. For some reason, it terrifies me.

When I worked as a healer in the borderlands, I mended injuries like this often. I repaired severed limbs and called back souls hovering on the precipice of oblivion. But that was before burnout. Still, I was able to save Hunter. I just need to remember how I did it.

My power swirls inside me, anxious and ready. I close my eyes and try to focus on it. I draw the golden light out, little by little, coaxing it forth. Sweat begins to prickle on my skin. The power resists me, like pulling a worm from the dirt. I lose my grip, and it snaps back into hiding.

Frustrated, I sit on my heels to think. I can feel Nalina's eyes on me, judging. No doubt wondering if she's made a terrible mistake in bringing me here.

I steady myself as I feel the weight of the room press in around me. Nalina, Elisandra, and the man are watching, waiting. The man's face isn't filled with fear anymore. It's filled with hope.

I lean closer to the boy and reach a trembling hand to his forehead. His skin is fire. Sweat clings to his pale skin, making his hair damp and matted. I press my palm against his chest, feeling the weak, shallow rhythm of his heartbeat. My own chest tightens in response. He should have died already, given the way his body is shutting down. But still, he clings to life, like a flickering candle in a storm.

"Please," the man beside me whispers again, his voice pleading.

I nod slowly, taking a deep breath. My power stirs inside me. I close my eyes and feel it hum in my chest, trying to break free. It pulls at me, struggling to be released. No more control, I remind myself. I need to let go.

This time, when I reach out toward the boy on the quilts, something feels different. My hands don't shake. I close my eyes, and instead of forcing my power, I feel it. It swirls and flows through my body, a warm, golden light. I don't try to tell it what to do; I just rely on instinct.

Energy swirls just beneath my skin. Sweat beads along my brow, and the temperature in the room shifts as a strange heat radiates from me. Serenity washes over me before the dam breaks.

My power surges from my core, rushing through my body and down my arms, seeping from my palms. It reaches into the boy, mending broken nerves, and fusing the shattered bones together. His body jerks beneath my hands, but I hold firm, not daring to stop.

I can feel his soul hovering near the edge of life and death. Somewhere deep in the recesses of my mind, I call to it.

Come back. It's not your time.

There's a long moment of uncertainty. Then, with a jolt, the boy's life force rushes back into his body. Finally, his breathing steadies. The fever that burned through him fades.

His eyes snap open. For a split second, his pupils are dilated with panic, but then they focus on me. The fear in them morphs into confusion. Elisandra rushes to the boy's side, and the man lets out a choked sob of relief. His hands tremble as he reaches for the boy, stroking his hair with shaking fingers.

"It's okay now. You're going to be all right," he whispers through tears.

The boy blinks up at me. "Why is the Fox Heir here?"

The man lets out a relieved laugh. "It's nothing to worry about. You're safe now. She helped you." He pats the boy's hand with a tenderness that makes my chest ache.

Elisandra looks at me with something like pride. "She helped us."

The praise makes my stomach clench. I rise to my feet and step back. A wave of lightheadedness washes over me, but it passes in an instant. The power that once hummed so fiercely within me now curls back into my core like a drowsy cat.

Behind me, a door creaks open. Tabitha steps through the

doorway. Her wild white hair is tangled around her face, and her eyes are wide with shock.

"Jona?" she breathes, her voice a mixture of disbelief and fear.

The boy turns toward her. His face lights up with recognition. "Grandma."

The old woman stumbles forward, dropping to her knees beside him. She gathers him in her arms, pressing him against her chest. Tears flood down her weathered face as she holds him tight, rocking back and forth.

I should be overjoyed. I've done a remarkable thing, saving this boy's life. But as I look around the room at the joy and love these people share, I feel out of place. After Grandmother disappeared, my family never loved me the way these people love each other. If I had fallen from a roof as a child, my father would have left me to die—and been glad for it.

I don't belong here. As I watch these people cry and clutch each other with a desperate love I will never understand, I see that I've already faded into the background. And that's fine by me.

I grab my damp cloak off the hook and throw it over my shoulders. Nalina doesn't make a move to follow me, but I can feel her eyes on the back of my neck as I slip out the door. The winter storm is cold and unrelenting as I walk back to the castle alone.

CHAPTER 28

WHEN I MEET Tristan at the castle entrance at dawn, I yawn and stretch my limbs, willing myself to wake up.

"Nice to see you're bored with me already."

I stifle my yawn. "No sleep."

"Yeah." He pushes himself up from where he's leaning against the cool stone wall. "Sleep and I haven't been well-acquainted lately either." His tone is light, but I sense a deeper meaning behind his words.

After I healed Jona, my power bloomed in my chest and stayed. It answers at the briefest call now, no longer timid or reluctant. It's back, and my mind can't stop thinking about the possibilities. What can I do with this power, now that it's returned? How strong can I become?

How will I use it to kill the Fox King?

"What unique torture do you have planned for me today?" I ask as I bend to touch my toes.

"We're practicing with power again."

I look up, lifting an eyebrow.

"You can do it."

I don't budge.

He crosses his arms over his broad chest. "Why does your face say you don't believe me?"

"After last time—"

"Forget last time, we're starting fresh."

I wonder if, by "forget," he means my accusation of jealousy ... or the look he gave me when he asked if I still love Hunter. The tension is too much to bear.

I huff in mock confusion. "And here I thought you were only interested in arrows, swords, and other pointy things."

A reluctant smile tugs at the corner of his mouth. "Yes, well, I do love pointy things."

"I know." I unsheathe my knife and give it a fancy little twirl for good measure.

Tristan watches the blade spin between my fingers. Something tells me the tightness in his jaw isn't just annoyance with my showmanship. His eyes study mine beyond the flashing blade. My skin prickles and I sheath my knife in one swift motion.

He clears his throat. "As you've reclaimed your power, we need to measure exactly how much of it you can control."

I narrow my eyes at him. "A test?"

He sighs, then waves for me to follow him. He leads me out into the early morning mist. Overnight rain has flattened the snow into icy patches. I focus on not slipping as we cross the field and head toward the wall of trees. The forest is wet and the branches hang low, burdened with melting ice. It's like the world is confused. It's not sure if it should be melting or freezing this time of year.

For the first time in my life, I wish the world would commit to winter a little longer, because spring means my father's soldiers can pass through the Spires. It means death is marching toward us and I am nowhere near ready.

The Wolf brings me to what might be a woodland meadow, if it weren't frozen solid.

"Why aren't we just practicing in the training yard?" I ask.

"I thought we needed a little distance from the castle. There's been a lot of distractions lately."

Hunter, he means. Not that Hunter and I are on the best terms.

Tristan stands in the center of the frozen meadow. "Get into position."

I ready myself, stepping into a fighting posture that's become natural to me now.

The Wolf strikes. Smoke bursts from his palms like a flying arrow. I deflect it with a burst of light, pushing it aside without even thinking.

"Good." Tristan nods, but his face is still grim.

A small twinge of pride rises in me, but he comes at me again before I can think much of it. Darkness engulfs the meadow like a wave on a stormy sea. It crashes down from above so fast, I don't see it coming.

"Gah!" Shadow engulfs me before I have a chance to ignite any light at all.

"Less good." The Wolf's voice cuts through the darkness.

After he summons his darkness back into his palms, I shoot him an irritated glare. My movements are slow from lack of sleep, and my mind is unfocused. I take a deep breath and step into position again.

This time, I attack first. I shoot a bolt of light toward him, but he sidesteps easily. The bolt crashes into one of the many boulders scattered around, leaving a deep dent in the rock. I wave a cloud of rock dust away from my face.

Tristan nods, as if appreciating the newly improved boulder. "Impressive, but your speed is lacking." Tristan steps back into position.

"I'm trying." My jaw clenches.

He doesn't answer. Just nods once, curtly.

The frozen meadow is silent except for the occasional rustle of wind and our blasts of light and shadow. Above, the sky is pale, the sun swallowed by hazy winter clouds.

Pride surges inside me when I manifest a crackling ball of energy. But the energy evaporates into thin air when I realize it's singeing my shirtsleeves. I wave my arms and pat out the fire, but luckily it didn't burn my skin.

"You're not paying attention," Tristan says.

"I'm doing the best I can," I snap.

"Well, your best is sloppy. Distracted. Slow." With the wave of his hand, he paints the world in darkness again.

I trip backward over a root.

Tristan heaves a long sigh and recalls his power.

I stand up, brushing the snow off my backside.

Tristan's voice is terse. "Do you think we've spent all this time just playing games?"

Shadows shoot past me. I stumble backward, then struggle to get my bearings again before another attack. The shadow swirls, taunting me.

His voice cuts through the darkness. "That this isn't serious?" A gust of dark wind blows my hair and cloak out behind me, like the gale of a tempest. "That people aren't going to die if you can't pull yourself together?" The entire forest turns to night in the blink of an eye.

"Stop!" I throw a ball of light at him. It bounces off his shoulder and dissolves in the frozen snow with a pathetic sizzle. My breath is coming in wild, angry bursts that turn to mist in the cool air. "I get it! Okay? I'm a disappointment!"

Tristan sucks in a breath and turns his back to me for a beat. Snow crunches beneath his boots. "Red ..."

"I'm not like you!" The words tumble out of me, hot and angry. "But I'm trying."

He looks back at me, jaw tight, eyes unreadable. His dark hair falls over his face, damp with sweat and melting snow. "I don't want you to be like me."

"That's not how it looks from here."

Something in his expression cracks, just a little. "I'm hard on you because if you can't fight, Sienna, you die."

"I know that." My voice breaks.

He says nothing. Just watches me. The wind shifts, catching a strand of hair across my cheek.

"Maybe I'm not as strong as you think. Maybe I *can't* be the weapon you need me to be."

His eyes narrow. And then, before I can blink, he steps forward, grabs my wrist, and pulls me toward him until we are chest-to-chest. My breath catches. His eyes are fierce as he stares down at me.

"Don't ever say that again," he says, his voice low. "You don't get to give up on yourself. Not while I'm still here."

I stare up at him, pulse hammering. He's close enough that I can see the flecks of darkness in his gray irises. Suddenly, I'm very aware of his body so close to mine.

"I'm not giving up," I say. "I'm just tired of disappointing you."

His grip on my wrist softens, thumb brushing over my pulse. His voice is quieter now, almost apologetic. "You don't disappoint me. You scare me."

I blink, taken aback. "Why?"

"Because I care about you." He swallows. "More than I should. And every time you're near, I can't help but think about what it would cost me to lose you."

The air between us shifts, thin as frost. I don't know if I want to kiss him or shove him away. He's both infuriating and intoxicating. Gently, I pull my wrist from his grasp. My hands are shaking. I don't look at him when I speak.

"I know what's at stake. Nalina told me."

Tristan freezes. "What did you say?"

I look back toward him. "I know about the fae in the dungeon. And I know how much you need to defeat my father. You once told me he would destroy the world. That wasn't hyperbole, was it?"

Tristan's face has gone pale. "No."

A sudden, violent need to prove myself rises within me. Deep down, I know who I am. Who I've always been. I'm a Fox. I don't run and hide. I don't let other people fight my battles for me. I have as much at stake as Tristan does.

I blast a wave of light at him with renewed energy. He blocks it with a wall of shadow, but I strike again. And again. Darkness seems to seep from every pore of his skin as he counters my attacks. We fight with all our pent-up frustration and anger. With each new attack, he circles closer, like a predator ensnaring its prey.

I stop my onslaught when his face is mere inches from mine.

His voice is a rough whisper. "For the record, I never said you were a disappointment."

I push him backward with my hands, knocking him off balance. He regains his stance in an instant, much to my irritation.

"You didn't have to. It's written all over your face." I swing a fist at him, momentarily forgetting about light and shadows. He dodges my swing, but it just makes the fire inside me flare hotter.

I shoot crackling bolts of light at him. My breath is heavy and ragged, my chest an infuriating mix of anger and passion.

"Every."

Bolt.

"Single."

Sizzle.

"Day."

Flare.

Tristan blocks my attacks with a shield made of darkness, but he's slower to meet my power. I dig deep into my core and call forth a glaring flash of light that paints the world in shades of white. Tristan drops his wall of shadow to cover his eyes with his hands.

"Red, enough!" Tristan's voice is far away, lost in this uncontrollable storm of emotions that's making me spiral.

I'm gasping and exhausted, fueled by a fire I can't smother now. It's like I don't know where I am anymore. Like I'm back in

Caerwen Palace, trying to survive in a den of foxhounds. I am never good enough. Never wanted.

"I am *done* being a burden to everyone." I extinguish the blinding light and send another lightning bolt that he barely blocks. "I'm not an inconvenience!"

The Wolf dodges every attack I send at him, but with less grace than he did moments ago. It's as if I'm actually besting him at his own game now. As if my anger matches his skill.

"I am not weak!"

"I never thought you were." His voice is sincere, and it catches me off guard, breaking through the fog of anger.

He's right. In every situation we've ever been in, he always believed in me. In the foxhound kennels, in Korrigan Forest, in the wraith-filled battlefields—he always believed I was capable of more than I believed in myself.

Then he shoots an onslaught of shadows my way. Each attack catches me off guard, but I manage to block every single one. Too late, I realize he's been pushing me backward. My heel grazes a boulder as his shadows press into my chest. He leans toward me, his eyes fierce. At first, I think it's fury. It isn't until his face is inches away from mine that I realize what it truly is.

Desire.

"You are *not* a burden, Red." His breath is shaky, trembling.

Slowly, he releases the shadows between us, but he doesn't step away. I should take advantage of his lowered defenses and attack, but I don't. I let him lean even closer until my back is pressed up against the boulder.

"You are infuriating." His voice is rough. "You're thrilling. Fucking intoxicating." He says these words like a swear, biting and hot. "I can't get you out of my head. It feels like I'm starving." His eyes are on mine, tortured. He looks at me as if I'm the only one who can release him from his torment.

Tristan leans forward, the tip of his nose brushing lightly against the shell of my ear. "I've wanted you ever since I first saw you, dancing with Hunter at your engagement ball. Dressed head to toe in scarlet."

My chest rises and falls like I can't get enough air. Heat surges through my body, pooling low in my belly.

"I can't get enough of you," he whispers, his breath hot against my neck. "*That* is why I find it so hard to be in your presence."

He puts a hesitant hand up to my waist, and the briefest touch ignites me like an inferno. He stares deep into my eyes, his eyebrows pinched together as he studies me.

I can't hide the longing in my voice. "You want to devour me, Wolf?"

He leans forward and brushes his lips over my jawline. "Every. Last. Inch."

Goosebumps prickle all over my skin. "Then do it."

His mouth crashes onto mine. This is nothing like our kisses in the cave. There is no hesitation, no vulnerability. No secrets or holding back. This is fire and flood and famine all rolled into one. This is pure animalistic need.

Tristan pushes his hips against mine, his desire fully evident. I moan at the luscious pressure of his hard length against me. Without thought, my thighs spread open to feel more of him. But even that doesn't feel like enough. He smells of cedar and salt and fire. And, gods, I need more.

Tristan weaves his hand through my auburn hair, loosening the braid that's come undone. He presses his mouth into mine as his hands roam roughly over my hips, my waist, my breasts. My back presses into the boulder behind me, and I relish the pain. I want him to push harder, deeper into me. To devour me until I'm nothing but bone.

"Tristan," I gasp between kisses. My chest heaves, unable to get enough air.

He laughs low in his throat. "Do you want me to touch you, Red?"

I nod. "Yes." My voice is unfamiliar, laced with hunger and need.

Tristan moves his hand between us and unlaces the front of my leathers. Then, in one swift motion, he spins me around to face the boulder. I can feel his hard length up against my backside.

He moves his fingers beneath my pants, hovering there above my sex. He kisses my jawline as his thumb brushes lightly over my most sensitive parts. A muffled sound escapes me, something between a gasp and a moan.

I can feel his self-satisfied smirk as he pushes his fingers inside me. I crumble against the boulder, gasping at the sparks of molten desire that shoot through me. He holds me tighter against his body. I gasp as he caresses me, making my legs tremble.

His mouth moves close to my ear as I lean against him, breathless and weak. "I can feel how much you want me."

Tristan strums me faster and, suddenly, I'm melting. My power surges inside of me, delicious and thrilling, as sparks flash behind my eyes. I cry out as waves crash over me again and again.

He holds me up against the boulder to keep my legs from giving out. His low chuckle rumbles against my neck where he runs his lips over my skin. It makes me want him more.

He removes his hand from my leathers and turns me back around to face him. He presses his body squarely against mine, his hand caressing the skin of my hip. Every inch of him is hard and hot with need, and despite my tingling limbs, that spark of desire rushes back.

I kiss him with a desperate fever that I've never felt before. I'm aching and wanting all over again. And I know, deep in my soul, that nothing will satiate me except this Wolf. It's like my body waited for him before coming fully alive. Despite the cold, I'm blissfully warm, heated by an inferno inside of me that threatens to burn us both alive.

My hands ache to reach down, to release him from his black leathers. I trail my hand down over the front of him, grasping the parts that strain against the fabric. He groans and presses into my hand. My fingers scramble to unlace his belt.

Fast as an adder, he grabs my wrist. He breaks our kiss and stares into my eyes. I wonder if I've somehow misread him, from his ragged breath, to the hard length I can feel pressing against me. I look up into his gray eyes.

"You have to beg me for it first." Tristan gives me a wicked grin.

I scowl. "I don't beg." Yet I can't deny that I'm deeply aroused at the thought.

His laugh is low in the back of his throat. "Don't worry, Red. I can wait."

I raise an eyebrow. "You'll be waiting a long time, then. Forever, in fact."

He smirks at me, dark and dangerous. "Beg."

My other hand grabs the straining front of his leathers again. He moans and leans one hand on the boulder behind my head. This game we're playing makes me feel powerful. I adore how I can make him crumble with just the touch of a hand.

I lean closer to whisper in his ear. "Keep dreaming."

"Oh, I do." He recovers enough to nip at my neck. "Every night as I stroke my cock. I dream of you whimpering, moaning. Begging me for more."

My heart skips a beat. The roiling heat between my legs flares again. My pulse throbs between my legs.

As if he can sense it, he gives me a wicked grin. "I'm going to keep you aching for me until you're so needy and desperate, you can think of nothing else but sinking your sweet, pink cunt over my thick cock."

In all my life, I've never heard anyone speak like this before. I stare at him openmouthed ... and desperate to hear more. The seductive pull this Wolf has over me is undeniable now. It has me, for once, at a complete loss for words.

His lips are swollen as he grins. He trails his mouth down my throat, taking special care to kiss the thin, silver scar that my father left. I feel the light scrape of his teeth against my skin, and I shiver.

Then, his lips move lower, over my breasts, and down my ribs. He pauses at my navel as he loosens my leathers further. My fingers run through his hair as my head tips back. Out of instinct, my knees widen to let him closer.

His laugh is low and smug. "Impatient."

He tugs the leathers down over my hips, stroking my skin all the way down. He nips at my hip bones, and warmth blooms there. With a grunt of satisfaction, he tosses my leathers aside.

It strikes me that I should be cold. Freezing, in fact. But my skin is hot. Hotter than it should naturally be in the middle of winter in the frozen north. That's when I realize my power is coursing through my entire body, like liquid heat. It even warms the stone behind my back.

At the sight of my bare legs, the Wolf growls. His eyes look up at me, almost pleading.

I nod at his unspoken question and grab his dark hair in my fist. He doesn't need any encouragement. He presses his face into my sex and devours me. He spreads me, licks me, enters me with his tongue, does things to me with his mouth that I never imagined were possible. The swirling sensations that fill my body make my toes curl.

"Gods, I want you inside me." My words are achingly desperate.

His laugh rumbles against my sex and he pauses to ask, "Are you ready to beg now?"

I can barely make myself speak, but I do. "Never."

My knees grow weak again as the Wolf presses me against the boulder. He continues to lose himself in my body. He reaches one hand up, under my wool shirt, and feels for my breast, but I've tied a linen wrap around my chest for support. He gives a grunt of displeasure and tears at the fabric, all the while licking and spreading me, until my breasts are free. The wrap unwinds and he throws it to the ground. He runs his thumb over my nipple as he works me like he knows my body better than I do.

When I scream with release, my voice echoes off the trees. This pleasure is the most powerful experience I have ever had in my life—and it's come from the tongue of a Wolf.

I'm left with my legs trembling and my hand tangled in Tristan's hair. He looks up at me with wicked gray eyes.

"Red," he whispers. "Look."

I blink down at him for several seconds before I realize what he means. Mist rises around us. No, not mist, I realize. Steam. All around us, the ice and snow have melted. And somehow *I* did this. My power is coursing through me, my skin radiating gold with light.

Slowly, Tristan stands, not taking his eyes off me for a second. "You don't need more control." His voice is hushed in awe. "You need *less*."

I blink at him, still at a loss. Fractured starlight still flickers at the corners of my vision as I shake my head. "That's not what everyone else thinks."

He squeezes my hips, insistent. "Everyone else is wrong." He meets my gaze. "Red ... All your life, they've told you to be smaller. Weaker. Less dangerous. Less you."

I'm still trying to catch my breath as I come back from that place of ecstasy. But even through the haze, some secret part of me aches with recognition. I draw in a slow breath as my head clears. "That's because it was easier to survive when I stayed quiet. When I hid."

"I know." He grabs me by the waist, drawing me close. His thumbs trail over my glowing skin. "They made you believe power meant control. That you had to cage everything wild in you to survive."

"My father told me I was too volatile, too unpredictable to inherit the Fox Throne."

"Your father is a liar."

When his lips brush mine, my eyes flutter closed. Tristan

kisses me slowly, deeply, with the taste of me still on his tongue. The emotion in his touch makes my heart race again. I want to live in this moment with him, bathing in the strength of my power.

Tristan breaks the kiss slowly. My eyes flutter open to see his grin.

"He lied because he was afraid of you," Tristan says. "And he *should* be."

Those words are almost as intoxicating as the Wolf who says them. I sigh and lean my head back to look at the great northern sky.

CHAPTER 29

FOR THE NEXT WEEK, when I do sleep, I'm haunted by nightmares. Where I used to dream of corpse beasts and Dead Queens, now my fear manifests in gleaming, copper armies marching into Annwyn. The surrounding mountains are still pounded by daily storms, but few make it past the fae barrier. It's a hint of the spring to come. And with the end of winter approaching, so is my father.

I kick off my heavy blankets, tired of lying in bed, wide awake. What I really need is a cup of tea.

In the dark, I throw my red cloak over my shoulders before making my way through the halls, toward the kitchens. Surely, I can manage to heat water over the embers in the hearth to make one small cup of tea. It doesn't seem like too much to ask.

The kitchen is predictably dark, so I ignite an orb of light to illuminate the space. Pots and pans hang from hooks over long countertops, casting shadows across towers of clay bowls for mixing and jars filled with cooking oils. It smells inviting, no doubt due to the spices that have been ground into the flagstones below my feet for centuries.

I turn my attention to the hearth and notice movement. The

embers crackle as a familiar black fae creature rolls around in the soot.

Despite my gloom, I smile.

I'm not sure if it's the same cinder fae from my room, but he's similar with his mouse-like body, short fur, and beady black eyes. I'm afraid I'll scare him away if I approach, so I lean against a table and watch him. He's having such a joyful time, wiggling among the hot coals and rubbing soot into his fur with tiny hands. Or, are they paws? I'm not certain about fae anatomy.

After a few minutes, he makes a bed or nest of some sort. He wiggles into it and closes his eyes to sleep.

So much for boiling water for tea.

Behind me, the kitchen door creaks. I turn, sending my light to illuminate the source. The wooden door sways slightly. Then I notice a small, pale hand holding onto the doorframe.

My heart stills. Tucked into the shadow of the corridor, another fae creature watches me. It can't be taller than three feet, with hairless skin and a humanoid shape. Its skin is pale blue, like its been carved from ice. The dark shapes of organs are visible through its nearly translucent skin.

My heart hammers in my chest, but I'm not afraid, merely curious. "Hello?"

It blinks at me with watery eyes. Then it opens its mouth and makes a popping sound.

"Did you need something?" I whisper, reluctant to wake the tiny cinder fae in the hearth.

The creature nods, then waves its pale fingers for me to follow. It darts back into the shadows of the corridor. I hesitate. All my life, I've heard that fae can be tricksters. While I suspect this creature is more like the cinder fae than the monster in the dungeon, I'm still not sure I should follow. I do anyway.

The short fae sticks to the shadows, skittering ahead, then pausing in dark corners. It makes tiny popping noises with its mouth while it waits for me to catch up. Then it turns and scoots further down the hall. Much to my relief, it doesn't lead me to any new dungeons or dilapidated wings. Instead, I follow it through the main corridors until it slips out the front entrance, into the cold night. I pull my red cloak tighter around my shoulders and follow.

It leads me passed the stables and up to one of the battlement wall's side doors. With great effort it pushes the heavy door, then wiggles through a crack. When I get there, I push the door open further and step outside.

Beyond the wall, the night is silent. The blue fae has disappeared, but my heart skips in my chest when I realize who it led me to.

A familiar wraith hovers above the blanket of snow. Her back is turned to me, so all I see is her waving dark hair and her long, white gown as it drifts in the still air. Deep down, I know she senses I'm here, but she doesn't turn to look at me. She just hovers, as quiet as the night. I look back toward the castle once more, then step out into the snow.

It's as if we're connected now, chained together on this terrifying ride of discovery. Given that she's nearly led me to my death twice now, I probably shouldn't follow her blindly anymore, but I do. Because each time she brought me into danger, there was a reason. She's trying to tell me something important. I just need to figure out what it is.

When I approach, she simply drifts further out into the night. I carve a path through the snow. Already my boots are wet and my feet are cold, but I won't turn back now.

I catch up with her along the edge of the wide field. The forest beyond is dappled with moonlight, but something feels off. It's too quiet. Normally, I'd expect to hear the sounds of night animals—the hoot of an owl, the scurry of a squirrel, the scream of a hare as a fox catches it in its jaws. But there's nothing, not even the rustle of wind. It's as if the forest is afraid of the wraith.

"Where are we—"

She takes off down a snowy path, further into the trees.

By the time I reach her again, I'm sweating and panting.

There's a small game trail that leads off the main path. I probably wouldn't have noticed it if my guide hadn't so pointedly brought me here.

I stop. It's one thing to follow a ghost woman into the forest at night. It's quite another to follow her off the beaten path, into the trees. Especially since she's been known to lead me into danger before.

"I don't think I will, thank you very much."

The wraith turns to me for the first time. Her eyes grow dark, and her mouth spreads unnaturally wide to reveal a mouth full of sharp teeth. She looks like she did the first time I saw her. Back when I first arrived in Gwyllion with Tristan, corpse wolves hot on our trail, and the first winter storm chasing us.

Only this time, I'm not afraid of her. Her scare tactics have grown old, and I am so, so tired.

"Fine." I say, stomping down the game trail. "But whatever you want me to see better be close by."

Her normal features return, and she floats ahead. Within minutes, we come to a clearing. Mounds of snow cover the ground, and the moonlight reflects so brightly, I have to shield my eyes until they adjust.

The wraith waits several yards ahead, expectantly.

I look around, but I don't see anything of note. Just a small clearing in an otherwise ordinary forest. Well, ordinary for Annwyn, anyway. The trees bend and sway around me in a gentle breeze. Not a single creature makes a sound.

"I don't understand," I call out to the wraith. She remains still, frozen in the center of the clearing with an expectant look on her face.

I spin in place, searching for anything out of the ordinary. This wraith has led me to forbidden rooms, dungeons guarded by human-eating fae, and crumbling cliffs. This is just an ordinary glade, in an ordinary forest.

"I can't do this anymore!" I yell at the wraith. Irritation burns inside me, making me forget the cold. I trudge further into the clearing, waving my hands around as I spin in circles. "There's nothing here!" I stomp toward her, as if I could catch her by the shoulders and shake her.

"There's nothing—" I tumble into the snow, face first. My toe throbs in my frozen boot. After I wipe the melting snow from my face, I look for what I tripped over. The tip of a stone sticks out of the snow near my feet. But something about it looks odd. It's smooth and has a right angle, as if it was carved.

I look up toward the wraith, but she's disappeared. With shaking hands, I reach out to brush the remaining snow off the mound.

It's a tombstone.

Frantically, I clear the rest of the snow away. With trembling hands, I ignite an orb of light to read the words etched there.

Isadora
2118 – 2138
Beloved daughter of Corrin and Ilsa
Devoted sister to Tristan
May the Moon Goddess forever keep you at peace.

I stare at the gravestone for a long while. All this time, I thought I was following the ghost of some vengeful, Llwyn-hating villager. Or maybe some castle dweller from centuries past. But it turns out I had no idea who I was dealing with.

I've been following Tristan's dead sister.

CHAPTER 30

THE NEXT MORNING, I'm waiting at the front gate when Tristan arrives. He approaches with easy confidence, his steps echoing off the stone walls. When he sees me, he stops. A small grin transforms his face.

"Eager for more lessons, Red?"

The implication makes my stomach tumble deliciously, low in my belly. I study his face. His shadowed eyes are brighter today. His skin looks a little less hollow. It's like the veil of despair has lifted, letting a hint of sunshine through. At this moment, I can finally see what Nalina meant when she said this man used to be happy. After last night, I think I know what destroyed him.

"We have to talk." My eyes dart toward the villagers arriving early for their work within the castle. "Somewhere private."

Tristan's smile fades, and I hate that I'm the reason for it. He leads me outside, around the castle, and toward the remains of old Gwyllion. Frost sparkles on the ruins as leaning towers stand tall against the receding night. Out here, only the ghosts can hear our secrets.

The dawn is vibrant pink and orange as we settle onto an old, toppled column. I tilt my head toward the rising sun. It's warmer today, promising a day of melting snow and dripping icicles.

There's a war raging inside me, fighting against the joy of the cloudless sky and the fear of what it will bring: spring. And with it, my father and his Fox Army.

For all I know, they've begun marching through the mountains already.

Tristan touches my hand lightly, and my power flares in my chest in response. We've kept our secret this past week. Whenever we're in the castle, I hardly dare to look at him. If I do, someone will see how I blaze with the need for more of him. Someone will notice how much I crave to have this Wolf's hands on me again. How I ache for him at night.

My skin grows warm, and it has nothing to do with the sun on the horizon.

Tristan clears his throat. "It's been my experience that nothing good follows when a woman says, 'We need to talk.'"

A breathy laugh escapes me. "No. I suppose you're right about that."

"So, what do I need to be worried about?"

"You mean beyond the fact that the Fox Army is on its way to murder us all?"

He nods.

I sigh, not sure how to break this to him, but there's no way through it but forward. "I discovered something last night. I think it helped me understand you a little better."

Next to me, Tristan shifts, turning a curious glance my way. "Oh?"

I nod.

"And does this have anything to do with Nalina stealing you away to the village?"

I tilt my head. "You knew about that?"

He leans back, his palms bracing against the stone. "I make it my business to know everything about you, Red. You should know this by now."

"Does Nalina tell you everything?" My voice comes out petulant, but I can't hide my annoyance.

He shrugs. "Sometimes. Other times, not so much. We have ... unresolved issues."

"You and me both."

The corners of his lips hint at the ghost of a smile. "She always forgives me though, eventually." He tilts his head as he watches my reaction. "She hasn't had it easy."

"So she mentioned."

He turns to face the rising dawn. "Nalina is a lot like your Golden Boy, you know."

I scoff. "Those two couldn't be more different."

He gives me a challenging look. "They're both unendingly loyal. They'll always do whatever they think is right, no matter the personal cost. And they will always choose the ones they love over themselves."

Above us, the sky has broken into a blue morning. I watch, captivated, as the last remnants of the blazing dawn evaporate before our eyes. All around us, animals begin to wake. Birds chirp and mice scamper through the tall grasses surrounding the ruins of old Gwyllion.

I pause, thinking. "Is that why Nalina's such a miserable bore around me? She's protective of you?"

He barks out a laugh. "Maybe. Nalina's methods can be ... unconventional. But she believes in them."

"She doesn't believe I can help Gwyllion."

"Oh, she does, in spite of herself." He huffs a laugh. "Otherwise, she wouldn't have brought you to the village, even if Elisandra asked her to."

I flick a pebble off the stone we're sitting on. It bounces off another fallen column. "If she believes in me, it's only on account of you telling her she should."

"Maybe so." He shrugs. "But I've made no secret of my faith in you, Red. Eventually, other people will believe in you too."

As if in response, my power flutters inside of me. My voice is edged with relief. "I thought my power was gone forever."

His voice is softer now, filled with something like earnestness.

"I knew it was still there. We just had to figure out how to reach it."

I turn to face him. "How do you do that?"

"Do what?" A slight breeze blows a lock of his dark hair across his forehead. I want to reach out and smooth it back with my fingertips. To feel the warmth of his face. To release the pain locked behind his eyes.

"How do you always have so much faith in me? Even when no one else does, not even me?"

He shrugs, tilting his head up to the rising sun. He closes his eyes, savoring the warmth. "Because you are worth believing in."

My throat tightens, threatening to smother me beneath the weight of emotion. I've never felt like this before. It's as if I can finally breathe. As if I can be myself, without reservations or hiding. It's empowering, and yet it leaves me distraught for all the lost time. All those years when I doubted myself. All the loneliness and anger that I've carried for so, so long.

"Hey, Red. It's okay." Tristan leans forward, reaching his hand to cup my jaw. He wipes away a stray tear that I didn't know I'd shed. His gray eyes are worried, his eyebrows pinched together with concern. "Whatever it is, we'll find a way through. You've found your power again. You're unstoppable now."

I laugh lightly. "It's not that."

"Then what is it?"

It takes me a while to find the words, but Tristan waits patiently. He scoots closer to me and puts an arm protectively around my waist. It's so simple, so beautiful a gesture that I hate what I must tell him next.

"I know what happened to you. At least, I think I do."

Around me, I feel his arm stiffen. "What happened to me?"

"I met someone last night. Or rather, they finally told me who they are."

His expression is wary. "Who?"

I study his eyes, watching for any hint of emotion. "Isadora."

He blinks rapidly several times before shaking his head. "That's not possible."

"It is," I whisper. "She's been visiting me all winter. She's the woman who led me to the sacred temple that first night. Who led me to the cliffs." I swallow. "To the room on the far side of the castle that night. It was her room, wasn't it?"

His face pales. He shakes his head again, his dark hair falling into his eyes. "I don't understand. Isadora is—"

"Dead. I know."

Tristan stares at me for a long time, barely breathing.

I shift to face him. "The first time I saw her, we were outside the castle grounds, when the corpse wolves chased us to the gates."

Tristan is so still, he could be mistaken for part of the stone column we're sitting on.

"She led me to the fae in the dungeon."

"You went down there?!" His eyes flash and he grabs my face in both hands. "Red, promise me, never go down there."

I've never seen Tristan lose his composure before. His panic makes me realize just how dangerous the fae in the dungeon really is. I may not fully understand everything yet, but two things are clear: First, the fae in the dungeon is a bigger problem than I realized. And, second, Tristan fears losing me like he lost his sister.

I draw his hands down and hold them. "It's okay," I whisper. "I'm okay."

He's breathing heavily now and sweat glistens on his brow. "No, Red. You don't understand. You can't possibly ..."

"Then help me understand." I squeeze his hands. "All of it. What is Isadora trying to tell me?"

Tristan looks down at our entwined hands and lets out a shaky breath. "Okay." He nods. "I'll tell you." He closes his eyes before squaring his shoulders. His face is wan again and his eyes are haunted.

I hate that I did this to him.

"This castle, Gwyllion, it's the only safe place we have

now. Further north, we can't survive the winter. And to the south ..." He doesn't need to finish that thought. To the south is my father. To the south are the territories stolen by Llwyn.

He takes a deep breath. "But this castle has a price."

"Nalina mentioned that."

He groans and mutters to himself. "Of course she did."

"But I want to hear it from you." I nod, encouraging him to continue.

He pinches the bridge of his nose. "For centuries, it was abandoned. Inhabited only by the fae in the dungeon. Moribund. He's ... revolting." Tristan closes his eyes in disgust. "He considers this castle on loan until we claim territory back from the Fox King. It's taken longer than expected."

"What do you mean, 'on loan'?"

"Moribund requires payment." He swallows hard. "Beauty and youth."

Ice runs through my veins, freezing me on the spot. "The hair ..."

Tristan nods. "He collects it."

"Not just any hair though."

"No." Tristan shakes his head slowly. "He has a preference."

"For blonds."

"Yes." His face is guarded, like he's hiding something. It makes me suspicious. I'm missing something important. Something he doesn't want me to know.

I tilt my head. "But Moribund said he wants *my* hair. It's auburn."

Tristan's eyes drift back over to me. They travel over my coppery hair, which I've tied into a thick braid that hangs over one shoulder. His eyes flicker up to meet mine.

"Yours is unusual in Annwyn. Exotic. Moribund covets unusual shades. I'm sure he'd consider yours a treasure."

"That's horrible."

Something defensive flashes across his face. "Yes. It *is* horrible.

In case you hadn't noticed, in Annwyn we sometimes have to do horrible things to survive."

His sharp tone catches me by surprise, but he's right. Conditions in Annwyn are deplorable because of the unending war. Because of my father.

Tristan tips his head up toward the sky and gathers his composure. "We hate this, you know. Even as we love our kingdom. There's beauty in this place, but ..."

"Also terror."

He nods.

But I still don't have all the answers. "What about your sister? You told me she died suddenly."

He swallows hard. "He killed her when I was twelve."

I shake my head. Something doesn't add up. "But that can't be. I've seen your sister many times. She isn't blond."

Tristan laughs humorlessly. "Moribund demanded my sister that summer. She had the palest blond hair I've ever seen. It was long and thin, like spider silk. It's why he desired her." Tristan's face hardens. "In my hubris, I thought I could trick him. I'd picked the darkest berries I could find and pounded them into a paste. We worked it through her hair until it was the shade of midnight. I thought he wouldn't want her anymore since her hair was spoiled." His voice catches.

My heart sinks. "It didn't work."

He leans forward and puts his head in his hands. "I insisted on bringing her to the dungeon myself, even though I wasn't a Wolf yet. I wanted to see Moribund's face crumble when he saw I'd outsmarted him." He scoffs at the memory. "At twelve, you think you're a man. That you're in control and you know everything there is to know about the world. But you're still a child in many ways, naïve and hopeful." He swallows. "Moribund just laughed. I'd forgotten about fae magic. He just turned her hair back to the shade of moonlight. Even terrified, she was so, so beautiful ..."

I'm too afraid to speak.

"He killed her. Right in front of me."

I reach out toward him and place a hand on his arm. "It wasn't your fault."

He shrugs my hand off gently. "I should have saved her. It was summer, so we could have survived a journey through the Spires. It was the only time I'd ever considered abandoning Annwyn. Of following the other refugees that hide throughout Llwyn."

"You couldn't have known Moribund would demand your sister."

"I knew he desired blonds. I knew my sister was beautiful. Everyone did."

I think of the wraith with her long, floating hair. Dark as midnight, just as Tristan said. She'd kept the shade in death. After the torture her blond hair brought, I can't blame her.

"It was only a matter of time," he says, as if to himself.

Something in his words makes me pause. "A matter of time? How many women has Moribund taken?"

"I can't be sure. We've lived in Gwyllion a long time."

That's not good enough for me. "When does he require payment?"

Tristan stills. "Every season we remain in his castle."

My eyes widen. "Every season?" I remember the corpses in the dungeon. The nest of blond locks. The snakes of pale braids woven through it. The urge to vomit rises in me. "I've lived in this decrepit castle for nearly three months now. That means—"

"Yes," he whispers. "He's taken someone since you've been here."

My mouth falls open in horror. "Who? When?"

Tristan looks away. "A girl from the village. On the night of the midwinter full moon."

"The night of the bonfires? The night you kissed me?" My voice is rising in pitch, but I can't restrain my horror. "How did he find her?"

"He doesn't leave the dungeon while we're here. It's part of the deal."

"Then someone brought a girl to him. Delivered her to be killed?"

He nods. I study his face. His jaw is clenched, his eyes tight on the horizon. A shiver runs down my spine as realization spreads through me.

"Who?" I ask, though I fear I already know the answer.

"It doesn't matter." He closes his eyes.

My resolve is firm in this. I need to hear him say it. "Who?!"

"It's one of the duties of a Wolf."

"*Which* Wolf?" My eyes are slits of rage, but I refuse to break my glare.

His head drops as he stares at the frozen ground. "I did," he whispers. "I always do."

My heart sinks into my stomach.

"And I will live with that horror every day, until I die." His voice is hollow, haunted.

I can't stop staring at him, searching his face for a sign that it isn't true. That he's lying. I'd begun to care for this man, this Wolf. He's my sworn enemy, yet I'd let him touch me in the most intimate ways. I'd craved him like the dying crave life.

And he's a murderer.

CHAPTER 31

I FEEL FROZEN IN PLACE, just another icy statue in this ruined castle. Then, a familiar voice breaks into the conversation.

"I tried to warn you."

I spin around to see Hunter step out from behind the ruins of old Gwyllion. His hair gleams gold in the morning sun. His brown eyes are pinned on Tristan in disgust.

"I told you not to trust the Wolf."

Tristan straightens slowly, turning his head to study Hunter. "I wondered when you'd stop sulking and start tormenting me again."

Hunter's cheeks redden. "I'm not here to torment you. I'm here to do my duty."

Tristan raises a dark eyebrow. "Since when are you a spy?"

"My duty isn't to spy. It's to protect Sienna."

"She isn't in any danger from me."

"That's not what it sounded like."

The Wolf bristles. "Then maybe you shouldn't have been listening from behind two tons of ancient stone."

My head aches, and I rub my temples. "Enough!"

Both men turn to look at me. For a moment, it feels like old times. Back when the biggest worry we had was escorting Tristan to the borderlands in one piece. It wasn't even three months ago, but it feels like ages. I force my hands into my pockets to keep from strangling the two of them, and my fingers brush the little green book.

Hunter stomps toward us. The copper-plated sword at his hip glistening in the morning light. He must have gone back for it after abandoning it in the throne room.

Tristan doesn't bother to stand up from the toppled marble column. Instead, he leans back on his elbows, as if settling in for a leisurely bout of sunbathing.

"If that fae has his eye on Sienna, we need to get her out of here."

I wave my hand dismissively. "I'm not afraid of the fae."

Both men turn to me and say in unison, "You should be."

I roll my eyes.

Hunter folds his arms across his chest. "And if this beast is the one delivering his meals, I don't feel comfortable with you training with him. Especially not alone."

I tilt my head at Hunter. "Oh, and you're here to boss me around now, are you?"

"I'm not trying to boss you around; I'm trying to protec—"

"I don't need your protection!" I throw my hand up in frustration.

Hunter straightens his spine. "The queen assigned me to—"

Tristan barks a laugh. "Look who's doing the dirty work of the Dead Queen now."

Hunter's face grows crimson. "I'm not doing this for *her*."

Tristan's cocky grin is back. "No. Of course not. You're spying on Red for her own good. Patronizing prick."

Hunter stomps up to where Tristan's still languishing on the stone column. "What did you call me?"

I groan. "I can't handle any more of this masculine pissing competition that you two have going on."

They both turn back to me. I clench my fists to keep from punching them both in their pretty, stupid noses.

I point toward the sun-bathed Spires. "We have much bigger problems to deal with."

They both glare at each other, but thankfully, don't open their damnable mouths again.

"Hunter, can I speak with you?" I ask.

Tristan makes a move to stand, but I give him a firm head shake. I give Hunter a pointed look. "Alone?"

Tristan shrugs and lies back on the stone. He tilts his face to the sun. "Be my guest."

By the look on Hunter's face, I can tell it takes a great amount of effort for him to back down from the smug Wolf, but he does. I turn and trudge through the melting slush, toward the tree line. Reluctantly, Hunter follows a few paces behind me. When we reach the cover of trees, I turn to him.

"Hunter, I'm glad you're here. I truly am. I missed you. But things have changed."

His jaw is set. "I can't help you if you keep doing dangerous things."

I sigh wearily. "Everything is dangerous here, Hunter. I need you to trust that I know what I'm doing."

He studies me, his brown eyes trying to read my mind. "All of this ... Annwyn, the queen, you and Tristan ... it hasn't been easy for me, you know. I'm trying."

I close my eyes and rub my aching temples. "I know."

Hunter thinks for a moment, then squares his shoulders, facing me. Something on his face is open, vulnerable.

"How do you think this makes me feel? I sailed the frozen sea and lost a hundred good men to save you ... only to see you with him. A Wolf."

I stare at him, my eyes disbelieving. "You knew I came here with him."

He shakes his head. "Not like that, I didn't."

"Like what? What's that supposed to mean?"

His voice is firm, but I don't miss the note of heartbreak. "You never looked at me the way you look at him. Never."

All around us, the frozen forest glitters in the sunlight. Squirrels hop from branch to branch, knocking the remains of melting icicles to the ground. Birds tweet, grateful for the warmth and the promise of spring, but I still feel cold inside.

"This isn't just about Tristan," I say. "You're clearly still angry with me."

Hunter looks at me as if he can't believe what he's seeing. "You betrayed me. Of course I'm angry!"

"You betrayed me first!"

And there it is, the splinter between us that's never come out. The one ghost that will forever haunt us.

"That was years ago." His voice breaks. "How long do I need to suffer?"

"You sold me out to my father because you were jealous." I pin him with a glare.

He sniffs and sets his jaw in defiance. "I was. I probably still am. But I'm trying to move on, Sienna. Why can't you?"

"What do you want from me, Hunter?"

All around us, the forest sounds have ceased, as if even the trees feel the brewing tension. As if they're afraid.

Hunter's face breaks into bewilderment. "Forgive me already!"

"I DO!" I don't mean to shout, but the pent-up pain that I've been tending for years bursts out of me. My voice echoes off the trees, sending my words into the still forest in an unending loop. I nearly choke on a sob. "It's myself I can't seem to forgive, not you."

We stand in silence for several long moments. A breeze shakes snow from a pine branch, and it glitters as it falls gently to the ground.

When Hunter speaks again, it's so quiet, I almost don't hear him. "I just can't stand to see you with him."

The truth of it is plastered clear across his face. Hunter is unendingly loyal, yes. But he is also jealous. Always has been.

"But I'm trying, Sienna. I truly am."

"Hunter, I—"

My words die in my mouth. The ground is shaking. I look to the trees around us to confirm. Leaves tremble on branches and melting snow rains down from the treetops. I listen intently. Beyond the sound of trees trembling, there's something else.

Hooves.

I turn to Hunter, my heart in my throat.

His face is pale, his eyes wide in panic. He stands with his feet apart, ready to fight. "What—?"

A creature leaps out from behind a clump of brambles. It's a doe, I realize. Her eyes are red and wild; spittle foams at her mouth. She doesn't even see us as she races past, her breathing strangled in panic. I turn toward the direction she came from. In the distance, through the trees, there's movement. It's so wide, I don't know where to turn to get out of its path.

Hunter grabs my hand. "Run!" We turn to follow the deer.

It takes a moment for me to realize what's approaching. It isn't just one thing. It's a stampede of forest creatures. I glance behind us. Rabbits leap over logs, their ears tilted back for speed. Squirrels dart from limb to limb, scrambling for purchase. Then, more deer.

I put one arm over my head as we dart between them, running in the same direction as we try not to get trampled.

Three bears thunder past, their paws indenting the soggy ground, spraying mud all over us. There's nowhere to go, only forward as we try not to fall.

I stumble momentarily, and the little green book falls out of my pocket, into the slush. Panic floods me, and I reach out to save it, just as a buck leaps over me, crashing to the ground in front of us. Hunter hauls me to my feet as I stuff the book back into my pocket.

"Don't stop!" He drags me forward with the tide of forest creatures.

They're not all normal animals. A lynx-like cat with human hands slinks past us, darting between the feet of beasts much larger. Its spotted tail is tipped in a lethal-looking barb. What appears to be a boulder rolls past us, crushing a chipmunk beneath its weight. As it passes, I spot limbs tucked in tightly to its core.

The boulder fae knocks into a tree as it passes. The pine comes crashing down, pinning another fae beneath its branches. Its scream is cut short as more creatures climb right over the tree trunk, pushing it deeper into the mud.

"Get down!" Hunter tells me as he drags me into a crevasse made by two trees held up by a pile of tumbled rocks.

Instinctively, I reach into my core. My power comes easily as I call it forward, then push it out from my body in a protective circle. It folds around us in a glimmer of light, where we crouch beneath the toppled trees.

We listen to the thundering hooves and scratching feet as what must be hundreds of animals leap and crawl over our hiding spot. A weasel-like creature with a human face scrambles up to us. It cowers in front of our shield until another bear lumbers past, then it scurries away after it.

Slowly, the rumbling stops and the sound of the stampede fades into the distance. Until all I hear is our ragged breath. I release my power with a gasp. It eases back into its hiding place, deep in my sternum. Relief makes me feel lightheaded.

Hunter crawls out first, slow and cautious. I follow him, my hands and knees sinking into the slick mud left in the wake of the stampede. All around us, the forest is a path of destruction. It looks like a storm tore the forest to shreds. Trees are overturned and branches are crushed to pulp. Here and there, the remnants of creatures that were too slow or too small are scattered throughout the wide path. I turn away, not wanting to look too closely.

"Red!" Tristan comes running through the trees. When he spots us, relief washes over his face.

"We're alright!" I call back.

He runs up to us as Hunter turns slowly in place, taking in

the scale of the destruction. Tristan grabs my shoulders, pulling me into his chest. I breathe in the cedar and salt smell of him, and I feel my heart rate slow.

"Why are they running?" I ask as the truth dawns on me like a wave of icy water.

Tristan releases me, his face grave. "They're coming."

The Llwyn army. My father.

Hunter shakes his head slowly, his face etched in disbelief. "What were those things!?" His voice is tinged with panic. There's a long gash in his hand, but he seems oblivious to the blood as it drips down his fingers.

I wonder if the shock has rattled him somehow. "Hunter, they were animals. A stampede."

"No." He shakes his head. "Not the deer and the ... the bear ... the *things*!" He gestures with his hands. "The creatures with spiny tails and human faces!"

"You could see them?" I ask, dumbfounded.

"What do you mean?" Hunter looks at me incredulously. "Of course, I can see them! They nearly trampled us to death."

"But Nalina told me most people can't see fae." I look to Tristan.

"They can't," he says flatly.

"Well, I saw them." Hunter stares in the direction the stampede fled, his expression laced with both wonder and fear.

I gesture to the Wolf. "The only other person I know who can see fae is Tristan."

The Wolf shakes his head once. "No, I can't."

"W—what?" I stutter, confused. "But you told me you saw Moribund. With your sister ..."

"I said Moribund killed Isadora in front of me. I saw her murder. I did not see her killer."

I shake my head. "That doesn't make any sense."

His lips draw into a firm line. "In Annwyn, we coexist with the fae, but we cannot see them. We hear them. We sense them. We even make ill-advised deals with them on occasion."

Goosebumps erupt across my skin. "Why do some people have the ability and others don't?"

Tristan watches me intently. "It's not that *some* people can. It's that no one can. They're invisible to the human eye."

I blink, stunned. My eyes drift to Hunter. "No. Hunter can. I can. Clearly, some people can. Nalina said so."

He turns to look at Hunter, who stands still as death. A drop of blood falls from the tip of his thumb into the muddy slush at his feet.

Tristan speaks carefully. "Only *royal blood* can see fae. Kings and queens who have the echoes of old magic in their veins. Nobility may give you the power to control light or shadows, but to see the fae ... That's an entirely different thing."

I'm a royal, so that makes sense. But Hunter? I turn to stare at him, trying to understand.

"What does this mean?" I ask hesitantly. My heart hums in my chest, almost as if I'm afraid.

"Come with me," Tristan says as he walks back in the direction of Gwyllion Castle.

"But what does it mean?" I call after him again.

Tristan turns to look back toward us. There's something frightening in the hard lines of his face. "It means Hunter is the Heir to the North."

CHAPTER 32

WE FIND the Dead Queen in the tower of moths.

She's standing with her back to us as she looks out the window toward the Spires to the south. Nalina is at her side, her face grave. She eyes us warily as we enter, but the queen doesn't turn to acknowledge us.

Tristan kneels. "My queen, we have news."

Nalina places a casual hand on the hilt of her sword. "Where have you been?" She shoots me an assessing glance. "I sent for you."

Tristan stands. "My apologies. We were in the ruins, then the forest."

Nalina raises an eyebrow. "Doing what exactly?"

Tristan bristles. "I don't answer to you, Nalina."

Nalina looks like she bit something sour, but she doesn't press him further. The Dead Queen still hasn't turned from the window. Next to me, I feel Hunter stiffen as he notices the rafters above us. Dead moths climb over each other, fluttering their wings and perching on old wooden beams.

"That's ... unnatural," he whispers next to me.

Unnatural, yes. But I don't miss the edge of awe in his voice. He's learning, as I did, that nothing is as it seems in Annwyn.

Inside the pocket of my red cloak, my fingers grip the little green book with the silver moth on the cover. So many moths, so many secrets.

Slowly, the Dead Queen raises one skeletal arm and points out the window, toward the mountains. She isn't wearing her long black gloves. Her fingers are little more than bone, her arm made of mottled flesh, like the corpse she is. I squint out the window. From this height, I can see what captured her attention.

Smoke rises from beyond the Spires, a surefire warning of the armies approaching.

"We know," Tristan says. "The forest is responding. The animals and fae are fleeing."

"They are wise to do so." The Dead Queen's voice rattles in her throat. The sound sends a shiver down my spine.

Next to me, Hunter squares his shoulders, as if anticipating a fight. "We can't run from them."

Slowly, the queen shakes her head and turns toward us. "No, we cannot."

"Why didn't you send your legion of dead monsters to attack them?" Hunter's voice is accusatory.

"I have."

Hunter's mouth snaps closed.

"If it were so easy to destroy the Fox Army, don't you think we'd have won this war long ago?" The Dead Queen turns only halfway toward us. "My corpse wolves can't keep legions out of Annwyn. They're being slaughtered by the hundreds. I can't spare any more."

My eyes dart to Hunter. He opens his mouth to argue, and I shake my head. Thankfully, he restrains himself.

"So, what do we do?" I ask.

The queen turns toward Nalina. "We've been making plans in your absence."

It's no more than a comment, but I feel the implication within it. While we were distracted, Nalina was here with the queen, preparing for the worst.

"I'll ready the villagers," Nalina says. "Everyone who is able to fight will."

The Dead Queen turns back toward the window. "I'll call the wolves."

Corpse wolves, she means. I've seen them in battle before, and I never wish to see them again.

"How long?" I ask.

Nalina squints out toward the mountains. "Three days, if we're lucky."

The midday sun streams into the tower, highlighting the moths above us. Their wings flutter like flower petals caught in a storm. White, orange, blue, green.

"That's not all," Tristan cuts in.

From the tone of his voice, I know what's coming. He's going to tell them he believes Hunter to be the Heir to the North, as impossible as that seems to me. I've known Hunter my entire life. Wouldn't I have suspected if the shy boy who loved adventure novels was a secret king?

Nalina gives him a sharp glance, then eyes Hunter and me with suspicion.

The Dead Queen doesn't respond, only waits. Her skeletal hand reaches up to grasp the silver moth necklace, like she used to do when she needed comfort in life. For a moment, my heart stills. Is it possible there's still some small remnant of my grandmother in her?

Tristan's voice is firm. "He knows."

The phrasing makes me blink rapidly. Next to me, Hunter stiffens.

"How?" Nalina asks.

"He can see them. The fae. I had to tell him."

The queen whirls away from the window. "That was not your place, Wolf!"

Tristan doesn't shrink away. He doesn't even flinch. "We came straight to you."

"Wait," Hunter interrupts. "You knew? You *all* knew?"

My heart thrums painfully in my chest. "I didn't. I swear." I reach out a hand to touch his elbow, but he shakes me off.

Tristan barely blinks at Hunter's rising anger. "It was best to keep you in the dark."

Hunter shakes his head violently. "No. It's not true. You're mistaken. I can't be royal. I barely even have power." He stammers. "I can hardly make my own light in the dark."

"That's because you're not from Llwyn," the Dead Queen says evenly.

My mouth falls open. This is nonsense. "Hunter and I grew up together in Caerwen Palace. Of course he's from Llwyn!"

Hunter steps forward. "My father was from a noble house!"

"And your mother?"

"She ..." Hunter's words fade away.

I know what he must be thinking. No one knew her well. And she died before she could tell him her story. Hunter was another motherless child, like me.

Hunter's face has gone pale. "My father said she was a poor village girl he met near the borderlands. He found her while collecting taxes for the King."

Tristan's expression is grave. "It appears that she was more than she seemed."

The queen speaks. "Like many refugees from Annwyn, your mother, Rhiannon, kept her heritage a secret. Llwyn villagers aren't picky about who shows up to help with the harvests." She steps toward Hunter. "You forget that I knew Rhiannon. Quite well, in fact."

Hunter's face looks stricken. My heart is hammering in my chest, and I'm beginning to feel light-headed. This can't be happening. It's not possible. My eyes dart to the dead moths where they flutter above us, oblivious to the fact that my world is fracturing below.

The queen continues. "Your mother had no family left after the Llwyn raiders set fire to her village. She was the heir before you. The final descendant of the human kings who used to rule

Annwyn before the Dead Queens took power five centuries ago."

Hunter's eyes are on the ground, his hand clenched over the copper fox on the pommel of his sword. "Did my father know?" he whispers.

The Dead Queen shakes her head slowly. "No. I don't believe Malen ever knew about Rhiannon's past. But I suspected. It's why I sent Tristan to Llwyn. To find you."

My ears are ringing. All this time, I thought the Wolf had been in the castle to find clues about a myth, the legendary Heir to the North. I never suspected it was real. That *he* was real. Especially not someone who I've known and loved my entire life.

Hunter shakes his head. "No. You're wrong about me. About my mother."

"I am not."

Hunter glares at the queen. "Why would a woman who was terrorized by Llwyn go on to marry the commander of the entire Fox Army?"

"People do strange things in the name of survival," Nalina says.

A thought hits me all at once. Grandmother was the leader of the Sympathizers before she became the Dead Queen. She was a member of the Llwyn royal family through my mothers' marriage to the Fox King. She used her position to spy on my father. Could there have been more spies in the court of the Fox King? The little green book in my cloak pocket feels ten times heavier than it should, as if the weight of its secrets grows by the moment.

"Or ..." I say, my thoughts whirring. "Maybe she didn't marry Malen out of pure survival. Maybe she knew *exactly* who he was." I turn to Hunter, my eyes wide. "Maybe she knew that by marrying your father, she'd be brought to the palace. To the king."

"You think she was secretly a member of the rebellion?" Tristan asks, one dark eyebrow raised.

We both look to the queen, the former leader of the Sympathizers. She offers one curt nod of confirmation.

My fingers grip the book in my pocket. I shake my head. "No, she couldn't have been. One spy in the royal court is outrageous." My eyes dart to the corpse that used to be my grandmother. "Two would be impossible."

"Impossible?" There's a curious lilt in the queen's voice. "You stand there in front of a dead queen and speak of impossibilities?"

"Hunter's mother was married to the Fox King's most trusted advisor. To the Commander of the Fox Army!" A bewildered laugh forces its way out of my chest.

"And my own daughter was the Fox Queen, however briefly."

Words fail me. It's true. As impossible and outrageous as it sounds, she's right. My mother, the Fox Queen, was the daughter of the leader of the Sympathizers. A pang of regret stabs my heart. We should have had more time together. She should have lived long enough to tell me everything herself. But Father killed her. And here I am, listening to the story through the undead lips of a corpse queen instead.

"You have proof," the queen says.

"I have proof?" I blanch.

She nods slowly. "Do you think I wouldn't recognize that little green book you've been carrying around ever since Hunter arrived?"

I stiffen, my heart beating rabbit-fast. My hands stop fidgeting with the corners of the book in my pocket. How had I given away my secret without even knowing it?

"How did you know?"

"My eyes may be dead, but they don't miss much, Fox Heir."

"But there are millions of books in the world. How could you possibly know which one this is?" My fingers curl possessively around the book's spine in my pocket.

There's a hint of pride in her voice as she says, "I could never forget it. I printed it."

"Printed it?" Hunter's words sound far away, like he's speaking into a south-facing wind.

The queen walks slowly toward me. "Before either of you

were born. Before my daughter married the Fox King and your mother was ensnared by the Commander of the Fox Army, I had a very different life."

"We already know you led the Sympathizers." Hunter's voice is sharp and distrustful.

"But I wasn't born a noble. I didn't become a rebel within the walls of Caerwen Palace. I lived in White's End."

Hunter's eyes shoot to mine. White's End is where we found the first moth carved into the wall of a dusty pawn shop.

The Dead Queen must recognize the looks dawning on our faces. "I see you've been there. Clearly, I'm not the only one with secrets."

The Dead Queen holds out her hand expectantly. With shaking fingers, I reach into my cloak, pull out the water-damaged book, and place it in her outstretched palm. Without hesitation, the Dead Queen opens the front cover to reveal the names written there, some blurry from water damage. With one skeletal finger, she points to the last name on the list.

"Rhiannon," she says. "In the language of the ancient north, it meant 'queen'."

I stare at the shaky signature. This is the handwriting of someone who wasn't used to holding a quill. Someone who may not have grown up with the luxuries of palace tutors. Could it be true?

"I am not what you say!" Hunter shouts.

I jump at the sound. The green book slips from my hands and lands on the stone ground with a thud.

Hunter's eyes are wild with disbelief. "I've spent my entire life hating Annwyn. My mother can't have been the Heir to the North."

The Dead Queen leans toward him. "Have you ever tried to summon shadows? Or hide in darkness?"

My heart seizes in my chest. We spent most of our childhood hiding from our ruthless fathers. Hunter was never talented in healing or light power. That was one failure on a long list that

Commander Malen held over Hunter's head for his entire life. So, we spent our childhood in hiding—the library, the gardens, anywhere we could escape our fathers' judgment. The only person who ever made us feel safe or loved was Grandmother.

I never saw Hunter create swirling shadows or summon darkness like Tristan, but now I wonder ... How were we able to hide so well?

When I glance over at Hunter's face, it's stricken. Does he remember? Deep down, did he suspect something about him wasn't normal? At least, not by Llwyn's standards.

Something about all of this doesn't feel right. I turn to Tristan.

"If you didn't suspect I was the Heir, then why did you risk your neck to take me across the border? Why didn't you just leave me behind?"

"Because your father would have killed you." Something dark flashes behind his eyes. It may not be a lie, but it's only half the truth.

"And?"

The queen's cold, dead voice rattles behind us. "And it was the only way to lure the Heir to the North across the border."

I whirl around to face her. "What is that supposed to mean?"

Behind her black veil, she lifts her chin in what looks like defiance. "It means I knew Hunter would follow you to the ends of the earth. Anyone could see that. If Tristan brought you to me, then Hunter would soon follow."

I turn back to Tristan, my eyes wide with indignation. "So, I was just bait?"

His jaw is set firm, but his voice is soft. "Not to me."

"You *used* me." The words come out like venom, tasting like poison on my tongue. My eyes are fire as I glare at the Wolf.

"I don't like defending the Wolf," Hunter says. "But he couldn't have known I'd follow you."

I nod. "Yes, he did." I tilt my head as I watch Tristan for a reaction. "What was it you told me? That Hunter is unendingly loyal. That he will do anything for the people he cares about, even at the detriment of his own safety? That he's the type of person who will do anything to save the people he loves?"

Tristan stares at me, his face blank as stone.

"I can't believe I've been so naïve." I laugh humorlessly. "I feel a little foolish now."

Nalina scoffs. "It's about time."

Tristan growls at her, like the Wolf he is. "It wasn't like that, and you know it."

Nalina grins at him like a predator. "All I know is, the queen sent you to fetch the Heir to the North. And you did. Like a good little Wolf. That one," she points to me. "Was a means to an end."

My power fizzles and pops inside me, fueled by my growing rage.

I point toward Tristan. "Why send him? Of all the people left in Annwyn, why send him to fetch me?"

"Because I trust my Wolves above all others." The queen folds her skeletal hands in front of her. "My Wolves would do anything for me. They helped create me."

The hair on my neck bristles. "No riddles. Tell it plainly."

"It's not a riddle. They were there in the borderland when I died."

I blink rapidly. "Explain."

No one moves. We barely breathe as we wait to see how much the queen will tell me. A moth floats down from the rafters, fluttering on gray wings. It settles on the queen's dead chest, unafraid.

"These two." She tilts her head toward Tristan and Nalina. "They were barely more than children, but they were soldiers nonetheless. It's something far too many Annwyn teenagers must become when we have so few soldiers to protect our land from Foxes."

I eye Nalina. When Grandmother died, I was twelve. She couldn't have been more than sixteen or seventeen. Just a few years older than Tristan and me.

More moths flutter down, as if drawn to the Dead Queen in her vulnerability. As if they're comforting her. Their wings open and close where they perch on her veil, her dress and along her skeletal arms.

"Your father didn't just murder me in the borderlands." The Dead Queen's voice is cold. "He tortured me, tied me down, and watched as his feral foxhounds tore me apart, bit by bit."

Her torn flesh, the exposed bone. I'd assume it was natural rot and decay, but she died that way. My father's beasts ate her flesh straight down to the bone.

"He left me there in the mud. He thought I was dead, but my heart still beat. Barely." She pauses, studying me. "As a reward for all of my service, the previous Dead Queen nominated me to take her place. Only one Dead Queen can reign, so she passed from this earth. She left me with this ruined kingdom and the endless torture that this war brings."

She sounds resigned, not what you'd expect from a woman given a throne. But I wouldn't want to be in her place either. It would have been kinder to let her die in peace.

"When you say Tristan and Nalina helped create you," I ask. "What do you mean?"

The two Wolves stiffen, glancing at each other.

Beneath her black veil, she shakes her head. "The secrets of reanimation are sacred in Annwyn."

I don't budge. "If you expect me to be a weapon for Annwyn, then you'd better start by telling the truth."

The Dead Queen takes a moment before she nods once.

Nalina begins to protest. "My queen, these rituals are secret for a reason. I don't trust the Fox."

"I know." The Dead Queen stares at me for a long time as the undead moths on her dress open and close their tattered wings in a silent dance. "But I do."

Slowly, she lifts her veil with her skeletal fingers. The moths on the thin fabric take flight, waiting until the veil settles again. They return to perch on my grandmother's corpse.

Every time I see her face, I struggle not to shrink back. But this time, I take her in. All of her. Every mark, every bared bone and torn shred of flesh. Now that I know how it happened, who did it to her, I feel a spark of pity. I know what it's like to feel my father's wrath, but not to this extent. She endured a brutal death.

My eyes drift out the window to the bonfire smoke drifting up from the Spires. I will make him pay for what he did to her.

The Dead Queen steps forward slowly. She raises her arm and traces my cheek with a cold, hard finger bone. "I want him to tell you." She turns to Tristan.

I turn and focus all my attention on the gray-eyed Wolf.

"What's the secret to eternal life?" I ask, my voice low, daring him not to tell me.

His eyes are sad, but they never leave mine. "To live eternally, there must be sacrifice. When the future queen gives up her life, she must be bathed in the light of the full moon, so the Moon Goddess can witness the act of devotion." He pauses.

"That can't be all there is to it."

"No." He swallows hard. "That's not all. Her heart must be stolen from her chest before it stops beating ... stuck in the moment between life and death. It must be stolen by someone devoted to her cause for the rest of their life."

Something hardens in my chest. "Who?" I ask, my voice low and threatening. "Who tore out my grandmother's still-beating heart?"

"It's not that simple."

"Then explain it to me!"

"Why does it matter?"

"Who was it?"

"You know who."

"Say it."

"It was me." His voice is barely a whisper.

My heart fractures like obsidian. "All this time. *You knew.* You knew I was looking for my grandmother's killer. You knew what happened. You lied to me."

He shakes his head. "I never meant—"

I push him full in the chest. He doesn't stop me.

"It doesn't matter what you meant, Tristan!" I hit him with my fists, as tears fill my eyes. "It's what you did. You should have told me!" I'm trembling with fury as I push him again.

"I couldn't. I'm bound to her, Red." His breathing is heavy now, his eyes wide, begging me to believe him. He almost looks afraid. "The person who steals the heart of the Dead Queen is changed forever. They're bound to serve the dead for the remainder of their lives. That sacrifice can never be revoked. Blood calls to blood."

"I don't care about your duty to your queen." Tears are falling in earnest now, trailing down my cheeks. I'm too furious to care who sees.

His voice is sharp, but there's an undercurrent of regret beneath it. "You can't possibly understand what that means. I can't betray her. I can't tell her secrets." He lets out a shaky breath. "Not even to the woman I love."

The word hangs between us, frozen in midair.

"You know nothing of love." Anger makes my voice tremble. My vision is blurry with hot tears. "You're a Wolf. I'm the Fox Heir. And this," I point between us. "This was never more than a fantasy."

My tears fall as fast as my feet pound the ground. I turn and run.

CHAPTER 33

EACH PASSING day feels like waiting for an axe to fall. At night, I watch for the telltale flickers of bonfires on the horizon. Until the third evening, when I see them. Fires speckle the nearest mountains. Hundreds of them.

Over the last two days, we've trained the villagers in basic combat and fortified the castle walls as best we can. Our defenses are mostly wooden pikes and rudimentary patches made from rubble found on the north end of the castle grounds. An old castle ruin now used in the defense of a castle that's soon to become a ruin itself.

Everyone operates under an air of desperation. It's as if we all expect to die. All of this—the extra weapons, the training, the pits laced with spikes—it will merely slow them down.

Each breath burns my chest as I heave a cart of broken timber toward the castle's crumbling gates. Around me, someone calls for rope, another shouts for more stones. The whole village moves with a frantic, shuddering pulse, as if we can somehow beat back the inevitable by sheer force of will. If Gwyllion is to crumble, we'll take down as many Fox Soldiers as we can in the process.

Tristan passes me without a word, carrying an armful of

rusted spears scavenged from the old armory. He doesn't meet my eye.

Hunter, not far behind him, hoists lumber over a shoulder. His face is grim, jaw set like stone. He's the newest member of this rebellion, but you'd never know it by the look of him. He's just as committed to resisting my father's army as the rest of us. His was a hard-won loyalty, but he still hasn't accepted that he might be—*is* —the Heir to the North.

To be honest, I find it difficult to believe too. The mythical Heir to the North is supposed to be descended from the human kings and queens who reigned long before the Dead Queens. Back when humans and fae lived side-by-side. While the Moon Goddess created the Dead Queens to restore the balance between humans and fae, the legendary Heir to the North is supposed to return the world to a time of prosperity. He's supposed to save Annwyn. Save us all.

It's a lot to believe in, especially about your childhood best friend. Hunter is the kindest, sweetest man I've ever known. He always wanted to be a great knight, but a legendary king? The man destined to change the world for the better? That's ... a lot.

I shove the cart harder, ignoring the ache in my arms. It lurches forward, wheels catching in the uneven dirt. A mud-covered boy scrambles to help me push the cart. His hands are raw and blistered, but he grins at me anyway, gap-toothed and proud to be useful.

"Thank you," I say as we park it near the front gate. My voice sounds as tired as I feel. The boy's smile beams wider, and he darts off, vanishing into the chaos.

Everywhere I look, there's motion. Women strip linen into bandages and boil water in battered kettles. Old men fashion makeshift spears from broom handles and melt scrap metal into silvery pools. Children scurry, ferrying messages and supplies, too young to understand the full horror of what's coming. Too young to understand that this might be the last battle they see.

This is all that's left of Gwyllion. We are an army of misfits.

I catch sight of Tabitha, her aged back bent over a sack filled with herbs. She tosses a few into a large mortar, then nods to Jona. He lifts the heavy pestle into the bowl and begins to crush the leaves. At their feet are small jars filled with oils and tinctures. No doubt they're preparing medicines for the wounds that we're bound to face. This isn't Llwyn. There are no healers with power here, except me. But I can't spend my time and energy healing the wounded when I need to fight. I am, after all, the Dead Queen's weapon.

My heart aches at the sight. People will die. There's no question about that.

Beyond Tabitha and Jona, a line of villagers hand stones, buckets, broken pottery, and any heavy scrap up to the battlements, to be thrown down when the soldiers arrive. My eyes drift to the distant Spires, where smoke from the Fox Army still drifts above the trees.

Someone places a gentle hand on my elbow. I turn to find Elisandra studying me.

"Here," she says, handing me a cup of water. "You look like you need it."

I take the dented tin cup in my shaking hands. "Thank you."

Elisandra surveys the scene while I drink the cool water. It tastes like the well, but Elisandra was right; I needed to drink. I feel my head grow clearer with each sip.

"We're a sorry sight, aren't we?" Elisandra says with a sigh.

"No," I say as I wipe my mouth with the back of my wrist. "The opposite, actually."

She raises an eyebrow at me. "You've seen the Fox Army, so you must know we're a pitiful sight compared to them. We've grown up with tales of their skill and strength. Their copper-plated armor and their training." She waves a hand out over the courtyard filled with villagers. "What would you call this?"

I study her for a moment, considering what to say. I settle on the truth.

"You're right that the Fox Army has greater numbers, better

weapons, and years of training. But—" I hand her the cup with a meaning-filled look. "We have the conviction of knowing that we're *right*. Every person here is willing to sacrifice everything in order to protect their home." I huff. "Sure, Fox Soldiers can follow orders. But they don't think for themselves. They don't have something to fight for beyond the will of the Fox King." At the mention of my father, my stomach wrenches with anger. So many people will die. All because of him.

Elisandra sniffs, and I realize her eyes are wet. She throws her arms around my shoulders and squeezes. I'm so shocked, it takes me several breaths to remember to wrap my arms around her too. We stay there, embracing, for a long time.

"Thank you, Sienna. For everything."

I squeeze her tighter. "I wish there was more I could do."

Slowly, Elisandra lets me go. "I know." She takes a deep breath and wipes the hair out of her face. Her cheeks are wet.

"What will you do when they arrive?"

"I wish I could fight those bastards." She points to her clouded eye. "But I'm a liability out there. I can't aim straight to save my life. So, I'll be in here." She points toward the castle. "Tending to the children. At least until the wounded arrive. Then I'll help Tabitha mend whomever we can."

"It's as noble a job as any."

She nods. "I know. I just wish I didn't feel like such a coward, staying back."

"Bravery takes many forms, Elisandra." I place my hands on her shoulders. "And you are one of the bravest people I know."

She gives me a weak smile before hugging me again. "I hope this isn't goodbye, Fox Heir. But if it is, it was an honor being your friend."

"I feel the same about you."

Elisandra straightens and tightens the apron tied behind her back. "Well, duty calls." She gives me a weak smile before she walks back toward the well, to bring water to the next weary soul.

Tristan's voice cuts through the noise. "Red, over here." It's not a request. It's barely even polite.

I hesitate, just long enough for it to show.

He hoists a splintered beam across a gap in the battlement wall. He's reinforcing it, though we both know it's a fool's hope. Still, I cross the yard toward him, heart hammering unevenly against my ribs.

Hunter is already there, driving iron spikes through the wood and into the wall's remaining mortar with quick strikes. He doesn't glance up as I approach, though I feel the tension in the air. It's thick enough to drown in.

Just look at us now, a Fox, a Wolf, and a knight. All barely on speaking terms. We've fallen a long way since our travels through Llwyn last autumn. I never thought I'd long for the days when we were running for our lives. At least as fugitives, we were a united front.

"We need more beams to brace the west wall," Tristan says, his back to me. "Someone needs to fetch more from the old stable." His words are clipped.

I nod, even though I know he can't see it. "I'll go."

For a heartbeat, neither of them acknowledges the offer. The only sounds are the steady thud of hammers on wood and the sharp hiss of whetstones as villagers sharpen blades.

Finally, Hunter says, "I'll go too."

He tosses his hammer to the ground and wipes sweat from his brow. His jaw is clenched. He doesn't want to come with me, but we both know I can't carry that timber alone.

We fall into step without speaking, weaving through the crowds toward the old stables. The ancient stone buildings are half-collapsed with gaping roofs, but the heavy beams inside are salvageable.

Inside what's left of the old stables, dust hangs in the air like mist. Hunter grabs an axe from the threshold and sets to work hacking at a beam already half-split by rot. I follow his lead, yanking the boards loose, piling anything that might work to patch the castle wall.

The silence between us stretches. I can feel it pressing down on me, the weight of everything we haven't talked about. How all along he's been the prize the Dead Queen wanted ... and I was just the trap that lured him here.

Finally, Hunter breaks. "I'm sorry."

I freeze; a board clutched in my hands. Those were not the first words I expected to hear from his lips. A lesser man would have had choicer words for me, chief among them being "liar," "backstabber," "traitor," and maybe even "whore".

His voice is tight. "None of this has been easy to wrap my head around."

"You think it's been easy for me?" I snap back before I can think better of it.

His mouth twists, as if he's biting back another sharp retort. Instead, he turns back to his work. Splinters of wood fly under each swing of his axe.

He rips a beam from where it's stood for a century, at least. The wall finally crumbles without it. Hunter tosses the beam onto the pile to be taken to the wall.

"I don't know where we go from here," he admits.

Suddenly, I feel exhausted, and not just from the manual labor. "I don't either."

We don't speak again as we pile wood into the cart. By the time we haul it back through the courtyard, dusk is curling over the hills like a slow tide. Above us, the first stars begin to pierce the darkening sky.

With the night encroaching, people are finally beginning to rest. They gather in small groups, whispering and sharing water-skins. Lanterns gutter in the wind. Their light casts long shadows, making everyone look even more exhausted.

Hunter and I drop the last load of beams near the north wall and, for a moment, we just stand there. The ache in my arms has sunk deep into my bones, matching the pounding in my head.

Across the courtyard, Tristan is speaking to the village leaders, gesturing toward the weak points in the battlements. His silhouette is sharp and black against the firelight, like he's made of shadows.

Hunter wipes the dirt from his hands and mumbles, "You should eat something." The words are gruff, but I know he's trying to be kind.

I shake my head. "Not hungry."

He hesitates, as if he might argue before his shoulders sag. He turns away without another word, disappearing into the crowd of villagers who huddle around the fires. I'm left standing alone, a splintered board still clutched in my hands.

I drop it and walk through the crowd, careful to avoid making eye contact with anyone. I don't think I have the strength to chat, knowing how many of us will be dead in the morning. I check the defenses we managed to scrape together. The gate is reinforced now, though the wood groans under its own weight. Makeshift barricades of stone and chopped trees line the walls. Every able-bodied man and woman carries a weapon, some little more than farm tools.

It's not enough. But it's all we have.

I climb a guard tower that leads up the outer wall. My boots trip on the crumbling stairs, but I don't summon my light. I'd rather not draw attention to myself. At the top, the wind hits me full in the face, cold and sharp with the scent of smoke. I lean against the guard tower, disappearing into its shadow as I watch the Spires fade into twilight.

Somewhere out there, the Fox Army moves ever north. And tomorrow they'll be here.

I grip the battlement's edge, the old stone rough under my fingers. Part of me wishes the soldiers were here already. That I could see their copper banners slicing through the mist, and feel their war drums shaking the earth. At least then the waiting would be over.

Behind me, I hear footsteps. I know it's Tristan before he speaks.

"You shouldn't be up here alone." His voice is quieter than I expected. Not the sharp-edged tone he used earlier.

I don't turn around. "I want to look my father in the eye when he finally gets here."

Tristan lets out a low grumble of a laugh. "I doubt he'll see you up here in the dark."

I shrug. "Fine. I can't stand waiting down there with everyone else."

"You've never been especially patient."

He comes to stand beside me, close enough that I can feel his heat through the chill. Close enough that it hurts. Something aches deep in my core. It feels like regret mixed with longing. We stare out over the dark mountains together.

Finally, Tristan exhales. "Red …"

I cut him off before he can finish. "It doesn't matter."

It does. But if I let him say it, then something inside me will crack open. And I can't afford that. Not now.

He turns to look at me, and I allow myself to take him in for the first time in days. His dark hair is windswept and tossed across his forehead. His black shirt is covered in dust and debris. His sleeves are rolled up, exposing strong forearms peppered with tiny scrapes and bruises from hard labor.

I can't help but remember how those arms were wrapped around me not long ago. How his large hands gripped my waist, my shoulders, my jawline. How his full mouth trailed down the length of my body. How it made me feel alive for the first time in so, so long.

Despite everything, I can't help but ache to be consumed by the fire of him again. To get lost in this Wolf's shadow. To feel safe with the man who, by all accounts, should be my enemy.

He *is* my enemy, I remind myself. That has never changed. He is still the Dead Queen's Wolf and I am still the Fox Heir, whether my father has disowned me or not.

The wind blows my hair from my messy braid. Tristan reaches out and captures a strand in his hand. He holds it between his fingers, almost reverently. When I finally meet his stormy gaze, I see fear in it. It's the same kind I feel, but it's not about the impending battle. It's the fear of having lost each other before we ever truly found a way to be together.

"You're not fighting him alone this time," Tristan says, voice low.

My throat tightens painfully. I look away, blinking hard against the sting in my eyes. "I know."

In the courtyard behind us, fires bloom. The villagers are settling in for the night, their voices mixing into the sound of the wind.

Tristan's hand brushes against mine where it rests on the stone wall. It's the barest touch, but his skin ignites mine. Neither of us pulls away. For a moment, we are simply two people standing on the edge of something too big and too terrible to name.

Tristan stares into my eyes with something like hunger, and I'm held captive by it. Here, on the precipice of death, nothing seems to matter but us. Nothing feels as real as the fire low in my belly and the desire I still feel for this Wolf, despite everything.

In one smooth movement, I grab the front of his shirt and press my lips to his. All else fades into shadow.

Tristan reacts instantly. He wraps his arms around me and turns our bodies into the guard tower. Feverishly, I remove my tunic, leaving no question about what I want from him. His hands move to untie the tight wrap around my breasts as I tear at his shirt, our arms fighting with the need for bare skin. We bump into old wooden shields that topple to the ground at our feet. I pull his dusty shirt over his head, unveiling his broad chest and shoulders in the moonlight.

I want to be angry. I *am* still angry, but that doesn't quench the ache I feel at the sight of his thick-veined biceps and rippled stomach. I trail my fingers over the scar on his chest, the injury that nearly killed him when we first met in Caerwen. His eyes travel to the thin silver scar just below my jawline. It's a reminder that Caerwen nearly killed me too. Yet somehow we both survived that place. Maybe we'll survive this one too.

He kisses me like a man about to die, like I'm his last breath of air. His teeth nip my bottom lip, and I feel it swell as I capture his mouth with mine. I have never been kissed like this. All my youthful fumblings, and even my love-drunk forest romp with Hunter couldn't compare.

Whatever this is, it isn't sweet. It isn't sentimental. It's intoxicating lust. It's primal hunger. It's two people, forbidden, and colliding on the edge of destruction.

He finally unwinds the linen wrap around my chest and the fabric drops to the ground. My skin prickles at the caress of cool night air on my bare breasts. Tristan sucks in a sharp breath at the sight of me.

I tilt my chin up, giving him a good, long look. My face flushes at the audacity of the simple motion, but I am not the woman who once hid. I'm a huntress. And I know that, with one look at my naked body, I have ensnared a Wolf.

I pull him toward me, starving. My desire for skin-on-skin contact makes me lose all self-control. I tug at his belt, feeling him strain against his leathers. When I push his pants down, freeing him, I wrap my hand around his length and give him a tight squeeze. Tristan lets out a muffled moan and leans into me.

With renewed urgency, he pulls at my leathers, tugging them over my hips and down my thighs. My skin prickles at the feel of his hands trailing down my legs. Finally freed, I kick them to the side. In moments, we're both bare, dressed only in moonlight and shadow.

Tristan lifts my hips, and I wrap my legs around his waist. His cock presses hard against my inner thigh, his need matching my own. He kisses down my neck. I arch my back, grinding against him, clenching my thighs tighter around him.

Tristan groans. "Red ..." His voice matches the ache I feel.

My nipples tighten as he takes one of my breasts and nips it with his teeth.

"I want you," I gasp. "Now."

His fingers grip my ass, hard. I'll have bruises there tomorrow. The thought sends a thrill up my spine.

He laughs low. "I need to hear you beg."

I grab his dark hair and pull it back, forcing his chin up. He closes his eyes and groans again as I lick the thick veins that trail up his neck. I lean in toward his ear.

"Listen to me, Wolf. I will never beg. Not for you, not for anyone." I can feel the Wolf's thundering heartbeat beneath the palm of my hand where I'm digging into his chest. His arousal makes my own heartbeat faster.

He groans. "Red, you can't play hard to get with me. I can feel how wet you are for me."

I refuse to let him take the upper hand in this conversation. "And another thing." I tug his hair back a little further. "I haven't forgotten your lies, Wolf." My power ignites inside of me in a dangerous flare. "You used me. Tomorrow, we might all be dead. So, tonight, I'm going to use *you*."

His eyes grow dark with a lusty sheen. "You think you can just order me around, Fox Heir?"

"Yes. I do."

In one swift motion, he pins me against the stone wall and presses the tip of his cock to my entrance, both a promise and a dare. A fluttering moan slips from my lips as a desperate need consumes me.

"You'd better commit this to memory," I say, breathless. "Because your lying tongue will never get a taste of me again."

He smirks. "We'll see about that."

Shadows erupt around us as he thrusts into me. There's no gentle easing with Tristan, no love-struck tenderness. This is pure instinct. I knew it was coming, but the sudden fullness makes me gasp. Warmth spreads throughout my body, from the tips of my fingers down to my toes. I'm glad for the cloak of his shadow, because I know I won't be able to control my power anymore. I am lit from within, my power surging through me.

I take what I desire. Every last inch of it.

The muscles in his neck strain as I work him like I own him, grinding my hips with wild abandon. His eyelids are heavy, and he's looking at me with an intensity that makes me squeeze my thighs tighter around his waist. With one hand, I brace against the stone wall for support as he plunges into me again, and again.

"Gods, Red," he gasps, his breath hot against my neck.

He groans as my body clenches around his thick cock. My hips grind against him, taking him deeper.

"Do you think you'll dream of this until your dying breath?" I nip at the shell of his ear, and goosebumps erupt all over his skin.

"Yes." He shivers.

I lift myself off his cock, pull his face toward mine, and whisper. "I want to hear *you* beg."

He laughs low, and the rumble of it sends a thrill of pleasure through me.

"For that pussy, I'd do almost anything."

He tries to pull my hips back down, but I'm not finished torturing him yet. "Beg." I nip his earlobe with my teeth.

"A Wolf is not a pet. I don't beg for treats."

"No?" I reach under my wet thigh, bending to take his tight testicles into my hand with a gentle squeeze.

The sound that comes from Tristan's chest is more animal than man. He leans his head forward, onto my breasts. When he looks up at me, his eyes aren't playful anymore. They're ravenous.

He turns away from the stone wall, taking me with him. In one swipe of his arm, he knocks debris from the tabletop as he repositions me on a rough worn table. Rolls of parchment, dried-up inkwells, and dusty gloves clatter to the ground as I lie back. My power is surging inside of me in a delicious, swirling heat.

"Fucking *please*." His words are tense, desperate.

"Oh, alright." I tighten my thighs around his hips and pull his hard cock back inside me. He fills me so much, I turn my head to muffle a scream of pleasure into my arm.

There's a wicked glint in Tristan's eyes as he grinding his hips, driving his stiff cock deeper into me with violent thrusts. Stars erupt in front of my eyes as I near that mounting, desperate release. I angle my hips to take him deeper.

We fuck without restraint, without control, without a care in the world outside of pushing each other to the limits right here on this table. Pleasure builds inside of me to a desperate peak, leaving me breathless.

I force myself to sit up on my elbows and grab his chin roughly, making him look into my eyes.

"Watch as I fuck you, Wolf," I say. "This is the only time you'll ever see it." I spread my knees, giving him a full view of where his body joins with mine as I grind into him.

He groans but obeys. "You'll fuck me again, Red. I promise you that." He rubs his hands over by belly, my breasts, and then
...

My body clenches around his. We stare at each other with a mixture of fury, desire, and desperation before my body is consumed by the delicious fullness of him inside me. My sex is throbbing and wet, dripping in a way I never knew a woman could as waves of pleasure crash over me repeatedly. I am breathless, drowning in light.

And then we do it all a second time.

I almost regret promising that he'll never make my body tremble like this again.

When we're spent, gasping on the cold, stone ground, I can't help but wonder ... How could anyone cower in the face of Death when you could shatter on the cock of a Wolf instead?

CHAPTER 34

AT DAWN, I wake to the sound of bells. A deep, persistent clanging echoes across Gwyllion.

Hazy morning light spills in through the open tower window, and spiderwebs sway in the corners above our heads. Next to me, Tristan jumps to his feet, all signs of sleep vanished. I'm momentarily distracted by his delicious nakedness before I remember what the bells mean.

They're here.

Tristan reaches out a hand to help me off the ground where we'd slept, warmed by the power purring inside of me. Of course, the first night I sleep wrapped in a man's arms, he's my enemy and we're hidden away in a ruinous watchtower. So be it. I will face the Fox Army with kiss-swollen lips and dirt smudged on my defiant face.

I tug my tunic back over my head as I run to the window beside him. Beyond the castle's defensive walls, mist clings to the ground. The field is nothing but swirling shades of gray in the early dawn.

Then, I see them. Shimmers of copper in the distance, caught in the first rays of morning sun. The Fox Army waits along the edge of the distant forest. And several yards ahead of them, sitting on the white stallion he favors, is my father. The Fox King himself.

My power flares like fury inside of me.

Part of me had expected he wouldn't come. That he'd stay behind in his gilded palace and let his army do his dirty work. That's his usual tactic, but this battle is different. This is personal.

I humiliated him by running away with Hunter and Tristan. I escaped his grasp again and again. Just like Grandmother did. And if there's one thing I know about my father, it's that he knows how to hold a grudge. And he'll want to be here to watch me suffer.

A smile grows on my face as I watch his copper banner wave in the distance. Because if Father is here, it means this is the day I finally get my revenge.

I'm going to kill that man today.

Finally clothed, Tristan and I run down the crumbling stairs and into the courtyard below. The villagers are awake. They're sharing final goodbyes and rushing to their assigned posts. I watch them one last time. A mother sobs on the shoulder of her young son, who stands with a rusted pike in his hand. The expression on his face makes my heart ache. He's trembling, but the hardness in his eyes makes it clear he's determined to fight.

At the front gates, still as stone, the Dead Queen waits. Her long veil blows in the breeze as she sits astride a black, undead stallion. It isn't Nell, and I find myself grateful for that small mercy. The horse's opalescent eyes stare blankly at the gate.

Beside the Dead Queen, Nalina waits on her brown mare. She doesn't meet our eyes as we approach.

I glance around, but I don't see Hunter. He's probably in the castle armory, giving last-second advice to the Annwyn fighters. I wonder how much Father knows about him. Does he think Hunter died in Ellyll last autumn? What would Father do if he found out Hunter is here, helping Annwyn?

A sudden thought strikes me. Is it possible Father *knows* Hunter is the Heir to the North? Is that why he kept him so close all these years? Could that be why he wanted me to marry him? If so, then Hunter needs to stay out of sight. Father can't see that he's alive. If I'm Annwyn's secret weapon, then Hunter is too, if not more so.

A groom brings out two more horses. He leads them toward us. The horses dance nervously, their eyes glancing toward the dead woman astride the dead horse. You'd think they'd be used to the Dead Queen, living in her stables, but it appears instinct is stronger than training.

I climb onto my anxious horse and gain control of the reins.

"What are you smiling about?" Nalina shoots me a disapproving glare.

"Committing patricide."

She shakes her head. "Not right now, you're not. If you kill the Fox King before the battle even begins, his army will capture you before you're able to be useful to us." She grips the hilt of her sword. "You're supposed to be our great weapon, not a reckless child."

I can't help but roll my eyes. "I'm not going to kill him *right now*." I move my head from side to side. "Eventually. Today, preferably."

Next to me, Tristan grins atop his black horse.

I can't see the queen's expression behind her veil, but I can feel her dead eyes on me. No doubt she's wondering if I'm too much of a loose cannon to parade in front of the Fox King. If I'll give away our biggest secret and show my harnessed powers too soon.

In front of us, the gate begins to rise, and a scout gallops through.

"They're waiting to parley," he says to his queen.

We'd assumed as much. Even the Fox King would prefer to have his demands heard before the battle begins.

Behind her veil, the Dead Queen nods. Nalina tightens her grip on her reins and urges her horse forward, ahead of the queen. Tristan takes the queen's right side, and I hover at her left. I've traversed this field many times over the last few months, but it has never felt so wide. My heart pounds in my chest as we get closer to my father.

Morning mist swirls around our horses' thudding hooves, scattering with each step. I feel very much like a child again, resigned to meeting the displeasure of my father. Only this time, I'm not helpless. This time, I'm not alone.

In front of us, the wall of copper-clad soldiers appears to go on forever in both directions. They've built a long, impenetrable wall of men. Their message is received: there will be no escape.

Ahead of them, my father waits, his copper crown gleaming atop his graying auburn hair. His armor, darker bronze than the others, is etched with a snarling fox with teeth sharp enough to cut.

As we near the parley point, our horses pant with excitement. Except for the undead horse, whose exposed ribs don't hold breathing lungs. Its dead flesh glistens in the morning light, punctuated by splinters of white bone.

Father hasn't changed in these past few months. I'm not sure what I'd expected from the man who always seemed so immovable, so put-together. I feel like an entirely different person now. I suppose I thought he would be too. But here on the battlefield, he's still remarkably calm. He's the perfect, poised Fox King, except for the barely restrained fury behind his eyes.

It must be difficult for him to look at us, his deceitful daughter and his loathed mother-in-law. Two women he tried to dispose of, both united against him now. It feels empowering. Despite the poor odds, I'm glad to be here fighting against him.

"Ah, at last," my father says as we approach. "I was beginning to suspect you hadn't seen us coming."

We halt our horses a few yards away from the Fox King and his guards.

His eyes narrow at the sight of me. "Daughter."

"Father." The word tastes bitter on my tongue.

"I never thought I'd see you here, in allegiance with our

enemy." His eyes flicker to Tristan. "The Wolf, however, I did expect."

Tristan gives him no reaction.

"Then you don't have much imagination," I say. "Or faith in my ability to learn the truth, despite your efforts to ..." I pause, considering how to word his years of obstruction and his attempts on my life. "Keep me in the dark."

His mouth pulls into a tight line as he redirects his attention to the queen. "It is polite to remove your veil in the presence of a king."

"The queen does not remove her veil upon request," Nalina snaps.

Father gives Nalina a patient smile. "Then how am I to know she is truly the Dead Queen and not some imposter?"

"How dare you—" Nalina begins, her hand shooting to the hilt of her sword. She stops mid-sentence when the Dead Queen raises a gloved hand.

"I will remove my veil for His Majesty." The queen's voice is as cold as a tomb.

She releases her horse's reins and slowly raises the hem of her long, black veil. She pulls it up over her face, allowing the wind to carry the fabric behind her.

The Dead Queen stares down the Fox King with pearlescent, dead eyes. The hole where her nose should be is black with rot. Her torn cheek flesh exposes broken teeth, giving her a permanent, gruesome grin. She raises her pale chin to give him a better look.

"After all, he has seen this face before," she says, exhaling her words with a death rattle. "In the borderlands, where he left me to die at the teeth of his foxhounds."

If Father is shocked at the sight of the queen's true form, he doesn't show it. His horse backs away, and his guards pale. But not Father. He merely smiles.

"The visage suits you."

The Dead Queen doesn't bite. "Why have you brought your armies into my territory?"

The Fox King takes a deep breath, tilting his face up to the rising sun. "Annwyn is such a gorgeous land. Truly. I thought I'd see it for myself."

The Dead Queen waits.

Father tuts. "You wound me. It's like we haven't known each other for decades. Like we're not *family*."

My nostrils flare. "How dare you use that word in front of us?" The words slip out of my mouth before I've had a chance to consider them.

Father's eyes slide back toward me, lazily. "You've always been a petulant child, but you're mine, nonetheless."

"Parents don't try to kill their children."

He shrugs. "Clearly, you haven't had any children."

I glare at him. "You locked me in a place of forgetting. You sicced your foxhounds on me." My eyes dart to the Dead Queen. "Just like you did to Grandmother."

He sighs. "Ah, so she told you, did she?" He shakes his head. "No matter. I'd assumed you'd find out sooner or later. I'd just hoped to acquire a new heir before that happened." He mimes a check mark in the air with one finger.

Tristan lets out a low laugh, speaking for the first time. "Odd how you use the word 'acquire' to describe a legitimate son and heir." Tristan's voice is light, almost contemplative.

Father's face grows dark. "What are you implying, Wolf?"

Tristan merely smirks.

"I grow tired of this game." Father sniffs. "Hand over your castle, return that rebellious daughter of mine, and I will let your people live."

The queen's voice is firm. "No."

Father gives her a disappointed look. "I'd thought death would make you come to your senses. It seems not."

I tighten my grip on my horse's reins. "What could you possibly want with a crumbling castle in a land that isn't yours?"

Father narrows his eyes at me. "You understand what she wants, don't you? Your precious grandmother and all the Dead Queens who came before her?"

"For you to leave Annwyn alone, I expect."

He gives me a patronizing smile. "Still so naïve. After an entire winter in Annwyn, you never thought to ask her?"

I don't respond. I can sense my father's traps a mile away.

"She wants to bring back the fae." He drops the words like a swing of a mace, but he miscalculates his aim.

"And here I thought that's what *you* desired with Annwyn." I say before I think to conceal my cards.

My father studies me for a long moment. I believe I've truly surprised him. He never suspected I'd know his true motives for marching on Annwyn.

He leans forward in his saddle. "And do you know what that means? To bring them back?"

I stare at him, refusing to play along.

He sits up straight in his saddle and tuts. "It means she wants the realm to go back two thousand years, to a time when humans were slaves. When we existed only to satiate the appetites of another species."

"It wasn't like that," Tristan says to me. "Don't listen to him. There was peace between the fae and the humans, Red. It was the humans who trapped the fae kings and queens, not the other way around. *We* were the ones who killed and tricked the fae."

My father watches me, his eyes waiting to see how I'll respond, but I keep my face a mask. He sniffs. "Well, I, for one, will not be a slave to the fae. I will not let the Dead Queen turn the hourglass back two thousand years."

"You'd rather be on the good side of the fae, you mean?"

"Better than their bad side." Father turns from me to address the silent Dead Queen. "I will have your bloody castle either way, you know. Either you hand it over without a fight, or I will take it by force."

The Dead Queen does not hesitate. "You know I won't do that."

"Do you want to watch your kingdom burn?" Father asks, his voice low. "To hear the screams of your people as they die on the end of a copper-tipped sword? I will show no mercy."

"You don't even know the word."

He grins; his mouth seemingly full of too many teeth. "Exactly."

My blood runs cold. He knew it would come to this. He's been looking forward to it.

The Fox King kicks his horse, and it steps back, turning toward his unending line of copper soldiers. He points one gauntlet-clad hand toward a distant mountain peak to the west. "You have until the sun reaches that point to change your mind."

He rides off, his copper King's Guards galloping at his flank.

Half a day. That's how much longer the people of Gwyllion have to live. By mid-afternoon, the copper axe will fall.

"You should have let me kill him," I say, staring as he retreats. Even as I say it, I know it isn't true. If the people of Gwyllion are to have any chance of survival, it falls on me, the Dead Queen, and the Wolves.

In the distance, thunderclouds gather at the edge of the Spires, rumbling and ominous.

Nalina ignores me and turns to the Dead Queen. "What are your orders?"

Through the hole in her face, I watch what remains of the queen's tongue as she speaks. "We fight."

Nalina nods once, then turns back toward the castle to ready the troops. When she's gone, I watch the Dead Queen for a long moment, wondering if she fully understands what she's asking of her people. They will be slaughtered.

If there was ever a time for honesty between us, it's now, on the edge of death. She needs to know who she's dealing with. Who I truly am. I will not slink off into the shadows to plot and kill in secret, like my father does. I will not hide in castle towers, creating undead creatures to do my bidding for me, like the Dead Queen.

I am not my father. And I am not what remains of my grand-mother. Secrets are what got us into this mess in the first place. I choose to live my life with brutal honesty.

"There's something you should know about me," I say, my voice unwavering.

"And what is that?" The Dead Queen barely even turns to acknowledge me.

"After I kill my father, I have other plans."

"I'd expect nothing less of a Fox Heir."

I turn to face her straight on. "Someday, I will end you."

Not even a hint of emotion crosses her face when she whispers her response. "I know."

At least, in that, we have an understanding.

CHAPTER 35

THE STORM CLOUDS bubble and rage along the edge of the fae-enchanted border as if they're waiting. As if they're impatient, like me. I've brooded all winter, locked up in this frozen cage. Now, I'm ready to fight. I'm ready to kill the Fox King.

Nervous villagers watch as the sun rises steadily overhead. It pauses at the zenith, as if holding its breath for the descent. When it hovers over the tip of the western peak, the tension finally breaks. Wordless, we all move toward our stations.

From atop the battlements, I can see everything. The open field stretches between Gwyllion's stone walls and the shadowed forest at the mountain's base. Somewhere beyond that veil, the Fox Army gathers.

My stomach twists with a mixture of fear and anxiety. So many people are about to die. And why has it come to this? Because my father cares nothing for human lives, that's why. He cares only about his own motives and ambitions. Now we all stand here on the edge of battle, waiting to see who will live and who will die. Cold rage laces through my veins.

A breeze blows my scarlet cloak behind me. It's foolhardy to wear bright red in battle. It makes me an easy target, but that's the point.

I *want* him to see me.

I want my father to watch as I use light power to rain death upon his men. I want him to recognize his own daughter as the one who burns brighter than he ever could. My hands grip the stone wall in anticipation.

Several yards away from me, the Dead Queen waits. She faces the horizon, veil rippling in the wind, her presence as cold and unmoving as the mountains. Below her, the castle gates stand sealed, and Gwyllion's fighters line up along the castle walls, waiting to hold back the Fox Army for as long as they can. The Dead Queen's Wolves are peppered throughout the mix, a few well-trained warriors among the farmers and townsfolk. Somewhere down there, Hunter and Tristan wait to fight alongside them.

My throat tightens. I try to spot Hunter's golden hair or Tristan's dark shadow among the others, but they're lost in the crowd. I tell myself they're strong fighters. That they'll make it through. But the words sound desperate, even inside my head. My only comfort is the fact that Hunter chose not to wear his copper armor, so he won't be mistaken on the battlefield for a Fox Soldier.

Down below, all is silent. The only sounds are the wind and my own pulse hammering in my ears. Every soul waits, staring toward the distant tree line.

And then—they come.

The first glint of copper flashes between the trees like a spark. Then another. Then hundreds. The Fox Army begins to march forward, their copper-plated armor glittering like beetle shells in the late afternoon sun. They move in perfect formation, row upon row of faceless soldiers, their swords rising and falling with every synchronized step. The earth shudders beneath them.

Below my battlement wall, white-knuckled hands clench around makeshift weapons. Old men stand shoulder-to-shoulder with boys barely strong enough to lift a blade.

And then I hear something ... Voices—no, screams—carried on the wind.

Corpse wolves.

They must be attacking the remains of the Fox Soldiers stationed in the trees at the base of the Spires. My eyes dart to the Dead Queen, but she shows no reaction. Her black veil blows behind her, blocking the late-afternoon sun where it falls toward the forest in the west. The silver moth on her chest glints in the sunlight.

On the battlefield below, the shimmering line of copper soldiers crests the final rise like a wave about to break.

And then it does.

The field explodes into motion. Shouts, war horns, and the thunder of a thousand boots echo as the Fox Army surges forward. Their front ranks break into a run, shields raised, arrows whistling ahead of them. The villagers brace behind overturned wagons and hastily built barricades. Just before the Fox Soldiers reach the Annwyn fighters, smoke and shadows swirl outward, blinding the Fox Army.

It's Tristan's power. I know it is. The shadows curl low and hungry, swallowing copper whole. Relief flickers through me, but it fades just as quickly.

The darkness doesn't hold them all back. A group of soldiers push through the wall of shadows, emerging into the sunlight, squinting. The villagers attack, using pitchforks and makeshift shields to push them back, but the soldiers recover quickly. Swords flash; screams split the air. The scent of blood rises almost instantly, sharp and metallic.

My hands tremble against the stone wall. I press them flat until my knuckles whiten.

Hold. Just hold.

If I break focus now, I'll ruin the element of surprise. My power builds and roils inside of me in anticipation. My eyes flicker to the Dead Queen a few yards away on the battlement wall. She stands emotionless as her people are slaughtered below. Her veil catches lazily in the breeze.

Below, wooden shields splinter beneath the force of bronze blades. One of Gwyllion's fighters drives her makeshift spear through the gap in a Fox Soldier's armor, only to be struck down by another before she can pull it free. An old man swings a scythe too wide and loses his grip; it clatters to the dirt. The air fills with the clash of swords and the thud of bodies hitting the ground. It's all motion and noise in a blur of mud, copper, and blood.

The Fox Soldiers advance step by step, driving the villagers backward toward the barricades. Arrows hiss through the air. A woman with a broken pitchfork throws herself at a soldier twice her size and takes him down. Black-clad Wolves dart in and out of the chaos, blades flashing like silver lightning, but even they're being pushed back.

Gwyllion villagers fight desperately. The sight claws at something inside me, hope and horror tangle together. I'm proud to be standing alongside them, and terrified that this is the end for Gwyllion.

My eyes search frantically for a copper banner or a white horse among the masses. I spot Father and curse. He's at the rear of the army now, where he can watch from afar as his Fox Soldiers murder innocent men, women, and children. Rage floods through me, burning away the fear, leaving only fire. I reach for my power, feeling it build inside me like a storm about to break.

"Wait."

It's the first word the Dead Queen has said since the battle began.

"But I see him!"

The Dead Queen doesn't look at me. "Wait."

I scramble to grab control of my power, to smother it back down. My heart pounds in my throat. What are we doing up here, standing around while our people are slaughtered?

Down below, another wave of pitch-black shadows erupts from the chaos. Screams follow. As the shadows move, several copper soldiers lie crumpled on the ground. Tristan uses his power to kill only if it's absolutely necessary for survival. Worry prickles my skin. We're losing this battle faster than I'd anticipated. I turn to the Dead Queen, ready to argue, but she's staring at the sky, her black-gloved arms outstretched.

"What are—" But I don't finish my thought.

A low hum builds from behind the castle, from the north. It grows louder as I turn to squint toward the trees, only to find them moving. A large, dark mass emerges from the old forest, twisting and turning like the wind. My breath catches in my throat. For a moment I think it's smoke. It isn't until the mass crests over the castle that I realize what it is.

Insects. Millions of them. All newly thawed from their winter graves and burrows beneath the once-frozen ground. They've been summoned somehow by the dark powers of the Dead Queen. Their wings thrum the air like billions of instrument strings. The sound is maddening, an undead symphony that claws at my skull. I flinch, covering my ears.

The swarm is so dense it blocks out the sun. The air turns thick, vibrating with the whir of wings. Dread surges through my chest. I turn to cover my head as they rush past us like a storm aimed for the battle below—from enormous cicadas and grasshoppers to the tiniest gnats and nymphs. And, of course, moths. Thousands of them.

My skin crawls as they brush against my hair and cloak, and my stomach twists in revulsion. But the Dead Queen hasn't moved. She hasn't even flinched. Her veil streams in the wind as her insects swarm past her.

I duck behind the barricade wall as they fly by, blackening the sky as thoroughly as twilight. Screams echo below. I scramble to peer through the cracks in the battlement wall. Dead insects swarm and dive at the copper-clad Fox Soldiers.

Only the Fox Soldiers.

I can feel the Dead Queen's power weaving through the

swarm, directing it like a conductor guiding an orchestra. It's terrifying. But it's also magnificent.

The people of Gwyllion watch with a mixture of horror and awe as insects crawl across copper armor, looking for gaps to sting and bite through. They fly into the soldiers' mouths as they scream, causing them to choke. They burrow into flesh, eating the Fox Soldiers from the inside out. The air hums with the furious beating of millions of wings.

Beetles attack, knocking grown men to the ground. Wasps sting any visible skin. Moths, delicate as lace, cling to eyes and mouths—blinding and suffocating. Horses scream and rear, throwing their riders. Soldiers toss their infested armor aside as they claw at their skin.

It's carnage. I should look away, but I can't. Every scream below is one less threat to Hunter. One less blade aimed at Tristan. The thought steadies me, even as my hands shake.

It is beautiful, in a terrible way.

I glance at the Dead Queen. Her veiled head is tilted slightly, as though listening to music. She looks almost serene, as if the massacre below is a hymn only she can hear. For the first time, I begin to truly understand what kind of creature she is. The Dead Queen is darkness made flesh, yes. But she is also so consumed by a single-minded purpose, there is no room for anything else: Revenge.

And I am more like her than I ever dared to admit.

Gradually, the swarm drops to the ground, one by one. Their corpses litter the battlefield. Alongside them, hundreds of dead Fox Soldiers lie. Some of their faces are so swollen from stings, they hardly look human.

Cheers rise up from below. Annwyn fighters hug each other and sob in relief, but I know it can't be over. I scan the distance for the flash of a white horse and a copper banner. I find Father, waiting.

"Why is he just standing there?" My words sound weak, as if I already know the answer.

Behind him, a second line of copper emerges from between the trees. More Fox Soldiers. At least twice as many as before. They rush toward the castle.

I turn to look at the Dead Queen. "That was just the beginning."

From behind her veil, she nods. "Now."

As if on cue, the wind picks up. It howls as the storm finally breaks through the enchantment along the mountain peaks in the distance. There isn't much time before it reaches the battlefield.

My auburn hair lifts from my shoulders, tugged by the wind, as I reach for my light. It pools like a torch in my outstretched hand. I close my eyes and feel the golden power as it surges within me. It claws to be released, fierce and wild. I don't force it. I don't make demands. I simply embrace it. My power knows my heart, and it senses my intentions.

Scattered all along the crumbling battlement wall, villagers take notice. They point to me, and beat their weapons against the stone, the rhythm rising like war drums. It creates a cacophony loud enough to rattle my bones. Loud enough for the fighters below to hear.

They were all waiting for this.

Below us, Gwyllion fighters retreat to take cover behind shields and overturned wagons. When the new wave of Fox Soldiers surge onto the battlefield, I release my light, holding nothing back. The power tears free in a searing rush, so blinding it momentarily burns my vision. The brilliant glow reflects off their copper and bronze armor, amplifying and redirecting the light back into their eyes a hundredfold.

Blinded, the Fox Soldiers fumble. Their shouts turn to screams as they clutch at their eyes. They stumble into one another, clatter to the ground, and trample each other in suffocating piles. The Gwyllion fighters hold steady in shaded huddles as I send every ounce of light into the faces of my father's men.

Then, our own second line of defense bursts through the castle gates. Their eyes are blackened with soot to absorb the light, and they're wearing a variety of wide-brimmed hats and veils to shade their faces. They sprint across the battlefield to impale the blinded Fox Soldiers on farm tools and pikes. Blood spatters and the air fills with an iron tang so strong, I can smell it high above on the battlement walls.

Beyond the blinding light, I sense my father's eyes on me. It's why I wore the red cloak, after all. So he could watch as I killed his men.

My blood sings with the thrill of power. The Fox King tried to extinguish my gift. He belittled me, berated me, tried to replace me, and then locked me up in a dungeon to die.

But I survived. And now, I'm the reason his men are dying. As my light power finally fades from my outstretched hands, I look beyond the battlefield. Even from a mile away, I can sense my father's fury. The Dead Queen was right. He *knew* I was stronger than he was. Even with all his armies and all of his rage, his power can't compare to mine. That's why he never fights on the battlefield. That's why he never deigned to heal soldiers in the borderlands. It's not just that he doesn't want to ... It's that he *can't*.

The realization makes me laugh. He may be the mighty Fox King, but he is weak. He's just a little man who hides behind a big army and a family name.

The wind tears at my cloak as thunder crackles toward us. The encroaching clouds block the sunlight as they move across the sky. But there's another boom, and it's not thunder. The wall lurches beneath me. The ground trembles, and the world tilts.

Too late, I realize I'm falling.

Chapter 36

The breath punches out of my lungs as I slam into the earth. Pain explodes along my ribs as I cough and try to catch my breath. Each gasp shoots searing pain through my chest. Grimacing, I sit up and blink through the dust swirling around me as I try to get my bearings.

The battlement crumbled beneath me. I should be dead, crushed beneath the stones, but I'm not. I'm bruised, and I'm fairly certain I cracked at least a few ribs in the fall, but I'm alive.

I'm also furious with myself.

In my hubris, I lost focus. I was more concerned with showing off for my father than with paying attention to my surroundings. There must have been a distant trebuchet pointed in my direction. My light and red cloak made me an easy target atop the battlements.

I was foolish and prideful, just like he always said I am.

I grit my teeth against the pain as I scramble down from the rubble. My red cloak snags on a stone, and I rip it off my shoulders. I leave it in the mud, stepping on it with my boot for good measure. I never want to see it again. Shame burns through my veins. I squint up through the dust, toward what remains of the battlement wall, but I don't see the Dead Queen anywhere.

The air is thick with dust, making me cough. My lungs seize painfully with each breath. I stagger, ears ringing, and my vision swims. The ground feels like it's tilted and shifting beneath my feet.

A Fox Soldier charges from the right, his axe held high. I dive, rolling through the blood-tinged mud. The impact jars every bone in my body. I land beside a corpse half-buried under rubble, and my fingers brush against the hilt of their sword. When I grab it, it's slick with mud and dust.

A shout tears the air behind me. I spin, barely raising the blade in time to block. The clang reverberates through my arms, nearly knocking the weapon from my grasp, but I stand my ground. I send a whispered thanks to Tristan for the past few months of training. Without it, I'd surely be dead. I try to reach for my light power to blind the Fox Soldier.

Nothing happens.

Horror fills my chest.

The soldier presses forward, his breath rank and hot against my face. I twist, using the moves Tristan drilled into me: pivot, slice low, step back. The edge of my stolen sword bites into the soldier's thigh where his flesh is exposed between plates of armor. He yells and falls to one knee.

I don't wait. I drive the blade upward into the gap between his armor and his helmet until his voice cuts short. Crimson blood streams over his copper chestplate. When I draw my sword back out of him, his body falls to the ground with a clatter.

My head is pounding, and my light power is flickering inside me like a dying flame. All around me, the world is chaos: soldiers shout, arrows shriek past, feet stomp through the mud-soaked earth. Fear claws at my throat, threatening to unravel me.

I have to stay calm. I grit my teeth to keep focused. My hands grip the hilt of my stolen sword tighter, even as a wave of dizziness makes nausea rise in my stomach.

Another Fox Soldier rushes toward me. I raise my blade, slower this time. His strike glances off my sword, knocking me back into the rubble. Pain blooms white-hot in my back. I heave my sword upward, catching him across the chest. He stumbles, armor screeching. Once again, I reach inside my core, calling for my power.

I'm met with hollowness instead.

"No, no, no, no, no," I say to myself as I scramble off the rubble.

The Fox Soldier raises his blade to swing again but stops short. Behind him, there's a flash of movement, followed by a sharp, wet sound. A pike shoots through the front of his chest. He blinks down at it, surprised, then collapses. So much for Father insisting Fox Soldiers don't need stronger armor than bronze and copper.

A young Gwyllion fighter stands behind the collapsed soldier. I recognize him instantly. He's the boy I saw with his mother before the battle began. He looks almost as stunned as the Fox Soldier did. His face is smeared with dirt and blood, but he's alive.

"Thank you," I say, my voice raspy. He nods, then turns and rejoins the fight, his boots sliding in the slick mud.

The first heavy raindrops fall, and thunder rumbles over the clang of battle. My arms are shaking, and I'm dizzy. I duck out of the path of a silver greatsword, wielded by a copper-clad giant. Somewhere in the distance, the roar of corpse beasts echoes along the outskirts of the fight.

I blink against the falling rain and try to focus. My brain is a jumbled mess, and blood trickles from my temple. Frustration builds in my chest. I can't fall apart like this! Even as I think it, I know it's not weakness that's making my brain muddled and my limbs weak.

It's burnout.

And most likely a concussion as well. Nausea swells within me again as rain streams over my face. Between my shaking arms and head injury, I can barely hold the sword. What was the point of those months of training if I can't even focus enough to use it?

Even as the thought crosses my mind, I know I'd be dead

already without Tristan's training. Still, I drop the sword and draw Grandmother's moth knife out from my boot. Thank the old gods, I haven't lost it in the chaos. The bronze hilt kisses my palm as I grip it. It's a poor weapon against an army, but I know how to use it on instinct. And right now, with my head a jumbled mess, I need to rely on a weapon that I can wield in my sleep.

The rainfall is steady now, dripping into my eyes, turning the ground into trenches of mud.

Another Fox Soldier spots me and lifts his sword to strike, but I twist away just in time. I try to call my power, but it's useless. Panic shoots through me like lightning.

The soldier turns toward me again. I rush at him, tackling him to the ground before he can strike. We land with a clatter that reignites the pain in my skull. Before the soldier can react, I slice my blade through his neck. I don't wait for the telltale gurgle of blood pooling in his mouth before I'm up again.

All around me, Annwyn men and women are dying. We can't stop the flood of Fox Soldiers, and even *I* can see our numbers are dwindling. We won't win this battle. The pain of crushing defeat and grief threatens to overwhelm me.

"Sienna!"

I whirl around, searching through the chaos. My eyes have trouble focusing. Finally, I see him. Relief washes over me with such intensity that a sob bursts from my chest.

"Sienna!" Hunter is sprinting toward me. He's soaked, and not just from rainwater. His exposed arms are coated in mud and blood. It streaks down in dark rivulets, dripping from his elbows as he swings his sword into the side of another Fox Soldier. It hardly slows him down as he runs.

When we collide in a breathless whirl, he wraps his arms around my shoulders. In the midst of death, all the anger and betrayal between us extinguishes. Nothing else matters now beyond this: Hunter is here, alive. The heat of him, slick with rain and blood, cuts through the surrounding carnage. Tears stream down my face as he squeezes me tighter.

"Thank the old gods," Hunter gasps into my rain-soaked hair. Then he steps away, grabbing my hand. "We have to get you out of here." He pulls me forward, and we weave through the piles of dead and dying.

Three Fox Soldiers spot us and charge in our direction. But instead of bracing himself to fight, Hunter surprises me by pivoting.

"What are you—"

He grabs me around the waist and tucks his face toward mine. "Trust me."

Suddenly, the soldiers stop advancing. Their eyes grow wide.

"What the ...?"

"They were just here!"

"Impossible!"

They whirl around, only feet from us, eyes wide and searching. As if they can't see us.

I stare up at Hunter, wide-eyed. "How ...?"

He presses a finger up to his lips.

I look back at the soldiers, my heart hammering in my chest. A swirling mist, thin as a spiderweb, dances along the edges of my vision. It's so negligible, it could easily be missed. For a moment, I think the head injury is messing with my vision. But no. Light and shadow bend around us in a shimmering ripple as the world distorts, hiding us in plain sight.

The soldiers locate a new target and run in the opposite direction.

Without a word of explanation, Hunter grabs my hand, and we run through the mud-slick battlefield, light and shadow swirling around us. We are little more than ghosts.

So, he *knew*. He denies being the Heir to the North, but he knew he was different. That's how we survived all those years, growing up in a hostile palace. The invisible children. He used his power to hide us.

How had I never realized?

An Annwyn fighter crashes into us, and Hunter drops my hand, dispelling the illusion.

"S-so sorry!" The fighter says, his eyes wide with panic. "I didn't see you! I swear." He scurries away, tripping over fallen bodies as he goes.

Hunter reaches for me again, but a surge of Fox Soldiers pushes more Annwyn fighters back. The press of bodies is suffocating. They flood between us, separating us farther. I can't reach him.

Then I hear another voice, sharp and clear: "Sienna!"

I whirl around to see a woman riding toward us on a dark horse. Her face is streaked with blood. Her long blond braid is soaked with rainwater.

Nalina.

In one swing of her silver sword, she decapitates a Fox Soldier in her path. His armor-clad body thumps to the ground. Blood spatters the horse's flank, washed instantly into red streams by the rain.

When she reaches me, her horse digs his heels into the mud, spraying muck in every direction. Without a moment's hesitation, Nalina reaches down and grabs my arm.

"Where's Tristan?" I yell toward her, terror seizing my chest.

Her only response is a quick shake of her head.

My eyes grow wide. "Tell me he's alive!" I don't miss the edge of panic in my voice.

Her mouth is a thin line. "I haven't seen him."

"Nalina!" Hunter yells above the crowd. "Take her!" He's fighting his way through the masses, swinging his father's sword at the soldiers.

"Hunter, no!" I gasp, twisting in her firm grasp.

With one final push, Hunter finally reaches us. He grabs the reins of Nalina's horse. "Bring her to the castle." His voice is urgent yet calm, like a well-trained commander.

"Not without you!"

Nalina's grip tightens on my arm. I dig my fingernails into her hand. She grimaces through her split lip, but she refuses to let go.

Hunter finally reaches me. He grabs my shoulders, his deep brown eyes staring intently into mine. "I'll find you."

In one swift movement, Hunter grabs me around the waist and kisses me so deeply, the world vanishes. The blood, the screams, even the rain dripping down my face fades away. I lose my breath, my thoughts, everything but him. His mouth is fierce and desperate, tasting of blood and sweat. His kiss feels achingly like a farewell. Like he knows this might be the last time. My heart breaks even as it soars.

He pulls away, his eyes staring fiercely into mine. "I promise."

"You'll die." An unexpected sob chokes my voice. I can hardly get the words out.

His gaze burns, unflinching. "I swore to protect you." His voice lowers, just for me. "But you know it's more than an oath, Sienna. It's you. It's always been you."

A sob builds in my chest. I believe him wholeheartedly. I trust Hunter completely. He will come back to me and we will find our way through this. All of it.

Nalina jumps down from her stallion and grabs my upper arm in an iron grip. Her voice is terse. "We're leaving. *Now.*"

She lets me go and draws her sword so suddenly, it makes me flinch. She cuts down two encroaching Fox Soldiers in barely more than a breath. Their bodies collapse in the mud at our feet, but all I can feel is the weight of Hunter's hand still pressed to my waist.

"I can still fight," I lie. My head is pounding, vision swirling. I can barely focus on Hunter's face in front of mine. The world is a blur of rain and blood, but he is painfully clear.

Hunter steps backward, eyes on me one last time. "You *will* fight. Just not here." He nods to Nalina.

She doesn't waste more time. She grabs my waist and practically throws me up onto her horse, then she leaps onto the saddle behind me. She clicks her tongue once, sharply, and the horse bolts, hooves cutting through muddy puddles swirling with blood, insects, and rainwater.

But I look back and see Hunter standing alone. It's a familiar sight, him on a battlefield. Me leaving him.

Only this time it's different. This time, he begged me to leave him. The irony of it is enough to break my heart in two.

Nalina grabs my head and pushes it down just as a spear whistles past, close enough to split the air beside my ear.

"Eyes open, Fox," she growls, kicking her heels into the horse's flank for more speed.

We charge through the battle and into the castle's splintered gates, narrowly avoiding colliding with Fox Soldiers and Gwyllion fighters alike. The horse skids through the castle grounds, leaping over fallen debris.

Nalina draws the horse to a stop at a wooden door along the castle's interior wall. She jumps down from the saddle, not even bothering to tie the stallion anywhere before she pulls me roughly from the horse.

"Where are we going?" I ask. My head aches so much, I fight the urge to vomit.

She draws out her silver sword. I turn to fight whoever's behind us, but there's no one there. When I turn back toward her, her eyes are on me, hard and dark. She spits a mouthful of blood onto the cobblestones and tightens her grip on her sword's hilt.

My stomach drops. Something is very, very wrong here. I reach down to grab my silver knife from my boot, but I can't see straight, and it clatters to the ground. My head is swimming. Nalina stares at me wordlessly.

My heart pounds through my skull. I have to get away from here. I look between her and an alleyway. I make a run for it.

I don't get far.

Nalina kicks her legs under my feet, knocking me to the ground. My knees crack painfully against the stone. This time, I do vomit. When it's over, I roll onto my back, gasping. She steps over me, looking down at me from above. Through the encroaching darkness at the edge of my vision, I see her face as rain drips from her hair, her chin, her nose.

This can't be happening. They need me. Tristan. Hunter. The people of Annwyn. I refuse to die like this. Not before I've killed the Fox King.

"Why?" I ask.

Without a word, she lifts the hilt of her sword and brings it down.

The world goes black.

CHAPTER 37

THE FIRST THING I feel is the cold.

It's not the crisp, biting cold of the courtyard. This air is musty, damp.

Stone bites into my spine, and I realize I'm lying on the ground. I groan. My head is throbbing. I lift my hands to cradle my skull, but find my wrists are bound in front of me with rusty irons. I'm shackled.

"Damn it, Nalina." My voice sounds distant in my ears.

Boots scrape across the ground ahead of me. I squint through the dim light. Chains pull against my shackled wrists, pulling my arms above my head, dragging me across the filthy ground. My shoulders pull painfully in their sockets as I'm dragged slowly down a long, dark hallway. I tug the chains and sit up. Someone releases the tension on the shackles, allowing me to scramble to my feet.

I blink hard, struggling to force my vision into focus. Nearby, water drips and rats scurry, their tiny claws scraping against the floor. The world swims around me: a rough stone floor slick with moisture, crumbling walls, a ceiling so low it nearly brushes my captor's head as she watches me.

Nalina.

The memory slams into me like a hammer. She turned on me. How long have I been unconscious? The sounds of battle are gone. Or maybe they're simply too far away to hear from wherever we are.

A few yards away, Nalina holds the other end of the chain attached to my shackles. My silver moth knife glints from her belt, and she's watching me, her face grim.

My mind reels. None of this makes sense. Is she working with my father? No, she would never align herself with the Fox Army. She'd rather die.

Dampness prickles my skin. The air down here has a wet, cloying stink of mold, rusted metal, and decay.

My heart lurches as panic claws up my throat. I *know* this smell. I know this place.

I jerk against the shackles and iron bites into my wrists. My light power flares instinctively, then sputters and dies, like a candle snuffed out.

Nalina gives me a patronizing glare. "So much for your mighty light power."

I say nothing as I try to access my light again and again. There are embers there; I can feel them burning in my core. I haven't reached complete burnout yet. So why can't I even make a simple orb of light?

Nalina crosses her arms in front of her chest impatiently. "Your shackles are made of iron." When I don't give her the reaction she's expecting, she straightens, studying me. "You don't know, do you?"

I just glare at her.

She lets out a bark of laughter. "How can that be? A Fox Heir with fae magic in her bloodline. And she doesn't know about iron?"

The realization crashes down. In all the old stories, the fae were weakened by only one thing: iron.

"But, those were fairy tales ..."

Nalina leans in close. "All fairy tales start from truth. That's what makes them so powerful."

"But there's iron everywhere." I stammer. "In wall sconces, even the door hinges! I've used my power around iron before."

Nalina tsks, as if I'm a naughty child. "Iron has to touch your skin to paralyze the power in your blood. Otherwise ..." She shrugs. "It's just a useful decoration."

My mind is whirling. My eyes dart to the skeletons and decaying corpses strung up along the hallway. They're all bound with iron shackles. Skeletal hands clutch at the air, their faces frozen in endless, silent screams.

"Why do you think all of our weapons are silver? Hm?" She raises an eyebrow. "So anyone can wield them, powerful noble or not." She taps the gleaming blade of her sword. "And what of your great Fox Army with its showy bronze and copper armor?"

Horror dawns on me. "There's no iron in copper ..."

Nalina nods slowly. "None. Your Fox ancestors figured that out, at least." She pauses, considering. "Though it's strange that your Fox King father never told you."

"No," I say as a hollow pit deepens in my stomach. "It isn't." The truth leaves a bitter taste in my mouth. Father didn't want me to know. My ignorance was one more advantage he held over me.

I look down at the iron shackles clasped around my wrists. My skin is rubbed red and raw against the rust. A memory rises to the surface of my mind: Tristan, chained in my father's kennels in Caerwen.

A humorless laugh bubbles out of me. He couldn't have used his power to hurt me, locked up in those irons. His power comes from the remains of fae blood in his veins too. When he was imprisoned in Caerwen, I believed he was a great, terrifying Wolf. But he couldn't have killed me with his shadow power, even if he wanted to. He was nothing but a man in chains.

I may not have known about iron, but Nalina did. She knew iron weakened me, and she still shackled me.

"Why ...?" I rasp, my throat dry. "People are dying out there! What are we doing down here?"

She doesn't answer. Her jaw tightens, and she turns, pulling the chains, and me, behind her. I pull and fight, but it's no use. Nalina is stronger than I am by far. Without my powers or my knife, I'm useless.

"They need you on the battlefield!"

Need *us*, I want to say, but I know I'm next to useless in my current state. I'm nothing but a liability. But Nalina could still fight. Why is she wasting precious time chaining me up and dragging me through the castle dungeon?

The corridor narrows, the stones growing slicker, blacker. More bodies line the passageways. All dead women. Some corpses are so old, they've crumbled into little more than mummified rags and bone.

I gag, bile rising in my throat, but Nalina doesn't slow. She pulls me past them as if they're nothing more than furniture.

A sound builds ahead, a faint scuffling. We pass through a broken archway that's coated in a layer of black soot as if it's been licked by flames. And there, in the farthest corner, I see it.

Moribund's lair.

A putrid scent wafts from the corner where his nest of burned human hair sits. It's far less impressive than it was the last time I saw it, with its long, blond strands escaping the towering mound of golden hair. Now, it's barely more than a pile of ash. Blackened bones poke out of the nest like flowers sticking out of a fresh grave. And at the center of it, half-shrouded in shadows, something shifts.

The revolting fae rises from his bed of ash, unfolding like a spider emerging from its web. He moves quickly and jerkily, all elbows and angles, scuttling over what's left of the burned hair with bare feet. His parchment-thin skin is covered in soot. As he grows closer, I see his flesh is bubbled and blackened in patches, with the unmistakable mark of burns.

When he grins at us, I grimace. My stomach lurches as revulsion mixes with fear.

"Well, well, well." His voice is childlike with interest. "Look what treasure you've brought me this time. Is that my little fox-haired bug?"

Nalina steps behind me, then shoves me forward. I stumble to my bruised knees, and the iron cuffs scrape hard against my wrists. Panic floods my chest. I need to get out of here. My eyes scan the walls, searching for something I might have missed before, some way out. A weapon, a door, anything. There's nothing down here but soot-painted walls, and what's left of Moribund's char-blackened nest.

I need to fight. But without my power or my knife, I'm nothing more than dead weight. And Nalina knows it.

"You said you'd help us," Nalina's voice is taut. "That you'd help save Gwyllion if I brought her to you."

Moribund's smile widens. His overlong fingers steeple together like a pastor deep in thought. "And so I did."

He crawls closer to us, a new tattered loincloth flapping with each movement. As he circles nearer, I can smell him. The stink of his breath is thick as rot.

"Such lovely copper hair," he purrs. "Such sweet blood singing beneath her bug skin."

I jerk away instinctively, but there's nowhere to go. His hand brushes a lock of my auburn hair. I flinch, but Nalina doesn't stop him.

"You can't do this," I hiss at her, fighting to keep my voice steady. "We're in the middle of a battle! We're fighting for the same people!"

Nalina's mouth twists, and something like guilt flickers across her face, but it doesn't stop her. "That's exactly why I'm doing this. My loyalty is to my people. To Annwyn. And, unfortunately, we need him."

"You can't be serious," I scoff.

Nalina whirls on me, her face inches from Moribund's. His wide, black eyes flick to her, and his grin widens.

"Listen to me, Fox Heir," she hisses. "Your life means nothing to me. Your family has slaughtered mine for centuries! As far as I'm concerned, your only worth is whatever I can haggle to save Gwyllion."

Moribund chuckles. It's a low, sick sound that seems to echo from everywhere. He runs his fingers through my hair again, slower this time.

My stomach sinks. It's like Tristan said, Nalina's methods may be unconventional, but she believes in them wholeheartedly. I'm nothing more than a bargaining chip to her. I clench my teeth so hard my jaw aches. My wrists bleed where the shackles bite deeper with every movement. I fix Nalina with a look of pure, seething hatred.

"You think this will save them?" I whisper. "You think *he* will save them?"

For just a moment, she hesitates. She looks toward the nest, but her eyes slide right over Moribund, who's only inches away from her face.

Suddenly, my fury clears enough for me to remember one important detail: Nalina doesn't have fae blood. She can't see Moribund. Only I can.

She steps back, then turns away from me. "I've come to make good on our deal." She calls out in the direction of the burned nest, where she assumes he's sitting. She unsheathes her sword and holds it flat against her palms in a peaceful gesture. "I'm not here to harm you."

At my left shoulder, Moribund's wide black eyes watch her with interest. He laughs lightly, and she turns to face the direction of his voice. She lifts her chin in defiance.

"An honest human?" Moribund asks. "Oh, how unexpected." He releases my hair reluctantly and crawls up into his flattened ash nest. The burned hair crunches under his weight as he wiggles down into it, like a child cuddling into his bedcovers. He narrows his eyes to slits, and his voice grows dark and menacing. "I needs to rebuild my nest since that sneaky fox-bug ruined everything."

Nalina pivots to face the sound of his voice again.

The fae recovers his composure in an instant and frowns dramatically. "But I already have a deal with your Dead Queen. Does she know you're here?" He asks his question with such delight, he must already know the answer.

"It's time to trade," Nalina presses on. "The Fox Heir for your help."

Moribund chuckles. "The humans want fae help now, do they? The last deal I made with your queen was to keep me away, to keep me out of sight." His voice drops low, haunting as a nightmare. "Your girlie bugs with the clean hair, for my castle."

"You can keep that deal," Nalina says. "In addition to this new one."

"No!" I struggle against my chains, but Nalina doesn't even look at me as I pull. "The Dead Queen would not approve of this, Nalina. You're her Wolf. You serve her! She'll see this as betrayal."

Finally, Nalina snaps her head toward me. "I cannot serve Annwyn if everyone who lives here is dead!"

Moribund cackles like he's enjoying this game. His black eyes move over me, inch-by-inch. My skin crawls.

"I do wants her hair." His voice quivers. This fae is positively unhinged.

If Nalina is as disturbed as I am, she doesn't show it. "I know," she says. "You can have it."

He looks up at her hungrily.

"For a price." Nalina's voice is sharp as a blade.

Moribund begins to salivate.

"I grew up hearing tales of your power," she says. "Of the terror you used to wreak over this land."

He smiles and nods, pleased. It seems the old stories were true —the fae adore flattery. "Yes, I am quite powerful."

"Could you kill an entire army?"

"Easily." He bats his eyes. "You are all but bugs for the squishing."

Nalina's face hardens. "Then help us save your castle. Protect Gwyllion and the people who live here. Kill our attackers, and you can have the Fox's hair."

The fae laughs gleefully. He crawls back out of his revolting nest on all fours and scurries back up to me. Slowly, he stands. A tremor runs across his thin skin in anticipation of having me. He presses the tip of one black fingernail to my navel. Inch by inch, he trails it up my body, between my breasts, and pauses at the hollow of my clavicle.

He leans in toward my ear, and the smell of rot makes me gag. I swallow hard.

"That is where I will slice you, I thinks." He sniffs the hair on my neck with a long, languid breath. "I can't wait to see if fox bugs look different on the inside. If that sweet blood tastes finer than the others." He lets out a low, hungry rumble from deep in his chest. Beneath his tattered loincloth, something moves.

"But first, I must taste your succulent parts." Drool drips down his chin as his eyes roam my body.

I think I'm going to be sick.

"Do we have a deal?" Nalina shifts her sword to one hand and holds the other out toward him to shake.

"No! You don't!" I shove Nalina with all my strength. She barely budges. "Nalina, listen to me. You don't know what you're doing." My voice is desperate, and I hate it. But right now, I have nothing to bargain with, no way out of this madness. I turn to Moribund, tugging on my chains with all my strength. "I scorched your lair, you filthy creature! Just think of what I'll do next if you don't let me go."

"She's in irons." Nalina says evenly. She tugs my chains so hard, I nearly fall to the ground. "She has no power."

Moribund considers us for a moment, his lips pursed in a

thoughtful expression. His eyes keep drifting over my long auburn hair. In one swift movement, the fae leans forward, grabs Nalina's wrist, and licks the length of her palm. Nalina's eyes widen with shock at the touch of the fae's tongue. For a brief moment, I see revulsion behind her eyes, but she recovers quickly.

Moribund releases her. "Now go, so I can play with my little fox bug first." He steps forward, pressing his body up against me. I can't breathe from the smell of him. His skin tremors along mine like a thousand eager fingertips. His hard length presses into my thigh, pulsing.

Nalina passes my chains to the fae.

"You can't do this!" My voice breaks and I scream at Nalina, all of my anger coming out in a snarl. I tug and pull at the chains with all my strength, but the ancient fae is far stronger than he looks. He grins at me with hunger in his black eyes.

Nalina turns to leave, then pauses. "One last thing."

Moribund steps back to glare at her. A low growl rumbles from his throat, all childishness gone from his voice. "I will help your silly castle when I'm through."

Nalina nods but walks back toward me. In one swift movement, she grabs my long hair in one hand and slices her sword clean through it. I'm so shocked all I can do is stare at the long auburn strands hanging from her fist.

Moribund screams. It's so piercing, I flinch.

Nalina grins and tosses the hair at his feet.

Moribund scrambles to the ground, trying to pick up each strand. He holds my cut hair to his chest. "You defiled my gift!"

Nalina shakes her head. "Not a gift. A trade. A deal."

Moribund's nostrils flare, and his black eyes pin her with a murderous glare.

It's Nalina's turn to grin. "I said you could have her hair. I never said you could take her body or her life."

Moribund growls. His lips flare over sharp teeth, like a rabid dog ready to bite. "You tricked me."

"A deal is a deal."

"How dare you try to fool the great Moribund!" Spittle flies from his mouth in his rage.

Nalina simply shrugs. "If you allowed your lust to cloud your judgment, that's no concern of mine."

Moribund glares between Nalina and me, back and forth, before shoving strands of my long auburn hair beneath his loin-cloth. "Filthy, stinking bugs ..."

Then, in a blink, he disappears.

Nalina and I stand in the darkness for several long moments. My heart is hammering, and my knees are weak.

"Is he gone?" she whispers. It's the first indication I've seen that she was really, truly afraid.

"Yes." My voice cracks on the word.

She nods once, then digs into the ankle of her boot. She withdraws an iron key and holds it out to me. Her hand is trembling.

I hold up my shackles. Nalina twists the key in the lock, and the iron clatters to the ground at our feet. We both stand there for a long, tense moment. As if remembering something, she takes my silver moth knife out from her belt and hands it to me.

"I imagine you want to kill me about now."

I nod and take the knife, gripping it so tightly my knuckles feel ready to split open. "I understand why you did it."

Something like relief transforms her face. Her shoulders relax, and what looks like genuine grief passes through her eyes. "He's the last card we have to play."

"I hope he's worth the price. He'll make you pay for tricking him."

She nods. "Me too, Fox Heir ... me too." She looks older than she did a day ago, as if this battle has taken more from her than just her strength. This couldn't have been easy for her, bringing me down into this dungeon. This is where she brought her own sister to die at the hands of that monster.

For the first time, I pity Nalina.

Nalina lets out a shaky breath. "I'm sorry I had to cut your hair."

I shiver at the memory of Moribund's long, bony fingers running through it. "I'm not." I sniff. "I'd have cut it off myself after that."

She nods, understanding me exactly.

CHAPTER 38

THE SCREAMS REACH us as we climb the spiral steps to the tower of moths. The door at the top is ajar, and when Nalina pushes it open, the sounds from the battlefield grow louder. They reverberate off the stone walls, echoing and multiplying. I glance to the rafters, but they're bare now, the moths dead and crunched underfoot on the battlefield below.

The Dead Queen stands, looking out an open window. Beyond her, the rain has stopped and the storm clouds have dissipated. Night has fallen, and she's haloed in the light of a full moon. Her face is barely visible through the sheer veil. Nalina and I stand beside her to view the carnage below.

The moonlight illuminates the chaos on the battlefield. Moribund multiplies before our eyes. His form doubles and triples until there are hundreds of him in the muddy field—all bent-backed, sallow-skinned creatures with long nails and wide eyes. He keeps true to his word. Each of his illusions tears Fox Soldiers limb from limb, but they only attack those in copper armor. The remaining Gwyllion fighters watch in horror.

As we watch, my heart stills in my chest. Tristan and Hunter might still be alive down there. I send silent thanks to the old gods that Hunter didn't wear his copper armor for this battle. If he had, he'd be dead.

I grip the stone edge of the tower window, my breath lodged somewhere behind my aching ribs. Below, the remaining Fox Soldiers try to run. Moribund's illusions attack, quick and unrelenting. One lunges and a man loses his face. Another rips open a ribcage with his bare hands. Another sinks its claws into a soldier's cheeks before he can even scream. The man's jawbone shatters, teeth scattering like lost coins in the mud.

I want to look away, but my body refuses to move. Of course, I knew the fae were powerful, but I had no experience with the sheer magnitude of that power. How easily a creature like Moribund carries that weight, like it's nothing at all to kill a man, or a hundred. It's sickening yet wondrous to behold. Now I can see why ancient humans both feared and worshiped the fae. And why they snuffed them out.

Further out on the battlefield, another Moribund leaps, landing on top of a man twice his size. The soldier's armor splits apart beneath black-nailed fingers. Moribund reaches up into the gaping hole and pulls. Something red and glistening spills out, trailing strings of sinew. Moribund doesn't even look at it, just tosses it aside and moves on to the next terrified soldier.

Somewhere in the chaos, Tristan might be bleeding. Hunter might already be dead. For the first time in my life, I close my eyes and send a silent prayer to the old gods. I beg for Hunter and Tristan to survive this night.

Beside me, the queen watches with interest.

"You knew, didn't you?" I say, turning toward her. "You knew Nalina brought be down to Moribund. You knew about her deal."

"Of course." She says this as if it's nothing. Like giving a once-beloved granddaughter to a monstrous fae is just the sort of thing a queen does on a daily basis. I'd be furious if I weren't so damn tired. If I weren't so relieved to see the tides turn on the battlefield.

"I try not to make deals with the fae unless absolutely necessary." The Dead Queen says as she watches Moribund devour men below. "It's not honorable to trick allies, even begrudging ones. He doesn't care if humans live or die, but now that we've used him, he will hold that grudge for a long time. Longer than any of us will exist."

"Will it come back to haunt you?" I ask.

"Most certainly."

We watch the horror for a long moment before the Dead Queen sighs. "He's always been a gifted illusionist." Her voice is reflective. "It's a shame he's only motivated by lust. Otherwise, he'd be a magnificent fighter in the borderlands."

Nalina scoffs. "He'd never fight for Annwyn. He only cares about his own hide. That and his precious blondes."

The queen shrugs. "What are human concerns to a creature as ancient as Moribund?"

Nalina scoffs. "He's a selfish, disgusting beast, and we never should've made a deal with him for this wretched castle. It's filled with nothing but misery and ghosts."

The Dead Queen doesn't respond. She stands, her eyes closed peacefully, as if relishing the sound of her enemy's violent demise. Down below, I don't miss the fact that several Moribunds pocket locks of blonde hair from fallen soldiers. I cringe, and my hand shoots up toward my short hair on instinct.

"Will he go back to the dungeons?" My voice is less steady than I'd like it to be.

"Oh, he'll crawl back into the dark." Nalina scoffs. "He likes it down there, as much as he hems and haws about needing sacrifices to keep him away."

"He's not a magnanimous creature," the queen says. "He will kill us all if we don't keep up our end of the deal."

"Then why haven't you killed him first?" I turn to her, wide-eyed with disbelief. "Why sacrifice your own people when you have the power to kill him with a glance?"

The Dead Queen stills. "For one, without him, this castle

would crumble around our ears. It's his magic that keeps it standing."

"There must be another way."

"There isn't." She turns to look at me. "Moribund has lived on this land longer than memory itself. We are not worthy of banishing him from it." She straightens her spine. It crackles like stones underfoot. "And besides that, we do *not* kill the fae. We live in harmony with them."

"Harmony?!" I blanch, astounded. I point out toward the blood-soaked, moonlit battle below. "You call that 'harmony'?"

The Dead Queen's voice is sharp. "Don't pretend to understand Annwyn's ways simply because you've lived here for a season."

I glower at her. "So, you'll keep feeding him innocent women? After all they've done to fight for Gwyllion? You'd still sacrifice them to that monster?"

"That monster is a fae." The Dead Queen's voice echoes off the stone and rafters around us. "They may be curious creatures, even cruel, but they are not, in fact, monsters. They do not understand righteousness. They know only how to satiate their own cravings."

"Forgive me if I don't see much of a difference."

"That's because you are a Fox," she says coolly. "Your ancestors ruled for hundreds of years believing they were better than everyone and everything else."

My mouth snaps shut.

The Dead Queen looks back toward the battlefield, where very few Fox Soldiers remain. Moribund's illusions make quick work of them, then pop out of thin air, as if evaporating. Eventually, only one Moribund remains. He scans the blood-soaked battlefield, then looks up toward the moth tower.

I stiffen.

As if he sees me, he grins, his tiny teeth glowing in the moonlight. He pulls something out of his loincloth and runs it beneath his nose slowly. I know in my gut that it's my hair, even though he's too far away for me to see it. Dread pools low in my stomach.

Then, in a blink, the final Moribund is gone.

"I daresay he's satiated for a little while, at least," Nalina says.

I'm not so sure.

Down below, the last of Gwyllion's fighters walk among the carnage, checking to ensure each Fox Soldier is dead. I wouldn't bother. Moribund doesn't seem the type to be sloppy about murder. Someone begins collecting swords and armor. No doubt they'll be reused in the borderlands. A haunting laugh escapes my chest.

Imagine that, Fox copper claimed to benefit the Dead Queen and Annwyn. My ancestors must be turning in their graves.

A thought ripples through my mind, too timid to creep out from the shadows. Too afraid to hope it's true ... We won.

Gwyllion suffered terrible loss, but the castle survives to stand another day. The people of Annwyn are safe. For now.

My smile fades as I remember my father. I lean forward, half out the window as I scan the moonlit field below. I don't have to look too far.

In the distance, on the crest of that damnable hill, an orb of light hovers. My father remains perched upon his white horse. His copper banner waves in the breeze. There are only a handful of King's Guards at his side, those he kept back from the fight for his own protection.

"That coward," I growl.

"And what did you expect?" Nalina asks. "He's a Fox. He would rather run than fight like a Wolf." Her voice is edged with steel.

I whirl on her. "Why didn't Moribund kill him?"

"Because your father isn't a threat to Gwyllion while he's out there on his stallion." Nalina's voice is laced with contempt. "The deal was to protect the castle. The Fox King isn't attacking."

"He's waiting." The Dead Queen's voice is cold.

"For me," I say. I know it in my bones.

Beneath her veil, the Dead Queen nods.

Good. A vicious grin spreads across my face. "I'm going to kill him now." My voice is firm, certain. If I've learned one thing this winter, it's this: I am a force to be reckoned with, even without my power.

The Dead Queen nods again.

"I'm coming with you." Nalina steps forward, unsheathing her sword.

I shake my head. "No."

"No?" she asks, as if she's not sure she heard me correctly. She shakes her head. "This isn't about vengeance. It's about the Fox Throne. You can't inherit it if you're dead."

"I need you to trust me."

Nalina turns to the Dead Queen. "My queen, it's too risky."

We both watch the Dead Queen, bathed in the light of the full moon.

"Please," I whisper. "I need to do this. By myself."

"Go," she says finally. "Make your grandmother proud." For the first time, I hear the echo of her true voice beneath the shroud of death. Even if it was only for a moment, I know I've finally heard the voice of my grandmother. And she's telling me to kill the Fox King.

I grip my moth knife tighter in my fist and nod. Nalina doesn't say another word as I walk out of the tower door to confront my father ...

And finally kill him.

CHAPTER 39

I RIDE out from Gwyllion's splintered gates on the first saddled horse I can find. He's fast and dark as midnight. The copper pommel on his saddle tells me he's well-trained in battle, likely the horse of an officer. No doubt his soldier is dead now, lying in a heap on the blood-soaked battlefield. The horse leaps over mounds of fallen Fox Soldiers and Gwyllion fighters alike as his hooves gallop through pools of blood.

The wind blows my short, choppy hair across my face. It's surprisingly freeing not to have a storm of auburn flowing around me anymore.

"Red!" a voice yells from the battlefield. "Wait!"

My heart splinters with relief at the sound of Tristan's voice, but I don't slow. Nothing matters more than this.

I can feel the Dead Queen's eyes on me as I ride across the ruined battlefield to meet my father. She's watching us from her tower of moths, waiting to witness the bloodshed that I have craved for so, so long.

Up ahead, the Fox King's orb glows, hovering at the crest of the distant hill. It's a beacon for me to come find him. When I draw near, I slow my horse to a trot.

My father and five King's Guards watch me approach. The

king isn't wearing his famous copper armor anymore. He looks almost like a normal man, sitting there atop his white stallion. But his casual posture makes me grit my teeth. I pull my horse to a stop in front of him.

"Father."

"Daughter." He nods. "I see you've had a haircut since this morning."

I don't give him the pleasure of engaging. In one swift movement, I swing down off my horse. I pull the silver moth knife out of my boot and step into the defensive position Tristan made me practice a thousand times this winter. "Let's talk."

Father gives me the briefest of smiles before he gets down from his own horse. He walks toward me with lazy steps.

"What has become of my Little Fox these past few months, hm? You've grown quite feral."

"I've learned the truth. The truth that you tried so hard to keep from me."

"Oh?" He raises an eyebrow. "And what truth is that?"

"That it was *you* who killed Grandmother. That she was fighting against you, leading the Sympathizers. That we, Llwyn, were the aggressors all along."

"We?" He tilts his head like a dog hearing an odd sound. "Do you still consider yourself from Llwyn?" He sucks his teeth. "You sound more like a flea-bitten Wolf to me."

His words make me pause, but only for the briefest moment.

He steps closer, and I hold up my knife, a silent promise to gut him if he tries anything. Little does he know, I plan to gut him either way.

"It's abhorrent. Unnatural." His voice trembles with disgust as he says the words. "You've sullied the Fox Throne. Ruined it with the stench of Wolves."

I refuse to take his bait. "This ends here."

He laughs and claps his hands together, his limbs loose and unafraid. "Oh, is that so?"

"Your men are all dead."

He tuts. "No. Not all. Llwyn is a large territory, after all. Growing larger by the day, in fact. Regardless of whether we take this measly little castle or not."

I grit my teeth and clench my fist around my knife's bronze hilt. "You don't deserve the Fox Throne. You're cruel. Selfish."

He raises an eyebrow, studying me. "And you're not?"

I bite my tongue at the truth in his words.

He grins, moonlight glinting off his canines. "We are both Foxes, you and I. The difference is I am a king." His grin dissolves into a snarl. "And you are nothing but an ignorant pup."

He takes a quick step toward me, but I'm faster. With one hand, I grab the back of his neck and stab my blade deep beneath his ribs. Hot blood gushes over my fist.

"This is for locking me up in that rat-infested dungeon." I pull out the blade and stab him again. He grunts and grasps for the bloodied hilt that's buried deep in his stomach. "This is for killing my mother and blaming me for it." I pull out the knife and stab him again. The color drains from his face. "And *this* is for what you did to Grandmother." I wrench out the knife, and stab him a third time, putting all my anger into it.

Tears prickle at the corner of my eyes. Finally, I feel the sweet release of vengeance that I've been searching for, ever since I was twelve years old. Ever since Grandmother disappeared and I was left alone with a man who hated me.

Up in her tower of moths, I know the Dead Queen is watching as I smile at my father for what might be the only time in my entire life.

Suddenly, I realize that none of his guards have stepped forward to save their king. My eyes flicker between them as unease settles over my bones. I look back at my father. His eyes bore into mine. He clamps both hands over mine ... and twists the knife, driving the blade deeper. Slowly, his lips grow into a self-satisfied sneer.

I know that face. I've fallen into one of his traps. I stumble backward, pulling my knife out of his stomach as I scramble away.

The Fox King struggles to stay standing. A wet gurgle erupts from his mouth as he spits blood across my face.

He stares me down with a bloody, unhinged smile. "Who needs an heir when you can live forever?"

Dread fills me.

"Red!" Behind us, I hear Tristan's voice.

"Sienna, no!" Nalina is with him. They're coming to save me. But they're too late.

A giant King's Guard grabs Father by the arms, steadying him on his feet. Deep red blood oozes from the wounds in the Fox King's stomach.

"Finally." He chokes out a laugh, his teeth stained red. "You've served me well."

With horror, I watch as another guard steps forward with a silver blade and slides it beneath Father's ribs. Father's grin falters as the guard reaches up into his chest cavity and tears out his still-beating heart. It glistens red in the light of the full moon.

A momentary shadow passes across the field, like a ripple in a pond, and I know that the Dead Queen witnessed the horror from her distant tower. With what should have been his final breath, Father looks back toward Gwyllion Castle, victorious.

What have I done? A memory of Tristan in the throne room flashes through my mind.

"To live eternally, there must be sacrifice ... When the future queen gives up her life, she must be bathed in the light of the full moon ... Her heart must be stolen from her chest before it stops beating."

Someone grabs my arms and pulls me back. Tristan. He's yelling something, but I can't hear him. I can't even see him through the shock. Horror blinds me to everything else but the pulsing, glistening heart bathed in silver moonlight.

Nalina rushes past me toward the Fox King, her greatsword swinging. Two King's Guards stop her before she can get close

343

enough to strike. They fight while I stare at my father, unblinking.

The bloodied guard hastily packs the still-beating heart into a velvet-lined case and closes the lid. The copper box glints in the moonlight before he leaps onto his horse and speeds away, south toward the Spires.

My father begins to writhe in agony as one King's Guard still holds him up. Father's eyes bulge in their sockets, and the veins in his neck turn black with death as he screams. The guard loses his grip, and Father falls to his hands and knees, gasping and vomiting up black bile. He digs his fingernails into the dirt as his limbs tremble.

But he does not die.

Finally, Tristan releases me. He jumps to his feet and unsheathes a bronze sword. He rushes toward Nalina, and together the Wolves fight, side by side.

Nalina runs at the Fox King again. She doesn't get far before the large King's Guard pushes her back. He swings his sword, his strong arms matching her brutality in a way that should leave me impressed. I know what a force Nalina is. But right now, she's worn down by battle. Sweat glistens at her temples, and the dried blood along her arms is dark. Her muscles tremble as she blocks each attack. Tristan is too busy with the other remaining King's Guards to help her.

I leap to my feet, finally snapping out of the horror-struck trance. I run at the guards attacking Nalina.

One guard breaks away from Tristan and runs to help my father up onto his white stallion. Nalina and I fight as the escaping guard gallops away with my father. Except he isn't my father any longer. He isn't even the Fox King.

He is a rogue dead king. And the entire realm is in peril.

I'm watching my father escape when I hear footsteps rush toward me. I whirl around to see a King's Guard, his bronze sword raised to strike me. Before I can react, Nalina throws herself between us, slicing her sword clean through the guard's neck. For a heartbeat, he simply stands there, stunned. Then, blood bubbles from his mouth. It fountains from the deep gash in his throat as his eyes go wide with horror. He collapses sideways with a thud.

Relief makes me dizzy. "Thank y—" But the words die in my throat.

Nalina turns toward me, a copper blade sticking out from her stomach.

"No!" Tristan yells behind us. He stabs his sword straight through the remaining guard and sprints through the mud, toward Nalina.

She sways, mouth parting soundlessly, and drops to her knees. She crumples to the muddy ground, scarred face slack with shock.

I scramble over to her at the same time Tristan reaches us. From around the blade, Nalina's stomach pulses with crimson blood. It's a death blow. I've seen enough of them to know.

Her eyes stare wide at the fox stamped into the end of the copper-plated sword. "Take it out of me." Her voice is strangled.

"We can't. You'll bleed out," Tristan says.

She gives him an impatient glare. "I'm dead anyway, Tristan. Don't make me die with a Fox sword buried in my belly."

He hesitates, his eyes darting between hers and the sword. After a beat, he nods, defeated. In one quick movement, he pulls the sword from her gut. Nalina gasps, blood spurting from her mouth. Her eyes are glassy with pain.

Tristan drops to the ground and lifts her head into his lap. "I'm here, Nalina. I'm right here."

He looks to me, panic clear across his face. I've never seen him like this, even in the middle of battle, even when faced by corpse wolves and foxhounds. I've never seen fear like this in Tristan's eyes.

I swallow hard and place my trembling hands over her wound as I try to call my power. It barely flickers in my core. I can tell by the defeat on Tristan's face that he already knows. I've used my power up fighting the Fox Soldiers. There's nothing left to save her. Gently, I remove my bloodstained hands from her stomach.

Nalina's face is pale, her eyes wide as they settle on me. She reaches up to touch a lock of my short auburn hair. "I see her," she whispers. "I see all of them."

It's her sister, I know. And all the other women sacrificed to Moribund to save what's left of Gwyllion.

Her eyes flicker to Tristan's. "Isadora, too."

Tristan closes his eyes and presses his forehead to Nalina's. He lets out a shaky breath. "Take care of them," he whispers.

"Always."

She drops her hand as her chest rises once, then stills. Remarkably, her face transforms. Her muscles relax and her eyes close. Her face grows peaceful in a way I've never seen it.

When death takes her, it's the only time I've ever seen Nalina smile.

CHAPTER 40

No FUNERAL SHOULD EVER BE this large.

All through the night, Gwyllion's survivors labor in silence, gathering the broken bodies of the dead. The old move stiffly, stooped with grief, hauling their neighbors and kin through ash-choked air. Children collect sticks and dried grass to build the pyres. Their small hands shake as they place offerings beside their siblings, their grandparents, their friends.

By the next afternoon, the eastern side of Gwyllion Castle is stained black with soot from so many fires. The wind carries the pyre smoke westward in a veil of ash that clings to everything. I wonder if the black scar will remain here forever, etched into the castle like a curse. Like a memento from when the Fox King invaded Gwyllion and was reanimated as the Rogue King.

I can barely see through the stinging haze as I drag the body of a fallen Fox Soldier toward the nearest pyre. My arms burn with effort. His copper breastplate is torn open, jagged and bloodied, likely from Moribund or a corpse beast. He may be my enemy, but I don't enjoy the sight. His mouth is still parted, frozen in a last gasp, his face slack with disbelief. One of his eyes is gone. The other stares blindly up into the ashy sky. Flies crawl across his face in greedy spirals.

I shoo them away, then lay a hand over his face to close the remaining eye. His skin is tacky with blood. I feel the moment his eyelid shuts beneath my palm, and something in me shudders.

The farther I drag him, the more rage grows inside me like a storm. I want to blame this man, to scream at him, to curse him and all the other men in copper armor. But I can't. Even as fury runs thick and black beneath my skin, I know the truth: he didn't choose this war. He didn't choose to become a monster or a martyr. None of us did. We're all just pawns in a game we never agreed to play.

Only one man chose this path. Only one player watched from afar while the rest of us bled for him: my father. And if there's an old god left in this ruined world, I *will* end him. One way or another, I will kill the Rogue King for good.

Out of the corner of my eye, something moves through the smoke. I blink through stinging eyes and realize it's a funeral march. The Wolves—or what remains of them, anyway—trail behind the Dead Queen as she walks past the burning pyres. The Wolves carry a plank on their shoulders. A body lies atop it, wrapped in a white shroud. I don't need to see her face to know who it is. The strong frame of her body, the careful way the others carry her—it can only be Nalina.

Tristan leads the pack, his face still as granite. I know how devastated he is to lose Nalina. And I also know he must be so, so proud. Because in the end, Nalina did exactly what he said she would. Her methods may have been unconventional, but she always did what she believed was right.

At the tail of the procession, I see a familiar golden head. Hunter follows the Wolves, his head bent in respect. And never in my life would I have expected to see Hunter fight alongside the people of Annwyn. Never would I have believed he'd mourn the death of one of their Wolves.

The scent of death is thick in the air, a bitter perfume of scorched flesh and dried blood. Flakes of ash drift down like snow, clinging to my hair and clothes. Somewhere out on the battlefield, my red cloak lies beneath mud and rubble. Good riddance. It's a reminder of my hubris and failure. I never want to see it again.

I abandon the Fox Soldier at the edge of the pyre without ceremony. His weight slips from my arms and hits the ground with a dull thud. My legs are leaden, and my boots drag through the mud as I fall into step behind the mourners. The world feels distant, muffled, as though I'm moving through water. My chest is numb, and each breath feels heavy.

The sky darkens with smoke, turning the sun into a dull glow behind the clouds. I keep my gaze fixed on the white shroud ahead, where a thin strip of linen billows in the wind. It's jarring, seeing something so boldly white in a muddied, blood-soaked battleground, but it feels appropriate.

Nalina hated me. But still, in the end, she sacrificed her life for mine. She saved us all.

I keep my distance as the Wolves set Nalina's plank down on a small pyre. For saving Gwyllion, she gets the honor of her own fire, rather than being piled on top of other bodies. A man carries a torch and kneels respectfully in front of the pyre. He lights the edge of Nalina's white funeral shroud. It catches, igniting the sticks and grasses beneath her within moments.

We all watch in silence as the linen burns away, revealing Nalina, her thick blond braid aflame. I'd expected to see her silver sword at her chest, but it isn't there. Even a death like Nalina's isn't immune to scavenging for the war effort. It'll be reused in the fight against the new Rogue King.

Eventually, the Dead Queen nods to her Wolves, wordlessly dismissing them to continue the cleanup efforts. Tristan's head hangs low as he stares at the pyre, unmoving. The Wolves place their hands on his shoulders or touch his arm as they retreat, off to continue the work of gathering the dead. They disappear into the smoke, but Tristan remains, his eyes fixed on Nalina's burning corpse.

Hunter remains too, keeping a respectful distance. His eyes meet mine, and I know he's waiting to see what I'll do. But I can't seem to make my legs move. I can't draw my eyes away from Nalina, the woman who was so infuriating, so confusing and complicated. The woman who saved my life.

"She didn't really hate you, you know."

I jolt at the Dead Queen's voice. My eyes are watering, burning with the sting of smoke and ash in the air.

I cough. "Fooled me."

"She was lost in grief." She turns to look at me through her sheer black veil. "I think you, of all people, can understand what that feels like."

I don't respond.

The Dead Queen sighs, as if her lungs need air. "The Fox King has presented us with a new problem."

"I should've seen it coming."

"You couldn't have known."

"Perhaps not. But I do know him. I should have suspected a trap."

The Dead Queen doesn't say anything for a long time. We watch as Nalina's clothes burn away and her hair curls and turns to ash.

Near the pyre, Hunter shifts on his feet. It almost feels like old times, him a King's Guard, following me around, protecting me, loving me. But this isn't Caerwen. We're not the same people we were back in Llwyn. We're not even the same people we were three months ago. Everything has changed. I look at his soot-smeared face and his filthy Annwyn clothes. His father's fox sword still hangs at his hip, but there's no other copper in sight.

I speak before I've had a chance to convince myself not to. "There's something you still haven't told me."

The queen turns to face me. "And what's that?"

My voice trembles, but I don't let it stop me. "Why did you choose Annwyn instead of me? Why was leading the Sympathizers more important than I was?"

It takes her a long time to respond. We watch as Nalina's skin grows charred and black. "It was for your mother," she whispers.

Beneath her veil, I can see her opalescent eyes close, as if she truly does still feel pain.

Her words trickle over my skin like spiders. Burrowing into me, nesting in my bones so that I can never, ever forget. No one speaks of my mother.

I shake my head, confused. "How?"

The Dead Queen stares at me, unblinking behind her sheer veil. "I had to make sure she didn't die in vain."

And somehow, I can understand that. It doesn't make it easy. It doesn't even make it right. But I can understand forfeiting your life in service of another. In that, we are the same.

There's something here between us, finally. Not a fondness, not by any means. It's not love or even friendship. It's more like an agreement. We don't have to like each other to fight against a common enemy.

A realization trickles over my mind like unexpected rain. I have finally come to terms with Grandmother's death. Her murder brought me great sorrow and pain. It brought me horror and death. It almost killed me. But it also brought me here, to Annwyn. It taught me that I am stronger than I knew. It taught me that I'm capable of both great and terrible things.

And I'll need both to end the Rogue King.

From the far side of the pyre, Tristan kicks a rock into the flames, then pulls his shoulders back. He walks toward us, finally ready to face the queen. He joins Hunter at my side. Together we stand in silence for a long time, each lost in our thoughts.

"There can only be one." There's a worried note in the Dead Queen's voice that I've never heard before. "Two dead rulers upend the balance. Two cannot be trusted with this level of power. Especially if the Rogue King doesn't respect the sanctity of life, both fae and human."

"There shouldn't even be *one*." My voice cracks, my throat scorched and dry.

I expect Tristan to react to this, but he doesn't. His eyes don't move from Nalina as she's swallowed by the flames.

"That may be," the queen agrees. "But the Moon Goddess created the first Dead Queen to preserve order, to restore the balance between the humans and the fae."

"It doesn't sound like you've done a very good job." I can't keep the bitterness out of my voice, but I hardly think it matters.

"In many ways, I've failed." She looks out toward the battlefield. "But all is not lost. Not yet."

I'm not so sure about that. Hunter's eyes watch me protectively. He's ever a King's Guard, even without the copper armor.

I hear my voice before I even register that I'm speaking. "Do you regret it? Becoming the Dead Queen?"

If Nalina were still alive, she'd protest my audacity. The thought makes a small smile flicker a cross my lips.

The Dead Queen pauses, then raises her thin black veil. It blows behind her, caught in a breeze. She sets her dead, opalescent eyes on mine.

"I regret being unable to feel the same emotions I did when I was alive. Peace, tenderness, love. I regret being unable to smile." Her gloved hand reaches up to her face, to touch the permanent grimace left after being torn to shreds in the borderlands. "Most of all, I regret not being there for you when you needed me."

I study her, but it's no use. You can't read a corpse the way you can read a living, breathing human. It's like staring at a stone and expecting it to cry.

"But I don't regret becoming the queen of these lands." She drops her hand slowly, then looks out toward the Spires. "I will never regret my mission. Tearing down the Fox empire and restoring balance to the world. It's what I lived for. What I sacrificed so much for. What I died for." She pauses. "I failed in life. Now, I have a chance at redemption in death."

We stare out toward the Spires, at the wild expanse beyond. Much of the snow has melted from the lower altitudes, but the jagged peaks are still tipped with ice. Annwyn is a treacherous land, the stories always said so. This winter has proven it to be true. But the stories never spoke of how strong and beautiful it is too. How the Annwyn people hold their wild secrets to their chests out of protection, not cruelty or spite. How this land carries magic, just below its surface.

My eyes flicker to Tristan, but he's lost to the flames and whatever dark thoughts consume him.

"If I'm to do this," I say. "If I'm to work with you to kill the Rogue King, then I need to know one thing." Smoke scrapes my throat raw and my eyes won't stop watering, but I don't waver. I stare right into the Dead Queen's eyes as I ask, "How do you kill someone who's been reanimated?"

She knows what I'm asking. And why. It's not just to end my father, it's to end her too. Beneath her grotesque grimace, I think I can see the hint of a smile on the Dead Queen's face. "You can't."

I narrow my eyes at her. "If that were true, then five centuries of Dead Queens would be roaming this castle."

She nods, as if pleased with the holes I stabbed in her story. "Cutting off his head won't do. We are not like corpse beasts. Our power will just make us whole again, to continue the torture of eternal life."

"I figured as much."

She nods in assent. "If I tell you, Granddaughter, you must promise me one thing."

I nod.

There's fire in her opalescent eyes when she speaks. "He must die first."

I snort. "You'd trust me to keep that promise?"

She lifts her chin. "I would."

"Why?"

"Why trust you? Or why do I ask you to wait?"

"The latter."

She steps slowly toward me through the shifting pyre smoke. "Because I want to watch as the shadows leech from his traitorous, murderous body for what he did to my daughter." She stares at me, as if challenging me to push back.

"Fine," I say. "It's as good a reason as any."

As much as I detest this woman—this corpse—I can't help but admire her. I'm in awe of this queen's immense power. How her fury consumes everything in its path. How her need for revenge will stop at nothing.

I see myself in her. It is both terrible and empowering at the same time.

"But first," she says, holding up one skeletal finger. "You must find his heart and stop it from beating. Only that will make him vulnerable to true death. No part of his body can live."

"So, *your* heart still beats somewhere then."

She nods slowly.

"I assume you have it hidden."

"In a place you will never find it."

It's a challenge; I can see it in her undead eyes. And we both know I've never been afraid of a challenge. We stare at each other for a long moment before I nod.

"Fine. If this is the only way to end my father, I'll do whatever it takes."

"You won't be able to do it alone." She turns her undead gaze to Hunter, where he lingers behind me. "And what of you, Heir to the North? Where do your allegiances lie?"

Hunter's mouth forms into a determined line. "I think I've seen enough of the Fox King's cruelty to last me a lifetime. I'm not interested in giving him the opportunity to do it for a thousand more." He turns to me. In one swift movement, he unsheathes his Fox sword and kneels. He places the tip of his sword in the dirt before him and bows his head to me. "I once vowed to protect the Fox Heir. I will keep that oath."

The Dead Queen raises an eyebrow. "Even now that you've learned you're the Heir to the North?" The Dead Queen asks, her voice pitched with curiosity. "In many ways, you are enemies."

Hunter's brown eyes dart up toward mine. "If I am truly the Heir to the North, as you say, then we aren't enemies at all." Hunter stands, sheathing his sword. "The human realms were not at war with each other. Only with the fae. And then," his eyes drift to the queen. "With the Dead Queens."

She nods, affirming.

Hunter looks back at me. "I will serve the Fox Heir. The *true* Fox Heir. Until she no longer needs me."

"And then?" I ask, my voice tense.

Hunter takes a deep breath and looks toward the crumbling Gwyllion Castle. "And then we'll figure out the rest. When the time comes."

My heart swells. I'm so glad to have him on my side again, I could cry. I reach forward and place my filthy hands on his cheeks. "Thank you," I whisper, my throat tight with emotion.

He gives me a shadow of a grin. "I'm sorry."

I sniff. "Me too."

"As touching as this is," the Dead Queen says. "You'll need more than a Fox and a knight. I cannot leave Gwyllion. I must maintain the border and protect what's left of our kingdom."

"But you will need to help us," Hunter says. "You're the only one with enough power to stop him."

She shakes her head slowly. "Power is made stronger by ruthlessness and cruelty. The Fox King knows no bounds. His recent transformation is only further evidence of his inability to control his lust for power." She holds out her hands, as if there's nothing else she can do. "I, quite simply, am not enough."

"Who else could possibly help us?" I ask.

The Dead Queen stares pointedly at Tristan for a long time, until he finally drags his eyes away from the fire. Understanding slowly washes over his face. "No."

"You must wake them." Her voice is unwavering.

Tristan clenches his jaw.

"Who?" I blink rapidly, certain I've misheard her.

"The high fae."

I blanch, coughing on ash. "The fae?" All I can think of is Moribund. I shiver. Then it dawns on me: the only stories about sleeping fae are the old kings and queens.

"But they're just fairy tales ... aren't they?" Hunter asks.

Tristan's voice is colder than usual. "The fae kings and queens are *very* real."

Hunter shakes his head, trying to dispel his disbelief. "But that would mean they've been sleeping for over two thousand years. Is that even possible? Could they be woken after all this time?"

The Dead Queen waves her hand toward the crumbling castle and the new storm that's roiling along the fae-enchanted edge of the Spires. "Anything is possible. You just need to be wise enough to believe it. And strong enough to fight for it."

"How many are there?" I ask.

"Once, there were twelve. Now, only six remain."

My jaw drops. "How are we supposed to find six sleeping fae monarchs who've been hidden for thousands of years?"

"The tapestries will show you."

I stare at her. "The ... tapestries."

"I've seen you studying the tapestries in the throne room. You know they're no ordinary artwork."

"That—I mean, sure," I stutter. "They change with the weather, but how could they tell me anything about the fae?"

"They're windows into prison cells," the Dead Queen says, as if it's an ordinary thing to peer across the expanse of time and space with needle and thread. "Each fae monarch lies beneath a black tree, trapped in iron. The tapestries are how the human kings of the north kept an eye on them during their imprisonment."

Our eyes move to Hunter.

"My ancestors," he says hollowly.

She nods.

"Are you sure this is a good idea?" Hunter asks. "I don't think they'll like me much, seeing as I'm allegedly from the family that imprisoned them."

"That's why my Wolf will accompany you." Her opalescent eyes dart to Tristan. He stiffens.

Behind me, Hunter lets out an involuntary groan. He shoots me a worried glance.

She continues, "He knows the ways of Annwyn. He was raised on fae lore. This is a journey for all three of you." Her voice is sharp and her undead eyes dart between me, Hunter, and Tristan. "Show them that both the north and south are allied in this. Free the ancient fae, and beg them to help us end the Rogue King."

We stare at her, slack-jawed and bewildered.

"Sounds like a suicide mission." Tristan grumbles as he kicks a copper helmet. It rolls toward the Dead Queen's feet. "Well," he pauses, eyeing the queen. "At least, it is for the living."

The Dead Queen's face grows grave as she turns to me. "You will need to become more wolf than fox if you are to succeed."

"How so?" I eye her with suspicion as shadows etch deeper into the creases of her decayed flesh.

"Foxes are solitary creatures ... but wolves are pack animals. If you are to find the fae, you will need to work together."

I glance between the two men and heave a shaky sigh. "So, we need to find and wake six angry fae kings and queens who were forcibly put to sleep over two thousand years ago, and beg them for help." I laugh humorlessly. "Should be easy."

All around us, the pyres crackle and burn as day turns to twilight.

Hunter pinches the bridge of his nose in irritation. "As much as I hate to say it, the Dead Queen is right. We have to find the high fae before your father does."

I look to Tristan. For the first time since the battle, a flash of life flickers behind his eyes. A slow grin spreads across his face.

"Chin up, Red." His canines glint in the firelight. "You know how much I love hunting."

Also by Briar Knightly

Want to read more of the Thrones of Ruin series?

The Dead Queen

A reluctant heir. A deadly secret. A Wolf who prowls the shadows of the Fox King's court.

In this dark fairytale retelling of Little Red Riding Hood, the line between predator and protector is as thin as a knife's blade.

The Fox Heir

Ancient fae lore. A castle in ruins. An heir who must survive winter in a den of Wolves.

Sienna escaped the Fox King, but there's more to fear than the Dead Queen in a crumbling castle haunted by ghosts and ancient fae with dark appetites.

———

Please consider leaving a review on Amazon or Goodreads

About the Author

Briar Knightly writes fantasy and romance. She is an award-winning author under a different pen name. When she's not working as a librarian, she spends her days writing, drinking tea, and pampering her giant cat. She lives in the Midwest.

———

Let's keep in touch!

You can find me on:

Instagram @Briar.Knightly
TikTok @BriarKnightly
BriarKnightly.com

Would you like to be the first to learn about new books, bonus content, and more?
Sign up for my newsletter!

Acknowledgments

To my husband, thank you for understanding how important writing is to me. And for upgrading my computer when my old one was on the verge of death. I didn't even have to ask for help. You just did it. That's love, right there.

For my family, thanks for being cool about it when I finally told you I write spicy romantasy. No one even batted an eye! But … maybe don't read it. 'Kay, thanks.

Thank you so much to my beta readers: Holly Baker, Irina Thompson, Corinne Hoag, and Terin Larkin. Your feedback is always incredibly helpful. You're all so smart!

And, as always, thank you to all the librarians and library workers out there. Preserving the right to read can be a thankless job, but we believe in the power of books to inspire hearts and change worlds.